VAMPIRATES

Black Heart

JUSTIN SOMPER

SIMON AND SCHUSTER

First published in Great Britain in 2009 by Simon and Schuster UK Ltd
A CBS COMPANY

www.vampirates.co.uk

Simon & Schuster UK Ltd
1st Floor, 222 Gray's Inn Road, London WC1X 8HB

This book is a work of fiction. Names, characters, places and incidents are
either the product of the author's imagination or are used fictitiously.
Any resemblance to actual people living or dead, events
or locales is entirely coincidental.

A CIP catalogue record for this book
is available from the British Library.

ISBN 978-1-4169-0103-7
2115414   JF
1 3 5 7 9 10 8 6 4 2

Printed by CPI Cox & Wyman, Reading, Berkshire RG18EX

www.simonsays.co.uk

For Peejay,
for too many reasons to list here.

The Story So Far . . .

The story begins in the year 2505. Sea-levels have risen. Whoever controls the oceans rules the world. The seas teem with pirate ships and other, more mysterious, vessels . . .

Twins Connor and Grace Tempest have grown up with their dad, Dexter Tempest, in Crescent Moon Bay, where their father is a lighthouse keeper. Neither Connor nor Grace ever met their mother and know next to nothing about her.

When Dexter dies suddenly, the twins decide to make a new life for themselves, and sail away in their dad's old boat. They don't get very far, however, before a sudden storm strikes, throwing them overboard to fight for their lives in the cold, dark water.

But Connor and Grace are each saved – rescued by different ships, with very different crews . . .

Connor is rescued by Cheng Li – deputy captain of *The Diablo*, one of the more notorious pirate ships. Its captain is the legendary Molucco Wrathe, the oldest of three brothers who form a charismatic and powerful, but unruly, pirate dynasty. Connor joins Molucco's crew and embraces a life of piracy, marking himself out as something of a prodigy on account of his strength, bravery and exceptional swordfighting. He grows especially close to crew-members Bart Pearce and Jez Stukeley, forming a trio affectionately known as "The Three Buccaneers".

Grace regains consciousness on board *The Nocturne* – a ship of vampire pirates (or Vampirates) which has been sailing through all eternity, largely undetected. For the early part of her stay, Grace is unsure whether she is a guest, a prisoner or a convenient parcel of blood for the crew.

Grace's dad used to sing her a shanty about the Vampirates, depicting them as "the demons of the ocean". Contrary to her expectations, though, for the most part the crew are well-disposed towards her. In particular, she forms friendships with Midshipman Lorcan Furey – the handsome Irish lad who rescued her – Darcy Flotsam – the ship's figurehead by day, who comes alive at night – and the mysterious captain, whose face is always hidden behind a mesh mask and who speaks in a strange whisper.

The Vampirates on board *The Nocturne* do not wantonly attack their victims but rather have a weekly Feast, during which each vampire feeds on the blood of their partner or "donor". But there is growing discontent among the Vampirate ranks about this system, and Lieutenant Sidorio is the first to rebel, resulting in his expulsion from *The Nocturne*.

Grace and Connor are briefly reunited but, though delighted to know that their twin is safe, new friendships and loyalties pull them in differing directions. Connor's life on board *The Diablo* takes a darker turn when Jez is killed in a duel, making Connor start to question Captain Wrathe's judgement, and his articles which he has signed up to for life. Meanwhile, Grace is drawn back into the world of the Vampirates and discovers to her horror that Lorcan has been blinded – and it may be her fault.

Sidorio is busy forging alliances and tempting Vampirates away from *The Nocturne*. His first recruit is Jez Stukeley, whom Sidorio sires to become his Vampirate lieutenant. Other rebels join their small but vicious band and together they carry out the brutal massacre of Porfirio Wrathe (younger brother of Molucco) and his pirate crew. This despicable act prompts revenge from the pirates, in an attack led by Molucco and Connor. They succeed in destroying several of the Vampirates, but both Sidorio and Stukeley return to fight another day.

Captain Barbarro Wrathe arrives to patch up a long-standing rift with Molucco, and to avenge the murder of Porfirio. Barbarro, captain of *The Typhon*, is accompanied by his wife (and deputy) Trofie – who has one hand made entirely of gold – and their teenage son, Moonshine, who holds a grudge against Connor after a previous run-in.

Grace journeys to Sanctuary – a place of healing for troubled Vampirates – with Lorcan, his donor Shanti and the Vampirate captain. They hope that Vampirate guru Mosh Zu Kamal will be able to cure Lorcan's blindness and advise the captain on the divisions emerging within the Vampirate realm. As Lorcan undergoes healing, Grace forms a new friendship with cowboy Vampirate, Johnny Desperado, who is also being treated at Sanctuary.

Molucco plans the mother of all pirate raids with Barbarro, but his nephew Moonshine endangers its success and forces Connor to make his first kill in order to save the boy. The killing shocks Connor to the core and he starts to question his allegiance to Molucco and his suitability as a pirate. He leaves the ship and heads off into the unknown, ultimately seeking out his former comrade Cheng Li, now teaching at Pirate Academy. She is preparing to become captain of her own ship and Connor decides to join her crew, if Molucco will consent. To his surprise, Molucco agrees, burning Connor's articles and dismissing the lad he once thought of as a son.

Sidorio's ambitions increase and he lures more vampirates from both *The Nocturne* and Sanctuary, including Grace's friend, Johnny. As more of the *The Nocturne*'s crew depart to join Sidorio's rebellion, the once invincible Vampirate captain collapses.

Grace and Connor assist Mosh Zu in a healing ceremony in which, at last, the captain's mask is removed. During the healing catharsis, a succession of souls rise from the captain's body. One of them is strangely familiar. It is the twins' mother, Sally, whom they have never met . . . until now.

READ ON FOR THE NEXT UNFORGETTABLE INSTALMENT IN THE VOYAGE OF THE TEMPEST TWINS!

For a more detailed version of "the story so far" go to www.vampirates.co.uk.

The middle of the ocean.
The year 2512.

CHAPTER ONE

Intruders in the Fortress

It was a calm, clear night. *The Typhon* charted its course through the ocean, sleek and confident as a killer whale. On deck, the pirates of the night watch performed their duties with time-honoured precision. Below deck, their crewmates variously rested, ate, relaxed and prepared for the business of the next day. *The Typhon* was a well-oiled machine: from the crow's nest to the galley; from the lowliest of pirate apprentices to the captain and his deputy.

In one of the smaller – but nevertheless grand – state rooms two levels below the main deck, four people sat around a circular table. The table was covered with a red silk cloth, from which arose a structure resembling the four walls of a fortress. Each wall was composed of small tiles – half wood, half bone – stacked tightly together. But evidently this miniature fortress was not impenetrable. The walls had been ravaged. Some of the tiles had made their way onto racks placed in front of each wall while other tiles lay bone side up on the table, revealing an array of intricate coloured symbols.

"Well," said Trofie Wrathe, a golden finger tapping the wooden rack in front of her. "This is fun, isn't it?"

1

Opposite her, her husband, Captain Barbarro Wrathe, was silent.

"Oh yeah, big fun!" grunted Moonshine, their son, positioned to Trofie's right.

"I think it's a marvellous game," said the elderly man on Trofie's other side.

Trofie nodded encouragingly. "Thank you, Transom. I believe it's your turn now."

"Is it?" The Wrathes' trusty *majordomo* seemed confused for a moment. Then he reached forward and, with quivering fingers, removed a tile from the wall. Turning the bone side towards him, he drew it up to his eyes to examine the symbol more closely.

Moonshine sighed loudly. "Get a move on, *Grandpa*!" he hissed.

His father gave him a stern look.

"Well, really!" the boy persisted.

"Moonshine . . ." said Barbarro Wrathe, his resonant voice loaded with warning.

Transom dropped the tile onto his rack and, with a sudden burst of energy, began shuffling the other tiles around as if he was performing an elaborate conjuring trick.

"Remind me," Moonshine piped up again. "Why *exactly* are we torturing ourselves in this particularly grim fashion?"

Barbarro sighed, shook his head, and lifted a glass of honey-coloured liquid to his lips.

Trofie smiled pleasantly. "Tuesday night is family night, *min elskling*. It was my idea, as you well know. I don't feel we've been spending enough time together." There was steel in her voice as she continued. "That's all going to change now."

In response, Moonshine rolled his eyes exaggeratedly.

Trofie glared first at her son and then at her husband. "Will *you* say something to your son?"

Barbarro shrugged. "Maybe he has a point. *He's* not enjoying this. *I'm* certainly not enjoying this and I can't believe that you—"

"I'm having a wonderful time," Trofie said, a wide grin immediately appearing on her face. "And so is Transom . . ."

The *majordomo* was still rearranging the tiles on his rack. As he did so, his face went through a series of contortions. Suddenly, his fingers ceased their miniature ballet. He looked up and gave a little smile.

"Mahjong!" he exclaimed, flipping forward his rack to reveal neat sets of different suits of tiles.

"Bravo!" cried Trofie, clapping her hands together. She did not make much sound since one of her hands was crafted from gold, the other of regular flesh – but her delight was plain to see. "Well played, Transom!" she said. "I think you're getting the hang of this." She glanced around the room. "Well now, shall we set up for another game?"

"No!" boomed Barbarro and Moonshine in unison. For once, they had found something to agree upon.

"All right," said Trofie, clearly deflated. "What *shall* we do next?"

"You tell us, Mum," said Moonshine. "Family night is your gig."

"If I might be so bold," Transom began, "I could have Cook prepare a light repast for you?"

"Yes," said Trofie, nodding. "That would be lovely. Perhaps some gravadlax, with cloudberries and cream to follow?"

"Very good, madam," said the ancient retainer, rising to his feet and heading towards the door.

After Transom had left, Barbarro rose and lifted a decanter, refilling first Trofie's glass then his own.

"Share the wealth, eh, Dad?" Moonshine said, grinning as he reached out for a glass.

3

Barbarro shook his head and put the cut-glass stopper back in the decanter.

"But it's *family* night!" Moonshine persisted. "The one night of the week where we share and share alike."

"Don't push it any further than you already have, my boy," said his father, sitting back down again. He reached for his wife's hand and tentatively caressed the golden fingers with their ruby nails. "We've given this a good go, Trofie, but what's the use in kidding ourselves? I could really do with going over those charts again. Would you mind . . ."

"Yes," said Trofie, abruptly withdrawing her hand. "Yes, *min elskling*, I would mind very much. No one is leaving this room. We're going to spend quality time as a family if it kills us." She folded her arms defiantly.

Barbarro grunted. Moonshine mimed stabbing himself in the heart and slumped, fake-dead, on his chair. And that's how they sat – in complete, suffocating, silence – until there was a knock at the door.

The relief in the room was audible. "Come in, Transom," called Trofie.

The door opened and a vast domed silver tray came into view.

"I thought you said a 'light snack'," Trofie laughed. But the smile froze on her lips as she saw that it wasn't Transom who had brought in the tray. It was carried by a tall figure, dressed in a dark cloak and hood.

"Who are you? What's going on?" Barbarro exclaimed, as the figure set the tray down on the table. Two further cloaked figures came into the cabin. They closed the door and stood like sentries on either side of it.

"I asked you a question," Barbarro boomed. "Who are you?"

In answer, the first figure threw back her hood, shook out her long dark hair and smiled at the three Wrathes. She was a strikingly beautiful woman with wide brown eyes, and razor-

4

sharp cheekbones. A centimetre to the side of her plump lips was a delicate beauty spot. Around her left eye was make-up – or perhaps a tattoo – in the shape of a black heart.

"Is it necessary that I ask you a third time . . ." Barbarro began.

At last the stranger spoke. "We're from the Oceanic League for the Defence of Elderly Retainers, O.L.D.E.R.," she said, in a clipped English accent. "It's high time you hired some younger staff, isn't that right ladies?"

Her two companions smiled enigmatically as they pushed back their own hoods. These two were younger women, both as strikingly beautiful as their mistress. Like her, they each had a black heart-shape inked around their eyes, though in their case it was on their right side.

"Seriously, who are you?" Barbarro persisted. "No one comes aboard *The Typhon* without invitation."

"Is that so?" said the stranger. "Well, I've never been the kind of girl to wait for an invitation. The kind of girl who stays home and pines for the phone to ring." She laughed. "Not my style. I mark my own dance-card, so to speak."

Moonshine grinned. There was something decidedly cool about this woman. And though she called herself a girl, from where he was standing, she was all woman. Her two companions were just as gorgeous. Whoever they were – whatever their business – they had certainly saved family night from being a complete wash-out.

"Well," said the stranger, "it's quite an honour to make the acquaintance of the great Wrathe family at last."

"You have us at a disadvantage," said Trofie, polite but steely. "You know who *we* are but we still have no clue as to your identity."

The woman removed her gloves to reveal long, delicate fingers, each sharp nail painted black. "My name," she said, her clipped accent somehow reminiscent of cut glass, "is Lady Lola Lockwood. And these are my crewmates, Marianne and Angelika."

"Crewmates?" said Trofie. "So you come from another ship?"

"Yes," nodded Lady Lockwood. "Not one as grand as *The Typhon*, I'll be the first to admit, but we call it home, don't we, ladies?"

Marianne and Angelika nodded. Their smiles gave little away.

Trofie moved across the room towards Lady Lockwood, her eyes never leaving the stranger. "I don't believe I've heard of you," she said with some finality.

"That doesn't surprise me," replied Lady Lockwood. "I'm a vagabond, you see. Born of high birth, some would say. Oh yes, the silver spoon was very firmly planted in my mouth . . . But really that was an awfully long time ago and it has little bearing on what I am now and how I choose to pass my time."

"Which is?" Trofie countered. Now the two women stood face to face, as if looking in a mirror, though one which utterly distorted its reflection. The women were of similar height and, each in their own way, beautiful. But Lady Lockwood was as dark as Trofie Wrathe was icily blonde.

"I'm a collector," said Lady Lockwood, her dark eyes fixed on Trofie's. "I like to acquire pretty things: jewels, *objets d'art*, rare and valuable things."

"So, in fact, you're a pirate?" persisted Trofie. "Like us?"

Lady Lockwood exchanged an amused glance with each of her comrades. "A pirate," she said. "Well, yes. That's part of it."

"Get to the point," said Barbarro, growing impatient. "It's been a long night already and I don't have the appetite for any further games."

Lady Lockwood gave a dismissive laugh. "Spoilsport," she said. "I've always rather enjoyed games. That's what comes of being an only daughter of the aristocracy, locked up in a damp, crumbling castle for days on end with no taste for tapestry—"

"I mean it," Barbarro said. "Get to the point or *I* will." With that, he drew his rapier and extended it menacingly towards her.

"Oh dear," said Lady Lockwood, a little sadly. "And I had so hoped we were going to be friends."

She laughed once more, glancing at Marianne and Angelika. Her two colleagues joined in, as if the three of them were sharing a private joke. Their laughter grew deeper and deeper, mutating from an expression of pleasure into a darker, more predatory sound. It was then that Moonshine Wrathe noticed the curiously long, and dangerously sharp, canine teeth protruding from each of their pretty mouths.

"Are you . . .?" he asked huskily, his voice disappearing before he finished the question. "Are you . . .?" Once more words failed him.

"Are we thirsty?" asked Lady Lockwood, smiling at him pleasantly. "Yes, my darling boy, we are very, *very* thirsty. Now, what can you offer us in the way of a drink?"

CHAPTER TWO

Flesh and Blood

"How long do you think they'll keep us waiting?"

Grace smiled at her brother. "My answer hasn't changed from the last time you asked me, three minutes ago. I just don't know."

Connor found the ante-room intensely claustrophobic. It was alien to him being in a room with no windows. Even the smallest cabins on board *The Diablo* had sported a porthole or two, giving you some glimpse of the world outside. The best this room could offer was a painting; the large, square canvas positioned as if to simulate a casement.

The whole of the Sanctuary compound induced feelings of claustrophia in Connor. He thought of the succession of winding corridors which marked the start of your journey underground. First the Corridor of Lights with its sickly-sweet smelling butter lamps. Then the Corridor of Discards or, as Connor had renamed it, of Junk. The walls of this corridor were lined with shelves, barely visible beneath their loads of bric-a-brac. They gave off an old, musty smell. Grace had informed him that these artefacts belonged to Vampirates who came to Sanctuary for healing. This thought made little sense to him.

Surely you either were a vampire or you weren't? And, if you *were*, there was no way to be healed.

The third corridor was the Corridor of Ribbons and as you walked along it, multicoloured strands of cloth brushed your hair and eyes. Grace had told him, rather breathlessly, that the ribbons were incredibly powerful, that they contained the emotions of the inmates here. But to Connor, they were just old, faded bits of cloth which, hanging in such close proximity to the lights, seemed something of a fire hazard.

It was strange, he thought, how he and his twin sister viewed the world so differently these days. He turned to look at her, lost in her own thoughts. She was sitting on the room's one chair. In time gone by, she would have curled her body into it like a little dormouse, her legs dangling over the side. Now, she sat with her back straight, feet on the floor and hands gently resting on her knees. Connor realised that he had left a girl at Pirate Academy and returned to find a young woman at Sanctuary. It hadn't been that long since he and Grace had last been together but experience was changing her, just as it was changing him. They were both growing up. But were they also growing apart?

Connor knew that whilst this place made him feel almost physically sick and aching to get back to the open ocean and fresh sea air, Grace seemed utterly at home here, amongst the Vampirates, their donors (the very idea of which made him decidedly nauseous) and their counsellors.

Grace suddenly looked up, evidently realising that he had been staring at her.

She gazed at him enquiringly. "What are you thinking?" she asked.

Deciding not to share the full range of his thoughts with her, he asked instead, "How can you be so calm, so patient?"

Grace shrugged, settling deeper into the chair. "Maybe I'm just enjoying having my brother back. It's been quite a while."

At this, Connor sat down on the arm of the chair and reached out his hand to her. "It's good to see you too, Grace. Not just good . . . well, I don't have to say it, do I?"

"No," she smiled, squeezing his hand. "You don't have to say anything."

"This takes me back," Connor said. "Back to when we were kids in the lighthouse."

"It was only a few months ago," said Grace. "But it feels a lifetime away, doesn't it?"

He nodded. "Sometimes . . . I wonder . . . Do you ever just feel like you want to go back? Back home?"

"I do think about going back," she said. "At least, I think about the life we had there. You, and me, and Dad. But even though it was only a few months ago, it feels like a dream. If we went back now, it wouldn't be the same. Dad wouldn't be there. The lighthouse would belong to someone else." She shivered. "To Lachlan Busby or whoever he decided to sell it on to. There might even be a new lighthouse keeper and his or her family. I don't think I could bear to see that. Could you? It would be as if we were ghosts."

Connor's eyes narrowed with pain. "No, I suppose not. And I know what you mean. The life we had before we were shipwrecked does seem like a dream, doesn't it? But it wasn't. It was real. It was our home. These days, I don't know where home is." He shook his head. "I thought that *The Diablo* could be my new home. I suppose I wanted it to be – and Molucco Wrathe to be some kind of father figure. But I was kidding myself."

"You have good friends there, though," Grace said. "Bart and Cate. Others too. I know you're angry with Molucco at the way he treated you, but maybe that *is* where you're meant to be."

"I didn't expect to hear you say that! Molucco Wrathe was never your favourite person."

10

"No," Grace agreed. The swaggering pirate captain had always been rather too smug and self-satisfied for her liking. "But what's right for you isn't necessarily right for me," she acknowledged now. "We're twins but we're different people."

"So we can never be together? Is that what you're saying?"

Grace shook her head. "I don't know. I wish I did. There's no one I feel closer to than you, Connor. But I never felt comfortable on *The Diablo*. And I know you could never feel at home aboard *The Nocturne* . . . or here at Sanctuary."

"But you do feel at home? On that ship of Vampirates and here?"

She shrugged. "Not at home exactly, but as though I'm meant to be here. I'm meant to be with them."

Connor's eyes widened at that.

"I know," she said, squeezing his hand again. "It's hard to understand."

He shrugged. "I don't see why it should be. After all, our mother is here, isn't she? She was on board the ship and then she came here, travelling within the captain's body somehow. It sounds weird when you try to put it into words, but I saw it . . . saw her . . . with my own eyes."

"Yes," Grace said, her own eyes bright with the image of their mother, sitting up and smiling at her. Her beautiful mother, with her emerald-green eyes and long auburn hair, opening her arms and drawing the twins into a hug.

"She was just as I always knew she would be," Grace said. "Just like in my dreams."

Connor leaned over to rest his head against Grace's. "Maybe that's all this is. Everything you and I have been through since the shipwreck. A dream, one we're dreaming together."

Grace smiled and snuggled in closer to her brother. Shutting her eyes, she allowed herself to retreat into her memories of happy times back in the lighthouse. But it wasn't long before

11

her restless mind threw up a fresh thought. "How did you find the climb up the mountain last night?"

"What? Oh, that. Nothing to it," Connor said. "A bit of a hike, but you know me. Super-fit and all that. Besides, there was a full moon. It was almost like daylight out there." He turned towards her. "Why do you ask?"

"*We* had the most arduous journey up here," she said. "The captain, Lorcan, Shanti and I. It was so dark and of course we had to lead Lorcan because he couldn't see then. Shanti lost her footing and almost fell. And just when we thought it couldn't get any worse, it began to snow. The path was so steep. Didn't you think so?"

Connor shook his head. "It was like a country road. Maybe you took a different route. It's funny though, I only ever saw one path at the foot of the rock."

"Yes," Grace agreed. "Yes, but it must be like Olivier told me once. That the mountain changes. That everyone makes a different way up here."

"Who's Olivier?" Connor asked.

Grace paused, remembering Mosh Zu's former lieutenant. He had been by turns indulgent and irritated with her: his moods as changeable as the weather. And he had betrayed his master, thinking that Sidorio would give him promotion, only to find himself betrayed and rejected by the renegade Vampirate in turn. "He was no one you need to know about," she said, at last. "He's gone now."

Connor slipped off the chair and drew himself to his feet once more. "How much longer do you think we'll have to wait? We only just got to say hello to her and then they took her away."

"They have to be careful," Grace answered. "She was one of the lost souls travelling with the captain. You saw how fragile they were, how bewildered at being set free."

"*Is* she our mother, Grace, or some kind of ghost?" He looked to his sister but she didn't have any answers for him. "She reached out her arms to us. She kissed us. I didn't imagine it, did I? She was as much flesh and blood as you or I."

Grace stood up and went over to him. "I don't have any answers for you, Connor. I wish I did. All I know is that Mosh Zu will do what is best. Until then, we just have to wait."

"I'm not very good at waiting," Connor said, starting to pace once more.

"We've waited for her for fourteen years," Grace said. "What's a few more hours?"

Connor smiled. "I guess when you put it like that . . ."

As he spoke, there was a knock at the door. It opened and Mosh Zu's assistant, Dani, poked her head around it. As usual, her face was impossible to read.

"Mosh Zu asks you to join him in his meditation room," she said.

"Is our mother with him?" Connor asked. "Is she all right?"

Perhaps Dani didn't hear his question. She had already begun walking briskly along the corridor.

"She'd tell us, wouldn't she?" Connor turned to Grace. "If something was wrong, they'd tell us, right?"

Grace could hear the rising panic in her brother's voice. "Come on," she said, reaching out her hand for his.

Grace felt her own heart beginning to race. She was every bit as anxious as Connor at the thought of what lay ahead.

CHAPTER THREE

The Queen of Hearts

"So, what *does* it take to get a drink around here?" Lady Lola Lockwood asked, her amber eyes skimming from Moonshine to Barbarro to Trofie Wrathe.

The three Wrathes were rendered speechless by the sight before them. Lady Lockwood and her two companions, Marianne and Angelika, were all smiling, revealing three pairs of exceedingly long canine teeth, which seemed only to get longer and sharper the more you stared at them.

Moonshine, who had been awed initially by the trio's beauty, now found his feelings towards them rapidly changing.

"We're thirsty," said Marianne, stepping towards him.

"Um, what . . . about . . . some . . . whiskey?" he faltered, reaching out for the decanter. But Marianne caught his arm and shook her head. "Can't drink whiskey. Doesn't suit my constitution." With that, she snaked her other arm around Moonshine and clutched him tightly to her, her mouth perilously close to his ear.

"Set him free!" commanded Barbarro. But Marianne seemed not to hear him. Barbarro turned to Lady Lockwood. "You, madam. You're their leader. Tell her to release my son."

Lady Lockwood smiled and shook her head. "She's just thirsty. And surely it's only courteous to offer a stranger a drink of welcome on a chill night such as this?"

"A drink of welcome?" Barbarro snarled. "Or a drink of blood?"

"Now you're talking!" said Angelika, stepping forward and snaking herself around the captain. He raised his arms and sword to defend himself but he was taken by surprise at her strength. In her clutches, he was frozen, though whether by his own fear or some magic, it was hard to tell. Trofie watched in wonder as Angelika removed the sword from Barbarro's fist as easily as a splinter and tossed it away out of reach.

She looked from side to side, to where her son and her husband stood helpless in the clutches of these women, these *demons*. What should she do? All normal rules of attack and defence seemed to be obsolete. Or were they?

Trofie turned to Lady Lockwood. "Perhaps I can make you a deal," she began.

At first, she thought Lady Lockwood might be too caught up in her own blood-lust to answer her but then she spoke. "A deal? What *kind* of deal?"

"Whatever it takes," said Trofie. "If it's blood you're after, then I can easily find some alternative crew-members for you."

Lady Lockwood smiled at that. "It's a charming offer, my dear, but blood is rather like wine. When you've supped on superior vintages, you lose your taste for cheap plonk."

"So," said Trofie. "Is that why you came here tonight? To claim the blood of the captain and his family?"

"My, I'm impressed," said Lady Lockwood. "There aren't many who could voice such a thought without plummeting into hysteria, yet you remain as cool as a glacier. It's clear to see who wears the trousers on *this* ship."

"Thank you for the compliment," said Trofie, "but if you

15

simply came with the intent to maim us, then let's not draw this out any longer."

On either side, Marianne and Angelika nodded at the thought, their grip on their two captives tightening. The fear currently being experienced by Barbarro and Moonshine was all too evident on the faces of both father and son.

"Wait!" commanded Lady Lockwood. Like well-trained dogs, her two comrades turned at their leader's voice. She held their gaze, then focused once more on Trofie. "You're as beautiful as they say," she said, running a finger over the curve of Trofie's cheekbone. Trofie remained as still as a waxwork at Lady Lockwood's ominous touch.

"I *will* make you a deal," Lady Lockwood announced. "I told you before that I like to acquire pretty things. Rare and *valuable* things."

As she spoke, her eyes never left Trofie's for a moment. "As thirsty as I am – as thirsty as we *all* are – I'm sure we could be distracted by a little treasure. What can you offer me, I wonder?" Lady Lockwood's bright eyes twinkled.

"Whatever it takes," said Trofie, unflinching. "Whatever it takes for you to let my son and husband go free with their lives."

"Well." Lady Lockwood raised an eyebrow. "You really *do* believe in family values, don't you?"

"Above all else," said Trofie.

Lady Lockwood reached out a hand once more to Trofie, but this time her fingers landed on the ruby necklace which dazzled like flame about Trofie's swan-white neck. "What a beautiful necklace," Lady Lockwood said, "and I'm quite sure it's unique."

"Yes," said Trofie. "Unique. Flawless. And worth a mint. If you want it, it's yours."

Lady Lola shrugged. "Why not? It's a little gaudy for my taste but I know someone on my crew who would adore it."

"If I give it to you, will you call them off?" Trofie asked.

Lady Lockwood folded her arms. "I'm afraid it's going to take a little more than that. But the necklace is a good starting point. Do you need any assistance unclasping it for me?"

"No," said Trofie, finally losing some of her froideur. "No, I can manage." She lifted her hands up to the back of her neck. As she did so, her golden fingers and ruby nails glimmered in the candlelight.

"Ah!" sighed Lady Lockwood. "There it is! The fabled hand of Trofie Wrathe!"

Hearing this, Trofie momentarily froze.

"Do you see it, ladies?" Lady Lockwood asked. "Why, isn't it a beauty? Such fine gold. Such perfect gemstones. It truly is a marvel. More fabulous even than we were led to believe! One of a kind."

Trofie unclasped her necklace and extended it in her golden hand to Lady Lockwood. But rather than taking the necklace, Lady Lockwood circled her fingers about Trofie's wrist where the flesh gave way to gold.

"Give it to me," she said, her eyes flashing with excitement.

"You want my *hand*?" Trofie said, incredulously.

"Yes, my dear." Lady Lockwood nodded, as if to a stupid child. "I'll take the necklace – it's a pretty trinket – but your hand is the real treasure."

"But what do you want with it?" Trofie said, bewildered. "It's no use to anyone but me."

Lady Lockwood still held the golden hand within her own. Now, she loosened her hold. "I told you before," she said. "I collect things. Pretty things. Unusual things. Sometimes I pass them on to my friends. And sometimes I keep them for myself. And this . . ." she caressed the golden fingers, "this I shall most definitely be keeping for myself."

"We have other treasures," said Trofie. "Let me show you.

17

Come to our treasure store and take your pick . . ."

"No thank you," said Lady Lockwood. "I'm not as greedy as all that. I'll go home tonight with the necklace and the hand and count myself a very lucky girl."

"But it's my mum's hand!" protested Moonshine. Angelika giggled and ran her fingers through Moonshine's hair.

Trofie kept her cool, her eyes fixed on Lady Lockwood's. "If I give it to you," she asked, "will you leave us? Do you give me your word?"

"I give you my word," said Lady Lockwood.

"Mum, you can't just give her your—"

"Be quiet, Moonshine. You've seen what Lady Lockwood is . . . what she is capable of. It's a small price to pay."

"It's your *hand*!" shouted Moonshine.

But Trofie's mind was made up. She reached across and released the catches with which the golden hand was fastened. It came free from her wrist. Trofie gave a nod. "It's yours. Take it."

Smiling, Lady Lockwood took the hand in her own, sliding it out from Trofie's sleeve. She lifted it to her lips and kissed it, then drew it into the folds of her cape. She clapped her hands in delight.

"Ladies, let the prisoners go. We have what we came for."

As Marianne and Angelika reluctantly released Moonshine and Barbarro from their clutches, Trofie stared at Lady Lockwood. "You wanted my hand all along, didn't you?"

"Perhaps," said Lady Lockwood with a smile. "Well, toodle-pip. Enjoy your midnight feast." She tapped the top of the domed platter she had carried in.

With that, she turned and pushed open the door. Marianne and Angelika followed their leader back out into the corridor. The door swung closed behind them and the three members of the Wrathe family were alone once more. They looked at each other, dumbstruck.

"I'm going after her," Moonshine said.

"No!" cried Trofie and Barbarro in unison.

Moonshine stopped in his tracks. "But Mum, your hand . . ."

"We'll get another," Barbarro said.

"Oh yeah," said Moonshine. "We'll just pop out to the golden-hand store!"

"She's a . . . she's a *vampire*, isn't she?" At last Trofie's voice betrayed some of the shock she had kept so well-hidden before.

"Yes, my dear," nodded Barbarro, taking his wife in his arms. "A vampire. Or Vampirate. Whatever they call themselves. The same monsters who killed my dear brother, Porfirio."

"All the more reason to exact a swift and terrible revenge," Moonshine said.

"This isn't something to be entered into lightly or alone," said his father. "We were lucky to get away with our lives tonight."

"All right," Moonshine persisted. "But what are you planning to do about it?"

"First, I'm going to talk to Molucco. He has some experience with these creatures. He talked me out of pursuing them for revenge before, but that's all changed now. I'll see to that. These monsters cannot attack us on our own ships! So we talk to Molucco. Then, I'm taking this up with the Pirate Federation. We will work together to purge the oceans of this menace." He bristled. "They chose the wrong ship to attack tonight! Let no one be in any doubt about *that*!"

Moonshine couldn't help but reflect that, stirring as his father's words were, the captain had been rather less combative during his encounter with the Vampirates.

Barbarro drew his wife and deputy closer to him and spoke more softly. "But right now, I'm taking your mother to our cabin," he said to his son. "If you want to make yourself useful, summon the entire crew to meet me on the main deck in ten

19

minutes sharp. I want to know just how those devils boarded the mighty *Typhon* in the first place." His orders given, Barbarro led his wife out of the state room.

Moonshine began to follow them, then stopped in his tracks, spying the domed tray which Lady Lockwood had carried in with her. His shock had given way to hunger. Was it too much to hope that there might be some tasty morsels under the lid?

But, as he lifted the lid, he was disappointed. The platter was empty, save for one item. A playing card.

Moonshine reached forward and lifted it into his hands. It was similar to a regular playing card but there was something odd about it. It was the Queen of Hearts . . . except that Hearts were always red.

And this card was black.

CHAPTER FOUR

Incomplete Reunion

"No need to linger in the shadows," Mosh Zu said as Grace and Connor entered the meditation chamber. He was standing in the centre of the room, facing them. In front of him was a wicker chair, its plaited twigs glowing pale gold in the lamplight. The back of the chair was turned to the twins. At its side, also made of wicker, was a round table, on which sat a pitcher of water and three glasses. As Grace watched, a small pale hand appeared from the other side of the chair and reached out for a glass. Grace's heart lurched. The hand belonged to Sally, her mother. In just moments, she and Connor would sit down and have their first proper conversation with her. Suddenly, the enormity of this meeting felt overwhelming to her. She reached for Connor's fingertips – she could feel him shaking too.

Mosh Zu remained matter-of-fact, asking Connor to help him bring two more chairs over to the centre of the room. Grace found herself alone, mere steps from her mother. Taking a deep breath, she walked forward. Sally's eyes met hers, the vivid green of her irises perfectly mirroring Grace's own.

"Hello again!" Sally said, smiling up at her. She looked weak but she was, just as Grace had remembered, flesh and blood.

She leaned forward and kissed her mother's cheek. It felt as smooth and cool as marble – but to Grace the important thing was that she *could* feel it. She remembered the visits she had received from Darcy when, though her friend had seemed to be in the same room, it had only been an astral projection and Grace's hands had moved right through Darcy's. This was different, very different.

Sally grasped both Grace's hands and their eyes met – green on emerald green. As they did so, Grace had the strangest sensation. It began like the onset of a vicious headache – a searing pain right through her skull. The pain was only momentary though and, as it gave way, a series of images flashed before her eyes. The first was of her father, but he was younger than she had ever seen him. It was night-time and he was outside, laughing. Grace felt Sally squeeze her hands once more. Now the image changed. This time, it was Sidorio she saw. He looked just the same as she remembered him. He was entering the long cabin at the bottom of *The Nocturne* – the cabin where the weekly feasts took place. Once more, Sally squeezed her hands and again the vision changed. This time, it was Lorcan Grace saw. He was looking at her closely, tears in his eyes. Then Sally took her hands away and the visions instantly disappeared.

Grace stood rooted to the spot, dazed, as Sally turned to face Connor. As she watched mother and son embrace, Grace wondered if Sally had any clue as to the effect her touch had had upon her. And what did this strange sequence of images mean? Was it a window into her past?

"Let me look at you," Sally said now. "Let me get a good look at both of you."

Grace turned and saw that Connor had come to a standstill beside her. Now, he reached out his arm and looped it around Grace's shoulder, though she was unsure whether he had done so in order to comfort her or to steady his own nerves.

"Grace and Connor," Sally said softly. "My twins. My angels!" It was clear from the rasp in her voice that these few words had not been produced without effort.

"Why don't you each take a seat?" Mosh Zu suggested, indicating the two empty chairs. As Grace sat down, she wondered why Mosh Zu had not brought over another for himself.

"Doubtless, you have many questions for your mother," Mosh Zu said. He turned to Sally, a soft smile sweeping across his face. "And I know she is eager to learn more about each of you. I shall leave you for a while. It is fitting that you should be alone together as a family. You have, each in your own way, waited a very long time for this reunion."

As Mosh Zu walked towards the door, Grace felt her pulse quicken. A raft of questions raced through her brain. How long have we got? How fragile is Sally's condition? What happens if she gets upset? She appreciated Mosh Zu's offer to give them space to get to know each other, but she wished he had better prepared her, for all their sakes.

She watched the door close behind him. As it did, she heard his voice, calm and clear in her head. "*Do not let these worries cloud the joy of your meeting. The answer to each of your questions is simple. I do not know any better than you do. But be assured, I will be close at hand if and when you need me.*"

Grace nodded, then turned back to the others, wondering if they had observed this gesture and thought it strange. Neither appeared to have noticed. Connor was looking down at his hands, which rested on his knees. Sally was watching him. She had, thought Grace, a childlike quality. It was hard to judge her age, given her current pallor. Even if she had been as young as sixteen when she had given birth to the twins, that would still make her thirty now. But she seemed younger than that. If Grace hadn't known otherwise, she'd have placed Sally in her mid-twenties or even younger. But that couldn't be the case. The numbers just didn't add up.

"Well," Sally said, "as long as we've all waited for this moment, it's actually kind of awkward, isn't it?" At these words, Connor looked up, staring at her through his fringe. Sally smiled at him, then turned to face Grace too. "Like the guru guy says, I'm sure you both have heaps of questions for me. Where do you suppose we should begin?"

Grace felt conflicted. She didn't want to ask anything too difficult or upsetting straight away. At the same time, she was conscious that, given Sally's condition, their time together might be limited and she didn't want to miss this opportunity to address the important questions. In the end, she hedged her bets. "I was just wondering," she said. "How long is it since you saw us? Besides that last time in the healing chamber. How long was it before that since we were together?" She paused. "I don't mean to sound rude or hurtful, but I don't have any memories of you in Crescent Moon Bay."

Sally started to speak, but her voice was hoarse – perhaps from lack of use – and she coughed, then asked, "Connor, would you be a darling and pour me a glass of water?"

Connor leaned forward and tilted the pitcher towards a glass, reaching out and placing it in his mother's hand.

"Thank you," she said, smiling up at him. For the first time, he smiled back. Sally took a sip of water, then continued. "Now, Grace, to answer your question. The truth is, I have never been to Crescent Moon Bay."

"Never?" exclaimed Grace. She could see that Connor too was surprised.

Sally shook her head. "I should like to go there someday." Some of the light drained from her eyes. "I suppose it would have to be someday very soon, now."

"But we've always lived in Crescent Moon Bay," Grace said.

24

"Right up until Dad died and we left and got caught in the storm. All our lives we were there."

"Yes," Sally nodded. "All your lives except the very beginning part." She lifted one small hand and gestured with her thumb and forefinger. "Just a tiny beginning sliver before you went to Crescent Moon Bay. That, my darlings, was the last time I saw you."

"When we were babies?"

Sally nodded.

"But why?" Grace asked.

"It's a long story," Sally said. "A long and sometimes difficult story." Her voice had grown weak again and she took another sip of water, pausing before she continued. "But it's your story and you must be told it."

Grace glanced at Connor, then back at Sally. Her fear had given way to excitement. It was as if they were little kids again, snuggled up in their twin bunks in the lighthouse bedroom they had shared when younger. Cosy and all set to hear a story before bedtime. Only, now they knew for certain that Sally had never been there in the lighthouse. It was their dad, Dexter Tempest, who had always told them stories before bed. Told them stories and sang them that strange shanty . . .

"I'll tell you a tale of Vampirates,
A tale as old as true . . ."

Grace felt sad that her dad wasn't here to share in this reunion. It made it incomplete.

"Your story begins aboard *The Nocturne*," Sally said.

"*The Nocturne!*" Grace exclaimed. "That's the Vampirate ship," she reminded Connor.

"Yes," he said, slightly irritably. "I know that."

"You sailed on *The Nocturne!*" Grace said, excitedly, shaking

25

her head. Now she had an answer to one of her big questions – how Sally and Lorcan knew each other. She felt a deeper sense of kinship with her mother. As if they had unwittingly walked the same path in life. "What were you doing aboard *The Nocturne*?" she asked.

"She was about to tell us," Connor said, with some force. "Grace, please let her tell us the story without interrupting every five seconds."

"All right," Grace said, turning from Connor back to Sally. "Sorry," she said.

"That's OK," Sally said, sipping a little more water. "I was always like you, Grace. Hungry for information. Couldn't wait to know everything. See everything. Do everything." She smiled, then set the water glass down again. "What was I doing on *The Nocturne*? Simple, really. I was a donor."

CHAPTER FIVE

Night Moves

Stukeley rode the wave expertly into shore, then jumped off into the shallows and flipped the surfboard into his arms.

He watched as Johnny followed him in. His balance was superb. He'd only recently learned to surf, under Stukeley's own tutelage, but already he was as good as his teacher. All his experience on horseback had given him a strong sense of how to balance and steer the board through the most powerful of waves.

Johnny was whooping with exhilaration as he scooped up the board and ran out of the water to meet his friend. "How'd I do?" he asked.

Stukeley smiled and reached out his hand to squeeze Johnny's shoulder. "You did good, mate," he said. "You're a natural."

"Thanks, *hermano*," Johnny grinned. *Hermano*. The word meant "brother" in Johnny's native tongue. And it was true that in the short time they had known each other, they had become like brothers. Stukeley had had close friendships before. His brain flickered briefly with an image of him on board *The Diablo*, clowning around with Connor and Bart. Such images were becoming harder and harder to conjure now, as if they were a dream he had once dreamed but could no longer return to. *This* was his life now – this world of pervasive darkness.

"You look distant. What are you thinking about?"

Stukeley shook his head. "I had just had this flashback to when I was mortal."

"Still getting those, eh?" Johnny gave a wry smile and set his Stetson back on his head.

"Yeah, I was thinking about—"

"Don't go there," Johnny said, with a shake of his head. "It'll only bring you pain." He slammed his surfboard into the sand. "Trust me. I've made that mistake too many times myself."

Stukeley watched the moonlit waves, reflected in Johnny's dark eyes. "Then what?" he asked. "Do I just let it all go? Everything I used to be?"

Johnny nodded. "Yes. Let it float away from you. Live in the here and now."

Stukeley looked at his friend. "Is that what you do?"

"I try to, man. It's not always easy but it's easier than filling your head with pain and regret and yearning."

Stukeley nodded. "There are people I cared about and people who cared about me. I didn't always do right by them . . ."

"Trust me," Johnny said. "The only way you'll ever be free is to live in the moment. On this beach. Right now. This is all we have."

Though Johnny looked a few years younger, on account of the age he'd been when he'd crossed, he'd been in this realm a whole lot longer than Stukeley. His journey had been long and often hard, Stukeley knew, from the few snippets he'd told him. When it came to giving advice on making fresh starts, the one-time *vacquero* knew what he was talking about.

"Look." Johnny spun Stukeley around and they watched the other surfers. Mortal eyes would have been blind to their serried ranks, even if any mortals had been brave enough to be out on the beach tonight, rather than shut up indoors, behind closed windows and locked doors.

The water was teeming with them. There was excitement in the air; not just from the exhilaration of the surf but also from the anticipation of what would follow.

"Where's the captain?" Stukeley asked. "I don't see him."

"Right there." Johnny pointed. "Right where you'd expect him to be – at the heart of the action."

And there was Sidorio, head and shoulders above those surrounding him, utterly in command of the tall wave which he rode in to shore. Seeing his two lieutenants awaiting him, he gave a roar and propelled his muscled body up into the air, turning a complete somersault, the surfboard still attached to his feet. Then he landed once more on the raging waters and latched onto another wave to complete his journey to the beach.

"Nice one, Captain!" Stukeley nodded in admiration as Sidorio strode up to join them.

Sidorio smiled. "Sometimes I even surprise myself," he said.

"Did you see Johnny surfing before?" Stukeley asked. "He's getting good. Really good."

"I saw him," Sidorio said, nodding at Johnny. "Nice work, Stetson."

Johnny basked in the captain's praise, which was rarely quick to flow.

Now the beach was filling up with the others – a massed rank of dark figures, emerging from the water and stepping onto land, immediately bone dry.

"Look at that!" Stukeley said. The three of them turned and looked along the beach, at the row of surfboards planted in the sand. Here was Sidorio's crew – the growing tide of Vampirates, recruited from the disaffected travellers aboard *The Nocturne* and those languishing at Sanctuary, as well as some recent

29

inmates of a prison ship. Fresh converts, thought Stukeley. And how readily they had crossed; more readily in many ways than he had. How could this be? How could they have crossed so easily, while he was still struggling? He gazed along the line at their expectant faces.

"They're waiting for you," Johnny whispered in his ear.

Stukeley heard the words and it was like a switch had been flicked inside his brain. Suddenly, he knew what he had to do, what he had to say. Suddenly, he knew who he was.

"OK," Stukeley clapped his hands, assuming authority and with it the semblance of confidence. "Welcome to Santa Demonica, guys. It's a friendly little town, so they say. But I can't promise that the locals will be too welcoming to you lot, at this time of night. Or, to be frank, any old time." He waited for their responsive laughter to settle before continuing. "You know the drill, guys. Do what you want. Take what you need." He zeroed in on a few choice faces within the crowd. "But try to play nice. No fighting between each other!" He addressed them all once more. "And most important. Be back here, ready for the ship, three hours from now."

Stukeley stood back. The ranks of Vampirates still lingered on the sand. Stukeley turned to Sidorio. "If you'd care to give them the command, Captain," he said.

Sidorio stepped forward without hesitation. "What are you waiting for?" he cried out. "Go forth and feast!"

At his command, they began to run, like hungry wolves released into the wild. Some ran together, in a pack. Others found their own way, preferring to track and take their prey alone.

Stukeley heard the first door being broken down, the first window being smashed. The first scream. These sounds had their immediate echoes, before the familiar discordant music grew louder, swelling into a sustained and violent rhapsody.

He shivered briefly, then turned to see Johnny standing at his side.

"Where's the captain?" he asked.

"Gone already," said Johnny. "Gone to feast with the others."

Another crescendo of breaking glass. Another chorus of screams.

"We should go too," Johnny said. "We need it as much as they do. We are all the same."

"Yes," Stukeley agreed. "Yes, we are all the same." Together, he and Johnny wandered off across the sand.

They hadn't got very far when Johnny nudged Stukeley. "Look," he said, nodding towards the dunes. "Looks like we could be hunting closer to home tonight."

Stukeley followed Johnny's eyeline. Over the dunes were two figures – two women, dressed elegantly in long, fitted dresses and, somewhat impractically, under the circumstances, high-heeled shoes. One of them was wearing a broad-brimmed hat and an extravagant ruby necklace, constructed rather like a spider's web. Both, rather curiously, had on large dark sunglasses.

"*Hola!* Good evening, ladies!" Johnny called, raising a hand. "You look like you're dressed for a party."

The woman wearing the hat turned to him. "A party," she said. "Yes indeed. Do you know where we can find one?"

"Right here!" Johnny said, emphatically. "Right about here!"

The woman smiled. Johnny could see his grinning face reflected in her dark glasses.

"Why are you wearing those shades at night?" Johnny asked.

The women laughed at this. Then they spoke simultaneously. "Fashion, darling!"

The way they said "darling" sent shivers up Stukeley's spine. This was going to be easy. It so often was. Few could resist a charm offensive by Sidorio's two charismatic lieutenants.

"So," said Stukeley, deciding to move things on. "Care to walk with us for a bit? I'm Stukeley, by the way, and this handsome fella here is Johnny." At that, Johnny removed his Stetson and bowed grandly.

The women smiled once more. "I'm Jessamy," said the hat-wearer.

"And I'm Camille."

"Beautiful names for beautiful ladies," Stukeley said. "Now, why don't you take off your sunglasses and show us your beautiful eyes?"

The women faced each other. Then, in perfect synchronicity, they lifted and removed their sunglasses. Turning back towards the men, they revealed faces that were far more beautiful than Stukeley and Johnny could have ever imagined. Their eyes were as bright as jewels and around each of their right eyes was a tattoo of a black heart.

Stukeley gasped. This was too perfect. His hunger was so strong now. He could sense it was the same for Johnny. He could see the fire burning in the depths of his eyes. As he shifted his gaze back to the women, Stukeley caught his breath. For the very same fire was burning in their eyes too.

Seeing his confusion, Jessamy smiled, opening her mouth a little wider than before, revealing a pair of over-long, razor-sharp incisors. Now Camille's incisors flashed white in the moonlight too.

"You mentioned a party before," said Jessamy. "I think we're all looking for the same kind of fun, don't you?" She extended her hand towards Stukeley. Like a mirror image, Camille reached out her hand to Johnny. "Come on," she said, hungrily. "Let's go and feast."

Stukeley awoke on the sand, feeling a deep sense of peace and relaxation, accompanied by a sense of disorientation. It took him a moment or two to recognise where he was. He turned and saw Johnny, snoozing away, his Stetson rising and falling on his chest. A broad smile was painted on Johnny's lips. There were a few spatters of blood between his lips and his chin.

Blood. It brought back a flash of memory. They had been feasting. For some reason, Stukeley could not summon up the full memory of it. But this was not unusual. It was often a blur on waking. Sometimes, it took a good while for the details of the feasting to return.

Stukeley watched as, at last, Johnny opened his eyes. He frowned. "Where am I?"

Stukeley chuckled. "You're on a beach, mate."

"I see that," his friend said. "But where – and why?"

"Well," Stukeley said, "judging by that little trail of blood above your chin, I'd hazard a guess that we've been feasting."

Johnny blinked at the word. "That's funny. I can't remember . . ." He brought himself up into a sitting position. "I feel kind of dizzy," he said.

"Me too," said Stukeley. "But it's a nice kind of dizzy." He climbed up onto his feet. His body felt like jelly. His limbs splayed out in each direction and he crashed back onto the sand, laughing.

Johnny laughed too. "That's the funniest thing I've seen in ages!"

"All right, smarty pants," said Stukeley. "Let's see *you* walk the walk."

Johnny accepted the challenge and clambered up onto his feet. "There!" he announced, standing perfectly upright for a moment. "Nothing to it!" As he finished speaking, his legs gave way and he tumbled back down onto the sand.

"Very impressive!" cried Stukeley, cracking up.

"*Man!*" exclaimed Johnny. "We must have taken a lot of blood tonight, don't you think?"

"Oh yes," Stukeley nodded. "I reckon we had one heck of a party. It's just a shame we can't remember a thing about it."

Lady Lockwood was waiting in her cabin for Jessamy and Camille to make their return. She was playing a form of Patience with a stack of unusual playing cards – unusual in that the only suit was Hearts and every card was black.

At the first knock on her cabin door, the captain called out. "Enter!"

Jessamy and Camille, wearing their cocktail dresses and finery, strode into the room. Both were smiling.

"Well?" said the captain. "You look like you had fun!"

"Oh yes," said Jessamy, removing her hat and shaking out her long, red hair. It clashed marvellously with her ruby necklace.

"Great fun, Captain!" agreed Camille.

"And did everything go to plan?" Lady Lockwood asked.

"Of course," Jessamy purred, with a smile. "They were putty in our hands!"

Lady Lockwood nodded in approval. "This calls for a toast," she said. By her side was a wine bottle and several glasses. Her own glass was already half filled but she lifted the bottle and poured a drink for her two comrades.

"What are we drinking?" asked Jessamy.

Lady Lockwood smiled. "A cheeky little Italian." She paused. "I think his name was Vincent. No, *Vincenzo*, that's right! An opera-singer, though not a terribly good one if truth be known."

Camille took a sip, savouring the fine vintage a good while before allowing it to slip down her throat.

"Is it to your taste, dear?" Lady Lockwood asked. "Or would you like something with more body?"

Camille shook her head. "It's delicious, Captain."

Jessamy nodded her own appreciation. "A worthy addition to the Black Heart winery," she said.

"I'm so pleased," said Lady Lockwood. "There are a few more bottles where that came from. Share them between you if you like. Consider it a little thank you for a well-executed mission."

The captain smiled, then lifted her own glass to her lips once more and drank. The first salvo across Sidorio's bows had been fired.

CHAPTER SIX

Different Realities

"A donor!" Grace couldn't restrain herself.

Sally nodded, reaching out and squeezing Grace's hand. But once more, though the touch was intended as reassuring, it caused a ricochet in Grace's head. In rapid succession, the three images she had seen before flashed by again – first Dexter, then Sidorio, then Lorcan. And this time, there was a fresh image – of the Vampirate captain himself, sitting at the table in his cabin.

As Sally removed her hand, the vision instantly died. Once more, apparently oblivious to the effect of her touch, Sally continued to speak. "I take it by your reactions that you both know what a donor is?"

Connor was silent. Grace, still shocked by the visions, nodded. She tried to focus on what Sally was saying. The fact she had been a donor explained the strange anomaly in Sally's age. The pact between Vampirate and donor prevented the donor from ageing. But surely Sally would have had to have stopped being a donor to give birth to the twins. Unless . . .

Grace's unconscious mind was whirring away. She felt she was close to a discovery but she wasn't quite there yet. Perhaps there was a clue in the strange sequence of images that had flashed through her head when Sally had touched her – Dexter, Sidorio, Lorcan and the Vampirate captain.

"Grace, are you all right?" Sally's voice cut through her feverish thoughts. Grace realised that her eyes were closed. She opened them again. "Sorry," she said, "I keep getting this jumble of images in my head." She gazed at Sally. "It happens every time you touch me." At this, Connor turned and looked at her curiously. Grace asked her mother, "Are you doing it on purpose?"

Sally shook her head. "No, Grace, I'm not. But tell me, what images are coming into your head?"

"They're people I know. Dad and Sidorio, then Lorcan and the Vampirate captain. But they're just flashes. I'm not sure what they mean – but I don't think they're my own memories. Dad's much younger than I ever saw him."

Sally smiled. "How amazing!" she said. "Do you want to try it again?"

Grace nodded. Sally reached out her hand and Grace took it. As soon as their flesh made contact, it happened again. Only this time, there was less initial pain and the vision was clearer. It was of her dad. The same vision as before. Night-time, out of doors. He was laughing. This time, the vision stayed with him. She saw that he was on the deck of a ship, then realised with a start that she recognised the ship. She gasped. Sally released her hand and the vision subsided as quickly as before.

"What did you see that time?" Sally asked curiously.

Grace opened her eyes, but she was still focused on the vision. She was reeling from the possibility it had led her to and uncertain whether to voice her thoughts.

"*What* did you see?" Connor asked, a note of irritation in his voice.

"It's OK, Grace," Sally said softly. "Whatever it is, you must share it with us. I told you this is a difficult story, but we'll make it through together – the three of us – I promise you." She turned to Connor. "I promise you *both*."

Grace took a breath. "It was Dad," she said. "He was so young and happy." She paused. "He was on the deck of a ship. It was *The Nocturne*. I saw the sails sparking with light behind him."

"That's impossible!" Connor said. "Dad was never on *The Nocturne*."

Grace shook her head. "No, I'm certain it was him." She turned to Sally. "I think I've figured it out," she said. "Our story, I mean. *You* were a donor. And our dad, Dexter, *he* was your vampire partner." Grace glanced at Connor, saw him frown, then faced Sally as she summoned up the words that she knew had the potential to change both twins' lives for ever. "Our father was a Vampirate."

Sally held Grace's gaze but, before she could respond, Connor jumped up from his seat and cried out. "No! I don't want to hear this! I don't want or *need* to hear this. Our dad was a good man. No, Grace – not a 'good man' like Lorcan or your Vampirate captain. A *truly* good man. He raised us on his own. He sacrificed everything for us for fourteen years and died way too young." Connor stopped and glared at Sally. "How dare you say these things about him!"

"I didn't say . . ." Sally began but her voice had grown weak again and, besides, Connor was already striding towards the door.

Sally coughed and reached for more water. "Go after him," she rasped at Grace.

Grace was torn. "What about you?"

"Go," Sally said, gathering all the force she could muster. "Bring him back. He needs to hear this as much as you do."

Her voice might be weak but her words were strong as steel. Grace ran to the door and chased along the corridor after

Connor. He hadn't got very far. He was leaning against the wall, his head in his hands.

"Connor, you have to come back in there with me."

He twisted his head and glared at her. "I don't *have* to go anywhere, Grace."

Grace was insistent. "You need to hear what our mother has to say. We both do."

Connor shook his head. "It's lies, Grace. A fairy tale." He shook his head. "No, not a fairy tale, more like a horror story."

"You might not like it, Con, but that doesn't mean it isn't true." She reached out an arm to him, but he shook her off angrily.

"You're actually asking me to believe that our dad was a vampire?" He shook his head, incredulous.

"Perhaps," Grace said. "And, if that is the case, then we ought to know." She paused, deep in her own spiral of thoughts. "I wonder . . . would that make *us* vampires too?"

Connor stared at her open-mouthed. "Listen to yourself!" he said. "Grace, you've completely lost your sense of reality. OK, so the Vampirates rescued you from drowning. They did a good thing there, no question. But that isn't enough for you, is it? No, you have to go and make *friends* with them! And now you want to be *family* too? It's not normal, Grace. It's weird. Deeply, horribly weird."

"I'll make friends with whomever I choose," Grace said, equally full of fire.

"Fine," Connor said. "That's *your* choice." Then he spoke very deliberately. "Our father was *not* a Vampirate. Dexter Tempest was a kind, normal, man with two kids and a job as a lighthouse keeper. Overworked and underpaid."

"You can keep telling yourself that," said Grace, surprised by her own calm, "but saying it doesn't make it true." She paused. "I haven't lost my sense of reality, Connor. I'm just open to *different* realities. While you've been away, living the pirate life,

I've had my eyes opened to the most amazing possibilities – things I would never have dreamed could be true." Her eyes flashed with fire as she continued. "You've even seen some of these things for yourself! You were there when Mosh Zu healed the captain."

Connor bristled. "I don't see what that has to do with Dad."

"Connor, you saw Mother and the other shades rise from the captain's body! Didn't that change your sense of what is *normal* and what is *possible*?"

"Maybe," he conceded. "Maybe I'm even ready to accept that she is our mother, or the ghost of our mother – though I'm really struggling with how she travelled around in the captain's stomach all these years." He sighed. "These things, they're too hard for me to get my head round and, frankly, I don't even want to. But I *knew* Dad. I lived with him for fourteen years, day and night. He was a regular guy. Dexter Tempest was *not* a Vampirate."

The more he tried to shut her down, the more impassioned Grace became. "You need to redefine your sense of what a vampire is," she said. "Vampirates can be *regular* guys too. Look at Lorcan . . ."

Connor nodded. "I thought it might come back to him. Look, Grace, I know how much you like Lorcan. He's the first boy you've ever been really interested in, but even so you have to face facts. He is *not* a regular guy . . ."

"He's kind," said Grace. "And thoughtful. And funny . . ."

"Oh yeah," Connor said. "A regular barrel of laughs is ol' Lorcan, I'm sure. But you're forgetting some of the more salient information about him, Grace." He paused. "Like, for instance, how he likes to suck blood."

"It isn't that he *likes* it," Grace said, vehemently. "Lorcan *needs* blood to revivify himself. He has an appetite for it but he has learned to control it."

"Well," Connor said, nodding. "You're right. That's *very* regular."

Grace reached out her hand to her brother, determined to give this one more try. "Connor, please, let's go back in there and finish this conversation with Sally while we have the chance. She's so frail. We don't know how long we have left."

He stared at her intently – his thoughts closed to her – then shook his head.

Grace sighed and turned away from him. Folding her arms tightly across her chest, she strode back towards the meditation room.

"Grace, wait!" Connor cried. "We need to talk! Just the two of us."

But there was no stopping her. She marched along the corridor and back into the meditation room. She went over to her mother's chair, then let out a gasp. Sally was slumped on the floor, her eyes closed and her body limp.

"No!" Grace cried. It couldn't end – not here, not now. There was too much left unsaid, unknown, between mother and daughter. She had to bring her back to consciousness.

Grace reached out to cradle her mother in her arms. As she did so, her head once more flashed with images. Dexter. Sidorio. Lorcan. The Vampirate captain. And now Mosh Zu and Shanti too. The vision flashed from one face to the next. It was like watching a pack of cards being shuffled really fast.

Not now! Grace pleaded. She had to save Sally . . . but there was no let up from the vision. Faces flashed before her, finally settling on the image of Dexter, as though his card had been selected from the pack. He was on the deck of the ship, just like before. And, in spite of Connor's nay-saying, there behind him was the main mast and *The Nocturne*'s vast wing-like sails, pulsing with light.

Dexter was laughing and reaching out his hand towards her.

41

Grace realised that she was seeing things from her mother's point of view. In the vision, she was standing up too, taking Dexter's hand in hers and walking across the deck. Her mother glanced behind her. There, on the deck was Lorcan and Shanti, *his* donor. They were smiling and waving as Sally and Dexter took their leave. Then, Sally and Dexter were walking inside. Grace could see the familiar corridor, with cabins on either side. Her mother's hand pushed open the door. Was she about to see her mother share blood with her father? This would be the confirmation that she had indeed been his donor: the irrefutable truth that Dexter Tempest *was* a Vampirate.

"Grace!" Connor's cry tore through her consciousness, but she clung on to the vision, desperate for it not to fade at this point. Then, she felt her brother's arms on her. He was pulling her away from Sally. "Let go of her!" he said. "You're holding her too tight. Grace, you're hurting her."

Grace came to on the floor, a distance away from Connor, who now cradled Sally protectively. "What have you done to her, Grace?" he asked.

"Me? I haven't done anything! How could you even think—"

"You were clinging on to her for dear life."

"She was like this when I came back into the room. I reached out for her, like you have, but as soon as I touched her, a vision began again."

Connor frowned. "I don't want to hear about it," he said, darkly. "And Grace, you have to *stop* touching her. I don't understand what's going on, but evidently it's not good for her."

He felt for a pulse, then stared up at Grace, panic etched across his face. "We need help, Grace. Go and fetch Mosh Zu or someone . . . anyone. Now!"

CHAPTER SEVEN

Friends and Secrets

Later that evening, several hours after her mother's collapse, Grace sat on the bench before the little fountain in the kitchen garden, trying to be patient as Mosh Zu and his assistants attended to Sally.

The fountain had become one of her favourite spots on the Sanctuary complex – the place she came to whenever she needed to calm her frazzled nerves. Something in the combination of the cool air, the fragrant scent of the wild herbs growing nearby and the sound of water tumbling back upon itself usually worked its magic upon her.

Right now, Grace's head was feverish with thoughts; her stomach coiled in knots. She thought about what Sally had told her – and what Sally had been on the *verge* of telling her. That she was a donor. That perhaps she was Dexter Tempest's donor. That the twins' father was a Vampirate and that, therefore, they too were vamp . . . But no, she mustn't let her mind race ahead of her. All Sally had said definitively so far was that she had been a donor on board *The Nocturne*. The rest, though it all made sense, awaited her confirmation.

Grace thought of the visions which had arisen, through her

contact with Sally. It had been amazing to see life on *The Nocturne* through her mother's eyes – to see her dad looking so young and handsome and carefree, and Lorcan too – though of course he was physically unchanged. Grace remembered the way Lorcan and Sally had looked at each other back in the healing chamber, when she had first reappeared. It was clear they had been good friends once and this confirmed it. Grace was pleased about that – it felt like another connection to two people she cared deeply for.

Seeing Shanti had been interesting too. Though Grace had mixed feelings about Lorcan's former donor, she still felt a deep sadness at her brutal murder at the hands of a renegade Vampirate.

Grace trembled. Her thoughts turned again to her mother. Were Connor's accusations fair? *Was* Grace actually hurting her by tapping into her distant memories? It was clear that Sally was in a deeply fragile state. The last thing Grace wanted was to make her weaker still. And yet, the way the visions rushed into her head the moment she and her mother made contact made Grace feel that Sally must want her to know them, even if only on a subconscious level. She seemed to be trying to tell Grace the full story.

Grace stared at the tumbling waters of the fountain. She wished that she was not alone, that she had someone close to talk things through with. But who?

Connor, though he had calmed down considerably, had said that he needed time to himself and had gone off to his room to get some rest.

The captain would have been a calm sounding-board for her, but there had been no sign of him since his healing.

She had sought out Lorcan but, according to one of the others, he had gone over to the donors' blocks and wasn't expected back any time soon.

44

Grace remembered other nights at Sanctuary when, in the lonely hours, she had sought out the company of Johnny Desperado. Now he was gone, lured away by the dark temptation of Sidorio. Though Johnny had turned out to be of questionable character, he'd been good company and a great listener. Now, sitting in front of the little fountain, Grace felt the absence of all the people she had grown accustomed to calling upon for support. She felt suddenly, achingly, alone.

"Grace!"

At first, she thought she had somehow conjured the voice herself – it wouldn't have been the first time.

"Grace!"

She glanced up to find Darcy Flotsam walking around the side of the fountain towards her. Darcy's warm smile was like the answer to a prayer.

Grace rose to her feet and hugged her friend. "Darcy! How wonderful to see you!"

Darcy hugged her back and laughed. "It's good to see you too, Grace."

"What are you doing out here?" Grace asked, her joy overriding her slight guilt at having omitted to think of Darcy, dear Darcy, in the same breath as the others.

"Much the same as you, I'd imagine," Darcy said. "Taking a breath of air. After nights on the deck of *The Nocturne*, it gets awful stuffy inside the compound, don't you find?"

"Oh Darcy!" Grace said, beaming, "It really *is* a treat to see you. I've been sitting out here worrying about my mother. And then I started thinking about stuff Connor said to me and about my dad and the captain . . . and I just got to feeling so alone." Tears welled in her eyes.

"Shhh," Darcy said, her voice as soothing as the waters of the fountain. "I'm here, Grace. You're not alone." She rested her hand on Grace's shoulder. "Come on, let's take a walk together."

Grace rose to her feet and looped her own arm through Darcy's. As they walked along in companionable silence, Grace thought how grown up Darcy suddenly seemed.

The two girls walked out of the garden and across the courtyard. Ahead of them was the wall where Grace had sat with Johnny Desperado on other nights such as this. She thought once more of Johnny – handsome, charming, wayward Johnny. His farewell words rang in her head. "*It ain't that I can't be good. It's just that I'm so much better at being bad.*"

She shivered to remember what he'd said. Was he still with Sidorio now? If so, then he'd have no shortage of opportunities to cultivate his bad side. Johnny had been something of a lost soul from the very beginning; an overripe fruit hanging from the vine, ready for Sidorio's rough hand to snatch.

"What are you thinking about?" Darcy asked, as they reached the wall which enclosed the courtyard.

"Someone I knew here before," Grace said. "One of the rebel Vampirates who went off with Sidorio."

Darcy smiled wryly. "Funny," she said, "if you want to know the truth, I wasn't only walking about outside to get some air. I was thinking about someone who went off with Sidorio too. Trying not to, of course, but the more you try not to, the more you can't help yourself."

"You're talking about Jez, aren't you?" Grace said, sitting down on the wall and gesturing for Darcy to join her. "He really hurt you, didn't he?"

"He really did," Darcy said as she sat down. "I thought he was the one, Grace. I thought he was my Mr Jetsam." Grace noticed there was a single tear, wedged like a pearl, in the corner of Darcy's wide, beautiful eyes. "How can someone be like that? So full of goodness and then so bad? Was it all a lie?"

Grace shook her head. "No," she said, thinking again of Johnny as well as Jez. "No, I don't think Jez lied to you. I think he really *did* care for you. He wanted you to go away with him and the rebels, didn't he?"

"Yes," said Darcy, her eyes wide. "But I couldn't! I just couldn't!"

"No, of course not," Grace nodded. "Because to you that would have been a betrayal of the captain. And you're not someone who trades loyalty lightly, Darcy. Jez is different. He's weaker than you. He couldn't resist the lure of Sidorio. But, even so, he still wanted you to go with him."

"Yes," Darcy said. "He did, didn't he?" Her face brightened. "In fact, *I* turned *him* down."

"Exactly," Grace said. "Because he wasn't good enough to be your Mr Jetsam. Jez loved you, Darcy, but he wasn't good enough for you. But one day someone else will come along and he will be the *real* Mr Jetsam. I'm sure of it."

Darcy smiled and squeezed Grace's hand. "Thank you," she said. "I feel a lot better hearing that. Next time, instead of tramping about outside in the cold and damp, I shall simply come and find you."

"Yes," said Grace. "You must! We're friends, aren't we?"

"Of course," Darcy said. "Surely you don't even have to ask *that* question! Now, tell me what's on *your* mind?"

Grace's face fell. "Oh, I don't know, Darcy. Connor and I had a big talk earlier, well an argument, to be honest. He doesn't think I should hang out with you or Lorcan or any of the Vampirates. He thinks it's wrong and – well, I'm sorry to use this word, but – *weird*."

Darcy didn't even flinch. "How can it be wrong and weird to have good friends?"

Grace thought perhaps she hadn't fully understood. "It's because you're a Vampirate," Grace said. "And I'm not." As she said the words, she heard her own voice inside her head. *Or maybe I am?* Should she share her thoughts – her visions – with

Darcy? No, it was too soon. Her visions were too fragmented to be sure of. Better to wait. This was too big.

"I get it," Darcy said. "Stick to your own kind. Like for like." She frowned and made a sniffing noise. "That strikes me as a somewhat narrow definition of friendship, Grace, if you don't mind my saying so."

"I agree," Grace said, nodding vigorously.

"Tell me," said Darcy. "Is our friendship so very different to the friendships you've had with other girls? I mean *normal* girls—"

"Don't say *normal*!" Grace interrupted her.

"Well, all right, then, with *mortal* girls. Back where you came from, in the bay?"

"To be honest," said Grace, "I didn't have any really close friendships with anyone back home. Connor was always my best friend then. I never had a proper girlfriend until you." She smiled. "It's one of the reasons you're so special to me."

"Well," said Darcy. "It doesn't *sound* wrong when you put it like that. And it's not just me you're friends with. There's the captain. And Mosh Zu. And Lorcan."

Grace shook her head slowly. "You don't even want to know what Connor had to say on the subject of me and Lorcan."

Darcy raised an eyebrow.

Grace hesitated. "Can I tell you a secret?" she asked.

Darcy smiled. "Of course, Grace. Isn't that exactly what friends are for?"

"Well," Grace said. "You know how I said that I never had a girlfriend like you before. Well, I've never had a proper boyfriend either." She glanced at Darcy, rather embarrassed. "You know what I mean?"

Darcy nodded. "I know what you mean, Grace. And now you're talking about Lorcan, aren't you?"

"Yes," Grace said, relieved to have got it out into the open.

"I just wish I knew how he feels about me. Does he ever talk to you about this kind of stuff?"

Darcy paused before answering, considering her words. "Lorcan's a very private person, Grace. He isn't someone who shares his feelings easily."

"No," Grace agreed. "That's certainly true. He's always been so good to me, Darcy, so protective of me. And I can tell he cares for me."

"He definitely cares about you," Darcy said, her voice brimming with passion. "There's no doubt about that." She broke off, then continued in a softer tone. "But perhaps he doesn't care about you in quite the way you want him to."

Grace frowned. "You mean that he just wants to be my friend?"

"Something like that," Darcy said. "Grace, I don't have any definite answers for you on this one. But I think you must tread very carefully. You said it yourself. You haven't had a boyfriend before and now you've set your sights on a . . ." She broke off mid-sentence. Grace's eyes met Darcy's.

"Say it," Grace said. "*Vampirate.* You were going to say that I've set my sights on a Vampirate." She frowned. "So it's one thing for me to be friends with you, but it's another thing altogether to have feelings for Lorcan?"

Tell her, the voice in Grace's head urged. *Tell her that you could be a vampire too. Wouldn't that change everything?* But somehow Grace couldn't do it.

Darcy shook her head. "Grace," she said calmly. "I was going to say that you've set your sights on a *challenge*." She hesitated. "Lorcan Furey is . . . complicated. I think perhaps you should just work on getting to know him better for now. After all, there's a lot going on at the moment. What with the captain's healing and Sally's return . . ."

Grace leaped at Darcy's words. "What has Sally's return got to do with Lorcan?"

Darcy averted her gaze. It was only a momentary thing but Grace knew her friend's little tics well enough to realise that she was hiding something from her. "Darcy, what has Sally's return got to do with Lorcan?"

Grace's mind flashed with the look Lorcan and Sally had exchanged when they had been reunited in the healing chamber. Then a second image – Lorcan on board the ship, smiling and waving to her mother.

Darcy turned her gaze back to Grace. "I meant for all of you, for all of *us*. Sally's your mother, Grace. And it's important that you take the time to get to know her, while you can. I'm not trying to alarm you. Like I said before, I'm your friend and, as your friend, I'm saying that right now Sally should be your focus, not Lorcan."

Grace nodded. Darcy's words made sense to her. All the same, she couldn't help but feel that her good friend was keeping something back. She decided to play along, for now.

"I'm going to go and find Mosh Zu," Grace said, feeling suddenly decisive. "And ask him how my mother is doing. Maybe he'll let me in to see her now." She turned to Darcy. "I could do with some moral support. Will you come with me?"

Darcy smiled back at her. "Of course I will." She stood up from the wall. Together, they crossed the courtyard and made their way through the heavy pair of doors into the Corridor of Lights, which marked the beginning of the internal compound.

They had moved through the Corridor of Lights and the Corridor of Discards and were walking along the Corridor of Ribbons, when a voice called out ahead of them.

"Grace!"

"Connor." She glanced up as he hurried over to her.

"Where've you been?" he asked. "I've been looking *everywhere* for you!"

His words, and the urgency of them, ignited an immediate

sense of fear in her. "What is it?" she asked. "Do you have news about our mother?"

Connor shook his head. It was then that she saw he was carrying his kitbag. And it was full. He hardly needed to speak. She knew just what he was going to say.

"I'm leaving," he said. "I've been doing a lot of soul-searching over the past few hours and I have to do this – for all our sakes. I was looking for you to say goodbye."

CHAPTER EIGHT

Journeys

"You're leaving now?!" Grace couldn't believe the body blow Connor had dealt her. Or rather she *could* absolutely believe it and, somehow, this made it worse. She realised that it was no longer a surprise when her brother disappointed her but, rather, the fulfilment of an expectation. She thought back, ruefully, to the night they had been shipwrecked. Once more she had the sense of a vast, raging ocean tearing them apart. It was as if the same process kept repeating itself over and over again.

While the storm raged within her, Connor looked back at her calmly. Nodding. Smiling. He was actually smiling!

Grace tried to hold it together. She felt a hand on her shoulder. "I'm going to leave you two to talk," Darcy said. "Grace, I'll be in my cabin if you need me." Darcy turned to Connor. "It was nice to see you again, Connor," she said, "albeit briefly." She made to leave, then looked back over her shoulder. "Oh and please don't worry about your sister. Her weird friends will look after her." With that, she turned again and strode off, her heels clicking angrily on the stone floor.

Connor stared after her open-mouthed. He looked back at

Grace. "You *told* her! You told her what I said? Are you out of your mind?"

"No, Connor, I'm not out of my mind. But maybe you are. You finally get to meet our mother and then she collapses and she's in a critical condition and you just have a nap, then pack up your old kitbag and decide it's the perfect moment to beat a hasty retreat!"

Connor sighed. "I can't deal with this," he said.

"With what? With me?"

He nodded. "With you. Like this. Yes, that's part of it."

"Go on," she said. "What about the rest?"

"The things you say. The things you want me to believe. That Sally is our mother . . ."

"She *is* our mother. It's a fact."

"She's a ghost, maybe . . ."

"She's our mother, Connor," Grace said firmly. "You have to stop dwelling on the stuff you don't understand and just learn to accept it."

"No," he said, his face a mirror of her stubbornness. "*You* have to stop being so accepting of the unbelievable – of the downright insane!"

"Stop being so closed," she said. Now she was the calm one.

"Closed?" He laughed, humourlessly. "You think I'm closed? To what? To the idea that my mother is a ghost who hitchhiked around the oceans in the captain's stomach? Or to the idea that our dad was a Vampirate and that you, me and Mum could make one happy vampire family?" Connor glared at Grace. "That's what you'd like me to believe, isn't it?"

"I'd like you to accept it's a possibility," Grace said.

"It *can't* be a possibility!" Connor cried.

"Why not? Because it scares you too much?"

"No," Connor said. "Because it doesn't make sense. Think about it, Grace. If you're so sure Dad was a Vampirate, how can he be dead? Isn't that the whole point of the gig? *Vampirates don't die!*"

These words stung her more than any others. Because she hadn't thought about this before. How could she have overlooked it?! If Dexter Tempest had been a Vampirate, he'd be immortal, like the others. So how could he have died? Her head was spinning. *Could* Vampirates die? The captain had certainly come close. Maybe it was too soon to walk away from the idea.

And what if . . . what if Dexter *hadn't* died? Maybe his death hadn't been exactly what it seemed. It was a crazy possibility but she had to remain open to it. Maybe there was a secret which Sally was going to tell her, when she recovered.

Or, Grace thought sadly, is Connor right? Am I tying myself up in these insane knots because I just won't accept the truth? That my father is dead. That he died too young of a heart attack. That I'm just a regular girl who happens to like hanging out with Vampirates.

When she looked back at Connor, she saw that the fury had drained from his face. She too felt different all of a sudden. The dark, poisonous rage was utterly gone. He was her brother again – her dear brother. And all she felt was sadness that he was leaving her, though now she accepted that he had to go.

Grace sighed. "Isn't there anything I can say to make you stay? Just for tonight? What if I said that *I* need you here?"

He considered her words, then shook his head. "If I really thought you needed me to stay, I would. That would be the one and only reason. But you *don't* need me here, Grace. Time and again you've proved how strong you are. And you're not alone. I'm sorry about what I said before. You have good friends here – Darcy, Lorcan, the captain . . ."

"I haven't even seen the captain since the healing ceremony," protested Grace. "I don't know where he is!"

Connor dropped his bag onto the floor and placed his hands

on Grace's shoulders, looking deep into her eyes. " I need you to know this, Gracie. I'm not in any way doing this to hurt you. I care about you more than I can put into words. When I'm away from you, not a day goes by when I don't think about you and worry about you and hope you're happy . . ."

His words came as a shock. He had never opened up to her to this degree before. If she needed further evidence that he was changing, here it was. She felt tears rising as he continued.

"But I can't be here with you. I have to go back to the real world. The world I know. A world full of life and light and adventure and—"

"Danger," Grace cut in.

"Yes," he acknowledged, "danger too. But someone once told me that the only journeys worth taking in life are those that test us to the very core." His eyes shone brightly as he remembered the exact words. "The journeys that strip the clothes from our back, mess with our minds and shake our spirits."

Grace frowned. "That sounds like something Cheng Li would say. You're going to find her again and join her crew, aren't you?"

"If she'll have me," he said. "Reckon she could make good use of a pirate prodigy like me!"

"Is that what you are?" Grace asked, feeling sad and powerless.

"Try to be happy for me, Grace. I think I've found the journey I'm supposed to take in life."

She locked eyes with him, the deep green of her irises perfectly reflected in his. "All right," she said. "But I think I've found my journey too. Try to be happy for *me*."

Once more they squared up to each other, then Connor broke the deadlock and swept her into his arms. "Of course I will," he said. "Of course I will. And we'll meet up again. Soon. Who knows where or when but that makes it all the more exciting, don't you think?"

Hearing his words and seeing his face flushed with optimism, Grace was momentarily caught up in his energy.

"Best not to drag this out, eh?" he said. Then, touching her arm lightly, he heaved his kitbag up over his shoulder.

"I'll walk you to the gate," Grace said.

He opened his mouth to say no, then changed his mind. Instead, he nodded and held out his hand. She took it. His touch felt reassuring. It reminded her of her dad's.

"Take care of yourself, Gracie!" Connor said, as the iron gates swung open for him and he continued onto the path leading down the mountainside.

Grace stood, bereft, as the gatekeepers pushed the gates back together. She couldn't deny the sadness she felt at seeing Connor go. She heard his voice in her head. "*We'll meet up again soon*." Would they? And, when they did, how would *that* reunion go? Wasn't there a danger that the gulf between them would only grow wider, harder to bridge, each time? Why did she torment herself so? Why couldn't she stop looking into the future and content herself with the here and now? Connor was happy in his life. He seemed to have found a sense of purpose. And he had been clear about his feelings for her. That should be enough. But it didn't comfort her in the way she felt it ought to. They were growing apart. Perhaps it had to happen, but it didn't make it any the easier to bear.

The Corridor of Lights seemed dark and claustrophobic after the daylight and open space outside. It was strange entering the internal part of the compound once again without Connor. Suddenly, Grace felt more alone than ever and sick with worry about Sally. She decided she could wait no longer. She would have to go and find out for herself how her mother was. She set off determinedly towards Mosh Zu's quarters.

She was just walking past the rec room, when she heard footsteps approaching along the corridor. As she turned the corner, she jumped to find Lorcan striding towards her from the other direction.

"Lorcan!" she said, delighted to see him.

He smiled back, but the smile faded fast. "Grace, I've been looking all over for you! Where have you been?"

"I was outside with Darcy and Connor," she said. "They told me you were over at the donors' block."

"I was," he nodded. "But I came back as soon as I heard about Sally – that she had collapsed."

Grace's pulse began to quicken. "Have you been helping Mosh Zu to heal her?" she asked. "How is she doing? Can I see her now?"

"That's why I was looking for you," Lorcan said, his voice low and controlled. "You need to come and talk to Mosh Zu. Right now."

The dark thoughts in her head grew more feverish. "Lorcan, you're scaring me. What's wrong?"

"Just come with me," he said. "Mosh Zu is the one you need to talk to." He took her by the hand and led her swiftly along the corridor.

"You're hurting me!" Grace cried, as he dragged her along.

"I'm sorry," he said, loosening his grip. "I just don't want to lose any time."

"Why can't *you* tell me what's going on?" Grace asked.

"It's best to talk to Mosh Zu," he said, pushing on towards the guru's quarters.

Mosh Zu met Grace and Lorcan at the threshold of his chamber. His tone was serious as he ushered them inside. Lorcan shut the door tightly behind them.

"I need to prepare you," Mosh Zu said to Grace, once they were sitting on cushions in the centre of the room.

"Prepare me?" Grace asked, feeling a wave of cold panic. "For what? Did something go wrong in the healing process?"

Mosh Zu shook his head and smiled at her. "No, Grace. Not at all. Sally is fine. She is in her room, sleeping. We'll go there in a moment."

"I don't understand," Grace said. "If she's all right, what do you need to prepare me for?"

Mosh Zu's dark eyes watched Grace intently as he continued. "Others of the shades the captain was carrying have begun to fade." He paused, allowing her to process his words. "In spite of my best efforts, I have not yet been able to reverse this process."

"How terrible," Grace said. She was sad for all the souls but, of course, her thoughts turned to her own mother.

"Terrible in some ways, yes," Mosh Zu said. "But the reason why the souls were travelling with the captain, why he rescued them in the first place, was because they were in torment. What I have managed to do for them is to release them from that torment and allow them to move on."

At last she understood.

"My mother is in torment too, isn't she?"

Mosh Zu continued to gaze at Grace carefully. "I would prefer to say that she has unfinished business," he said. "I believe that once that business is concluded, she too will move on." He paused. "It will be hard for her to leave you and very hard also for you to let her go. But she must embark on that final journey with joy."

"How much time *does* she have left?" Grace asked.

"I can't tell you," Mosh Zu said, shaking his head. "I just don't know."

Grace's head was spinning. "Isn't there a chance that Sally could be different, that she could beat this and become fully mortal once more?" They were difficult questions but she had to ask them.

Once more, Mosh Zu shook his head. "I'm sorry, Grace. I know you are looking for definitive answers but, on this occasion, I don't have any for you."

Grace trembled but took a breath. She had to be strong. And she didn't want to lose any more time.

"Can I go and see her now?"

Mosh Zu smiled. "Yes," he said, heading towards the door once more. "Yes. Let me walk with you."

Sally was propped up in bed, sleeping. She still looked very frail. Grace lingered in the doorway. Her head was racing with everything Mosh Zu had told her but she didn't want Sally to witness her upset. She couldn't bear the thought of adding to her mother's torment.

"Why don't you sit with her while she sleeps?" Mosh Zu said, resting his hand on Grace's shoulder and pushing her gently into Sally's chamber. "I'm sure she'll be delighted to wake up and find you here."

Grace nodded, stepping forward and walking towards the bed, careful to do so as quietly as possible so as not to disturb her mother. She stood by the chair at Sally's bedside. Gazing down at her, Grace thought how peaceful Sally looked in the soft candlelight. As Grace sat down, Sally stirred under the bedclothes. At first, Grace thought she was about to wake up but she must have simply moved in her sleep. One of her hands now rested above the counterpane. It was as if, even in sleep, her mother was somehow reaching out to her.

Instinctively, Grace extended her own hand. But as her fingers interlaced with her mother's, she realised her mistake. Immediately, her head was filled with a searing pain. It was so strong that she almost broke contact. But then, she thought: *No. I have to ride this out.* She didn't know how much time they had left. She didn't know how much strength her mother had to continue her story. But this way, even while Sally was sleeping, Grace might find out more about her past and perhaps help to ease her mother's burden. She gripped Sally's hand, waiting for the head-pain to subside, which it swiftly did. Then, as before, the vision took her on a journey back to *The Nocturne*.

This time, she was looking straight into Sally's face. Then she realised that she was still seeing things from her mother's point of view, it was just that she was looking into a mirror. In its reflection, she saw Darcy too! Grace smiled to herself as she watched Darcy fussing around with her mother's hair. She was putting it up, fastening the auburn tendrils with delicate combs. Her mother must be getting ready for a smart night out. Only, Grace reflected, there were no nights out on *The Nocturne*. But there *were* nights *in* – Sally must be getting ready for Feast Night.

Now she heard Darcy's voice at her mother's ear. "You look beautiful, Sally. He'll be so happy that you're his donor. Don't be nervous! It'll all be fine."

She saw her mother's face in the mirror, attempting a confident smile. It was only natural that she should be nervous. This must be her first Feast and, although she was paired with Dexter, she didn't know him properly yet. Grace had no idea what Sally's life had been like before joining the ship – but it must have been a difficult journey to lead her to make the choice to become a donor.

Now Sally stood and smoothed down the gown she was wearing – no doubt one procured from Darcy's bottomless closet. She looked very pretty, very innocent. She saw Darcy nod behind her. "Told you I'd make you look like a fairy-tale princess!"

The vision shifted and Grace found she was downstairs in the long cabin where the Feast took place. She was still seeing things from her mother's perspective, as she sat between two other donors, waiting for all their Vampirate partners to arrive. In the background, she could hear the music which accompanied the Feast – the strange, percussive music. And then the Vampirates began entering the room.

Grace watched them file in, eagerly awaiting her first sight of Dexter. This would be the final confirmation that her dad was indeed a Vampirate. In her previous visions, he had looked recognisably like the father she remembered, albeit younger and a little slimmer. She was filled with wonder at how he might look at the Feast, dressed up in his finery. Through Sally's eyes, she saw Lorcan enter the room, smile at her, and take his place opposite Shanti, who was sitting close by. Then she saw Sidorio enter, followed not far behind by the captain. The door closed behind them.

That was strange, thought Grace. Had she missed her dad's arrival? There was still a gaggle of Vampirates in the centre of the room. Perhaps he was amongst those?

The gaggle began to disperse and the seats filled up on the Vampirate side of the table, but still the place opposite Sally remained vacant.

She turned to glance along the table and found Shanti smiling and winking at her. Then, as she turned back, she saw that at last the chair opposite her had been filled. Her Vampirate partner had arrived.

Grace's heart was pounding as Sally's eyes traced up his shirt-cuffs and jacket, past his shoulders, to his neck and, at last, his face. But though the face was indeed familiar, it was not the one she had expected or wanted to see.

The Vampirate grinned at her. "So, you're my new donor! Funny little thing, aren't you?"

Grace felt a cold chill spread throughout her body as, through Sally's eyes, she looked up into the unmistakeable face of Sidorio.

CHAPTER NINE

House of Cards

Another night. Another dead-end coastal town. Another beach.

The two women stood on the cliffs, looking out to sea. One wore a mini-dress and tall leather boots. The other was dressed in a tight bodice and figure-hugging leggings. They both had on very large, very dark sunglasses.

"Look," said the first. "I think our ship has come in." She pointed at a vast prison hulk which had just turned into the bay.

"Right on cue," said the other. "Shall we go and meet the boys?"

The two women watched from the shadows as the Vampirates made their way to shore. It was just the same as the previous two nights. The ship dropped anchor out in the furthest reaches of the bay. Then the crew made their way into land. Some surfed. Others swam. There was a riotous atmosphere. They were hungry and ready to feast.

"May I borrow your field-glasses, Jessamy?" Camille asked her companion.

"Of course." Jessamy passed the glasses to Camille, who lifted them to her eyes and scanned the ranks gathering on the sand.

"There they are! Our two special friends," she said, with a smile. "I'm looking forward to seeing them both again. Aren't you?"

"Oh yes," said Jessamy, running a hand through her hair. "Yes, indeed. Every night it's as if we are meeting for the very first time, don't you think? It never loses its excitement."

She laughed. Camille nodded and joined in her laughter.

They waited for Sidorio to give his command, then lingered at the fringes of the beach while the crew ran off to pillage the town.

"They look very, very hungry, don't they?" said Camille.

Jessamy nodded. "They certainly do. But I'm afraid they're going to be disappointed again tonight." She drew her lips into a pout.

"Come on," said Camille. "There's Johnny and Stukeley, waiting till last, as usual. Let's go and introduce ourselves."

"Good evening, ladies!" Tonight it was Stukeley who noticed them first.

Jessamy raised her hand but said nothing as she and Camille continued their approach.

"Where are you two off to, all dressed up like that?" Stukeley asked.

"We're just looking for some fun," said Camille.

"Well, you've come to the right place!" said Johnny. "Fun is my middle name."

"Really?" said Camille, coquettishly.

Johnny grinned. "Actually, my name's Johnny. Johnny Desperado. And you're . . .?"

"Camille," she said, reaching out her hand.

"It's a pleasure to meet you, Camille," Johnny said, kissing her hand. "Tell me, why are you both wearing sunglasses in the middle of the night?"

Camille turned to face Jessamy, then both women looked at the boys. "Fashion, darling!" they said in unison.

Much later, the quartet walked back across the sand. Johnny felt light-headed from the feasting the four had embarked on together. He could see that Stukeley was in a similar state.

"That was amazing!" Stukeley said, turning to face Jessamy and marvelling again at the strange heart-shaped tattoo around her right eye. "We should do this again."

"Yes," Jessamy said, with a smile. "Perhaps we should."

"We ought to get going now," said Camille.

"So you're from another ship?" Johnny said. "What's it called? Where is it?"

Jessamy shot a warning glance at Camille.

Camille shrugged and leaned over to whisper in her ear. "What does it matter? They won't remember any of this. They never do."

The women turned back to their companions. "I'm afraid we really must be going now," said Jessamy.

Stukeley looked crestfallen. Jessamy walked over to give him a hug goodbye. At the same time, Camille drew Johnny into her arms. The couples embraced for a moment. Then, the women stepped backwards and the numb bodies of their dates slumped down onto the sand. Their eyes were closed.

The women stood back to check on them. "Don't they look sweet?" Camille said, wrapping her arm around Jessamy's waist.

"Yes," agreed Jessamy. "Like sleeping puppy-dogs."

Camille reached into her trouser pocket and produced a playing card. The Jack of Hearts. She brought it to her lips and kissed it, leaving the imprint of her lipstick on it. Then she let it flutter down to come to a standstill on Johnny's chest.

"Nice touch," Jessamy said.

"You don't think the captain will mind, do you?"

Jessamy shook her head. "She always encourages us to improvise on a theme." Saying this, she took a playing card from the pocket of her skirt, brought it to her own lips, then crouched down and slipped it between Stukeley's fingers.

Camille giggled and helped Jessamy back up onto her feet. "Come on," she said. "Let's get back to *The Vagabond* and report back to the captain."

Johnny woke first. He let out a yawn, then glanced around, taking a few moments to realise where he was. He raised himself up into a sitting position.

As he did so, something fluttered away from his chest. At first, he thought it was a moth but, glancing down, he saw that it was a small card – a playing card – which now lay face down on the sand. He reached out and turned it over, lifting it up to the moonlight. It was like no playing card he had ever seen. It was the Jack of Hearts but the hearts were black. And so too was the lipstick mark which covered the design. Where had the card come from? What did it mean?

Stukeley was stirring beside him. Johnny could see another playing card in his hand. What had happened to them both? Why couldn't he remember? Lately, their bouts of blood-taking seemed to be inducing some kind of amnesia.

"*Hola*," he said, as Stukeley sat up beside him.

"All right, mate," Stukeley said. "I just had the best sleep ever. Really deep and peaceful."

"Me too," Johnny said.

"Why are you frowning, then?" Stukeley asked.

Johnny pointed. "What's that in your hand, *hermano*?"

"In my hand?" Stukeley glanced down curiously. "Some kind of playing card." He lifted it up close. "The King of Hearts. But it's black. I was never much cop at cards but Hearts aren't supposed to be black, are they?"

Johnny shook his head slowly. "Hearts are not supposed to be black," he said.

"Where did we get these?" Stukeley asked him.

Johnny shrugged. "I don't know. The last thing I remember was you and me, setting off across this beach. How about you?"

"The same," Stukeley nodded.

Suddenly, the air was filled with a deafening noise.

"The ship's siren!" Stukeley exclaimed, jumping to his feet.

"It can't be shipping out already!" Johnny said. "Not without us."

"Come on," Stukeley said. "Something's wrong here. We need to get back onto *The Blood Captain* now!"

The Vagabond was a much smaller ship than *The Blood Captain*, which gave it certain advantages. One was speed. Another was the ability to hide itself in the shadows of an inlet. All the same, Lady Lockwood had conjured a veil of mist to ensure the ship was screened from prying eyes. Fortunately, this would not prevent her from looking out.

She stood in her cabin, her telescope trained out to sea.

There was a knock on the door. "Enter!" called the captain, standing up and rearranging her full skirt.

Marianne and Angelika entered, followed by Jessamy and Camille. Between them, the four women were carrying four wine bottles and five glasses.

"We thought you might like to taste some of the latest harvest," Marianne said.

"Absolutely!" Lady Lockwood said. "Would you be an angel, my dear, and pour?" Marianne nodded. Assisted by Angelika, she poured a small measure of liquid from the first bottle into each of the glasses.

Jessamy and Camille stepped forward.

"Another successful night?" Lady Lockwood asked them.

Jessamy nodded. "It's almost too easy," she said.

Lady Lockwood smiled and nodded. "Don't worry, my dear. I have plans to up the stakes very soon." She reached out and accepted the glass offered by Marianne. "So tell me," she said, swirling the glass to unleash the bouquet, "where is *The Blood Captain* headed next?"

"Well," said Camille, "according to our sources . . ."

The siren sounded a second and last time as Johnny and Stukeley jumped down onto the main deck. They both knew the implications of this. They were supposed to be the ones who sounded the ship's siren, calling the straggling Vampirates back to the ship, bringing the night's feasting to a close. They were not meant to be the last ones to return.

All about them were their crewmates. They seemed restless, almost feverish. This was not their usual state after feasting. Usually, at this point, the crew were slumped around the deck or down in their cabins.

"Something's wrong," Stukeley said to Johnny again.

"Where's the captain?" Johnny asked.

Stukeley looked around. "I don't know – but let's just hope he hasn't noticed we're late."

But he had. At that very moment, the captain was observing his two lieutenants from high up in the crow's nest. Now, he decided to make his presence felt. He climbed out of the platform and somersaulted down onto the deck, landing right in front of them.

"Good of you to join us," Sidorio said, his voice full of darkness.

"Hello, Captain," said Stukeley, nervously.

"And where have you two been?" Sidorio asked. "You're late back. Again."

"We were on the beach," Stukeley said. "We went to feast, just like everyone else."

"I see," Sidorio said, staring deep into Stukeley's eyes. "So, tell me, did you find anything to feast upon?"

His lieutenants were silent.

"Well?" Sidorio's voice boomed out across the deck.

"I think so," Johnny said.

Sidorio raised an eyebrow. "You think so, Stetson. What do you mean – *you think so*?"

Johnny trembled. "It's just that . . ."

Stukeley took over. "I'm really sorry, Captain, but the truth is we're having trouble remembering. Maybe we took too much blood or something . . ."

Sidorio gazed from one lieutenant to the other, his eyes blazing. "I'm getting mightily tired of you two rolling in hours after everyone else, with a dazed look on your faces. You're supposed to be my deputies, remember?"

"Yes, Captain," said Stukeley. "I'm sorry."

"Me too," said Johnny, hanging his head.

"You said that last night," Sidorio said. "And the night before that. And on each occasion, neither one of you has had a clue where you've been or what you've got up to. Either that or you're lying to me." He shook his head. "And lying to me would be a very big mistake. *Huge* mistake!"

"We're *not* lying," Johnny said, shaking his head.

Stukeley frowned. "Something strange must be going on."

Sidorio scowled at both his lieutenants. He was still furious with them.

Stukeley's eyes scanned the deck. "Captain," he said, "what's up with the rest of the crew? They don't look like they've feasted tonight."

"Ten out of ten for observation," Sidorio snapped. "They *haven't* feasted. Someone else got to that town first."

"Someone else?" Stukeley said, confused. "What do you mean?"

Sidorio glared darkly at his two lieutenants. "You had better come with me," he said.

As they stepped inside the captain's cabin, Johnny walked straight over to the table. It was covered with playing cards. All Hearts. All black.

"Look!" he said to Stukeley. "Just like . . ."

Stukeley's eyes blazed a warning, which silenced Johnny instantly. "What are these?" Stukeley said, turning to the captain. "Where did they come from?"

"We found them in the town tonight," Sidorio said. "The streets were littered with dead bodies and on each one was one of these cards."

Stukeley stepped closer. The cards were exactly the same design as the ones secreted in his and Johnny's pockets. The only difference was that, whilst the lieutenants' cards were marked with black lipstick, these ones were smeared with red blood.

Stukeley's brain finally kicked into gear. "There's another Vampirate ship! That's what you're saying, isn't it? Another Vampirate ship is getting to the towns ahead of us."

Sidorio nodded. "This is the third time it's happened. My crew is going hungry. And the hungrier they get, the more out of control they become. Except the two of you. You two seem to be getting blood from somewhere, only you don't seem able to remember it." He looked at them suspiciously.

Stukeley gazed at the blood-tinged cards, then lifted his eyes back to the captain. "It wasn't us, Captain! And it doesn't look like the work of *The Nocturne*. Not unless things have radically altered in the way they do things."

Sidorio shook his head. "This isn't anything to do with *The*

69

Nocturne," he said. "A new Vampirate ship must have taken to the seas. Maybe they think they're having a little fun with us – second-guessing where we're headed next and then beating us to the pass."

Stukeley frowned. "Maybe they're not guessing," he said. "Maybe they've found a way of getting the information first-hand."

"What do you mean?" Sidorio asked.

It was a risky move but Stukeley decided to play it. He reached into his pocket and removed the playing card, then nodded at Johnny to do the same. Both lieutenants placed their cards on the table.

"We found these on us," Stukeley said. "When we woke up on the beach. We don't know where they came from or who gave them to us, but it seems like a mighty big coincidence, don't you think?"

Johnny nodded. "It's as if someone is getting the information out of us, then drugging us so we don't remember a thing about it."

Sidorio raised his eyebrow. "It certainly looks that way."

Stukeley reached out his hand. "Captain, you have to know that neither Johnny nor I would do anything intentionally to disrupt the workings of this ship. We are absolutely committed to it, and to your command, aren't we, Johnny?"

Johnny nodded. They both waited on their captain's next word.

At last, Sidorio spoke. "It's OK, boys. I think I see what's been happening here. Someone's been playing us. Some new ship is making a bid to rule the waves. Well, they've had their fun, but it ends here, tonight!" He brought his fist down to the table. The pile of playing cards flew across the room. There was the sound of wood cracking.

"There's only room for one crew of renegade Vampirates,"

Sidorio said. "Mine! I'm going to find out who's in charge of this other ship. And then I'm going to take it over." He smiled, his twin incisors glinting ominously in the lamplight.

"Change the ship's course," he commanded. "This crew needs blood. And I intend to give it to them. Then, we'll see what happens to those who play games with a killer shark."

CHAPTER TEN

Sidorio's Donor

At last, Sally awoke. She turned her head and smiled warmly to see her daughter at her bedside. "Hello, Grace," she said, sitting up. But, seeing her daughter's expression, she paused. "Grace, you look awful! Whatever's wrong?"

Grace's voice was weak. "Sidorio!" she exclaimed. "You were *Sidorio's* donor!" She felt sick at the thought. Of all the Vampirates she might have chosen to have been her mother's partner, Sidorio was the last . . . the very last.

Sally did not deny it. "How do you know?" she asked. "Did Mosh Zu tell you?"

Grace shook her head. "I had another vision," she said. "I saw it all for myself."

Sally's eyes were wide with fear. "What exactly did you see?" She pulled herself up to sitting, propping pillows behind her back.

"I saw you getting ready for your first Feast Night," Grace said. "You were with Darcy, in her cabin. She was putting up your hair." Sally's expression softened at the memory. "You looked very beautiful, Mother. You were wearing a pale yellow

72

dress. Do you want to know a funny thing? It was the very same one I wore to *my* first Feast."

"You!" Sally said. "You went to a Feast? But you're not a donor, Grace, are you? You can't be!"

"No." Grace shook her head. "I'm not a donor. But I wore that same primrose-yellow dress, loaned to me by Darcy, and I went to the Feast and Sidorio tried to take me as his donor . . ."

"Sidorio did *what?*" Sally's eyes popped. Grace felt torn. The last thing she had wanted to do was to cause her mother distress, but nor did she want to hide things from her. If Sally kept asking these questions, she would just have to try to answer them as best she could.

"It's all right, Mother. It doesn't matter about that night. The captain intervened and it was all all right." She decided, for now, to spare Sally the details of how Sidorio had trapped Grace in her cabin and how she'd had to fight him off alone until the captain had rescued her a second time.

"Go back to the vision," Sally said. "What did you see?"

"I was sitting there, seeing it all through your eyes," Grace said. "Next, I – you – were in the long cabin at the bottom of the ship. You were sitting on the donors' side of the table. You looked to one side and saw Lorcan and Shanti. Shanti winked at you . . ."

"Shanti," Sally said, smiling. "Dear, sweet Shanti. Such a good friend. I should love to see her again. Do you know her? Well, you must – you recognised her, after all!"

Once more, Grace ran the risk of hurting her mother very badly. How could she tell her her friend was dead? She decided to brush over it for now. "Let's come back to Shanti later," she said.

"Yes, all right," Sally said. "Go back to your vision, Grace."

"You turned back and waited for your donor to arrive. I was

73

expecting to see Dad. But instead, it was Sidorio who sat down opposite you. And he said—"

But before Grace could continue, Sally spoke his exact words. "So you're my new donor! Funny little thing, aren't you?" She had never forgotten them.

Grace nodded. "I let go of your hand, Mother, and the vision ended. I wasn't ready to see any more. But I can't get what I did see out of my head." She turned to Sally. "What was Sidorio like when you knew him? What was it like being his donor?"

Sally closed her eyes for a moment and Grace wondered if she was too weak to continue. But then her mother's eyes opened, brighter than before. "If you want to know the shocking truth, Grace – and it is shocking when I think of everything that happened later – I rather liked Sidorio in the beginning."

"You *liked* Sidorio!" Grace shook her head in disbelief.

Sally shrugged and smiled. "No question, there was always something dark and brooding about him. I suppose I always knew he had the . . ." She searched for the right phrase. "The possibility of violence about him. But I thought he was very handsome. And I suppose I was swept up in the dark romance of it all. Here I was, aboard a ship of Vampirates, and he was to be my partner. It was like a marriage, of sorts." She shrugged. "At least that's how I saw it in my foolish little head." She paused. "Is there any water left in that jug? I'm parched."

Grace filled a glass and passed it to her mother, eager for her to continue her story.

"I had heard about Sidorio's connection with Julius Caesar and I thought it gave him a certain epic quality. It made him all the more attractive to me." Sally's green eyes danced in the candlelight. "Oh, Grace, you're clearly a very sensible young woman. You have your head screwed on just right. But I was full of strange ideas. And I confess that as I got ready for my first Feast Night I felt as if I was going on a date."

74

"A date!" Grace exclaimed. "With Sidorio?" Grace had never imagined she'd even hear those two words in such close proximity. It was hard for her to even contemplate someone thinking about Sidorio in that way.

"Of course, when I arrived at the Feast, it was a complete letdown. I took my place opposite Sidorio and waited for him to begin to ask me some questions. I thought he'd be as keen to get to know me as I was him. Around me, I could hear the chatter of other Vampirates and their donors. But after a few opening words, Sidorio remained stonily silent. It seemed that he had no interest in getting to know me at all."

Sally turned to Grace. "I realised that all I was to Sidorio was a source of blood, nothing more. My poor foolish delusions! After the Feast, we went to my cabin for the sharing. And, actually, he was surprisingly gentle and precise. Certainly, he only took the prescribed quantity of blood. Afterwards I slept. I don't know how much you know about the sharing, Grace, but it is customary for donors to need to sleep afterwards. Generally the Vampirates remain with their partners at this time. It's a mark of respect for the gift."

Sally shook her head. "Only Sidorio didn't stay with me. Not that night, nor any other – with one exception." She sighed. "When I woke, I was on my own. I have never felt so alone as I did then, in that small cabin on that strangely silent ship."

There were tears in Grace's eyes. She hated to think of her mother in such distress. She reached out to squeeze Sally's hand and felt her squeeze hers back. She paused, expecting – but not wanting – a fresh vision to come. But thankfully, this time, her head remained clear. She remembered Mosh Zu's words about Sally having unfinished business. Maybe her story needed to emerge under its own rhythm. Enough secrets had been shared for one day.

"I'm so sorry, Grace," Sally said. "This must all be very hard for you."

Grace smiled through her moist eyes. "I'm sure it's not exactly a walk in the park for you, either."

"No," Sally agreed. "But I want to make things right for you, before . . . Well, I just want to make things right for you. And for Connor, too. Where is he, anyhow?"

Grace considered this question but decided not to cover up the truth. "He left," she said, "earlier today."

"Because of me?" Sally asked.

Grace hesitated again. "In part," she said. "Because of what you began to tell us. That we are connected to the Vampirate world, that we always were." She looked at her mother sadly. "Connor doesn't want that."

"Whether he wants it or not is immaterial," said Sally. "It isn't something he can escape from."

"I know," Grace said, with a sigh. "But that won't stop him from trying. Even now, he's gone in search of a pirate captain to ask her to sign him up to her crew."

Sally shook her head. "He can run as hard and as far as he likes, but the truth will catch up with him. It always does."

These ominous words were Sally's last before she drifted off to sleep once more. Grace remained at her bedside for a time. She was still shocked by Sally's revelations but, at the same time, she felt strangely calm. She marvelled at how connected she and her mother were by the paths they had taken in life, by the ship they had sailed on and the people they had each encountered there. It made her feel less alone somehow.

At last, quietly so as not to disturb her mother's much-needed rest, Grace climbed down from the bed. She smoothed out the counterpane so Sally would be protected from the chill evening air. Then she blew her mother the gentlest of kisses and made her way back towards the door.

CHAPTER ELEVEN

The Interview

Connor wove his way through the shipyard, doing his best to follow the instructions he'd been given at the reception gate. It was late afternoon but the sun was still blisteringly hot and as he walked along the jetty, beads of sweat formed on his forehead and trickled down his neck and shoulders. He had changed into a fresh T-shirt after the arduous sail, but already a deep V of perspiration had formed over his chest.

In spite of the intense heat, everywhere he glanced was a hive of activity. Men and women worked away tirelessly on ships, from those in the early stages of construction – resembling a whale's skeleton on display in a maritime museum – to others which were almost complete, being given a final sanding down or coat of varnish. He watched a pair of shipwrights hoisting a taut new mainsail. Connor was used to battered sails and rigging heavy with salt and tar. He'd never seen canvas or rope as virginal as this before. He inhaled deeply. Fresh-cut timber. Drying paint. The shipyard exuded the heady scent of new beginnings.

At last he came to a vast dry-dock where a tall, elegant ship seemed to float on air. Connor couldn't help but gasp as he took in the pure majesty of the vessel. His pulse began to race. He felt an instant connection with the ship, as though his own veins and sinews were part of the rigging: as if its lanyards and sheets were clipped onto his heart. He hoped that one day very soon the ship would be his new home. It seemed all but complete, ready to break free from its shell of scaffolding. Standing on one of the uppermost platforms, a man was carefully painting the ship's name in gold paint. Connor squinted to read the words but the sun was too dazzling to make it out.

"What a beauty!" exclaimed a woman's distinctive voice.

Connor turned and found a tall, elegant woman at his side. She was a vision in white, from the pristine plimsolls on her petite feet to the precisely cut bob of white hair. Connor wondered if it was naturally white; she didn't look that old. Her lightly tanned face was stretched as taut as the sail he'd seen hoisted onto the ship just now. Her expression of mild disdain barely altered as she addressed him in a superior drawl. "Jacinta Slawter, editor-at-large, *Ship-shape* magazine." She fixed Connor with a glare. "And *you* are?"

"Connor Tempest," he said, shaking her hand.

"You're a little moist, Connor Tempest," said Jacinta Slawter, swiftly withdrawing her hand and reaching into her clutch bag for a cloth. "Well, never mind that. More to the point, where's your equipment?"

"My equipment?" What was she on about?

"Your cam-e-ra," said Jacinta Slawter, breaking up the word, as if he was a complete idiot or perhaps new to the English language.

"My camera?" Connor stared at her blankly.

Though her expression did not change, Jacinta Slawter was clearly growing impatient. "Now look, Connor Tinpot or whatever your name is, I'm here to do a profile of Cheng Li and her ship. It's a print exclusive, for the August issue. And I assume you're here to shoot the pictures for the *seven-page-spread*?" She articulated every syllable of the words. "Which rather begs the question, where is your apparatus?"

Connor shook his head, grinning. "I'm not a photographer," he said. "I'm an old friend of Cheng Li's."

"A friend?" Jacinta Slawter's voice changed instantly. She produced a small gold pencil from behind her ear and a notebook from her bag. "Care to share any special memories or insights?"

"Maybe later," Connor said, pointing up to the prow of the ship, where Cheng Li stood, hands resting on her hips, resembling a bird of prey, surveying the world below.

"Connor!" she called down. "What a nice surprise! And Ms Slawter. You're here! Why don't you both come on up?"

She temporarily disappeared from view and Connor followed in Jacinta Slawter's slipstream as she power-walked around to the gangplank. He felt a momentary flash of vertigo as he made his way across it but he controlled his breathing and kept his focus straight ahead. He wasn't about to show any weakness in front of Jacinta Slawter, of all people. Cheng Li was standing on the other side, watching him. This was a further inducement to remain calm and strong.

"Welcome aboard," Cheng Li said, extending a hand to help Jacinta Slawter down onto the deck.

"Thank you, Captain Li," drawled the editor-at-large.

"Oh, I'm not a captain for a few more days," Cheng Li said. Connor could see she was glowing with pride and excitement.

"Cool ship!" he said.

"Isn't she?" Cheng Li smiled.

Connor wondered if he should hug her but he missed the moment as Jacinta Slawter started up again. "Mistress Li, I'm terribly sorry, but there seems to have been a mix-up with my photographer. I'm sure it's easily explained but—"

79

"Yo, Slawter!" came a voice from up above. "Strike a pose!"

They all craned their necks up to the crow's nest. A camera clicked several times in rapid succession from high above. "Beautiful!" called the voice.

"Fabrizio? Dahling, is that you?" drawled Jacinta Slawter.

"The one and only," called the photographer, a highly-muscled man, with long black hair in a ponytail. He nimbly descended the rigging, several cameras dangling from his tanned and toned limbs. "What took you so long?" he asked, jumping down onto the deck. "I'm almost done here."

"I wasn't sure who they were sending . . . I thought the meet was due for three," Jacinta drawled. "Don't rush off, dahling. I'd like to get a few shots of myself with Cap . . . with Mistress Li. Oh and perhaps with this young man, Connor Pestilence." She hissed to Fabrizio. "Apparently, they're old friends."

"*Fabalous!*" said Fabrizio, not wasting any time and shooting several shots of Cheng Li and Connor there and then.

"Well," said Cheng Li, "who's for the grand tour?"

"Lead the way!" drawled Jacinta Slawter, managing to inject just a modicum of excitement into her voice.

As Connor followed Cheng Li, Jacinta Slawter and Fabrizio around the ship, he was awed at every turning. It really was an amazing piece of craftsmanship. Cheng Li had, unsurprisingly, been highly involved in the ship's design. As she pointed out its key features, she talked with complete assurance about why certain decisions had been made and how the craft married the best of the old traditions with cutting-edge innovation. Jacinta Slawter nodded authoritatively and scribbled furiously, while Fabrizio leaped about here, there and everywhere, snapping away. Connor found a new level of respect for Cheng Li as he listened and observed her. She seemed to grow in stature each time they met.

"Now forgive me for asking this question," said Jacinta

Slawter, her golden pencil at the ready, "but I owe it to the readers of *Ship-shape*. Undoubtedly, there will be some amongst the pirate community who will say that you are too young to be a captain. How do you respond to that?"

Before Cheng Li had a chance to answer, Connor found himself leaping into action. "Cheng Li *is* young," he said, "but what she doesn't know about being a pirate isn't worth knowing."

"Thank you, Connor," Cheng Li nodded, with a dignified smile. She turned to Ms Slawter. "If the old guard has a problem with my youth, then they are also going to be challenged by my crew as a whole. I have recruited several young people into key positions of responsibility. Some would favour age and experience over vitality and freshness of vision. I believe in finding ways to balance the two. That's the kind of ship I'll be running. Am I a visionary? That's for others, and the annals of history, to decide."

"Marvellous, dahling!" rasped Jacinta, scribbling away. "I assume I can quote you on that?"

Cheng Li nodded, winking at Connor. He grinned back. Her words in support of youth seemed a good omen for their pending conversation.

"And this," said Cheng Li, pushing open a pair of simple but elegant wooden doors, "is the captain's cabin!"

Jacinta Slawter clapped her hands. "Bravo! Oh *bravissimo*, Mistress Li."

"*Fabalous!*" agreed Fabrizio, diving fearlessly onto the floor and snapping away at an unusual angle.

"Wow!" Connor said, following them into the cabin and noting the generous-sized windows on both sides. Sunlight filtered in through gauze blinds, sending a soft light across the blonde wood floorboards.

"An inviting room," murmured Jacinta Slawter, scribbling away, "beautifully designed . . . simply but elegantly furnished."

It was exactly the sort of cabin Connor could envisage for himself one day. Given that it was the captain's cabin, it was actually pretty low-key. Yes, it was definitely larger than the cabins allocated to the other senior personnel, but this seemed largely functional – to accommodate a meeting table and chairs, plus Cheng Li's many regimented shelves of books. There didn't seem to be a volume on pirate history that she didn't own! Nevertheless, the cabin was not, like Molucco Wrathe's, a vast temple to the captain's insatiable appetite for treasure and excess. This felt altogether more pragmatic and businesslike.

The room was dominated by a large painting of an athletic male pirate, which hung behind Cheng Li's desk.

"Chang Ko Li," droned Jacinta Slawter. "I don't believe I've seen this portrait before. Fascinating style, if perhaps a little *naïf*? Who's the artist?"

"I painted it myself," Cheng Li answered. "I was nine years old."

"Too mahvellous! Fabrizio, we must get some shots in front of this. Just Cheng Li and her father, I think. Nice and tight."

"*Fabalous*!" Fabrizio nodded, whirring off the shots.

"And that's a wrap!" declared Jacinta Slawter.

"Can I offer you a drink before you go?" Cheng Li asked.

Jacinta Slawter glanced at her platinum wristwatch. "Actually, no. I have cocktails with John Kuo at seven-thirty, and I must dash back home first to change outfits. The loyal readers of *Ship-shape* would be devastated to see me in the same fashion twice!"

Cheng Li nodded. "Well, thank you so much for coming to see me."

"No, thank *you*!" said Jacinta Slawter. "This will make a sensational spread." She shook Cheng Li's hand, then turned and gave Connor something approaching a smile. "A pleasure to have met you," she said.

Connor grinned and extended his hand. Jacinta Slawter gazed at it, then trembled slightly and turned, looping her arm around one of Fabrizio's tree-trunk biceps. "Come on, dahling! Walk me to my launch. I'm desperate to hear all the latest goss."

With that, the editor-at-large and her daredevil photographer exited the captain's cabin.

Cheng Li waited until their footsteps receded along the corridor. "Well, that wasn't *quite* as gruelling as it might have been," she said. Smiling at Connor, she gestured to one of the chairs in front of her desk, then turned and pressed a buzzer. At once, a section of the wall parted and a small but well-stocked bar shot forward.

Cheng Li shook her head. "Seems unnecessarily flashy to me but the architect was very insistent. Would you like a drink?"

"Some water would be great," Connor said.

"Just water?" said Cheng Li. "It's not much to toast the return of an old comrade and a good friend."

Connor smiled at her words. "Water is just fine," he said. "And I was hoping we might make a slightly different toast."

"Really?" Cheng Li's right eyebrow darted up in the shape of an inverted tick as she poured water into two glasses. "Go on then," she said, sliding one glass towards him.

Connor raised his glass. "To new captains, new beginnings and –" he paused and took a breath "– reunited comrades." He watched carefully for her response. His heart was hammering beneath his sweat-soaked shirt.

"A nice toast." Cheng Li lifted her glass.

Connor found he was trembling. Drops of water spilled onto the pristine wooden desktop.

"Sorry!" he said, lifting his hand to mop up the water.

"No problem," Cheng Li said, a cloth already in her hand. "My, my, Connor Tempest. Jumpy, much?" Grinning, she mopped up the spill. "Anyone would think your very life and happiness depended upon this meeting."

"In a way it does," he said. He clearly wasn't going to pull off anything approaching nonchalance so he might as well be straight with her. "You know why I'm here," he said. "When we last met you said that if I talked to Captain Wrathe, and if he agreed to release me from his articles, you'd consider having me join your crew."

Cheng Li set down her glass and scrutinised Connor intently. "So you went to talk to Captain Wrathe?"

"Yes," he said. "I told him how I felt. That I needed to leave *The Diablo*. And that I wanted to join your crew."

Cheng Li's almond eyes widened. "I'm sure he was just thrilled to hear that."

Connor smiled. "Not exactly. He accused you of inciting me to betray him, but I told him, in no uncertain terms, that it was my choice and mine alone."

This time Cheng Li said nothing, but he could tell from her silence that he had her complete attention and, perhaps also, her respect. "Anyway, the long and the short of it is that he has released me from my articles. And so, I've come to ask you formally if you'll consider me joining your crew."

His pitch finished, he looked up at the grand painting of Chang Ko Li. What word had Jacinta Slawter used to describe the painting. *Naïf*? Connor wasn't sure what that meant, but from her tone he didn't think it was flattering. From his perspective, he thought it was a very impressive painting and incredible to think that Cheng Li had been just nine years old when she had painted it. The famous pirate captain seemed almost to be gazing out of the portrait at him, his expression undeniably ferocious but, at the same time, somewhat amused. Connor glanced back at Cheng Li, finding that she too was smiling.

"I'd be delighted to have you join my crew," she said. "You're hired!"

Connor was speechless. Somehow he hadn't expected it to be this easy. "That's brilliant!" he said, grinning. "I'll do you proud, I promise."

"I know you will, Connor. It's a shame, however, that you gave me the abbreviated version of your encounter with Molucco. According to *my* sources, he burned your articles in front of you and nearly set fire to himself and poor Scrimshaw into the bargain!"

"You knew?" Connor said. But of course she knew! She had eyes in the back of her head and tentacles of sources stretching throughout the pirate world.

"Well, now you're part of the crew, perhaps you'd like to meet your comrades?" Cheng Li said. "I've arranged to see some of them over at Ma Kettle's this evening. I have a few pieces of business to finish up here, then we can head over together."

Connor nodded. "I'd like that very much." He felt the doors of the old, familiar pirate world opening up again. Only it was *better* this time. This time, he had made a conscious choice about which crew he was joining. He might have had his doubts about Cheng Li in the past but now they were long gone. She was going to be a great captain and a superb mentor.

"Why don't you have another look around while I go over these papers?" Cheng Li said, slipping on a pair of half-rimmed glasses. "They're *just* for reading the fine print," she said, catching Connor's surprised expression. "Now off you pop. Pick out a cabin for yourself."

Connor rose to his feet, but lingered in front of her desk. "I already know which cabin I'd like."

Cheng Li stared up at him, her glasses balanced on the tip of her delicate nose. "I'm listening."

"The one marked Deputy Captain," he said. It was aiming

high, he knew, but so far today, the universe had been good to him. Why not ask it for just one more thing?

Cheng Li slipped off her glasses but kept her eyes focused on him. "I'm afraid, Connor, that the position of Deputy is already taken."

He could feel the flush flooding his face. "I knew it," he said. "I knew I should have got back here sooner!"

"No," she said, quietly but firmly. "No, on this occasion, it wasn't a question of timing. You're a good pirate, Connor. You learn fast and you're a team-player. Your courage is unquestionable and your swordskills are very fine indeed. But your talent is raw and your experience limited. Doubtless, you have an amazing career ahead of you, but you're not there yet."

Given how sharp she could be, as sharp as her twin *katana* blades, Cheng Li had chosen her words with care. Connor couldn't argue with the sentiments either. She had made an accurate assessment of his abilities at this point. She wasn't saying that he'd never make the grade, only that it was too soon. There and then, he committed himself to learning everything he could from her, and from whomever she had chosen as her deputy.

"You're disappointed," Cheng Li said.

"Yes." There was no point in denying it. "But I understand your reasoning. And I want you to know that I'll support you and your deputy one hundred per cent. I'm looking forward to meeting him . . . or is it *her*? Will they be at the tavern later?"

Cheng Li smiled once more. "You've already met. In fact, you know each other quite well." She paused. "Connor, my deputy captain is Jacoby Blunt."

Chapter Twelve

When Sally Met Dexter

Grace stood in the crisp morning light, looking down the mountainside. She had already been up more than an hour. It was a beautiful morning. The sun was strong and the sky was clear. Far down below, the ocean glittered as if sequins had been thrown into the pool of turquoise. It all gave Grace a fresh sense of optimism about the future. It also gave her an idea. Deciding not to waste a moment, she walked quickly back into the internal compound and made her way to Mosh Zu's chamber.

Grace wondered if Mosh Zu *ever* slept because he, alone of the Vampirates, seemed to be around and active during both the night-time and the day. Perhaps this was because he was currently on crisis alert, given the condition of the fading souls, including her own mother. Then again Mosh Zu was such a master of energy that perhaps he simply needed very little sleep.

At the door of Mosh Zu's meditation room, she knocked softly – loud enough to alert the guru if he was awake but not so loud as to disturb him if he was resting. She was delighted to hear him cheerily cry, "Come in!"

As she entered, he nodded and smiled warmly at her. "Hello, Grace. How are you today?"

"Very well," she said. "I've just been outside. It's a lovely morning. The sun is so strong already! The view down the mountain is incredible!"

Mosh Zu smiled to see her in such good spirits.

"I wonder . . ." Grace asked, "it's so beautiful outside. Do you think it would be all right to take my mother out?"

Mosh Zu considered her request for a moment, then nodded. "Yes, I think that would be an excellent idea. It will be good for Sally to feel the sun on her skin once more."

Grace was elated. "I'm so pleased. I thought I should check with you first, but I so want to show her the gardens and everything." Already she was back at the door, keen not to lose a moment. But suddenly, a dark thought crossed her mind and her earlier, fragile, optimism slipped away.

Mosh Zu saw her face drop and walked swiftly over to her. "Grace, you're thinking about our previous discussions, aren't you?"

She nodded. As hard as she tried to put it out of her mind, she couldn't escape the brutal truth that she and her mother were already on borrowed time.

Mosh Zu looked her in the eyes. "Grace, I have only one piece of advice for you. Try to see this time with your mother as a gift." He paused, smiling. "Not just for you but also for her."

Grace sighed. He was right – she knew he was. She walked soberly across from the guru's quarters to Sally's room, her thoughts becoming calmer with every step.

"Mother," she said, knocking on the door, "it's Grace. May I come in?"

"Yes, of course, Grace." The voice was faint but cheerful. Grace pushed open the door.

Sally was sitting on the bed, propped up against a hillock of pillows. Something about her mother's manner alerted Grace to the fact that they were not alone. She turned and saw Lorcan sitting on a chair by the side of her mother's bed.

"Good morning!" he said.

Grace could not disguise her surprise to find Lorcan there. It was so unusual for him to be up and about at this time. She had the feeling she had interrupted the two of them, somehow. "Lorcan," she found herself blurting out, "what are you doing here?"

He smiled, his blue eyes sparkling. "Catching up with a very dear old friend."

"Less of the old, thank you!" said Sally, grinning nevertheless. "I'd lob one of these pillows at you if I had the strength! But don't be lulled into a false sense of security. Reinforcements have arrived!" She grinned at Grace. "Haven't they, my darling?"

"Yes," answered Grace, sitting down on the bed, excited to see her mother in such good spirits. She turned back to Lorcan. "So *you* had better be on your best behaviour!"

"All right, you win!" he said, producing a white handkerchief from his pocket and waving it in surrender.

Grace laughed. Her initial discomfort had evaporated. It was good being here with Lorcan and Sally. She felt a sense of completeness that had been missing from her life for too long.

"Look at the two of you," Lorcan said. "A perfect pair. Your hair, your eyes, that same sprinkling of freckles, the identical way your noses wrinkle when you smile. You're a complete match!"

"Yes," Sally agreed, turning Grace's face gently towards her. "When I look at you, my darling, it's like I'm gazing into a magic mirror. I see myself at your age." She sighed. "I want so much for you to be happy and safe and cared for. After I'm . . . After I'm . . ." She couldn't finish the sentence.

Lorcan stood up and approached the bed. He reached out his arms and enfolded mother and daughter. "Grace will be well

89

looked after, Sally. Always. Have no fear of that." He planted a kiss on first Sally's head, then Grace's. Then he tenderly released them both and stepped back towards the door. "I'd better go," he said. "I was supposed to be in Mosh Zu's quarters ten minutes ago. Besides, I think you two deserve some time alone together."

"Yes," agreed Sally, with a nod.

"I'll see you both later," Lorcan said, smiling as he made his exit.

As the door closed behind him, Grace turned back to Sally. "I thought we might go out into the gardens, Mother. It's a beautiful sunny day. Would you like that?"

"Yes," said Sally. "Yes, Grace, I should like that very much." The mere idea seemed to give her a fresh pulse of energy. She eased herself up against the bedhead and swung her feet down on to the floor. Grace watched as Sally slipped on her shoes and fastened her cardigan around her. It had a pattern of shells and coral lightly embroidered in pale blue on white, with tiny mother-of-pearl buttons.

"That's so pretty!" Grace exclaimed. "Where did you get it?"

"I'll give you one guess!" said Sally.

Laughing, both mother and daughter spoke as one. "Darcy!"

"It's so wonderful to be here with you," Sally said as they crossed the courtyard, having taken in the view from the gates.

"For me too," Grace said, feeling somehow at peace now, arm in arm with her mother. "But how are you feeling? Would you like to sit down for a bit?"

Sally nodded.

"I know the perfect place," said Grace, leading her mother gently towards her beloved fountain and one of the benches positioned around it.

"What a beautiful spot!" Sally declared.

"I'm glad you like it," Grace said. "This is my favourite place here at Sanctuary. It's where I come to think. It's very peaceful, isn't it?"

Sally nodded. "Yes, it is. And shady too." She sat down and stretched out her arms, luxuriantly. Then she wrinkled her nose. "Is that lavender I can smell?"

"Yes." Grace nodded. "There's a herb garden just over there, see? It's where Mosh Zu grows many of the herbs he uses for healing."

"Oh yes," Sally said, wrinkling her nose. "I can smell lemon grass and rosemary and cardamon and curry leaf. How delicious!"

"Yes," Grace nodded, beaming. She was glad to see the garden was working its restorative magic on Sally too. She hoped the time was right to continue with her mother's story.

She turned to Sally. "Do you feel up to talking again, Mother? About your time on *The Nocturne*?"

"Yes," Sally said. "Yes, I think so. Now, where had we got to?"

Grace sighed. "You were telling me about being Sidorio's donor. And how he didn't live up to your expectations."

"Ah yes," Sally said. "That's right." She paused, reaching out and snapping off a stalk of lavender. She twisted it in her hands as she continued. "Well, I soon grew accustomed to Sidorio. I understood that all he wanted from me was a regular portion of blood and, after the initial period of disappointment, I was happy enough to give that to him." She shrugged. "In a way, him having no other interest in me gave me a certain freedom. It was only occasionally – very occasionally – in the darkness and the stillness after the sharing, when I felt just a little weak, that I'd have liked him to have been there. Those were the only times I felt low."

She turned her face to Grace. "Sidorio had very definite ideas, and a fierce pride. Other Vampirates – Lorcan for instance – saw their donors as equals. Sidorio didn't. At least, that's what I thought then." She hesitated, looking off towards the fountain for a moment. A delicate white butterfly had caught her attention as it hovered above the water. When she resumed speaking, her tone of voice was different. "My life aboard the ship was just fine. I had made a deal and what I got in return for my weekly donation of blood more than justified it. It really was a life of ease . . . and fun! We donors were always well looked after. And the food! After the rations I'd been on back home . . . Well, I ate like a horse – so much so that I soon began to balloon in weight. I had to take myself in check and start exercising."

"Exercising?" Grace asked. "Aboard *The Nocturne*?" The notion seemed strange, somehow.

"Don't sound so surprised!" said Sally. "I had made good friends with some of the other donors. Two of them especially . . . You saw one of them in your vision – Shanti . . . do you remember?"

"Yes." Grace nodded.

"Such a beautiful girl. And she's so much fun, isn't she?"

When Shanti's name had come up previously, Grace had brushed over the truth, but now she could no longer lie to her mother. Sally could see the sadness in her daughter's eyes. "What's wrong?" she asked. "Grace, whatever is it? Tell me!"

"I'm afraid I have some sad news," Grace said, reaching for Sally's hand and giving it a light squeeze. "I'm afraid Shanti died. I'm so sorry, Mother."

"Oh no!" Sally brought her hand to her chest and closed her eyes for a moment. When she opened them again, she saw the concern in Grace's eyes. "It's all right, Grace. Truly. Of course, I'm upset – Shanti was such a dear friend – but I don't want you to hide the truth from me. Please, tell me, what happened to her?"

Grace took a deep breath. "Shanti was killed. By her Vampirate partner."

"By Lorcan!" Sally exclaimed, incredulous.

"No!" Grace shook her head. "No, of course not! Lorcan would never be so brutal."

"I don't understand," Sally said. "Lorcan was Shanti's partner."

"Yes," Grace said, "they *were* partners, until Lorcan went blind and we had to bring him here to Sanctuary for healing. Shanti came along too but she hated it so much the captain finally agreed to take her back to *The Nocturne* and find another vampire to pair her up with."

"It isn't easy for a donor to switch from one Vampirate to another," Sally said.

Grace's ears pricked up at these words. Was her mother trying to tell her something? Sally had started out on board the ship as Sidorio's donor. But had she switched when another Vampirate had arrived on board? Was her mother telling her that she had been Dexter's donor after all? That he had been a Vampirate too?

The question was on her lips, but before she could ask it, her mother spoke again. "Looking back, it seems such an innocent time," she said. "Shanti, Teresa and I doing our daily round of keep-fit exercises up on deck. We had such a giggle. We really did! It was like being on a cruise ship. All day, every day, we'd be up on deck, without a care in the world. One of the other donors – Oskar, that was his name! – he was the most wonderful musician. He used to play his guitar up there. Such beautiful music! We'd sunbathe all afternoon." Sally turned to Grace, her eyes bright. "Why, it was on just such an afternoon that I met Dexter."

Grace's heart missed a beat at the mention of her dad's name. It was as if her mother had read her mind.

"I'd love to hear about *that*," Grace said.

"Oh Grace," Sally said, "I'm afraid the exercise and fresh air has made me a little tired. I think I'm going to need to rest before I carry on – and this is such a lovely spot for it . . ."

Grace couldn't conceal the look of disappointment in her eyes.

Sally put her arm around Grace's waist and reached for her hand. "Besides, why would you want to hear it from me," Sally said, "when you can see it all for yourself?" With that, she clasped Grace's hand and closed her eyes. As her mother fell asleep on her shoulder, Grace smiled. Suddenly, her head was filled with a vision of the deck of *The Nocturne* on a sunny afternoon.

The deck was crowded. Grace was once again seeing things through Sally's eyes. She was dressed in an old-fashioned swimsuit, sitting on a rug, rubbing sunscreen onto her arms. Opposite her, Shanti was doing exactly the same, chattering away. And there was a third girl close by – this must be Teresa. In the centre of the rug was a plate piled high with fruit, glistening jewel-like in the afternoon sun – fresh figs, succulent white peaches and icy slivers of watermelon. They looked delicious.

Grace could hear guitar music, just as Sally had mentioned before. She glanced beyond Shanti and saw a young man leaning against the mast, strumming away at a guitar. He caught her looking and smiled. Evidently, he knew her. What had Sally said his name was? Oskar, that was it!

Suddenly, she felt a hand on her shoulder. At first, Grace thought she was being jolted out of the vision but quite the reverse was true – it was sucking her in even deeper. Now, to all intents and purposes, she *was* Sally.

She felt Shanti's hand on her shoulder, and heard her distinctive voice. "Do as I say, girls and make a wish! But make sure you close your eyes first or it won't work!"

Within the vision, Grace closed her eyes for a moment. Everything went black. Then she felt Shanti's hand on her shoulder once more and heard her excited cry. "Open your eyes, Sally! Open your eyes! I think your wish has already come true!"

She opened her eyes and found herself being dragged – by Shanti on the one side and Teresa on the other – over to the edge of the deck. "Look!" they both cried, simultaneously. They were pointing out over the deck-rail to the shore. There sitting on a rock, a red-and-white striped towel laid out beneath him, was Dexter Tempest.

Grace felt her heart race. Her father looked so handsome. He had a picnic basket by his side and he was eating something. A peach. No, an apple! His eyes met hers and he stopped mid-bite and waved. Grace felt a shiver, but it was of delight – for this was the moment that her father had met her mother.

As she reconnected with the vision, Grace found herself standing on the edge of the deck-rail, once more with the girls at her side.

"Do it," Shanti repeated. "Go on, Sal! I dare you!"

Sally turned, her bare feet burning on the wooden rail. "But it's against the rules!"

"Do it!" Shanti repeated, more forcefully.

Suddenly, Sally was diving off the side of the ship into the wonderfully cool, clear ocean. As she surfaced, she smoothed back the strands of her hair and got her bearings. She saw the ship, and the girls above giving her the thumbs up and laughing to themselves. Then she turned in the water and looked over at the rock where Dexter had been sitting. There was his red-and-white striped towel, but he was no longer on it. Sally frowned. Then she saw that Dexter was swimming towards her, a powerful freestyle stroke bringing him ever closer. Smiling, she decided to meet him halfway.

They met in the middle of the ocean.

"Hello," he said with a smile. "I'm Dexter. Dexter Tempest."

"And I'm Sally," she said.

"Is that your ship?" he asked, nodding towards it.

"I'm travelling on it," she said, skirting around the full story for now.

"How glamorous!" he said. "I'm travelling too. All over the place. I'm the lighthouse keeper of a small town called Crescent Moon Bay, but lately I've had the travelling bug – I just knew I had to take off and see something of the world."

She smiled. "I know just what you mean. I had the exact same feeling."

Dexter smiled, his eyes boring deep into hers. "Maybe we were given the same feeling so we'd both come here, to this place at this very moment. So that we'd find each other . . ."

It was a bold thing to say. Sally's first thought was to smile and dismiss it. But there was something about him – such an honesty and openness in his eyes. So she did not dismiss it. His words made complete sense to her. She smiled back at him and nodded.

"Come on!" he said. "Come on, beautiful Sally! Swim back to my rock with me and share my lunch."

They swam back to the rock and dried off from their swim, then Dexter opened up various packages of food and offered them to her. Sally was too excited to eat much and anxious too. On the one hand, she felt a deep happiness. But mixed in with it was a dark sense of foreboding.

Dexter had a pair of binoculars with him and now he picked them up and looked back at the ship. "That's a very beautiful figurehead on the front of your ship," he said, lowering the binoculars.

Sally stopped eating mid-bite.

"But she has the strangest expression," he continued. "It's as if she's frowning at us! Aren't most figureheads painted with smiles?"

"Yes," Sally nodded, her heart beginning to race. "But she's no ordinary figurehead. And it's no ordinary ship." Suddenly, she stood up, flustered. "I shouldn't have come. I have to get back."

"Wait!" he implored, but she had already dived back into the water and begun swimming back to *The Nocturne*.

She heard a splash behind her and knew Dexter was following. There were tears in her eyes and she shook her head. "Don't follow me!" she warned. But he ignored her and soon caught up. She hoped he wouldn't notice her tears.

He swam back with her to the ship. "I'm afraid you mustn't come up," she said, reaching for the ladder. "I wish you could, but you can't. I'd be in big trouble. Worse trouble . . ."

"It's all right," he said. "I don't want you to be in *any* kind of trouble." He smiled. "But I must see you again, beautiful Sally. That's non-negotiable."

Her hands and feet were on the ladder. She shook her head. "We mustn't," she said. "I told you before. This is no ordinary ship."

"No," he agreed. "It's an extraordinary ship. It brought me extraordinary you."

Once more his words filled her with a bittersweet sense of joy and sadness. Shaking her head, Sally began climbing the ladder. "I'm sorry," she said. "I can never see you again, Dexter Tempest. You have to forget about me."

"*Forget* about you? Impossible!" he cried. "I'll follow the ship. I'll do whatever I can. But I *will* see you again."

She continued to climb but as she did so, her vision grew blurry. Suddenly, Grace found that her eyes were open and she was back, fully back, on the bench in the Sanctuary gardens, her heart pounding from what she had seen. What an extraordinary thrill to have experienced her parents' first meeting!

She turned to Sally, whose eyes were also open again. "Did you see it?" she asked Grace.

Grace nodded. "Yes," she said. "Right up to when you climbed back onto the ship. I can't wait to see what happened next. How he found you again."

Sally smiled. "That's a whole other story," she said. "We'll come to that."

"I wish Connor was here," Grace said. "I wish he was able to hear or see this too."

"It will be your job to tell him," Sally said, a shadow falling over her eyes. "When he's ready to listen."

CHAPTER THIRTEEN

Comrades

"Hey, Connor!"

"Jacoby." Connor stretched out his hand. "Congratulations on being made deputy captain."

"Thanks, man," Jacoby grinned at him. "I'm so stoked you've joined the crew. Best news we've had all week. Isn't it, Min?"

Jasmine Peacock stepped forward and nodded. "It's going to be good working with you, Connor," she said, giving him a little hug. As he held her in his arms for the briefest of moments, and smelled her sublime coconut-scented hair, Connor felt that this was his instant reward for being magnanimous towards Jacoby.

"Here you are, guys," cried a familiar voice. "A round of Dark and Stormys!" Connor turned and saw Sugar Pie setting down the tray of cocktails. Seeing him, she rushed over and gave him a hug. "Connor! You look great!"

Grinning, he took her in his arms. He noticed, to his intense satisfaction, that Jacoby's eyes were on stalks.

"Hello Sugar Pie," Connor said. "Let me introduce you to my new comrades, Jacoby Blunt and Jasmine Peacock. It's their very first time at Ma Kettle's!"

Sugar Pie beamed at them. "Any friends of Connor's are friends of mine. Welcome to Ma's. Anything you need, just holler for Sugar Pie!"

"Could you define 'anything'?" Jacoby couldn't help but ask. Jasmine grinned and dug her elbow sharply into his ribs.

"Nice work, girl!" Sugar Pie grinned, high-fiving Jasmine. "I think you're gonna fit in very well around here." She turned back to Connor, tucking her arm around his waist. "So it's really true? You've finished with Captain Wrathe and his crew? You've signed up with Mistress Li?"

Connor nodded. "It's complicated," he told her. "But I know it's the right decision."

"Well, for goodness' sake, stop looking so worried then!" Sugar Pie smiled. "And remember what I told you the last time we met. You'll always be welcome around here, whichever crew you're on. You're good people, Connor Tempest." Her kind words touched him more than he could say. "Well, I'd better get going. It's a thirsty crowd tonight. And I just *might* be doing a new song and dance routine dressed as a mermaid later." She winked at Jacoby.

"Wait!" Connor said. "Before you go . . . if you see Bart and Cate – I mean, *when* you see them – will you tell them . . . tell them I said hi?"

Sugar Pie grinned. "Tell them yourself," she said, nodding towards one of the VIP booths. "Looks like *The Diablo* and *The Typhon* are in for the night."

Connor looked across the bar. He saw Ma Kettle leading Molucco Wrathe into his favourite booth. They were followed by Molucco's brother Barbarro and his wife and deputy Trofie, who was, as usual, dressed to kill. Connor looked over, his heart hammering, to see if Bart and Cate were with them. He really ought to go and say something, but he didn't want to risk an encounter with Molucco. He couldn't see Bart or Cate in the crowd but, just his luck, Molucco looked straight over at him. The captain held his gaze for a moment but didn't smile or make any gesture of familiarity. Connor remembered what his former captain had told him when last they had met. "*You're nothing to me now.*" The words sent a fresh chill down Connor's spine as Molucco simply turned his head away. Evidently, those words held true.

"Hey, Connor," said Jasmine, appearing at his side with a drink. "Try one of these Dark and Stormys. They're heaven in a glass!"

Connor turned and saw that Jacoby and Cheng Li were also close at hand. Cheng Li winked at him and raised her glass. "To new comrades," she said.

The others echoed her toast and they all chinked glasses, before sipping Ma's delicious new cocktail.

Inside the VIP booth, Barbarro and Molucco Wrathe were deep in conversation. Trofie sat beside the two captains, deaf to their words, locked in her own dark thoughts. On the table in front of her, an untouched glass of oyster champagne bubbled away furiously, but Trofie felt as flat as stagnant swamp-water. She knew that fundamentally nothing had changed in terms of her wealth, power or legendary beauty. And her family, which she treasured above all else, was safe. Nevertheless, she felt deeply self-conscious about her missing hand and was wearing a stunning silver dress with exaggeratedly long sleeves, so that both of her arms were completely covered. In spite of the superb cut and exceptional expense of the dress, she felt as dowdy as a nun. If only she could find some way to lift herself out of this grim mood.

"Hello, Mother," said Moonshine, grinning amiably at her as he stepped over the velvet rope into the booth.

The appearance of her darling son, who seemed to grow

taller and more handsome with each passing day, was just the thing to make her smile. She lifted her face for him to kiss. As he drew back from her, she saw that his long fingers were looped through a string bow, connected to a brown paper package, which he swung back and forth in his hands.

Trofie nodded towards the parcel. "What's that, *min elskling*? Have you been shopping?"

Moonshine smiled. "It's a gift, Mother. For you."

"For me? Whatever for? It's not my birthday, or even a pirate's name day . . ."

"It's to make you feel better," Moonshine said, extending the package towards her.

Trofie waved her excessively long sleeves in front of him. "Perhaps, *min elskling*, you would open it for me?"

Moonshine nodded, beaming as he began untying the string.

"Look, husband." Trofie prodded Barbarro. "Our darling boy has brought me a gift."

Both Barbarro and Molucco turned to watch. Moonshine untied the string and then the layer of brown paper. Inside was a square box. He opened the lid. Trofie looked down excitedly as her son carefully lifted something out from within. It was still wrapped in tissue paper but the sprinkling of glittering powder, which fell from its layers, was a pleasing sight. Like silver rain.

Finally, with an emphatic gesture, Moonshine cast off the final swathe of tissue paper and revealed his gift.

Barbarro, Molucco and Trofie all gasped in unison.

"It's your new hand," Moonshine announced, then added, rather unnecessarily, "I made it myself!"

There, cradled in his arms was what had started out as a shop mannequin's hand, roughly sawn off and painted silver (somewhat unevenly).

"Well? Do you like it?" Moonshine asked, his eyes glancing up at Trofie expectantly.

Trofie gulped. "I'm . . . I'm speechless," she said.

"What a kind and thoughtful gesture!" Molucco boomed. "He's a good boy, your Moonshine," he said, nudging Barbarro.

"Look!" Moonshine held the silver hand right under his mother's nose. "Do you see how I painted the nails?"

She stared down, registering that each of the nails had been painted with the skull-and-bones insignia. Clearly some considerable effort had gone into this. Trofie felt hot tears sting her eyes.

"Now see," said Barbarro, "you've moved your mother to tears!" He massaged his wife's shoulder. "There, there, my darling. I can see how touched you are by our son's gift." Through her sobs, Trofie nodded.

"Let me fit it on you," Moonshine said, excitedly. Before Trofie could protest, Moonshine lifted the voluminous folds of her sleeve and pushed them back to reveal her truncated wrist. He had fitted a thick leather belt to the wrist of his DIY hand and now he pressed the silver hand to his mother's wrist and gently but firmly buckled the belt. The entire Wrathe family watched with bated breath to see if it would hold. Miraculously, it seemed a perfect fit. Moonshine removed his hands, surveying his craftsmanship with great pride.

Trofie glanced down at her strange new hand, which was still shedding shards of silver, like premium-grade dandruff, all over the floor.

"Thank you," she stammered. "Thank you, *min elskling*. I'm so very . . . so very . . ." As she spoke, she lifted the hand towards her son but, as she did so, the weight of the hand pulled the belt away from her wrist. The hand came free and shot to the floor. The thumb broke clean off and flew out beyond the velvet rope. More silver shards sprayed everywhere. Moonshine cried out an exceedingly colourful word and received an immediate clout from his father.

"It's ruined!" Moonshine cried. "That took me and Transom two whole days to make!"

"Never mind, lad," said Molucco. "It's the thought that counts. And if you go and retrieve the thumb before someone steps on it, we can try to repair it."

"What's the point?" Moonshine shook his head. "I'm not stupid! I can tell she didn't like it! She dropped it on purpose!"

"It matters not," Barbarro boomed with fierce authority. "We're going to recover your mother's real hand. And soon."

Trofie reached out to her son. "Oh, *min elskling*, I did like it. Of course I did!"

But Moonshine broke free from her vast phantom sleeves and kicked back the velvet rope, heading out of the VIP booth into the main bar. His head was filled with a familiar black fog of tension and anger. He wanted to punch something, or *someone*, very very hard. As luck would have it, as he looked up, he saw a familiar face heading straight towards him.

For once, Moonshine's fist was completely on target. *Thwack.* The advantage of surprise enabled him to land a knockout blow. Connor Tempest slumped down onto the tavern floor like a dead weight. The noise he made as he landed on the rotten wooden boards was quite possibly the most enjoyable sound Moonshine had heard since the latest release from thrash-shanty gods, *The Dark Spaces.*

"He's coming round!" Jacoby said. "Guys, he's coming around!" They all watched as Connor, who was laid out on a velvet chaise, opened his eyes.

"Those smelling salts never fail," said Ma Kettle.

Jasmine grinned. "Erm, I don't think it was the smelling salts!" She nodded towards Sugar Pie. "She kissed him."

"She did?" Ma Kettle grinned. "How did I miss that? Well, whatever it takes."

Connor stared groggily up at them all. "What's going on?" he asked. "Why's that huge silver skull-and-crossbones spinning around like that?"

Jacoby turned to the others, his features grave with concern. "He must be worse than we thought," he said. "He's hallucinating."

"No he's not!" said Ma, pointing up above the dance-floor. "See my new skull-and-bones glitterball? I saw it in a ballet production and I thought: I'm having me one of those! Gorgeous, isn't it?"

Relieved, Jacoby turned back to Connor. "Do you know who you are? *Where* you are?"

"Yeah, yeah," Connor nodded. "I'm Connor Tempest, I'm in Ma Kettle's Tavern and that drongo Moonshine just attacked me for no reason."

"Looks like he didn't inflict any major damage," Jacoby said. "That's good news, at least." He turned to the others. "Move back, everyone. Give Connor some room to breathe."

Ma Kettle laughed. "Better yet, give him a strong drink. That'll buck him up." She turned to Sugar Pie. "Let's fetch this lot another round of Dark and Stormys. On the house!"

"Aye-aye, Ma."

As Ma and Sugar Pie headed off, an exaggerated cough heralded the arrival of Barbarro Wrathe, closely followed by his brother, Molucco. "How is he?" he enquired.

"He'll recover," Cheng Li said. "No thanks to your wayward son."

"I'm sorry," Barbarro said. "His behaviour was quite uncalled for."

"Yes," Cheng Li agreed, "it was. Let's just hope there are no broken bones."

"Come, come, Mistress Li," piped up Molucco. "I don't think it's as serious as all that."

Cheng Li drew herself up to her full height, fixing Molucco

with her dark almond eyes. "*You* may be somewhat lax in treating assaults on members of *your* crew, Captain Wrathe, but *I* take these matters very seriously indeed."

Molucco waved his hand, dismissively. "It's horseplay," he said. "Connor was simply in the wrong place at the wrong time. Moonshine has a lot on his mind right now. We all do. I assume that you've heard about the attack on *The Typhon*? By the Vampirates?"

"Yes." Cheng Li's tone was more circumspect. "Even so."

Molucco clearly thought he'd now gained the upper hand and proceeded with the subtlety of a steamroller. "I think you'll understand then how this puts things into sharper perspective. We must all focus now on addressing the Vampirate threat." He paused. "To which end, we'd like a word with young Mister Tempest about the Vampirates. I seem to remember he has some knowledge and experience of them."

Molucco pushed past Jacoby and Jasmine to clear his path towards Connor, who was now sitting upright on the chaise-longue, but still looked somewhat dazed.

"Excuse *me*, Captain Wrathe," Cheng Li said, stepping protectively in front of Connor. "But what on the oceans do you think you are doing?"

Molucco frowned. "I thought I'd made myself perfectly clear. We wish to consult Connor about the Vampirates."

Cheng Li rested her hands on her hips. "I've noted your request," she said. "But now is not the appropriate time."

"I'm sorry—" Molucco began, sounding very far from being sorry.

Cheng Li continued, unabashed. "You appear to be under the illusion that Connor is still part of your crew. He isn't. And nor, for that matter, am I. Connor is under my command, now. And, therefore, it is I who will decide when and *if* you can talk to him."

"This is outrageous!" Barbarro glared down at Cheng Li over his brother's shoulder.

"Hardly more outrageous than a random assault on one pirate crew by another. Why, I've a mind to file a report with Commodore Kuo and the Pirate Federation. It would be another strike against Moonshine's name."

"Don't threaten us, Mistress Li," blustered Molucco. "File any report you care to. We *will* have our interview with Mister Tempest."

"Perhaps you will," Cheng Li said. "But not here and not tonight." She folded her arms. "Make an appointment!"

Molucco held her intent gaze for a good few moments then turned on his feet and marched off, his angry feet reverberating along the floorboards. Barbarro followed, close at heel.

"Go, Captain!" said Jacoby. He and the others all turned to Cheng Li.

She nodded at them soberly. "I want you to understand something," she said. "I'm not on some kind of power trip here. You've all signed up to my articles but in return, I vowed to look after each and every one of you. And that's exactly what I intend to do once I become captain in a few days' time."

CHAPTER FOURTEEN

Deadlock

Stukeley knocked on the door of the captain's cabin.

"Come," called Sidorio from within.

Stukeley pushed open the door and stepped inside, closely followed by Johnny.

Sidorio nodded at his lieutenants. "Are we on course as planned?"

"Yes, Captain," Stukeley nodded. "We should arrive at the bay presently."

"Excellent," Sidorio said. "Now we'll find out who's been playing games with us and bring this matter to a close."

"Yes, Captain," Stukeley said once more. "But before we arrive in the bay, Johnny and I have been doing some thinking, which we'd like to share with you."

Sidorio raised an eyebrow. "All right then," he said. "Start talking."

Stukeley nodded. "We think it's time to get a bit more organised, more regimented."

Johnny nodded. "We've expanded so fast," he said, turning to Sidorio. "We have what, two hundred, three hundred on the crew now?"

Sidorio waved his arm dismissively. "We'll have five hundred by the end of the month . . . a thousand next . . ."

"Exactly!" Stukeley said. "That's our point. If we're going to grow that fast, we need to get organised. We'll need more ships, for starters . . ."

Sidorio shrugged. "So, we'll get more ships. Starting with the one we're taking tonight. We'll build a fleet . . ."

"Great idea," Stukeley said. "And each ship will need a captain."

"Sure, sure." Sidorio's attention was fading.

Stukeley knew the captain's thoughts were elsewhere, but he forged on. "But not just a captain. We need a more regimented command structure on each ship."

Sidorio laughed. "Next you'll be suggesting that we have a crew of donors and a weekly Feast Night!"

"No!" Stukeley said. "No, I'd never suggest that. We don't need to replicate the ways of *The Nocturne*."

"Dead straight," said Sidorio, firmly. "That's not how things are going to be run around here. Not in my army." He nodded at Johnny. "What do you call it, Stetson?"

"*El ejército de la noche!*" repeated Johnny.

"Very poetic!" Sidorio said, with a grin.

Stukeley stood up. "Captain, I'm not suggesting that we set things up remotely like *The Nocturne*. You're originally from Roman times, right?"

This brought Sidorio's attention instantly back. "Roman times, yeah."

"Well," continued Stukeley, "I've been doing some research, see. Into the Roman army and its command structure. Did you know that the Roman army had—"

Sidorio waved his hands dismissively. "Believe me, I know all there is to know about the Roman army."

"So, what do you think?" Stukeley pressed on patiently. "To

setting up our ships – ahem, *your* ships – along the lines of a Roman legion?"

"Hmm," Sidorio said. "Maybe. I'll think about it." It was clear to Stukeley that the window had closed. "Let's go up on deck," said the captain. "I have a feeling we're getting close to our destination."

Stukeley nodded. He had done his best.

"There's the ship," Jessamy said, lowering her sunglasses.

"Oh yes," said Camille. "Time to go and meet our boys."

"For the last time," Jessamy said sadly, her mouth down-turned.

"That's what the captain said," agreed Camille. "I confess – I'm going to miss them. They're such pretty playthings." She smiled at her companion.

The two women waited on the cliffs as the crew of *The Blood Captain* gathered on the sand. They watched as Sidorio gave the command: "Go feast!" and all but two of the Vampirates raced off into the town – the town already decimated by Lady Lockwood and her crew.

Then, as Johnny and Stukeley walked towards the dunes, Jessamy and Camille went to meet their prey.

"Good evening, gentlemen," Jessamy called as Johnny and Stukeley walked towards the dunes. She had taken off her shoes in order to skim down the side of the dune. Camille followed in her wake.

"*Hola!*" Johnny called, smiling and walking over. "Where did you two spring from?"

"We were just up on the cliffs, taking in the night air," Camille said. "How about you?"

"We just came into shore from our ship," Johnny said, pointing to the prison hulk, out in the waters of the bay.

"So," Jessamy said, smiling at Stukeley. "What brings you gentlemen into town tonight?"

Stukeley shrugged. "We've come to let off some steam. You know how it is."

Jessamy nodded.

"What about you?" Stukeley asked. "Do you live here or are you visitors too?"

The women glanced at each other. Then Jessamy spoke again. "Visitors," she said.

"Hey," said Johnny, "how come you're wearing sunglasses? It's pitch black out here!"

The women smiled once more. Then they both spoke at once. "Fashion, darling!" They smiled at their companions.

"Take off your glasses!"

The smiles froze on the women's faces. Neither Johnny nor Stukeley had spoken.

"I said, take off your glasses!" The voice became more forceful.

Camille turned to Jessamy for guidance. They glanced around.

Sidorio stood behind them, his arms folded. "Do I have to ask you a third time?" he said. "Take. Off. Your. Glasses."

As he walked down the dunes, the women removed their sunglasses. They stared at the men, their black heart tattoos revealed.

"Very eye-catching," Sidorio said, coming to a standstill between his two lieutenants. "No wonder you've managed to entrance these two night after night." He nodded.

"Who are you?" Jessamy asked. In spite of Sidorio's brooding presence, she did not seem perturbed.

"I'll ask the questions around here," Sidorio said. "And we'll start by hearing who *you* both are and which ship you hail from."

He stared at them. The women stared back. For a time, there was deadlock between them. Then Sidorio spoke once more. "You've been having a little bit of fun with my lads these past

111

few nights, haven't you? Pumping them for information about where we're heading next and then working some magic to make them forget they ever met you." He paused. "That's right, isn't it?"

Jessamy placed her hands on her hips, defiantly. "Perhaps it is right, sir."

"At last, we're getting somewhere," Sidorio said. "Now, which ship do you come from?"

Jessamy looked him directly in the eye. "I'm not authorised to share that information with you," she said.

Sidorio frowned. "Not authorised?" He stepped closer. "*Not authorised?* You might want to rethink that. Fast."

But Jessamy shook her head. "I don't think so," she said. "Loose lips sink ships."

"What?" Sidorio stared at her blankly.

Once more, there was a stand-off.

"All right," Sidorio said. "I gave you the opportunity to do this the easy way. But there are other options." He turned to his lieutenants. "Bring them to the ship," he commanded, turning and walking off towards the water.

Johnny and Stukeley stepped forward. "Come with us, little ladies," said Johnny.

Jessamy looked at them both disparagingly. "We've overpowered you three times before," she said. "What makes you think tonight will be any different?"

"Yes," Camille nodded. "And, by the way, *sir*, that 'little lady' spiel grows tired really quickly."

The four Vampirates squared up to each other. Each had fire burning in their eyes. This time it was not hunger for blood that drove them on, but the need to do battle.

Suddenly a fresh voice entered the fray. "Is there a problem?"

Lady Lola Lockwood strode across the beach, the full skirt of her tight-corseted gown trailing across the sand.

112

Sidorio turned towards her. "And who might you be?"

"Lady Lola Lockwood." She nodded towards Jessamy and Camille. "These are two of my crew."

"*Your* crew?" Sidorio said incredulously.

"That's right," Lady Lockwood said. She pointed out to the side of the inlet. "My little ship is moored over there."

"Really?" Sidorio said, pointing to the vast prison hulk looming in the bay. "That's *my* ship."

"Golly," said Lady Lockwood with a smile. "It's enormous!"

Sidorio nodded, disconcerted.

Lady Lockwood continued affably, as if she had bumped into Sidorio at a cocktail party. "I'm afraid *The Vagabond* is a mere minnow, compared to your great whale of a ship! *The Blood Captain* – is that what it's called? How thrilling!"

She had a very strange way of speaking. Like nothing Sidorio had heard before. It was mesmerising, as were her eyes. And the strange tattoo of the black heart.

Which reminded him . . . Sidorio reached into his pocket. "I suppose I have you to thank for these?" He produced a cluster of playing cards and tossed them onto the sand.

"Oh, you found those, did you?" Lady Lockwood said. "Our little calling cards."

"Yes," said Sidorio. "We found them. Night after night. Just like you wanted."

Lady Lockwood frowned. "What on earth do you mean?"

"Don't play the innocent with me," said Sidorio. "We know what you've been up to, you and your *crew*." He spat out the words dismissively, nodding towards Camille and Jessamy, who were still squaring up to Johnny and Stukeley. "Your little handmaidens have been tricking my lieutenants into telling you where we're heading next. And then you've been beating us to the pass and attacking the town before we get there."

Lady Lockwood's expression gave nothing away at first. Then

a smile broke across her bow-shaped lips. "Well, I suppose there are advantages to being a minnow, after all," she said.

"You admit it," Sidorio said. "So now we can stop playing games."

"Oh, it was never a game, Sid. May I call you that?"

Sidorio's face darkened. "No, you may *not* call me Sid. My name is Sidorio. Quintus Antonius Sidorio. King of the Vampirates."

Lady Lockwood smiled. "How rude of me. I quite forgot myself. What a great honour it is to meet you." She curtsied, her body dipping low on the sand. Then she rose up. "I'm so sorry that we appear to have got off on the wrong footing."

Sidorio shook his head. "What footing did you *expect* us to get off on, acting the way you and your crew have?"

Lady Lockwood shrugged. "I was just trying to get your attention," she said. "It's not easy for a minnow to signal a whale."

Sidorio frowned once more, strangely unnerved by her words, her distinctive voice and her rare beauty. "You wanted my attention?" he said, confused.

"Why, of course," Lady Lockwood replied, with a smile.

"So this is just a game to you?"

"Oh no, sir," said Lady Lockwood, lowering her head. "Not a game at all."

"You're not trying to rival me?" Sidorio said. "To take command of these waters?"

"Oh no, sir," said Lady Lockwood. "That would be preposterous."

"Yes," Sidorio nodded. "It *would*!"

"Perhaps we should call a truce between our crews," suggested Lady Lockwood. She gestured towards Johnny and Stukeley, who were still squaring up to Jessamy and Camille, ready to fight.

114

Sidorio considered for a moment, then came to a conclusion. "Leave it, boys," he said.

"Stand down, ladies," Lady Lockwood called.

The four Vampirates stepped back into their pairs. Johnny and Stukeley came to stand by Sidorio, whilst Jessamy and Camille walked over to Lady Lockwood.

"But this feasting has to stop," Sidorio said. "I have a large, growing crew. They need blood."

Lady Lockwood nodded. "Agreed. But surely there's room for more than one ship of Vampirates on these oceans?"

"There's room for any number of ships," Sidorio said. "But only one Commander-in-Chief." He tapped his chest, in case the point needed emphasising. "Me!"

"Of course," Lady Lockwood nodded. "I told you before, Sidorio, I'm in no way attempting to rival you. I was just, perhaps in a rather gauche fashion, attempting to parlay an introduction."

Sidorio looked at her blankly for a moment. Johnny stepped forward and whispered in the captain's ear. "I think she just wanted to meet you, Captain."

Overhearing this exchange, Lady Lockwood nodded. "That's right. I just wanted to meet the great Sidorio, King of the Vampirates."

At this flattery, Sidorio grinned openly. "Well, now you've met me."

"Yes, indeed." Her eyes glowed. "And you've far exceeded even my expectations."

He smiled once more.

Lady Lockwood glanced at him guiltily. "I'm afraid, sir, that my crew has feasted on this town already tonight. But I vouchsafe to you this will not happen again."

Sidorio shrugged. "No problem. My crew has feasted elsewhere. We only came here to confront you and bring this matter to a close."

Lady Lockwood nodded. "And are you satisfied that it is now closed, sir?"

He stared down at her, thinking what a rare creature she was. "Yes," he said at last. "Yes, it ends here."

Lady Lockwood made to leave. "Come, ladies. Let us wend our way back to *The Vagabond*." Jessamy and Camille nodded and, stealing a final glance at Stukeley and Johnny, began to walk off.

Then Lady Lockwood turned and came back. She reached out her hand to Sidorio. "I hope we'll meet again," she said. "Under somewhat different circumstances."

Sidorio looked down at her hand, unsure at first what to do. Then to everyone's surprise, including his own, he leaned down and kissed it. "We'll meet again," he said. "I'll make sure of it."

Lady Lockwood withdrew her hand and walked off to join her crewmates.

When she was out of earshot, Stukeley turned to the captain. "What just happened?" he asked. "I thought we were taking over her ship."

"It's just a minnow," Sidorio said, echoing Lady Lola's words. "I have no need of a minnow. Let her have her plaything." He stared after her. "I like her. I like the way she talks."

Stukeley was about to protest but Johnny dug him in the ribs. Stukeley got the message loud and clear. "Would you like us to go sound the sirens, Captain, and summon the crew back on board?"

Sidorio nodded. "Make it so, Stukeley," he said, striding off across the sand, with a final glance at Lady Lockwood's fast disappearing figure.

Stukeley turned to Johnny. "He said he was a killer shark," he said, shaking his head. "But he backed down like a sea-slug!"

Johnny grinned. "I hear you, *hermano*. But I think the captain's in love!"

116

"Don't be daft," said Stukeley. "Sidorio doesn't know the meaning of the word. He isn't interested in such things."

"Trust me," Johnny said, shaking his head. "You are wise about many things, my friend, but I know how it is between men and women. And there's some kind of connection between those two. For sure!"

"That was a close call!" Jessamy said to Lady Lockwood.

"Yes," agreed the captain.

"Is that guy for real?" asked Camille. "I mean, I've heard the rumours, but he was even more Neanderthal than I expected."

Lady Lockwood smiled. "I found him rather charming in his own way," she said.

"Charming!" Camille exclaimed.

"You were very accommodating to him," Jessamy said, "if you don't mind my saying so, Captain?"

Lady Lockwood smiled. "Was I? Did I seem that way?" She stretched out her arms and laid one hand on Jessamy's shoulder and one on Camille's. "The thing is, my dears, sometimes you have to lose a battle to win the war." Her smile grew broader. "And the war is a very long way from over!"

She sighed. "Now, all that chit-chat has made me thirsty. Let's hasten back to the ship and break out the Argentinian!"

"Oh yes!" agreed Jessamy. "The Argentinian ambassador. He *was* rather tasty, wasn't he?"

"Yes," said Lady Lockwood. "Indeed he was . . ."

CHAPTER FIFTEEN

Sally's Request

The next time Grace visited Sally's room, she found her mother in surprisingly high spirits.

"Oh, my darling, I have news, wonderful news!"

"What is it?" Grace asked, marvelling at the change in her mother.

"We're going on a journey together." Sally's eyes were bright. "I've asked Mosh Zu and he says it's all right. We're going to Crescent Moon Bay!"

"Crescent Moon Bay!" Grace exclaimed. "But why?"

"I want to see where you and Connor grew up," Sally said. "And I want to visit Dexter's grave. To be close to him again. Oh, Grace, please be happy about this."

"I *am* happy," Grace reassured her. "It's just very sudden. Are you sure you're strong enough . . ." She let out a deep breath. "Oh Mother, of course, I'd love to show you Crescent Moon Bay!" She took Sally in her arms and hugged her.

"You must go and pack your things. We're joining *The Nocturne* tonight!"

"*The Nocturne*?" Grace repeated. A fresh thought occurred to her. "Does that mean that the captain is coming too? Is his recovery complete?" The possibility was an exciting one.

Sally shook her head. "I'm afraid I don't know the answer to that. You'll have to ask Mosh Zu."

Grace glanced at her mother once more. Sally looked as excited as a young child on the eve of her birthday.

"You're sure you're all right about going back?" Sally asked her now. "About visiting Dexter's grave? And the lighthouse? You must show me the lighthouse."

Grace nodded instinctively. It would be strange going back, especially without Connor. But it would be great to show Sally, and Lorcan and Mosh Zu – and *hopefully* the captain – where she had grown up. And it would be good to visit her dad's grave once more and to feel close to him again.

Thinking of her dad, she turned back to her mother. "I don't suppose," she said hesitantly, "that we could we pick up the story again, could we?"

"Yes," Sally said. "Yes, of course." She patted the bed. "Come up here, next to me. That's it. I want you nice and close."

Grace didn't waste a moment, clambering quickly up beside her mother.

"So Shanti and Teresa were waiting on deck for me," said Sally. "They were desperate to hear all about my encounter with Dexter. It was strange but though I'd only spent a short amount of time with him, I somehow knew he was the one I was supposed to be with."

Grace smiled. She had felt it was love at first sight for her parents and Sally's words just confirmed it.

"Over the next few days," Sally continued, "we talked of little else and we all agreed that we had to leave the world beyond the ship behind. It was, after all, the deal we had made when we became donors. We all had our reasons for coming aboard, though we didn't necessarily choose to share them with each other. And, though it was nice to daydream, we knew that we could never go back to the other world. It had been fun to visit, but that was an end to it."

Grace frowned. "But it *wasn't* the end. It couldn't have been."

Sally smiled at her daughter. "No, my darling, of course it wasn't. Life, as they say, is what happens to you while you're making other plans."

"So how and when did you see Dad again?"

Sally stroked Grace's hair as she continued. "It was a few days later. And in those days and nights, I felt such sadness – as if I was in mourning. But for what? For my past life? For the path I hadn't taken? For a man I had met in the middle of the ocean and swum with for, what, half an hour? It seemed too ridiculous but my feelings were deeper and truer than any I had previously experienced." She sighed. "Even Sidorio noticed something was wrong. I remember him asking me about it at Feast Night. Just before we began to share, he asked if I was all right. It was such a shock that I burst into tears. I couldn't stop sobbing." Sally shook her head. "I'm sure Sidorio regretted having said anything, but – you know what? – he did his best to comfort me. And then he took my blood. That night, for the first and last time, he offered to stay. But I said no. I wanted to be on my own."

Grace thought of her mother, alone in her cabin. It was heartbreaking.

Sally continued her tale. "The following day, I woke up feeling even more wretched. The girls were intent on distracting me. The ship was docking on land to pick up fresh food supplies for us donors. And, well," she paused, "it turns out that it wasn't just food that we picked up that day, but also a new kitchen porter . . ."

Grace turned to face her mother, her eyes wide with expectation. "Dad?" she asked.

"Dexter," Sally confirmed with a nod. "I didn't find out until the next day, mind you. I was walking along the corridor, minding my own business and this voice suddenly says, 'Hello again, beautiful Sally'. I nearly jumped out of my skin! I couldn't believe my eyes. I asked him what he was doing, how he had found me, how much he knew about the ship . . . and, oh, about a hundred more questions." Her eyes were bright as she recalled the encounter.

"And what did he answer?" asked Grace.

Sally shook her head, a soft smile playing across her lips. "He said, 'I told you I'd find you, Sally. I said I'd find a way for us to be together.'"

"Go Dad!" Grace said. She was so proud of him. He had been so romantic and so bold too – to hunt out the Vampirate ship and join its crew. There were few roles for mortals on board, but she remembered her own first days aboard *The Nocturne* and her time in the kitchen with the young kitchen porter, Jamie. How strange to think that her own father had once worked on *The Nocturne*. It was wonderful to know that at varying times Sally, Dexter, Connor and Grace had all travelled on the same ship.

"You must have been so happy," Grace said, turning back to her mother.

Sally considered this. "Happy? Perhaps. Excited, certainly. But I was also frightened – very frightened. Don't get me wrong, Grace, I was thrilled to see Dexter again, but I felt like we'd boarded a rollercoaster together. And, I couldn't help but wonder where it would end."

Grace saw the look of remembered fear in her mother's face. She also saw tiredness there. It seemed as if telling her story was depleting her energy reserves again.

"I'd better go," she said. "I should sort out my things for our trip."

"Yes," Sally said, the thought restoring the light to her face.

121

"Oh, I'm so looking forward to seeing all the places that are special to you, Grace."

Grace nodded, planting a kiss on her mother's cheek. "And I'm looking forward to showing them to you. I'll see you later."

"So I gather we're all going on a voyage," Grace said, stepping into Mosh Zu's chambers. "Back to Crescent Moon Bay."

"Yes, indeed," Mosh Zu said. "There's no time to lose. We set sail on *The Nocturne* tonight, after sunset. Darcy and Lorcan are coming too."

"What about the captain?" Grace asked, full of hope. "Is he going to meet us there?"

Mosh Zu shook his head. "No, Grace. The captain will not be joining us on this voyage. I shall stand in for him."

Grace couldn't mask her disappointment. "How is he?" she asked. "I really miss him."

"You have a special relationship, don't you?" Mosh Zu said.

Grace nodded. "We always have, from the first time I joined *The Nocturne*. It will be strange travelling without him."

Mosh Zu nodded. "For us all."

Grace paused, barely daring to ask the next questions. "Is he going to recover? Will he ever return?"

Mosh Zu reached out his hands and laid them on Grace's shoulders. "I hope and believe that he will, Grace. I know that he wants to. But he was very sick and we have to give him the time and space to heal properly."

"I understand," Grace said. "And I know you'll do a great job of commanding the ship."

Mosh Zu nodded, gratefully. "That's very generous of you to say so," he said. Then he frowned. "If I could have postponed this voyage, I would have. But it's very important that Sally makes this journey now."

"I know," Grace said. She saw Mosh Zu hesitate. "Is there something else?" she asked.

"Your mother is in a fluctuating state," said Mosh Zu. "She's been talking to you about her past, hasn't she?"

"Yes," Grace said. "I've been asking her about it. She's been telling me about her time on *The Nocturne*. And I've been able to channel some of it for myself."

"It seems that your powers are continuing to develop, Grace," Mosh Zu said.

"It is all right, isn't it?" Grace asked. "My mother does seems very frail. I so want to hear my story from her, but is it OK? Or is it weakening her? Because if it is, I'll stop."

Mosh Zu smiled tenderly at Grace. "Don't blame yourself," he said. "Yes, talking about the past and sharing her secrets is, I think, weakening her – as you phrase it." He paused, reaching out his hand once more. "Grace, I told you before that the other souls were fading more quickly than your mother. That she was holding on for you."

"Yes." Grace said, her heart feeling now as heavy as a stone. "So what now? Can she not hold on any longer?"

"What I have observed in the other souls is this," said Mosh Zu. "When they emerged during the healing catharsis, their torment, which the captain had been sheltering them from, was still fresh. Perhaps you remember how startled they seemed?"

"Yes." Grace nodded, vividly picturing the scene of the disorientated shades wandering through the mist.

"My assistants and I have worked with them to bring peace to each of their troubled souls. What we have found in every case so far is that, as they release their torment, they grow lighter." He paused. "They fade faster." He smiled softly at Grace. "They are letting go – of their torment, but also of their physical self. At long last, each of the souls is journeying towards a lasting peace."

Grace felt herself trembling. Mosh Zu pressed his hand a little more firmly onto hers, sharing some of his strength with her.

"And that's what's happening to my mother," Grace said, feeling the tears well up. "As she shares her secrets with me, and comes to terms with what happened to her, she too is moving towards peace."

"Exactly so," Mosh Zu said, his voice calm and serene.

"And the more she tells me, the lighter she becomes. And once she has told me everything, she'll . . . she'll fade from here." Grace's eyes filled with tears.

Mosh Zu gazed at her for a long time before answering. "That is what I think," he said at last.

Grace frowned. "So I have a choice. Either I let her tell me everything and she finds peace and . . . I lose her." She trembled. "Or . . . or I stop her from sharing these things and prevent her from ever finding true peace, selfishly keeping her here with me." She shook her head and sighed. "It's not much of a choice, is it?"

"No," Mosh Zu said. "No, not really."

Grace rubbed her eyes. "Tell me one thing," she said. "Does she know what's happening? This voyage to Crescent Moon Bay. Is it her last request?"

Mosh Zu weighed the question up carefully. "I think so," he said. "I think she is holding on to make things right with you. And then I think she will have the most long and beautiful rest, safe in the knowledge that her life, her dreams, continue in you. And in Connor too, of course."

"But I've only just found her," Grace said, shaking her head. "I really don't know if I'm strong enough to let her go."

Mosh Zu leaned forward. "You know what I think, Grace? I

124

think you are a whole lot stronger than you give yourself credit for. And, though it may be hard for you to accept this now, I believe that everything is unfolding just as it should."

Grace sighed. She wanted to believe him, but it seemed to her that, this time, he was asking the impossible.

CHAPTER SIXTEEN

The New Captain

Cheng Li's heart was beating fast as she made her way down the hillside steps towards the Pirate Academy harbour. As a student at the academy, she had watched this scene many times before: the stands filling up with the great and the good – and the notorious! – of the pirate world, dressed up in all their finery; the royal-blue carpet stretching out on the quayside, running up to and over the central platform. She could hardly believe that this time all the fuss and bustle was in her honour. But it was! By the time she climbed into her bed tonight, she would finally bear the name of Captain and, more importantly, the concomitant responsibilities.

"Mistress Li!"

She turned to find Commodore Kuo bounding down the steps from his study. He cut an elegant figure in his full commodore's uniform – his waistcoat emblazoned with medals indicating his elevated rank, and a long blue tail-coat swishing about his tight britches. In his hands he held his legendary sword, the Toledo Blade. Cheng Li was surprised and delighted. Usually, the sword only appeared once a year, at Swords Day. It was a great honour that Commodore Kuo had broken protocol to use it to perform her investiture.

"Well!" said John Kuo, catching up with Cheng Li and pointing to the bustling scene on the harbourside. "Is it everything you hoped it would be?"

Cheng Li followed his gaze, watching the men in their dress coats and the women in feathered hats making their way to their seats, as the academy orchestra played the fourth movement of Rubinstein's *Ocean* symphony – a firm Federation favourite. "It's perfect," she said, her eyes glittering like the afternoon sun on the harbour waters. "Absolutely perfect."

"The Pirate Federation never scrimps on its brightest stars," said Commodore Kuo, with a wink. "And how are *you*, Captain?"

"Now don't be premature," she smiled, finding it easy to relax in John Kuo's company. "There's the small matter of my investiture."

"Procedure, that's all. Pomp and circumstance. You've been a captain since the day you arrived here at the academy, when you were knee-high to a seahorse."

His words pleased her greatly. She felt as if she were walking on water. "I do feel as if every event of my life has been a stepping stone to this moment," she said as they descended the hillside together.

"You're excited but nervous, yes? Raring to go but wondering if you can live up to everyone's expectations . . . to your own expectations?"

She nodded. "Yes!" How clever of him to put it into words. "Yes, that's exactly how I feel."

He smiled. "That's just how I felt, all those years ago, when I took my first command. And it was the same for Platonov and Grammont and Lisabeth Quivers and the rest. There's no need to be fearful. As I said before, you're more than ready. But the fear shows me how much you care about this. It proves how passionately you want to make this work. The fear confirms that the Federation has put its faith in the right pirate."

"Thank you, John. That means a lot. Especially coming from you."

He smiled and stretched out his arm, giving her shoulder a squeeze. "I'll always be here for you, Cheng Li. Just remember that. That was always the case and nothing changes now."

"Thank you, John," she said, as they arrived at the quayside. "Oh, and I should have said so before, but good luck in the race."

He grinned. "Can I count on your support?"

Cheng Li smiled enigmatically. "My deputy, Jacoby, is racing with Captain Quivers. And Captain Platonov has signed up Jasmine, another key member of my crew."

"I see," said Commodore Kuo. "So your loyalties are divided."

"I'm sure I don't know what you mean," she said, with a smile. "But I understand that you are, just for a change, the favourite."

"Am I?" John Kuo asked with a twinkle in his eye. "I'll be happy simply to beat last year's time."

"Yes," Cheng Li grinned. "And to break another academy record."

"Ouch!" Commodore Kuo made a sudden grab for his shoulder. "As ever, your darts are brutally accurate, Mistress Li."

She laughed, but then a rogue thought entered her head. A rogue thought she had anticipated but had vowed would not trouble her today. And yet, it was impossible for it not to.

"What's wrong?" John Kuo asked her.

Cheng Li sighed. "I was just thinking about my father. It's folly, I know, but I wish he could have seen me here today."

"Not folly," John Kuo said, reaching out his arms to Cheng Li. "Not folly at all. Chang Ko Li was like a brother to me. I knew him better perhaps than anyone but you and the rest of your family. And I know, my child, that he *is* watching you today and that he is the very proudest of men."

"Thank you," Cheng Li said, burying her face just for a moment into John Kuo's powerful chest.

"I mean it," Kuo said, kissing her lightly on the head. "Now, come on. We must hasten to the foreshore. It wouldn't be good form to be late for your own investiture!"

As the orchestra played the opening notes of the Pirate Federation anthem, the crowd of dignitaries, teachers and students rose in unison. Cheng Li felt a shiver along her spine as she sang the familiar words . . .

> *"I pledge my life to adventure*
> *I submit my soul to the sea.*
> *I shall fight both wind and weather*
> *For the dream that burns in me.*
> *And the dream that burns in me*
> *Is simply to be free.*
> *And there is no greater freedom than*
> *To be a pirate!"*

The words and music resounded loudly in Cheng Li's head. As she sang the second verse, she turned to stare at the platform, from which Commodore Kuo would shortly begin the ceremony. Behind it hung the ancient sailcloth bearing the Pirate Academy logo. The logo was composed of four symbols — the sword, the compass, the anchor and the pearl. One of the very first things Cheng Li had been taught on her arrival at Pirate Academy was the meaning of the four symbols: the sword

129

representing the ability to fight; the compass signifying skill in navigation; the anchor acknowledging the importance of pirate history; and the pearl celebrating the capacity to forge on through the toughest situations to find the treasure within. These, in the view of the Pirate Federation, were the four core talents any pirate must master and Cheng Li knew she had mastered them all.

> ". . . And the honour that I seek
> Is a title beyond compare.
> For there is no greater title than
> To be a pirate!"

As the third – and most stirring – verse of the anthem approached its close, Commodore Kuo gave Cheng Li's hand a squeeze, then rose from his chair and walked over to climb the steps up to the podium.

"Good afternoon, ladies and gentlemen," he said, addressing the vast audience on the ranked stands with his natural confidence. "Welcome back to the Pirate Academy. This, like any harbour, is a place of connections. Many of you were formerly students here. Now you are captains and deputy captains of your own ships. Others amongst you are teachers here at the academy – you, like me, have left the oceans in order to pass on your knowledge and experience to the pirate captains of the future." He nodded towards the ranks of students. As he did so, a ripple of applause broke out amongst the crowd. The headmaster waited for it to subside before continuing. "Yes, I think of our little harbour here at the academy as a place to depart from and return to – and to keep returning to, throughout your days as a pirate." He paused. "We are gathered here once more for the investiture of a new pirate captain. Such occasions always fill me with pride, but today this is especially true. We are about to see a truly remarkable young pirate take to the seas as captain of her own ship."

He exchanged a reassuring glance with Cheng Li. Standing there, she was already glowing with pride as he continued. "Cheng Li is, as you all know, the daughter of the great pirate captain Chang Ko Li. He was known as the best of the best – and for very good reason. Tragically, he died before Mistress Li was of an age to learn his skills at first hand. Whether piracy is in the blood is a matter for debate. Whatever one concludes, no one can deny that Cheng Li has been the most conscientious of students of piracy. During her illustrious career as a student of this academy, never once did I hear her invoke her parenthood as a reason for preferment. Never once did she use it to win favour with her classmates. No, because Cheng Li is a worker. She applied herself to the lessons here with absolute focus and diligence. She graduated top of her class and, as is customary, left this school to take up an apprentice post as deputy captain on board a pirate ship – *The Diablo*, captained by Molucco Wrathe."

Cheng Li wondered if others would note that neither Molucco, nor indeed any member of the Wrathe family, was present today. No matter. If they did, they would doubtless put it down to the recent incident on board *The Typhon* and the Wrathe brothers' determination to reclaim Trofie Wrathe's stolen hand. Remembering her recent run-in with the brothers Wrathe at Ma Kettle's, Cheng Li was relieved that they were absent from today's ceremony, though she knew that her investiture would have made Molucco squirm rather satisfactorily.

She turned her attention back to Commodore Kuo. "We were lucky to borrow back Mistress Li to assist our teaching body for a few months – the first time, I might add, that a non-captain has been asked to work here. It will come as no surprise to you that not only did Cheng Li rise to the challenge but she exceeded all expectations. She is a naturally gifted teacher and, had we the luxury of two lifetimes, would I'm sure make a very valid contribution here. But the rightful place for Cheng Li is out on the oceans and, with no more ado, I would like to ask her to join me on this podium so I can perform her investiture as captain."

There was a spontaneous outburst of applause as Cheng Li climbed the steps to join Commodore Kuo on the platform.

They bowed before each other and Teagan, a rather serious student from the Reception class stepped forward with a cushion – fashioned from an antique *joli rouge* flag – bearing the captain's chain. This chain, made from gold and the finest gems, bore the same four symbols of the Pirate Federation – the sword, the compass, the anchor and the pearl. Every captain certified by the Federation was given one, and wearing the chain would not only be a huge honour for Cheng Li but a potent link to the great pirates who had come before her. There was rapturous applause as the child presented the cushion to Commodore Kuo and he lifted the chain, then draped it around Cheng Li's bowed neck.

Now, Teagan stepped back again and Cheng Li knelt before Commodore Kuo. There was absolute hush in the crowd as he removed his Toledo Blade from its holster and held it in readiness.

"By the powers invested in me by the Pirate Federation, I, Commodore John Kuo grant Cheng Li the title of Captain in perpetuity."

He took the Toledo Blade and extended it until the blade rested on one side of Cheng Li's neck. As the metal touched her pale skin, he spoke. "Plenty and satiety."

Then he moved the sword over her head to the other side of her neck, saying, "Pleasure and ease."

Finally, he rested the sword-tip on her heart. "Liberty and power."

He returned the blade to his holster and the final part of the ceremony began. The entire congregation chanted together the words of the investiture:

> "In your head and in your heart, may you uphold the
>   traditions of the Pirate Federation.
> Honour those who have come before you.
> Give those who come after reason to honour you.
> May the oceans sustain you and the weather be good to you.
> May you teach your crew and allow them to teach you.
> May you be steady both in glory and adversity.
> And at the setting of your sun, may you travel home in
>   peace and harmony."

He bowed to her and extended his hand to help her up. As he did so, he kissed her lightly on the cheek and whispered in her ear: "Congratulations, Captain Li." Then he stepped back to give her centre stage. Once more the applause was rapturous.

"Thank you," said Cheng Li, her face as bright as the afternoon sun. "I promise not to detain you long but I would like to take this opportunity to thank a few people. Thank you to Commodore Kuo for performing my investiture and for saying such kind words about myself and my father. Thank you to the academy tutors who taught me so well and –" she paused "– who worked me so tirelessly!" There was a ripple of laughter at this. "But if I thought the students worked hard here, that was as nothing to the work the teachers put in, as I now know!" She clapped her own hands together to honour her teaching colleagues. In the crowd, she saw Captain Quivers acknowledge her praise.

"Today is a wonderful day for me, but piracy is a team event. I feel blessed to have such a wonderful new ship provided by the Federation – and yes, very soon, I shall unveil the name I have chosen for her. But before I do, I want to acknowledge the crew

I shall be working with. Thanks to all those who have signed up to my articles. I hope I will serve you well as your captain. I know how talented you are and I look forward to working with each and every one of you." She glanced to where Jacoby, Jasmine, Connor and the other members of the crew sat in the stands, smiling at their dynamic leader.

"And so to the name of my ship. I thought long and hard about this. But, as I filled a notebook with ideas, I kept coming back to one name. There was just no getting away from it. I had to ask Commodore Kuo if we could bend Federation regulations. I'm delighted to say that the Federation has agreed and so I give you my new ship, *our* new ship, *The Tiger*!"

There was a communal gasp as the ship's plaque was revealed.

"I know!" Cheng Li said. "I know that it is not usual practice to take the name of a former Federation ship – and I need hardly tell you that *The Tiger* was the name of my father's vessel. My father, Chang Ko Li, was cut down in his prime. People talk about him as being the best of the best. But he was only a young man when he died and I think there was much we had yet to see from him. I want to continue his work. I hope that you will understand that I chose this name not to ride upon his reputation but to honour it and, I hope, in the fullness of time, to enhance it."

As she finished speaking, there was absolute silence once more. Cheng Li glanced nervously about the crowd. She caught Jacoby's eye. His hands began to clap. Then Jasmine and Connor joined in. Then the rest of the crew of her newly named ship. Behind her, she heard John Kuo bringing his own hands together. Cheng Li dared not turn around but glanced instead up to the row of captains. She saw with relief that they too were clapping her. Within an instant, she faced a wall of applause. Many of the audience had risen to their feet in a further demonstration of support.

"There," Commodore Kuo whispered in her ear, "I told you they'd fall into line, didn't I?"

Smiling, Cheng Li nodded her appreciation as Commodore Kuo addressed the crowd once more. "Ladies and gentlemen, Captain Li and her crew will now sit for the crew pictures that are customary prior to the maiden voyage. As for the rest of us, please do join me on the academy terrace for our deservedly famous tea. And then we shall resume our seats – at least *you* will resume *your* seats – for the Captains' Race!"

Out at sea, Lady Lola Lockwood's face was pressed tight against the high-definition periscope which enabled her to see outside without ever actually having to venture into the daylight. She adjusted the focus until she had a crystal-clear view of the scene in the Pirate Academy harbour. She watched for a moment, then stepped back and stood up to her full height, brushing a stray tendril of raven hair away from her eyes.

"Well?" inquired Marianne who was sitting across from her, on a beautiful silk-covered chair, working away on her needlepoint.

"The race is about to begin," announced Lady Lockwood.

Marianne grinned and set down her tapestry. "Shall I go and ready the others?"

"Yes, my dear," smiled Lady Lockwood. She rubbed her hands together briskly. "Goody, goody! I'm in the mood for some sport tonight."

CHAPTER SEVENTEEN

The Captains' Race

Smiling gracefully at the many well-wishers around her, Cheng Li took her seat in the stands, grateful to find a familiar face waiting in the neighbouring seat.

"Hello Connor," she said. "Mind if I sit next to you?" she asked, though the seat already had her name on it.

"Be my guest," he said with a smile.

As she sat, Cheng Li opened the race programme she'd received from one of the juniors.

"Now," she said to Connor, "I assume you know how this works?"

"Ten captains, in an eighteen-foot skiff, each with two assistant crew," Connor said. "It's a race of two halves – the race out to Spider Island in daylight; the race back in darkness. First skiff back wins."

"Very good." Cheng Li smiled. "You're a quick student."

"I learned from the very best," Connor said, turning to watch as the captains and their crews took to the water.

Jacoby gave him and Cheng Li the thumbs up, before escorting Lisabeth Quivers down to their skiff. They were accompanied by one of Jacoby's mates, Bastian, who made up the complement of their crew. Connor smiled – leave it to the unorthodox Captain Quivers to have nabbed the strongest lads in the graduating class as her assistants!

Jasmine was already seated inside her skiff, alongside a guy Connor vaguely recognised from his first visit to the academy. Aamir, that was his name. They were both listening intently as Captain Platonov gave them his final instructions.

Across the harbour, Commodore Kuo seemed in amiable form as he chatted to his two young assistants – Zak and Varsha. Kuo exuded the confidence of the headmaster and the race favourite, but he had to know that you couldn't be complacent with nine other former pirate prodigies all hellbent on glory. Connor's eyes scanned the remaining captains' faces – Rene Grammont, Francisco Moscardo, Apostolos Solomos, Kirstin Larsen, Floris van Amstel, Shivaji Singh, Wilfred Avery. Together with Kuo, Quivers and Platonov, these were ten of the most celebrated captains of all time. Each one a legend.

One day, Connor thought. *One day, I'll join them.* He smiled and turned to his side. Cheng Li was staring out at the harbour even more intently than he had been. He thought he knew exactly what she was thinking.

As the six o'clock cannon sounded, the ten boats and their crews flew into action. Immediately, Connor was transfixed and wished he was out there sailing on one of the teams.

"They're so fast!" he exclaimed to Cheng Li as he watched the small skiffs skimming across the harbour.

"Better believe it!" Cheng Li said. "The eighteen-footer is the ultimate sailing boat. Its flat hull means there's almost no resistance in the water."

Captain Singh's boat led the fleet. Commodore Kuo was in second position, followed a length behind by Captain Grammont. Captains Solomos and Moscardo jostled for fourth position.

"They're getting awfully close, aren't they?" Connor said.

Cheng Li laughed. "Apostolos and Francisco are arch rivals. But they'd better clear some space between them or they'll take each other out of the race. It's happened before!"

The boats had gained such speed so swiftly that most of the crowd were already reaching for their field-glasses to monitor the race's progress as the fleet raced out towards the stone arch, marking the boundary of the academy harbour. Looking through his own binoculars, Connor saw Captain Quivers and her team making good progress. To prevent the eighteen-footers from capsizing, the crew had to use every ounce of their weight strategically, leaning out far over the side to achieve an optimum position. Connor hadn't seen Captain Quivers in action before and he was surprised at how agile she was. With Jacoby and Bastian supporting her, she looked like she had a very strong chance at victory. Good luck to them!

He searched through his viewfinder for Jasmine. There she was! Captain Platonov's boat was trailing a few lengths behind the leaders but they were gaining fast. Connor watched Jasmine letting out the spinnaker.

"Look at Jasmine go!" Connor cried.

"Yes," said Cheng Li. "You see what she's doing? The spinnaker is like a wall of silk. You need as much of its surface as possible to connect with the wind. That way, the skiff can sail just as fast as the wind is blowing."

They both watched as, thanks to Jasmine's prowess, Captain Platonov's skiff zipped up to the leaders, just as they reached the academy arch. They gained a good angle and overtook Captain Singh into second place. But there was no catching Commodore Kuo yet. His skiff had already darted through the arch. If he kept up this pace, it would be impossible to catch him. Connor could no longer make out the expression on the headmaster's face but he knew that Kuo wouldn't be complacent, even with such an early advantage. There was plenty of this race to go.

Suddenly, there was a huge gasp in the crowd, followed by a communal sigh. What had happened? Connor dropped his glasses for a moment, scanning the full scene out in the harbour. One of the boats was languishing far behind the others, dead still. But which one was it? Lifting his binoculars again, he zoomed them straight into the irate face of Kirstin Larsen. He watched as the captain dropped her head into her hands.

"That's Kirstin out of the race, I'm afraid," sighed Cheng Li. "Forced out by a broken spinnaker pole. She won't be happy about that. But it could happen to anyone. It's a tough north-east wind this evening. They're going to encounter big seas on the way out to the island and back."

Connor watched as a rescue craft set out to assist Captain Larsen and her crew. He noticed that several other vessels were also taking to the water.

"Are those more rescue boats getting prepared?" he asked. "Just how dangerous does this race get?!"

"No." Cheng Li shook her head. "They're *not* rescue boats. They're scouts going out to light the fire-beacons, to guide the boats home during the second half of the race. They've been waiting for some clear distance so they don't get in the way of the competitiors."

"Ah!" Connor turned his focus back to the race, watching as the final two skiffs – those belonging to Captains Avery and van Amstel – sped towards the arch. As they swept through to the other side, it was no longer possible to distinguish one vessel from another. The leaders were out in the open ocean and the fleet was starting to fan out as the captains embraced the wider channels open to them. Connor wished he could continue to follow the race but, short of flying overhead, there was no chance of that.

"What do we do now?" he asked, setting down his glasses.

"Oh, there's plenty to keep us entertained until the skiffs return," Cheng Li said. She turned over her race programme and tapped it. "Up next is a combat demonstration from the Reception class, then the Second Years will perform a short play inspired by the history of the Pirate Federation. Then it's the Third Years' turn and then we break for supper. By then, the skiffs should have made it to the island and be turning back. That's when things *really* start getting exciting."

After the combat demo (quite impressive actually), the play about the Federation (a major snooze) and the Third Years' performance of an original shanty (no comment!), Connor was more than ready for the supper break. He accompanied Cheng Li up the hill to the terrace, where an array of tempting food had been set out for the academy students and their VIP guests.

Connor noticed that a row of telescopes lined the terrace. "Take a look!" Cheng Li said. "They're very high-range. You might just be able to catch one of the boats beginning its return now."

Connor pressed his eye to the telescope and searched for signs of life out at sea. All he could see were the blazing fire-beacons lit by the scouts. As the sun fell away and the day slipped into twilight, the fires seemed to blaze brighter and brighter.

"Nothing yet," he announced, stepping back from the telescope.

"Oh well," Cheng Li said, passing him a plate. "Better stock up on protein then."

Connor needed little encouragement. He hit the buffet with a vengeance, while Cheng Li found herself suddenly surrounded by well-wishers. As Connor piled his plate high, he

140

watched her chat to each and every one of them – from a gaggle of over-excited juniors to a doddery old pirate intent on joining her crew. She dealt with all of them with equal grace and enthusiasm. She was on fine form. It was her big day and it was good to see her enjoying it. All in all, Connor had never seen her so happy and relaxed.

For the boats pelting towards Spider Island, there was no time to relax. The seas were as big as Cheng Li had predicted, and a momentary lapse in concentration could prove very costly indeed. Commodore Kuo was still enjoying a healthy lead but this did not stop him from urging his crewmates to work harder and faster.

"Come on!" he cried. "Give me everything you've got! And then more!"

"Aye-aye, Captain!" cried Zak and Varsha in unison, throwing their weight once more out to the side.

Commodore Kuo laughed. "We've left Singh and his crew for dust! At this rate, we'll be back at the academy before they finish supper!"

"Stay focused, Jasmine!" Captain Platonov commanded. "You too, Aamir. We've had some bad luck so far but we can still catch up and win this."

Jasmine nodded, her face as determined as that of her captain. Her hands had been burned by the force of the ropes. The pain was intense but she pushed it to one side. Nothing mattered at this point besides gaining on the leaders.

"Isn't this marvellous?" Captain Quivers beamed at Jacoby and Bastian as they leaned out, riding the crest of a wave. "I just adore the Captains' Race. I really should get back out on the oceans more often."

141

Jacoby laughed. "Makes a change from Knots class, eh?"

"Indeed it does," said Captain Quivers. "So, tell me, are you excited about becoming deputy captain of *The Tiger* . . ." Her words were drowned out as a tall wave threw water all over them. In spite of the drenching, Captain Quivers merely whooped and waited for Jacoby to answer her question.

He grinned back at her. "Can't wait!" he said. "I truly cannot wait!"

Out at Spider Island, *The Vagabond* idled in the dark waters. The sun had finally set and Lady Lockwood and several members of her retinue bestrode the deck. Most of the crew were simply relaxing and enjoying the fresh air and the promise of night. Lady Lola stood alone at the prow of the ship, her antique field-glasses trained across the ocean.

Arriving at the captain's side, Marianne gave a light cough. "You requested a pot of tea, Captain," she said.

Lady Lockwood lowered her field-glasses and smiled to see the fluted silver tray, which rested on a small table nearby. "Mother's silver tea-tray," she murmured with some pleasure.

The tray was set not only with a silver teapot and a china cup and saucer and matching milk jug but also with a proper tea-strainer and its rest. Lady Lockwood was, as her crew had come to know, exceedingly particular about how she took her tea.

"Shall I pour?" offered Marianne. "It has steeped for three minutes exactly."

"Very good," said Lady Lockwood with a nod.

Carefully, Marianne lifted the teapot and strainer and poured the honey-hued tea into the china cup, which was decorated with a quaint scene of shepherds and lambs gambolling on a river-bank. Nestling beside the cup and saucer was the matching china milk jug. It was not, however, filled with milk.

Lady Lockwood preferred something a little stronger in her tea. Marianne, who was well versed in these matters, lifted the jug and poured a precise measure of the liquid into the cup. A swirl of crimson cut through the golden tea. Marianne placed a silver teaspoon on the saucer and passed it to Lady Lola.

"Thank you, my dear," said Lady Lockwood with a smile. She gave the cup a stir then lifted it to her nose and inhaled its aroma. "Nectar," she murmured. Then she took the cup and drank down the liquid in one.

"Would you care for a second cup, Captain?" asked Marianne.

Lady Lockwood shook her head. "Watch this," she said. "I think it might rather amuse you."

Intrigued, Marianne stepped closer. She watched as Lady Lockwood lifted the empty teacup and saucer in one hand and, with the other, stirred the spoon once more. Marianne was puzzled. No liquid remained inside the cup.

"No, my dear," said Lady Lockwood. "Don't watch the cup."

Whatever did she mean? Marianne turned her head. As she did so, she heard the susurrus of rustling branches above. The trees lining the island had started to blow in the ocean breeze. It sounded as if a storm might be approaching.

As Marianne stood there, she felt the breeze grow stronger. She glanced at Lady Lockwood, whose trance-like face was fixed out to sea, as she continued to turn the silver spoon round and round the china cup, faster and faster.

Marianne watched, amazed, as the waters beyond the ship grew choppy, then began swirling and spitting like a miniature maelstrom.

"That should just about do it," Lady Lockwood declared at last, setting the spoon back to rest on the rim of the saucer.

Marianne pointed out to the swirling ocean. "*You* did that," she said, "didn't you?"

Lady Lola nodded, smiling. "It's a little trick I've grown rather clever at. I call it my storm in a teacup."

"But what's it for?"

Lady Lola grinned. "Watch and wait," she said. "Not much longer now."

CHAPTER EIGHTEEN

Spider Island

The eighteen-foot skiff captained by Commodore Kuo was caught in the heart of the maelstrom.

"Captain, the sea's getting rougher and rougher," cried Zak.

"I know," called Commodore Kuo. "But we're nearly at the island now. I can see the fire-beacon."

"The boat's out of control," Varsha shouted, gripping so tight on the ropes that her hands were red raw.

"Focus!" commanded Commodore Kuo. "We've hit an isolated spot of aquatic turbulence. That's all. We can ride it out!"

Varsha's eyes were as red as her hands and stung from the constant assault of salt-water. Why couldn't Commodore Kuo admit that they were in trouble? Big trouble!

"Captain, look!" cried Zak. "Ship to starboard!"

John Kuo turned. A moment too late. The eighteen-footer crashed into the hull of the pirate galleon. The vessel seemed to have come out of nowhere – perhaps due to the raging ocean and the thick sea-mist which hugged the waters close to the island.

"Pull her around!" Commodore Kuo cried.

"We're trying!" answered Varsha.

"Captain, look at the spinnaker pole!"

Three pairs of eyes glanced up at the pole, which had rammed into the ship. They had all watched from a distance as Captain Larsen's spinnaker pole had snapped and forced her out of the race. Now, they watched as their own pole fractured before their eyes. They had lost any chance of finishing the race.

"Are you in trouble?" A woman's concerned face appeared at the side of the ship and called down to them.

"Yes," answered Commodore Kuo. "I'm sorry but we've crashed into your ship. I don't think any damage has been caused to your vessel . . ."

"Don't worry about that," came the soothing answer. "How about your boat?"

"Our spinnaker pole is broken. Other than that, I think we're OK. We got caught in a sudden maelstrom out there."

"Yes, we saw you. You fought it as hard as you could. Sometimes the elements are just too strong."

"Captain!" Zak said. "I think the skiff is sinking."

Commodore Kuo turned back. The small boat was letting in water. The collision must have caused more damage to the skiff than had first been evident.

"You had better all come up," said the voice from above. "Can you reach the ladder or should I send help?"

"We can reach," said Varsha, her hands already stretching out towards the steel ladder which led up to the ship's deck.

"But our skiff . . ." protested Commodore Kuo. "The race . . ."

"The race is over, Commodore Kuo," said Zak sadly, following Varsha onto the ladder. He watched as the skiff slipped down further into the dark water. Commodore Kuo was still holding on to his dreams of victory.

"Come on, sir," implored the voice from above. "Come up with your comrades and we'll take care of you."

Shaking his head sadly, Commodore Kuo reached out for the ladder just in the nick of time. The skiff ducked deeper into the ocean and swiftly disappeared from view.

As the three wet pirates climbed onto the deck, the captain, flanked by her two deputies, hastened to meet them.

"Welcome to *The Vagabond*," the captain said. "I'm Lady Lola Lockwood and these are two of my crew, Marianne and Angelika."

"I'm Commodore Kuo, headmaster of the Pirate Academy. And these are my students, Zak and Varsha. We're competing in a race."

"So you said," answered Lady Lockwood, nodding her head sadly. "What terrible bad luck that you got caught up in the freak weather out there."

"It's called the Captains' Race," said Commodore Kuo. "It runs every time the Federation appoints a new captain. All the captains who work at the academy each crew an eighteen-footer . . . Well, you'd know about all this of course, being a pirate captain yourself."

Lady Lockwood smiled indulgently. "Oh, but I'm not a *pirate* captain, Commodore Kuo. This isn't a pirate ship."

"It isn't?" said Commodore Kuo, glancing up the mast and seeing that the flag did not bear, as he had first thought, a skull-and-bones, but instead a design not unlike a playing card. "What kind of ship is this, then?" he asked.

"A private sailing vessel," said Lady Lockwood with a smile. "Now look, you're drenched and your poor charges are shivering. Angelika, would you go and fetch some towels and blankets? And Marianne, I think we'd better have some more of your famous tea!"

"We don't want to impose," said Commodore Kuo.

"It's no trouble," answered Lady Lockwood, her voice as

clipped as her vowels. "We like to look after our guests aboard *The Vagabond*, don't we, ladies?"

"Aye-aye, Captain," answered Angelika and Marianne in unison, before departing to perform their duties.

"Come," said Lady Lockwood, leading them to a seating area, sheltered from the breeze. "Let's sit here and wait while the girls sort out your things. I'm sure they'll be back in a jiffy."

As Zak sat down, he saw more members of Lady Lockwood's crew arrive up on deck. "Captain, are all the members of your crew women?" he asked.

"Yes indeed," said Lady Lockwood. "I'm afraid that you and Commodore Kuo are quite outnumbered!" She laughed lightly. "But don't worry, though no men are allowed to join the crew, we welcome them as guests."

Zak smiled. He could think of worse things than being rescued from the icy waters by a crew of beautiful young women, who even now were hastening to his side with towels and blankets.

But as Angelika arrived, Lady Lockwood raised her hand. "On second thoughts, Angelika, these two youngsters are soaked through. Why don't you take them inside and find some dry clothes for them?"

Varsha stood up gratefully, but Zak shook his head. "Thanks all the same but I'd rather stay wet than put on a dress."

Lady Lockwood laughed again. "Very amusing! But don't worry, my dear. I'm sure Angelika can find you something to suit. As I say, we've welcomed men as guests onto the ship many times before."

"OK, then," said Zak, following Varsha and Angelika, who were already setting off inside.

"I'm sorry, Commodore Kuo," said Lady Lockwood. "I'm sure we can find some clothes for you too if you'd like?"

He shook his head. "I'm fine thank you, Lady Lockwood.

But it's kind of you to look after the students. I'm afraid they are a bit shaken up by what we've been through."

"Of course," said Lady Lockwood. "Quite understandable. But a man of your years and experience is made of stronger stuff. It takes more to rattle your cage, I'm sure."

"Well, yes," said John Kuo, with a smile.

"Look," said Lady Lockwood. "Here's Marianne with our tea. Thank you, my dear. You can leave it and I'll pour. Now, let's see. Do you prefer milk or lemon, John?"

"I drink my tea black," he said.

"Very good," said Lady Lockwood, lifting the tea-strainer in one hand and the pot in the other.

Commodore Kuo watched her as she poured. "You know my name," he said.

"Yes." She passed him the cup and saucer. "You introduced yourself to me earlier."

"I introduced myself as Commodore Kuo. But you just called me John."

Lady Lockwood laughed. "Well, perhaps that was a little informal of me. Though you are quite welcome to call me Lola."

"You misunderstand, Lady Lockwood." Commodore Kuo scanned her face. "How did you know my name was John?"

Lady Lockwood blushed. "You've caught me out." She raised her hands. "*Mea culpa!* I knew who you were. The exceedingly famous Commodore John Kuo, former captain and now headmaster of the academy and leading light of the Pirate Federation. And, if I'm not mistaken, you're carrying your legendary sword, the Toledo Blade." She nodded her head towards the hilt of the sword, which poked out from its holster. The distinctive stingray bindings on the hilt shimmered in the moonlight.

Commodore Kuo was wide-eyed. "You knew all this?"

"You're a very famous man," she said. "I've seen pictures. Though, if I may be so bold, they don't quite do you justice."

Commodore Kuo smiled. "I'm sure I'd say the same if I'd seen a painting of you," he said. "How come I haven't heard of you, Lola?"

"I'm a very private person, John. I've led quite a colourful existence, so I suppose now I naturally migrate to the shadows."

"Hmm," said Commodore Kuo, sipping his tea. "A rare bird of prey such as yourself should not be caged up, shrouded in darkness."

Lady Lockwood smiled, stirring the spoon in her teacup. "Are you flirting with me, John? How sweet!"

Commodore Kuo grinned and took another sip of his tea.

Suddenly he noticed that she hadn't touched the tea herself.

"What's wrong? Why aren't you drinking?"

"Oh, I had a cup not long ago," she said. "Besides, tea's not my drink of choice."

"No?" he said, his interest piqued.

She shook her head. As she did so, he saw her eyes change. It happened in a moment. At first, he thought it was the fire-beacon reflected in her dark brown eyes but, turning, he saw that there was no beacon in range. The fire was in her eyes, as if it burned in a very deep well. For once in his long and illustrious career, Commodore John Kuo was speechless.

CHAPTER NINETEEN

Mercy

"This tea," Commodore Kuo said, "you put something in it, didn't you?"

Lady Lockwood nodded. "A mild sedative. Something to take the edge off your troubled mind."

"My mind wasn't troubled. But now it is. You're a vampire, aren't you? This is a Vampirate ship."

Lady Lockwood smiled. "Names, John. I was christened Lady Lola Elizabeth Mercy Lockwood but I've been called many names over the years. Adventuress. Highwaywoman. Pirate. So yes, why not add Vampirate to the list?"

"What do you want from me?"

The fire burned in her eyes once more. "It's quite simple," she said. "I want your blood. I'm sure it has a powerful flavour. Full-bodied and dry would be my guess."

Commodore Kuo blanched, then stammered, "You want my blood?"

"That's right, John. You'll fill a half case. And it will be highly prized, you being such a famous pirate and headmaster and leading light . . . and so forth."

"You're mad," he said, though words were no longer easy to come by. "You're quite mad."

"Call me what you will, John. Like I said before, I've been called many things."

Commodore Kuo slumped in his chair. Clearly the sedative was taking a deeper hold on him. He had little fight left but, with an obviously great effort, he pulled himself upright again. "What about the students – Zak and Varsha?"

"What about them?" asked Lady Lockwood. "Oh look, here they come now!"

Sure enough, Angelika was leading them back across the deck. They were dressed in dry clothes and were laughing and joking with Angelika and a couple of other members of the crew.

"Spare them," Commodore Kuo said, his voice suffused with urgency. "Do what you want with me but let them go free. I've had my years of glory. Theirs are still ahead . . ."

"Yes, yes," said Lady Lockwood, cutting him off mid-flow. "Of course I'll spare them if that's what you wish. Besides, young blood is a little too coarse for my palate, though others of my crew might disagree."

"Others . . ." The words died on Commodore Kuo's lips as he saw Angelika's eyes burn with the same hellfire as Lady Lockwood's. Thankfully, Zak and Varsha appeared oblivious to this.

"Are you all right, Commodore Kuo?" Varsha asked.

"You look a little pale," said Zak. "Maybe you should change clothes? Look at the sharp suit they found for me."

Utterly oblivious, thought John Kuo. In spite of everything he had taught them about *zanshin* – the Samurai warrior's heightened sensibility to danger in every situation. But then, he himself had been slow to identify the danger here. And now he would pay the price.

"You must go," he rasped. "Lady Lockwood and I have business to conclude."

"Go?" said Zak, incredulously. "Where?"

"The skiff sank, Commodore Kuo," said Varsha. "Don't you remember?"

"Yes," he said, but his voice was distant, disconnected.

"He's right," said Lady Lockwood. "You two really should leave."

"We can't leave without Commodore Kuo," said Varsha. "He looks terrible."

"You must," Commodore Kuo said. "Swim to shore. Wait at the beacon for the next crew. They'll fetch help and you'll go back to the academy."

"Swim?" protested Zak. "In my new suit? But why?"

"No more of this!" announced Lady Lockwood. "Angelika, remove them from the ship."

"Aye, aye, Captain." Angelika turned and beckoned over three of her comrades. Between them, they led Zak and Varsha towards the edge of the deck.

"Jump in, little fishes," Angelika hissed, her eyes flashing fire.

Zak caught sight of it, but Varsha missed it. In a flash, he realised what was happening. He grabbed Varsha and pulled her away from the ship, plummeting down with her into the icy waters.

Angelika led her comrades back across the deck. "They're gone," she informed Lady Lockwood.

"Free?" Commodore Kuo rasped.

"Yes," said Lady Lockwood. "As per your last request. That *was* your last request, I trust?"

"Yes," gasped Commodore Kuo, slumping to the deck.

Angelika glanced at Lady Lockwood, awaiting orders. The captain rose from her seat. "Take him to the pressing room," she said. "But be careful with him." She smiled. "I want the corpse in prime condition later."

153

"Aye, Captain," said Angelika, turning once more to summon assistance.

As she turned her back, Commodore Kuo seized his opportunity. In one seamless motion, he rolled forward, withdrew the Toledo Blade from its holster and lunged directly at Lady Lockwood. He had no idea if a blade through the heart would destroy her; but at the very least it must inflict a deep wound.

But Lady Lockwood was faster than him and, as he lunged, she simply stepped backwards. "My, my, Commodore Kuo," she said. "You appear to have made a remarkable recovery."

Commodore Kuo wielded the blade menacingly in the direction of her heart. "Your sedative had no impact on me. I drew on the Samurai's skills of willpower to overcome its effects."

Lady Lockwood smiled. "The Samurai's skills of willpower and some decidedly hammy acting," she demurred. She folded her arms across her chest. "So, what's the plan now, little man? Are you going to slay me and my crew single-handed?"

Commodore Kuo looked her in the eye. "It wouldn't be a first," he said.

"Well, bravo!" Lady Lockwood said. "Full marks, John. I'm starting to see how you built your impressive reputation. You *do* have a few tricks up your sleeve." She unfolded her arms. "But, unfortunately for you, so do I."

She began circling one hand about the other, first slowly then gaining pace. As she did so, Commodore Kuo felt the Toledo Blade vibrating in his hand. It was as if Lady Lockwood was exerting some kind of magnetic field, drawing the sword free from his grip. Using every last grain of determination, he gripped onto the stingray-skin hilt.

Lady Lockwood's hands spun faster and faster, until it was impossible to separate one from the other.

Commodore Kuo could feel his grasp on the sword loosening, but even he was not prepared for what happened next. The Toledo Blade came free but, instead of dropping to the floor, it remained hovering in mid-air, a little distance away from him. Then, as Lady Lockwood continued to spin her hands, the sword spun around so that its blade was threatening Commodore Kuo himself. He stood, transfixed. Was this the end, then? Felled by his very own sword? When they spoke of the great pirate, Commodore John Kuo, was this the story they would tell?

Lady Lockwood's clipped voice cut through his thoughts. "You said before that you had the skills of a Samurai, so why not choose to die like one? Fall on your own sword. Isn't *seppuku* the most honourable way for a Samurai to die?"

Commodore Kuo watched as the Toledo Blade threatened its master. Now he knew what his hundreds, perhaps thousands, of victims had felt in the very same position. Perhaps she was right. Perhaps this was the best, most honourable way to die. He found himself transfixed by the glittering hilt of the sword, made all those years ago by the master craftsman of Toledo.

"I've known Samurais, John Kuo," said Lady Lockwood. "And you're no Samurai."

He thought of Zak and Varsha, swimming their way to freedom. He thought of the other captains, racing home to the academy. He thought of Cheng Li, who had just assumed the rank of Captain. His work was done. The glory that had once been his was passing to the next generation. This *was* the fitting end.

He felt a sudden surge of adrenaline as he threw himself towards his sword. He was laughing as he fell upon it and slumped onto the deck, smiling in death wider than ever he had in life.

Lady Lockwood beckoned her crew around her. "Take him

below," she said. "I don't want a drop of his blood wasted." As they lifted him, she took the sword and drew it out from his flesh. It was coated in his hot blood. She dipped a finger to the blade, then lifted it to her lips. She let the taste roll around her mouth, before declaring her verdict. "Complex and exquisitely well-balanced. Explosive, sweet, with an exotic pomegranate note in the finish. Delicious." She passed the sword to Angelika. "Have this cleaned. It will make a nice addition to my collection. I'm going to my cabin. I don't wish to be disturbed." She began walking away.

"Captain," Angelika called after her.

"Yes." Lady Lockwood turned.

"The two students. Did you *really* want them to go free?"

Lady Lockwood considered for a moment. "I'm really not fussed either way," she said. "I shall leave that decision, my dear, in your very capable hands."

Zak and Varsha swam towards the island.

"We'll never make it," Varsha cried. "It looked close but it seems to be getting further and further away."

"It's because we're tired," said Zak. "But we're doing good. Keep swimming! There's the beacon. Keep your eyes fixed on that. We'll wait there for whichever crew comes next."

"What if they attack them, too?"

"It's over," Zak said. "Put it out of your head."

"But what they did to Commodore Kuo. What they're doing to him . . ."

"Stop!" Zak said. "He wouldn't want you to think about that. Remember his lectures. *Zanshin* and all that. We need to be strong and direct our entire focus on getting home safe. It's what he'd have wanted."

Varsha heard his words and, as she watched Zak swim on, she thought perhaps he was right. Perhaps they *could* make it.

Just then, there was a popping noise in the water. A head bobbed up a couple of metres away from them. A woman's head. Then another, a few metres to the other side. Then two more. Then another two. And two more. Zak and Varsha found themselves surrounded by Angelika, Marianne and six other members of Lady Lockwood's crew.

"Hello again," said Angelika with a smile. "How are you enjoying your swim?"

"Leave us alone," said Zak. "That was the deal. Commodore Kuo sacrificed himself in order that we could go free."

"We're just swimming," said Angelika.

"It's a free ocean," added Marianne.

"Come on," Zak said, pushing Varsha forward. "Keep swimming."

The two students pushed on towards the shore. Lady Lockwood's crew swam on, keeping pace, maintaining a perfect ring around them. It was almost as if they were protecting their young charges.

"It's no good!" Varsha said. "I can't do this, Zak."

She stopped. Zak had no choice but to pause and reach out for her. "Rest your arms a moment, here," he said. "But keep treading water."

The eight women had stopped with them. Suddenly, they began swimming around Zak and Varsha in a perfect circle. Their beautiful faces were smiling. Perhaps then this was some strange game, but one which might not necessarily end in danger. Zak wondered how long it would last. His legs were growing numb in the icy water. He could sense Varsha's remaining strength sapping away.

Suddenly, Varsha let out a sneeze. Then a second. And a third.

The women giggled. Then, in unison, they began singing as they swam around and around . . .

"Ring a ring o' roses,
A pocketful of posies.
A-tishoo! A-tishoo!
We all fall down."

As they finished the last line, they laughed and shot down under the water, out of sight.

Zak was taken by surprise. He and Varsha were alone again. It was over. The island was only ten metres or so away, maybe less. He felt a fresh jolt of adrenaline rising. He smiled reassuringly at Varsha. "Come on," he said. "Not far now."

But as he tried to pull away, Zak felt a pair of hands clamping around each of his ankles. There was a brief moment of terror as he realised the fate about to befall him and Varsha. Then he felt a merciless tug from below and was utterly powerless to resist.

CHAPTER TWENTY

Winners and Losers

"Here they come!" Excitement spread like wildfire as the first of the returning skiffs was sighted entering the academy harbour. "Who is it?"

"It's Captain Platonov!" Connor exclaimed. "Way to go, Jasmine!"

"Better watch out," Cheng Li said, "there's another skiff coming through the arch now. It must be Commodore Kuo."

"No," Connor cried. "It's Captain Singh. And he's gaining on Platonov fast."

Another two skiffs approached the arch, barely a length separating them. "I don't believe it!" said Connor. "Captain Solomos and Captain Moscardo are still neck and neck after all this time."

Cheng Li lowered her glasses and frowned. "That means Commodore Kuo's in fifth place. That's a low ranking for him."

"He *isn't* in fifth," Connor cried excitedly, pointing. "It's Captain Quivers and Jacoby."

As he spoke, Lisabeth Quivers' skiff skimmed through the arch, taking advantage of the following wind to narrow the distance between her vessel and the skiffs just ahead. The waves in the harbour were illuminated by the final few fire-beacons. There was so much happening at once, it was hard to know where to look. Another skiff approached the arch, but it was surely too far behind the others to be a serious contender.

Captain Platonov still had the lead, closely pursued a single length behind by Captain Singh. Captains Solomos and Moscardo were fighting it out for third place, but Captain Quivers was gaining on them every second.

"Come on, Jasmine! Come on, Jacoby!" Connor cried.

Around him, the students and the guests were all calling out to their friends and favourites. The waves in the harbour were high and choppy. One of them threw Captain Moscardo's skiff up in the air. As it landed, it crashed into Captain Solomos' boat, before cartwheeling off to the side. The crowd gasped. Both skiffs had, in the very last moment, been taken out of the race. The arch-rivals had neutralised each other's threat.

The crowd's attention turned back to the front runners. Barely a length separated Platonov from Singh and there was no more than a half-length between Singh and Quivers. Connor was hoarse from yelling but he wasn't about to stop. "Go, Jacoby! Go, Captain Quivers!"

As he shouted, he was delighted to see Captain Quivers' boat draw level with Captain Singh's. Platonov was still a length ahead, as the skiffs flew into the final section of the harbour and approached the finish line.

"Come on!" The cries of the crowd rose to a crescendo.

It was Captain Platonov who crossed the finish line first, a half-length ahead of Captain Quivers, with a clearly disgruntled Captain Singh forced into third place.

"They did it!" Connor cried excitedly. "Jasmine and Jacoby did it!"

"Yes," said Cheng Li. "Captain Quivers certainly pulled out all the stops at the eleventh hour. Kudos to her."

"Look!" Connor said. "The next two skiffs have come through the arch."

"Let me see!" Cheng Li raised her binoculars. "Captain Grammont and Captain van Amstel," she said.

"That only leaves Captain Avery and . . ."

"Commodore Kuo," said Cheng Li. "It's unthinkable for Commodore Kuo to finish in ninth or tenth place! Something's wrong here. I'm going down to talk to Platonov. Perhaps he knows something."

"I'll come too," Connor said, not giving her an opportunity to refuse.

They moved as fast as they were able through the jubilant crowd. At the harbourside, the winning teams were disembarking from their skiffs. Connor saw Jasmine, thirstily drinking from a bottle of water. He ran over to her and impulsively swept her up in a hug. "Congratulations!" he cried. "You won!"

"Thanks," she said. "It was tough out there, but we nailed it."

To their side, Captain Platonov was leaning towards Cheng Li and shaking his head. "I don't understand it," he said. "Commodore Kuo led all the way out. He got to the island so far ahead of us, we didn't even see him when we made the turn around. I just assumed he would win by a mile. When we sailed through the harbour arch, I really thought we were fighting for second place. Until I looked up and saw the faces of the crowd and realised that Commodore Kuo's skiff wasn't already here."

"Do you think he's in trouble, Captain Platonov?" Cheng Li asked, her brow furrowed; her eyes searching.

Platonov shook his head. "I don't know what to think. Let's talk to Shivaji, see what he has to say." Captain Platonov pulled Captain Singh over.

"Congratulations, Pavel," said Captain Singh, managing a smile. "You fought well out there."

"Thank you. You were a worthy adversary. Now look, Cheng Li and I are discussing Commodore Kuo. You didn't see any sign of him and his skiff out there, did you?"

Captain Singh shook his head. "No, you were just about the only other skiff we had in our sights for the duration of the race. Right until Captain Quivers pulled through at the end."

"Did someone mention my name?" Captain Quivers, flanked by Jacoby and Bastian, joined the group. "Sorry that I had to punish you at the last, Shivaji."

Captain Singh frowned. "Captain Quivers, when and where did you last see Commodore Kuo's skiff?"

Lisabeth Quivers' face became serious at once. "Is he not back? I haven't seen him since the beginning of the race. After he shot through the academy arch, I really didn't think any of us had a chance of catching him up."

"Something's wrong," said Cheng Li once more. Her face was ashen.

Connor could see that the other captains had come to the same conclusion. And the talk had spread from the cluster on the quayside up through the stands. Everyone, whether a student at the academy, or a guest, knew that for Commodore Kuo to come in last, his skiff must have got into trouble out beyond the harbour arch.

As Captains Grammont and van Amstel crossed the finish line, with Captain Avery sailing in a few lengths behind, the applause was muted. As far as everyone was concerned, the race was over. The really important question was: where was Commodore Kuo and what had happened to him?

"There's no need to panic just yet," said Captain Grammont, who in spite of coming fourth in the race (Captains Moscardo and Solomos having been ruled out of the rankings) naturally now assumed charge as Commodore Kuo's longstanding deputy.

"We must send the scouts out now to search for him," said Captain Platonov, urgently.

"Why just the scouts?" argued Kirstin Larsen. "We should all go!"

"Does it really require nine of us, plus the scouts, to form a search party?" asked Captain Singh. "There's probably a simple explanation for this. A broken spinnaker, perhaps?" His words seemed directed at Captain Larsen, who frowned and turned her back on him.

"This is Commodore Kuo we're talking about," said Captain van Amstel. "I vote we *all* go and look for him. Let's not waste any more time arguing."

"I'm inclined to agree," said Captain Avery.

"*Moi aussi*," nodded Captain Grammont. "Time is of the essence."

"I'd like to come too," said Cheng Li. "If that's all right with you."

The captains turned and looked at her, their faces suddenly frozen.

"Oh dear," said Captain Quivers. "What a dreadful thing to happen on your investiture day."

"Now, now, Lisabeth," said Captain Grammont. "We don't know that anything dreadful *has* happened."

Captain Larsen put her hand on Cheng Li's shoulders. "Nevertheless, it has put a tear in the proceedings. And I know, Cheng Li, that John was not simply your commander, but a close friend."

"Please," said Captain Grammont, "do not speak of John in the past tense."

"Is it really necessary to correct my grammar at this time?" barked Captain Larsen, rather missing the point.

"Of course you can come with us, Cheng Li," said Captain Grammont. "We'll take the academy launches."

"Wait!" It was Captain Platonov who spoke now. "I'm sorry to sound a note of discord. But what if something *is* wrong here? Let us take seriously the notion that Commodore Kuo *has* been attacked. I think we're making a mistake if all of us race back out to sea. What if there's a bigger plot to attack the academy? In that case, we'd certainly be assisting whoever's masterminded this by removing all the senior captains from the scene."

The other captains were shocked by his words, but Captain Grammont took charge once more. "As ever, your words are brutal but wise, Pavel. I suggest then that we divide up. Myself, Captains Larsen, Moscardo and Solomos will head out to sea. With Cheng Li, of course. The rest of you will wait here."

"Not just wait," said Captain Platonov. "If the academy is in danger, we need to evacuate or at least prepare for a possible attack."

"I don't think we need evacuate the students," said Captain Grammont. " Just get them together in the Rotunda and try to keep their anxiety levels down. Pavel, you will announce our plans to the crowd." He glanced sadly at Cheng Li before continuing. "And I'm afraid you had better send our guests home."

Captain Platonov saluted Captain Grammont. Then the party of captains divided up to put their plan into action.

In the end it fell to Captain Quivers to make the announcement to the crowd – her interpersonal skills being judged a little softer than Captain Platonov's. Nevertheless, the panic and speculation amongst the crowd was rife.

Amid the anxious chatter, Connor sought out Jacoby and Jasmine. "Isn't this awful?" Jasmine said.

Jacoby pulled her into a comforting hug. "It could all still be OK, Min," he said. "There could be a thousand explanations for this. Even if Commodore Kuo got into trouble out there—"

"And Varsha and Zak," Jasmine said. "No one seems to be talking about them."

"Yes," agreed Jacoby. "But they are strong sailors, *really* strong. Commodore Kuo wouldn't have selected them otherwise, now would he?"

"What do you think has happened out there?" Connor asked him.

But Jacoby just shook his head sadly. "I don't know, man. I just don't know."

In the end, it was decided that it would make more sense to gather the students in the Refectory than in the Rotunda. What had started out as a day of celebration had ended as a vigil. The remaining captains tried to keep up the spirits of the students but the overall atmosphere was mournful and claustrophobic, as a tropical rainstorm broke overhead.

Everyone kept asking the same questions, over and over. What do you think has happened out there? When will the search party return?

Every time one of the captains entered the room, there was an instant hush in readiness for an announcement. But news was hard to come by and as the minutes, then hours, ticked by, Captain Quivers had to take the stage once more and call the faculty to attention. "It's late," she said, "and there's nothing more we can do here. The search for Varsha, Zak and Commodore Kuo will continue through the night. Go back to your dormitories and try to get some sleep. Hold them in your hearts. Say a prayer for their homecoming, perhaps, but try not to get swept up in fears. I speak on behalf of all the captains when I say that I remain confident that tomorrow morning we'll have good news for you."

The students drifted off to their dormitories, exhausted from the events of the day and the ongoing anxieties.

Connor, Jasmine, Jacoby and Aamir walked down to the quayside. It was wet after the brief but violent rainstorm. Around them stood the podium and empty stands erected for Cheng Li's investiture, now soaked through. In the moonlight, it looked like a ghost town. But the four pairs of eyes were closed to it, all their attention focused out on the harbour, hoping against hope that the search party would return with good news at any moment.

"Look." Aamir pointed. "Here comes one of our boats."

Their excitement was high as they watched the academy launch weave its way through the academy arch and back across the harbour. The launch was strung with lights and its arrival was noticed by other students and staff-members crossing the academy gardens. They changed direction and hastened down to the quayside once more.

The launch contained the captains: Rene Grammont, Kirsten Larsen, Francisco Moscardo, Apostolos Solomos – and Cheng Li. Their wan faces as they stepped onto the quayside told the story even before they opened their mouths.

"There's no sign of them," Captain Grammont announced. "And it's too dark to effect a meaningful search. The scouts are making camp out at the island. We'll all renew our efforts in the morning."

Connor looked at Cheng Li. Her face seemed empty somehow. He considered how happy and relaxed she had seemed hours earlier, during the investiture. Now, everything had changed.

"I can't help but fear the worst," she said, unable to maintain a façade before Connor and the others.

There was nothing any of them could say to comfort her. Captain Grammont took Cheng Li by the arm and led her back up the hill. It was not, reflected Connor, at all how her day was supposed to have ended.

*

The next morning dawned bright and hot with the bluest of skies. Connor woke early and, though he had slept little, he felt full of energy and ready to get up and moving. Jacoby, who had the neighbouring bunk, was snoring away, dead to the world. But then Jacoby had competed in a two-hour race the previous day, Connor reminded himself, as he dressed and slipped quietly out of the room.

As he crossed the academy gardens once more, he noticed a diminutive figure standing on the podium at the quayside. It was Cheng Li. She was staring out to sea.

"Everything is ruined," she said. "Today is my first day as captain, but I'm too worried about Commodore Kuo to think of anything else."

Connor nodded, thinking how vulnerable she suddenly seemed alone up there. He was tempted to go up beside her and put his arm around her but, as ever, he found it difficult to know the right way to act around her; she could flip from vulnerable friend to scornful commander in a matter of seconds.

"Mistress Li! Mister Tempest!" Captain Moscardo called to them, from the academy terrace. He was beckoning them enthusiastically.

"Quick!" Cheng Li said. "He must have news." They raced up the hill.

Captain Moscardo was breathless. "I got here as fast as I could. There's a rumour that Commodore Kuo has returned! Apparently he's in his study."

Cheng Li's face broke into a smile and it was, thought Connor, like the sun appearing through clouds. Whatever her frustration about her wrecked investiture, he knew that her chief worry had been about her old friend.

"Let's go!" she said, pulling Connor along with her.

The door to the headmaster's study was ajar and Francisco Moscardo stepped back to let Cheng Li and Connor enter first.

Stepping inside, they found Captain Grammont had beaten them to it. He was standing in front of Commodore Kuo's desk. His expression was not one of joy but of shell-shock. Connor was confused.

"I don't understand," Cheng Li said, voicing Connor's own thoughts. "Captain Moscardo told us that Commodore Kuo had returned. That he was back here, in his study."

"That's right, *to a degree*," Captain Grammont said. "He wasn't to know in what form. I want you to prepare yourselves for a terrible shock."

A shock? What was he talking about? All became clear as he stepped to one side. Behind him, Commodore Kuo was indeed sitting in his chair, just like always. Except . . . except that he was frozen still with a glassy expression in his eyes. And his body was entirely drained of blood.

"I'm sorry," Captain Grammont said, bowing his head. "I wish I could have prepared you better for this."

But how could any words have prepared them for the horrific, absurd sight before their eyes? Commodore Kuo was dead, there could be no doubt about that. But he was dressed as he would have been in life and had been arranged in a lifelike pose, his hand stretched out across the desk, as if he wanted to show them something.

"What's that?" Cheng Li asked. "He's holding something in his hand."

"It's a playing card," said Connor.

"Yes," nodded Captain Grammont. "And a strange one at that. Do you see? It's the Queen of Hearts, but it's not red like it's supposed to be. It's black."

CHAPTER TWENTY-ONE

Morning Light

It was the fifth day of the voyage back to Crescent Moon Bay. Grace stood on the upper deck of *The Nocturne*. In some ways, returning to the ship itself had been the most natural thing. But it had been an adjustment coming back without the captain. Grace could only hold on to what hope Mosh Zu had given her that he was taking the time he needed to heal his wounds properly. Then again, she was seeing the ship through new eyes after everything that Sally had told, and shown, her. It was strange, but wonderful, to think of her mother being here, up on the deck, sharing sun-cream with her friends and listening to guitar music. Sally seemed so frail now, but Grace had seen how full of life she had been back then.

Leaning against the deck-rail now, she thought again of her mother's first sighting of her father, sitting out there on that rock, on his red-and-white striped towel. Thinking back to the vision, she suddenly made a fresh connection. She had seen that towel! She had held it in her hands one time when she was clearing out the linen cupboard. The red had faded to the palest pink and the fibres had grown brittle with age and sea-salt. She had put it out for the rubbish collection, but the moment her father had glimpsed it lying there, he had scooped it up into his arms, as tenderly as if he was lifting an infant. "I reckon this towel has a little more life left in it yet," he'd said to Grace, with a wink. She had watched in puzzlement as he had folded it up carefully and placed it back on the shelf, without further explanation. Now it made perfect sense.

Grace was so deep in thought, she was utterly oblivious to the young man jogging along the deck towards her. As he ran by, he slipped on a slick of ocean spray and careered into Grace. They both toppled to the ground.

"I'm so sorry," said the young man, helping Grace back up onto her feet. "Are you hurt?"

"No," she said. "I'm fine. Don't worry. It was my fault – I was in a bit of a daze."

"You certainly looked lost in thought," he said. "What were you thinking about, I wonder?"

"It's a long story," she said.

"My favourite kind!"

Grace's eyes turned to get a better look at the young man in front of her. He was good-looking, with short cropped hair, grey eyes and a lean body.

"Do you run every day?" she inquired.

"Without fail!" he said. "Well, they like us to keep fit."

"Us?" Grace echoed.

"Us donors," the young man clarified.

"So, you're a donor?" she asked. *Like my mother*, she thought.

"Yes," the man nodded. "But my Vampirate recently jumped ship to go off with Sidorio and the rebels." He pulled at his T-shirt and revealed a nasty wound at the top of his chest. "Didn't stop him getting a bit nasty beforehand!"

Grace frowned. "That looks sore."

The donor shrugged. "It's OK. A lot of the donors had it worse than me. I'm told it will heal pretty quickly."

Grace had another thought. "If your Vampirate jumped ship, where does that leave you?" She thought of Shanti. "Isn't it dangerous to be a donor without a partner Vampirate?"

The man nodded but smiled. "Fortunately, I've already been paired up with another Vampirate. And this time, I'm confident I won't get mauled. He's a really nice guy, called Lorcan Furey."

"Lorcan!" Grace exclaimed.

"You know him?"

Grace nodded.

"Wait a minute!" said the donor. "I bet I can guess who *you* are." Without missing a beat, he exclaimed. "It's Grace, isn't it?"

She flushed. "Yes, that's right. I'm Grace. And who are you?"

"Oh, I'm sorry." The donor extended a hand. "My name is Oskar. It's lovely to meet you, Grace. Lorcan has told me a lot about you." He smiled. "I really hope we can be good friends."

"Yes," Grace said, thinking of her tense relationship with Shanti. "Yes, that would be very nice."

"Well, what are you doing right now?" Oskar asked. "I'd like to get to know you better and there's no time like the present!"

Grace hesitated.

"What's wrong?" Oskar asked. "Is there somewhere you have to be?"

Grace made an instant decision. After all, it would be a while before they reached the bay, and Sally was still sleeping.

"No, I don't need to be anywhere just yet," Grace said. "But I need to make one thing very clear to you, Oskar. I don't do running!"

He laughed heartily. "That's OK," he said. "I've clocked up enough distance already this morning. Let's just take a seat and shoot the breeze! It's a glorious morning, don't you think? A day to celebrate just being alive!"

Grace grinned. Oskar's presence was as warm and energising as the morning light. Just what she needed.

Grace spent a very enjoyable few hours with Oskar. Indeed, he was such easy company that, after only a morning with him, she felt she knew him better than she had ever known Shanti.

I've made a new friend, she thought to herself, with some pleasure. *And, better yet, he's one who'll be awake in the day so I won't be alone any more.* But then, she mused, she had always had the option of socialising with other donors aboard *The Nocturne*. Why had it never occurred to her to do so until now? It was as if her fascination with the Vampirates had clouded her reason. Certainly, her determination to keep to the Vampirates' daily rhythms had made it hard for her to function through the day as well as the night. But maybe it went deeper than that, she mused. Maybe deep down, if she was given a choice between donors and Vampirates, she would always choose the Vampirates, just like Connor had said.

Grace shook herself. Oskar was looking at her quizzically. "What are you thinking?" he said. Grace wasn't sure she was quite ready to tell him, so she changed the subject.

"It's so funny you being Lorcan's donor," she said.

He raised an eyebrow. "Funny how, exactly?"

"I mean, you being a boy and being Lorcan's donor," Grace said, blushing. "I suppose I just assumed that because Shanti was a girl, her replacement would be a girl too."

Oskar shrugged. "Plenty of the Vampirates are paired up with donors of the same gender."

She nodded. Now that he said it, she remembered seeing this for herself at the Feast Night she'd attended.

"Grace," Oskar said. "I know that you and Shanti didn't get on. Lorcan *did* tell me that. He was very concerned to find a new donor who would get along with you."

172

Grace was surprised. "He said that?"

Oskar nodded. "You're very important to him, Grace. And no, he didn't say that in so many words, but he didn't need to. His feelings for you are abundantly clear." He smiled. "Grace, I meant what I said before about us being friends. Lorcan's a great guy and all but, when push comes to shove, I'm just his MBS."

"His 'MBS'?" Grace asked, unfamiliar with the term.

Oskar smiled. "Mobile Blood Supply."

"No." Grace shook her head. "Don't put yourself down."

Oskar shrugged. "It's OK, Grace. I'm not under any illusions. I know how I fit in around here. I have my reasons for doing this and I understand the deal I'm making."

Grace stared at Oskar. "Why *are* you doing this?" she asked. "If it isn't too personal a question." Though she was interested to hear his answer, she was also thinking of her mother's motivations. The one thing she declined to talk to Grace about was what had led her to the ship in the first place.

"It's OK," Oskar said with a grin. "Look, Grace. I'm a pretty OK specimen, right? And I've been given this golden ticket to immortality. In other words, I get to travel the world and stay this young and cute for ever!" He winked at her.

Grace smiled. Her first instinct was to dismiss his sentiments as shallow, but maybe that would be hasty. The world today was a harsh place. She knew something of that, growing up close to the breadline in a dead-end town. Hadn't she stood in the lamp room of her father's lighthouse, looking down to the waters of the bay, longing for escape and adventure? In her case, adventure had come and found her. But what if things had been different? Maybe she would have sought it out anyhow. Maybe she'd even have made the same pact Oskar had, as Sally had before him. Who was she to judge them? When push came to shove, who *didn't* want to stay young for ever and have a life of excitement and ease? Once more, Grace thought of Sally. Things hadn't lived up to their promise for her. But why? Why had things gone wrong? Was it because of her dad? Or Sidorio? Or both, perhaps? Grace hoped this voyage was going to give her some answers.

"How come you're so interested in the relationship between Vampirates and donors, anyhow?" asked Oskar. "Thinking of becoming a donor yourself?"

Grace shook her head, remembering the time when she had offered to become Lorcan's donor. "No, I'm not thinking of becoming a donor, but my mother was one. I guess I'm just interested in finding out more about how it works."

"Your mother?" Oskar said, surprised. "You know I thought you looked kind of familiar."

Grace beamed. "You knew her!" Suddenly it clicked. "You're *Oskar*!"

"Yes, Grace, I told you that before."

"You play the guitar. You used to have much longer hair but I recognise you!"

He shook his head in confusion. "You recognise me? You're losing me."

"It's complicated," she said. "But my mother's name was Sally. She was friends with Shanti and another donor called Teresa . . ."

Oskar stared, open-mouthed. "Of course! I remember Sally! And you look so like her. I don't know how I didn't make the connection before. How is she? *Where* is she?"

"She's right here on the ship," Grace said.

Once more Oskar's face betrayed his confusion.

"Do you know about the souls the captain was carrying?" Grace asked him.

He nodded, his face filled with concern. "I always wondered what had happened to her. Is she OK?"

"She's doing all right, under the circumstances," Grace said. "But she's weak, very weak." She paused. "You probably know this, already, but most of the other souls who came back with her have now faded." She felt a lump in her throat. "But although she's frail, Mother is holding on. We're headed back to Crescent Moon Bay to visit my father's – Dexter's – grave." She paused. "She asked to . . . I think it will help her . . ." It was impossible to keep the emotion out of her voice.

"I remember Dexter too." He smiled at Grace. "A wonderful guy. Really genuine." He paused. "So you're taking Sally home?" Oskar asked Grace.

She shrugged. "It's not her home. She never went there. I'm not even sure it's *my* home any more. It's the place I came from, and I have some good memories of it. But there's no one there for me now. Dad's gone. Connor's out at sea. There's no life for me to go back to there." She turned to face him, feeling a wave of cold panic. "Oskar, I don't think I *have* a home any more."

He smiled at her. "I understand how you might feel that way," he said. "I've thought the same thing myself. But maybe home isn't a place. Maybe it's a feeling you have, inside of you, being around the people who matter to you. Maybe your home is right here, on board this ship."

Grace thought about this. "Yes," she said at last, feeling suddenly reassured. "Yes, I think that might be true."

For a time, Grace and Oskar sat there in companionable silence, watching the waves and lifting their faces to the soft breeze and the warm sun.

Then, Grace noticed something up ahead. "Oskar!" she cried out excitedly, leaping up.

He laughed and clutched his chest. "Careful, Grace! That was a cry to wake the dead."

"I'm sorry," she said. "I'm sorry, but I think we're nearly there. Look, that's the lighthouse! My lighthouse!" It surprised her to feel such a wave of emotion sweep over her. Perhaps Crescent Moon Bay held more importance to her than she had acknowledged.

A red-and-white striped lighthouse was becoming visible high on the cliffs around the next bay.

"I must go and fetch my mother! I'm sure she'd like to see this. Come with me – quick!"

They raced across the deck and through the door into the labyrinth of internal corridors. Grace was out of breath as she rapped on Sally's door.

"Mother! Are you awake? Can I come in?"

"Yes, yes!" Sally called excitedly from inside.

As Grace entered the room, she found that her mother was not, as she had expected, lying in bed. She was sitting, fully-dressed, in a chair by the porthole, looking out to sea. She turned to Grace and smiled. "We've arrived, haven't we?"

"Yes," Grace said. "Can you see the lighthouse?"

Sally nodded. "Yes, my darling. Yes, I can!"

"The view's a whole lot better up on deck," Oskar said, poking his handsome face inside the doorway.

"Oskar!" Sally exclaimed, delighted to see him.

"Sally!" He walked over and kissed her on both cheeks. "It's wonderful to see you again, after all this time." There were tears in his eyes.

"Still the sensitive artiste, I see," Sally said, shaking her head with a smile. "Now look, if the view's so much better up top, why are we three drongos dragging our heels down here?"

"You're right!" said Grace. "Let's go!"

They made it up to the deck just as *The Nocturne* passed the last rocky outcrop between them and their destination.

Sally gasped as the little coastal town came into view. She gripped Grace's hand tightly. "So this is it. This is really it! Crescent Moon Bay!"

CHAPTER TWENTY-TWO

The Mission

The Tiger was still moored in the harbour at Pirate Academy, its maiden voyage delayed by the tragedy at the Captains' Race. Connor, in common with the rest of the crew, felt an increasing sense of claustrophobia. It was time to set sail out onto the open ocean. What good could they do here? No question, what had happened was terrible. Horrific. Beyond words. But pirates were meant to be out at sea, not banked up in the academy harbour. The place had too many bad memories for Connor ever to feel comfortable here, even before the slaughter during Cheng Li's investiture day.

"Tempest," he heard one of the crew call. "Is Connor Tempest about?"

"Over here!" he shouted, jumping up so he could be seen more easily.

"Captain Li wants to see you," said the pirate. "In her quarters. ASAP."

"Aye-aye," Connor said, with a smirk. Was there ever a time when Cheng Li did not expect her orders to be met ASAP?

He jogged along the deck and down into the corridor leading

to the captain's cabin. As he knocked on the door, it was pulled wide open.

"Connor," said Cheng Li. "What kept you?"

"What's up?" he asked, then remembered that he probably ought to address her with a little more formality now she was his captain and he a mere lieutenant on her crew.

"We've been summoned to a meeting," Cheng Li announced.

"All right," Connor said. "Where? When?"

"At the academy," she said. "In approximately three minutes. Think you can make it to the top of the hill in that time?"

"Sure!" he grinned. "But what's it all about?"

"It's Federation business," Cheng Li said.

"Oh." Connor's excitement dwindled. His previous encounters with the Federation had instilled in him little enthusiasm for the organisation. "Shouldn't Jacoby accompany you? He's your deputy. I'm a mere lieutenant."

"I'm well aware of the ranking of my crew-members," answered Cheng Li, bluntly. "Jacoby would, in the usual scheme of things, accompany me but, as it happens, he is engaged on a separate expedition this morning."

"So I'm deputising for the deputy, am I?" asked Connor with a grin. "Does that make me third in command?"

"Actually, your attendance at this meeting was specifically requested," said Cheng Li. "Now let's get a move on. We don't want to keep them waiting."

The drumming of Cheng Li and Connor's footsteps on the marble floor alerted the headmaster's secretary to their presence. Miss Martingale raised her head and smiled weakly at them. Her face, Connor noticed, was streaked with tears, which had caused her make-up to run. As they approached her desk, she reached for a tissue and began blotting her face.

"Hello, Frances," Cheng Li said. "How are you today?"

"Not so good," the secretary answered. "It's all been such a shock."

"Yes," Cheng Li said. "For us all. John Kuo was an exceptional man – a superlative pirate, an irreplaceable mentor and a wonderful friend."

Her words were intended to soothe but seemed to have the opposite effect on Miss Martingale, who reached for the tissues. Cheng Li waited patiently, then continued in a soft voice. "Frances, I'm sorry to bring things back to business at a time like this, but we were called here for a meeting with the Federation."

"Yes." Miss Martingale nodded. "Yes, they told me to expect you. I'll just pop my head around the door and see if they're ready."

As she disappeared off, Connor asked Cheng Li, "Do you know exactly *who* we're meeting?"

"No." Cheng Li shook her head. "John was the most senior member of the Federation I ever dealt with. And he was *very* senior. My guess is that Rene Grammont has succeeded him." Hearing Miss Martingale's returning footsteps, she added, "Looks like we're about to find out!"

"They're ready for you now," Miss Martingale announced. "If you just follow the corridor round . . . well, you know the way to the headmaster's . . . study." She broke off sadly.

"Yes," Cheng Li said. "Don't you worry. We know the way!" As she marched off with Connor in her wake, she turned and muttered, "Poor dear. She was utterly devoted to John. Well, I suppose we all were." Connor nodded, deciding that this was definitely a time to keep his thoughts to himself.

Cheng Li knocked on the door and, after a brief pause, it was opened and the familiar face of Captain Rene Grammont greeted them.

"Mistress . . . Do forgive me – *Captain* Li. And Mister Tempest. Do come inside."

So, thought Connor, it appeared that Cheng Li had guessed right. Grammont had succeeded Kuo in his Federation role. Well, Connor had a better liking for Grammont. He exuded a more trustworthy air. Even so, he intended to be careful and watch his back at all times.

"It's good to see you again, Captain," said Cheng Li, as he kissed her hello. "Even under such dire circumstances."

"Yes," agreed Captain Grammont, reaching out to shake Connor's hand. "Tell me, how are the rest of your crew holding up?"

"They're all a bit shaken," said Cheng Li. "But ready to set sail. I think it's what John and the other students would have wanted."

"Quite so," agreed Captain Grammont. "Well, I'm sure *The Tiger* won't be detained here too much longer. Indeed, I think we may have some pertinent news for you on that front."

"We?" Cheng Li said, an eyebrow rising inquisitively.

In answer, Captain Grammont gestured towards a figure neither Cheng Li nor Connor had clocked as they had entered the room. A man was standing with his back to them, in the shadows by the French doors behind Kuo's desk. Now, he turned around and surveyed them. He was wearing a steel-blue uniform. Even as he stepped out of the shadows and into the light, it was hard to determine his age. His face was curiously unlined, but he had a moustache and goatee beard. Across his left eye was an eye-patch. The pupil of his right eye was a deep shade of violet.

"Captain Li, Mister Connor Tempest, may I introduce to you Commodore Ahab M. Black?"

Connor knew that Cheng Li was as surprised as he was by this turn of events but, as ever, she took it in her stride.

"Commodore Black. How do you do?"

"Captain Li," he said, shaking her stiffly by the hand. "I've heard good things about you."

"Thank you," she said. "I wish I were able to return the compliment but I'm afraid I've not come across your name before. Are you new to the Federation?"

Commodore Black gazed at her, but said nothing. It was left to Captain Grammont to step forward and explain. "Commodore Black was John's senior line of report within the Pirate Federation. The fact that you have not heard of him until now is a result of the Federation's desire for anonymity at the highest levels."

Commodore Black nodded. "That's about the sum of it. Thank you, Rene." He did not raise a smile as he addressed the elder captain once again. "You may go now. I'll take this solo from here."

Connor could tell from Captain Grammont's expression that this was an unforeseen development but, ever the diplomat, Grammont only smiled and murmured, "Of course." He smiled at Cheng Li and Connor. "I might pop down to the ship later," he said. "Perhaps we can have some tea?"

Cheng Li nodded. "I'd like that."

Then Captain Grammont and Commodore Black exchanged salutes and Grammont exited the study. Ahab Black, who, in Connor's opinion, seemed even less well-versed in the basics of human interaction than Cheng Li, turned again and walked back towards the window.

"Shall we sit down?" Cheng Li asked, raising her eyes in exasperation. Connor tried not to laugh.

"Sit or stand," Commodore Black said. "This won't take long."

"Very well," said Cheng Li, sitting down in one of the pair of leather armchairs which faced Commodore Kuo's old desk, and gesturing for Connor to take the other.

"Times are changing. And changing fast," announced Ahab Black in his increasingly grating monotone.

"Evidently," agreed Cheng Li.

Suddenly Ahab Black spun around, his one visible eye fixing them both in its grip. "The Federation has a mission for you," he said. "For some time now, we have been aware of the existence of a ship of vampire pirates or 'Vampirates'. I believe you are both also aware of this phenomenon?"

"Yes," Connor acknowledged.

"I've heard tell of it," Cheng Li answered, hedging her bets. Connor vividly remembered her telling him in no uncertain terms that the ship could not possibly exist. It was a credit to her that she could shift position so effortlessly.

"In the main, the Vampirates have caused us very little trouble in recent times," continued Ahab Black. "The occasional incident, perhaps, but nothing which has proved difficult to contain. For our part, we have adopted a policy of quiet tolerance. We have, to coin a phrase, turned a blind eye."

Perhaps an unfortunate expression to use when you were sporting an eye-patch, reflected Connor.

"Everything has changed!" Ahab Black's good eye blazed and his voice dripped with vitriol. "The attack on Commodore Kuo and his young crew was a direct affront to the authority of the Pirate Federation."

"And you think that the *Vampirates* were responsible?" Cheng Li asked.

"Affirmative," said Black. "It was a direct salvo sent to wound us at a high level. Well, we got the message and we're gonna send a reply."

The commodore had seized both Cheng Li and Connor's full attention. "The time of quiet tolerance is over," he said. "From hereon in, the Federation will pursue a policy of direct aggression towards the Vampirates. We will excise this scourge from our seas and eliminate the threat to this and future pirate generations." He brought both his fists down hard onto the desk. "We will purify the oceans."

"What is our role in this to be?" Cheng Li asked.

"You'll be at the forefront of delivering this policy," Black said. "*The Tiger* will be the first ship of dedicated Vampirate assassins. And your first mission is to eliminate the murderer of John Kuo and the students."

"I have a question," Connor said.

"So do I." Cheng Li spoke over him. Already her eyes were bright with excitement. "What level of support do we get for this initiative?"

"Top level," Black announced. "Whatever you need, you get. You already have an elite crew. If you want to add further personnel, no problem . . ."

"Budget?" inquired Cheng Li.

"Open," answered Black. "Whatever it takes to get the job done."

"We'll need new swords," Cheng Li said.

Connor thought of the boxes of swords they had just recently brought back from Master Yin's workshop. So far, the weapons had only been used for combat practice.

"We're fighting Vampirates now," Cheng Li said, as if reading his thoughts. "We'll need new weaponry and we'll need to research both weapons and attack strategy."

"Agreed." Black nodded. "Our thoughts are as one, Captain Li. I can see you are indeed the right captain for this job." He smiled, at last. "You mentioned research just now. We can help you there." He moved to the other side of the desk. Opening a drawer, he took out a mosaic octagon and passed it across to Cheng Li.

"This puzzle is the key into a hidden cache. This store contains several secret files containing our research to date on the Vampirates. I think you, in particular, will find it quite enlightening," he said, grinning at Cheng Li. "It's hidden beneath the floor of the Rotunda."

Cheng Li nodded, turning the strange mosaic octagon over in her fingers. "To think the cache was here under our noses, all this time!" She looked up at Ahab Black. "So the Federation has been keeping tabs on the Vampirates over a number of years?" she asked, her intrigue all too clear.

"Affirmative. Like I say, we've had them in our sights for a good while now. And we've all jogged along just fine. But now, they've crossed a line. It's time to remind them who rules the oceans."

Connor felt sick. He had to say something. "Wait!" he began. It came out stronger than he had intended and succeeded in capturing both Cheng Li and Ahab Black's attention.

"I'm sorry," he said. "I don't mean to be disrespectful – to either of you. But I've had some contact with the Vampirates."

"Yes," said Black. "That's why I called you in. You led the attack before. Quite the hero, according to my sources. You burned their ship and took them out."

"It wasn't as simple as that," Connor said. "We destroyed some of them. But not all. The main one, Sidorio, survived."

"That's OK," Black said. "Call it a teething problem. A learning parabola. But we're expecting a one-hundred-per-cent hit rate from this point in."

"Even if we are able to find ways—" Connor began.

"You'll find ways," Black said. "I have no doubt about that."

"Even so," Connor persisted. "Not all the Vampirates are so brutal. There's a breakaway crew, yes. But they're the exception to the rule. The others, well you said it yourself, you've shared the seas with them for a good time now."

He was sweating, all too aware of how high the stakes were. He thought of Grace, not knowing exactly where she was but certain she was with the Vampirates. And he thought of the Vampirate captain, of their meeting that time at Ma Kettle's, when he had told Connor to attack the rebel Vampirates with fire. It had worked. Perhaps not a hundred per cent but it had worked. And he remembered something else. The strange sensation he'd had when shaking the captain's hand: that somehow he had held that hand before; that on some level he too had a connection to the Vampirates.

Ahab Black's voice pulled him back into the present. "I hear what you're saying, Tempest, but as I told you before, we've changed our policy. The Federation has decided."

"Here's the thing," Connor tried one last time. "Not all Vampirates are bad Vampirates . . ." The words surprised him. So Grace *had* got through to him. He could hardly believe it, but now he knew she had been right. Not that the Pirate Federation was likely to agree with either of them.

"You'd better keep those kind of thoughts to yourself, my friend," snarled Black. "In fact, you had better eradicate those very thoughts from your mind. You're a young pirate who's been handed an important mission. And, while you're in the pay of the Pirate Federation, as far as you're concerned, the only good Vampirate is a dead Vampirate. They must all be eliminated, starting with the guy at the top of the pack. The one who assassinated John Kuo and the students, *your fellow students*, here at the academy."

Connor could have argued that he had never really been a student at the academy but he could see there was no point in doing so. As Black had noted, he was a young pirate, who had already, against all odds, been released from one captain's command. Now here he was at the beginning of a fresh employment – one that he had vigorously sought – being given a mission from the Pirate Federation itself. He ought to be filled with pride and excitement.

Instead, he felt sick to the core. There must be a way through this, he thought. What if he helped Cheng Li implement the Federation's mission and get rid of the rebel Vampirates? That would buy him more time – and the influence to persuade the Federation that there *were* good Vampirates, like the captain and Lorcan Furey. Yes, and it would also give him time to persuade Grace that she had to make a break with the Vampirates once and for all. He could make this work. All he needed was time.

"I have a question for you," Commodore Black said. He was looking at Connor now, not at Cheng Li. "Do you know which Vampirate killed John and the students, here at the Pirate Academy?"

"I think so," Connor answered. "I'd say Sidorio. None of the others . . . Well, I'm sure it was Sidorio."

"Good," said Black. "Then you have your first target. Take out this Sidorio guy and we'll proceed from there."

"We won't let you down," Cheng Li said, keen to reassert her own role in the mission.

"I should think not, Captain Li. Let us know what you need and we'll get it to you."

"And I'll contact you here or at Federation HQ?"

Black cracked another grin. "We'll stay in regular touch, Captain Li. Have no fear on that score. This is too important to the Federation to play things any other way. Succeed in this mission and your meteoric rise is guaranteed. Fail and . . . well, failure isn't really an option."

"Failure isn't a word in my vocabulary," said Cheng Li with a smile.

Saying nothing, Ahab Black walked over to the window, once more turning his back and broad shoulders on them.

Connor and Cheng Li stayed seated in their chairs, unsure what to do next. At last, Black looked back at them over his shoulder and scratched his goatee with mild irritation. "What are you two still doing here?" he inquired. "This meeting is over."

CHAPTER TWENTY-THREE

Lady Lola's Blood Bath

It was a matter of routine that the guard changed upon the hour aboard *The Vagabond* and so it was that at twelve o'clock sharp, Marianne and Angelika emerged onto the upper deck to assume their watch. They exchanged only the merest of pleasantries with Jessamy and Camille before the other two, relieved of their lanterns and their duties, went back below.

"Port or starboard?" Marianne asked her crewmate.

Angelika pondered for a moment. "You take port, I'll take starboard."

Marianne nodded and began moving to the left of the vessel. Meanwhile Angelika walked off to the right. Their lanterns swayed in the breeze like fireflies.

"Angelika!" Her comrade's sudden, piercing cry made Angelika turn instantly, and retrace her steps. She was just in time to see a large, well-built man propel himself up and over the guard-rail of the ship. He landed on the deck with a thud. Though he must surely have come from out of the water, his clothes and close-cropped hair were bone dry.

"Halt, stranger!" cried Marianne. Her lantern illuminated the

188

man's broad grin and twin gold incisors. "Who are you? Where have you come from?"

"Cut the performance," he said. "You know very well I'm Sidorio, King of the Vampirates. Now, take me to your captain."

Marianne and Angelika exchanged a look, then turned back to the intruder.

"You can't see the captain now," Marianne said. "She's otherwise engaged."

Sidorio shrugged. "I'll wait," he said.

Angelika frowned. "She gave us very clear instructions. She's not expecting you, is she?"

Sidorio grinned. "Just because she isn't expecting me doesn't mean she won't want to see me," he said.

"It's a little early for social calls," said Marianne, politely but firmly. "Perhaps you'd care to leave a calling card and we'll pass on your message . . ."

Deciding not to waste any further time, Sidorio simply pushed past them and strode towards the stairs.

"Outrageous!" complained Marianne.

"Come back!" cried Angelika.

But Sidorio did not heed their words. Instead, he descended below-deck and proceeded along the corridor, pushing open doors and eliciting shocked and anxious cries from within. Members of Lady Lockwood's crew pushed their heads out into the hallway inquiringly.

"What's going on?" cried one.

"Who is he?" shouted another. As a rule, men were forbidden entry aboard *The Vagabond*.

"His name's Sidorio," Marianne shouted as she ran after him.

"Says he's here to see the captain," added Angelika.

At this, a loud voice, as sharp as crystal, rang through the air. "Who says he's here to see me?"

Marianne and Angelika opened their mouths simultaneously but it was a deeper voice which sang through the air in response.

"Sidorio, King of the Vampirates!"

At last, he stopped walking, coming to a halt before a pair of gilded doors at the end of the corridor.

From behind the doors came a loud laugh. "What a lovely surprise! Welcome to *The Vagabond*, Sidorio! Just one moment. I'm a little unprepared."

The voice kept Sidorio rooted to the spot, giving Marianne and Angelika the chance to finally catch him up. After a minute or so had passed, the double doors opened.

"Come in!" called Lady Lockwood from inside.

Sidorio stepped into the dark cabin, his nose wrinkling at the heady scent within. There was no lamplight inside, only candles – hundreds of candles. They smelled like flowers. It wasn't a smell he was accustomed to or particularly cared for.

"I'm so sorry, Captain," said Angelika, following in Sidorio's wake.

"We tried to detain him," Marianne added. "But he was *very* insistent."

"It's quite all right," Lady Lockwood said, stepping out from the darkness, "I'll take it from here." She smiled at her deputies, then directed her focus solely towards the stranger. "Sidorio," she said, lifting her hand. "You lived up to your word. We meet again!"

"Yes," he said. "I came to thank you for your little gifts. I take it *you* are the Black Heart Winery?"

"One and the same," Lady Lockwood said. "Won't you come inside? I'm a little chilly out here in the corridor."

It was then that Sidorio noticed that Lady Lockwood was dressed only in a silk robe. Sensing his unease, she smiled. "You must forgive my *déshabillé*, sir. I wasn't expecting company and you arrived at my bathing hour."

She gestured to the tub in the corner of the room. It was

filled with rose-coloured water. Or surely, *not* water. Once more, Sidorio wrinkled his nose. A familiar scent cut through the floral aroma of the burning candles.

"Yes," Lady Lockwood nodded. "It's blood. I bathe in it every night. How else do you think I've kept such a rosy complexion all this time?" She placed a hand on his arm. "But for heaven's sake, don't tell anyone else. A girl has to have one or two secrets up her sleeve!"

Sidorio smiled, a little awkwardly. "The, erm, wine, was very tasty," he said, a little flummoxed now.

"That's right! I sent you a few bottles of our recent vintages, didn't I? I thought you might enjoy them after our little run-in." She smiled once more. "Well, let's not stand on ceremony. Won't you sit down?"

She reached out her hand and led him to a pair of silver chairs, rather like thrones. As he sat down, she took a crystal decanter and poured from it into two crystal goblets. She set one on the table in front of Sidorio, then took the other in her own delicate hand.

"We should make a toast, don't you think?" she said.

Sidorio shrugged, sniffing the liquid she had given to him.

"Don't worry, sir. This is one of our better blends. Young and fruity. Now, what shall we toast to? To friendship? No, that's a little bland, under the circumstances. To greatness? No, I think that we already have that covered, don't you? Oh I know!" She lifted her goblet until it met his. "To eternity!"

She lifted her glass and took a sip.

"To eternity," Sidorio mumbled. He took the goblet and drained its contents in one. He licked his lips.

"My, my," smiled Lady Lockwood. "Thirsty boy! Well, there's more where that came from, but you might want to savour the taste a little longer this time." She took the decanter and topped up his glass.

"Would you care for a sweetmeat?" She presented Sidorio with a platter of what looked like small globs of dark red jelly, dusted in sugar crystals.

"I'm a Vampirate," he said, somewhat unnecessarily under the circumstances. "I have no need for food."

"It's not a question of *need*, sir. These are just treats. And we all need a treat every now and then. Try one. I assure you they are quite delicious."

Rather gingerly, Sidorio took one of the jellies in his fingers and dropped it into his mouth.

"You like?" asked Lady Lockwood, arching an eyebrow.

He nodded, already reaching out for a second.

"Yes, do have another," she said. "In my experience, one blood jelly is never enough." She giggled, then added, almost casually, "Have you heard the latest news on the grapevine? The slaughter of the headmaster and his little pirates at Pirate Academy? A terrible business."

Realisation dawned, as Sidorio reached for another jelly. "*You* killed them, didn't you?"

Lady Lola laughed and raised her palms. "Guilty as charged. What can I tell you? I was a little bored. Frankly, I'm a danger to myself when I'm bored – and to everyone else around me." She smiled brightly at Sidorio. "But now the Pirate Federation is all hot under the collar and I fear they're fingering *you* as the villain. Rumour has it they're building an elite force of bounty hunters to come and seek you out."

"Let them try!"

"That's the spirit!" Lady Lockwood said. "Well, I'm delighted to hear that you're taking this in your stride. It's very sporting of you, I must say."

"Sporting?" Sidorio looked puzzled.

"You taking the rap for my misdemeanours, when I appear to have slipped under the radar, so to speak."

Sidorio shrugged. "Mortals and their piffling concerns are of no interest to me."

"Quite so, quite so." Lady Lockwood smiled. "Here's my philosophy. If you're under a hundred and fifty, what could you possibly have to say for yourself? I'm afraid there's far too much emphasis on youth over experience these days."

Sidorio grinned. "I like you," he said. "I like the way you speak."

"How sweet you are," said Lady Lockwood. "I'm *so* glad that you came over tonight. Do let's try to see a bit more of one another, in spite of our hectic schedules." She lifted her goblet to her lips and took a sip. Her dark eyes glittered in the candlelight.

Sidorio glanced at the bathtub, full to the brim with its glutinous contents. "I should go," he said. "Your bath is getting cold."

"Oh blow the bath!" cried Lady Lockwood. "I haven't had such a hoot in decades. Besides, blood retains its temperature for hours. Now, tell me *all* about yourself. I'm desperate to know every last detail."

Sidorio smiled. "Well, I'm from Roman times," he began. "You've heard of Caesar? Julius Caesar?"

"You bet, darling. You bet I have." She beamed. "And I suppose *you've* heard of Cleopatra?"

He nodded.

"Well, then," Lady Lockwood said, smiling once more. "I have a feeling we're going to get along notoriously well."

CHAPTER TWENTY-FOUR

The Commodore's Challenge

"Captain, what exactly *is* that thing Commodore Black gave you?" Jacoby asked Cheng Li. "Some kind of puzzle?"

Marching briskly towards the Rotunda, flanked by the youngest members of her crew, Cheng Li shook her head. "It's a key," she said. "To a secret cache. The door is somewhere in the floor of the Rotunda. Beneath the octopus mosaic, would be my guess."

"It doesn't look like any kind of key I've ever seen," said Jacoby. "And I've never heard anything about a secret door."

"Of course you haven't!" Cheng Li said. "If *you* knew about it, it wouldn't be a secret, would it?"

"Why didn't Commodore Black give us full instructions?" Connor asked.

"Either he doesn't know where the door is himself," said Cheng Li, "or he's testing us."

"You mean," said Jasmine, "that if we can work out how to use the key, then he'll be confident we're ready for the next part of the task?"

Connor shook his head. "This doesn't seem like the time for games, when we have three unsolved murders to contend with."

194

But Cheng Li nodded at Jasmine. "Sometimes," she said, "the Federation works in mysterious ways."

"May I take a look at the key, Captain?" Jasmine asked.

Cheng Li nodded and tossed the mosaic octagon up in the air. Jasmine deftly caught it. As she walked along, she began twisting it, rearranging the alignment of its faces. "Have you ever heard of Rubik's cube?" she said.

Jacoby looked blankly at her. "*You're* the puzzle princess." He turned to Connor and Cheng Li. "Jasmine loves nothing more than a brainteaser," he said, grinning. "It's the secret at the heart of our relationship!"

Jasmine's hands were furiously spinning the moving parts of the octagon around. "It's made up of interlocking pieces," she explained. "It's designed to be moved."

"But if it's a key, Min," Jacoby protested, "shouldn't you have left it the way you found it? The way it was when Commodore Black gave it to Captain Li?"

Without missing a beat, Jasmine executed a neat sequence of twists. "There!" she said, passing the key back to Cheng Li. "Good as new!"

Cheng Li, Connor, Jacoby and Jasmine made their way to the Rotunda – in so many ways, the heart of the Pirate Academy. Each of them had powerful memories of this room. Cheng Li, Jacoby and Jasmine had gathered here many times during their years as students of the academy – listening to the captains' lessons, hearing stirring tales of their pirate forebears. Connor had only been to the room a handful of times, each as a guest at the academy. For him, the dominant feature was the tangle of swords hanging down in glass cases from the central dome. As he followed the others inside, his eyes were once more drawn, as if magnetically, towards the swords in their cases.

When he had first visited, one sword above all others had

195

drawn his eye – the Toledo Blade belonging to Commodore Kuo. Now that sword was conspicuously missing and Commodore Kuo, so long the dominant presence at Pirate Academy, was dead. Whatever Connor's personal feelings towards Commodore Kuo, his murder was a profound shock; the *manner* of the murder an even greater one. A seismic shift was occurring within the pirate universe and Connor seemed to be caught right at its epicentre.

"All right," Cheng Li said. "Let's take a fresh look at this mosaic floor."

Connor hadn't properly noticed the mosaic before, due to his preoccupation with the swords. But now, as he walked over to join Cheng Li, he saw it. It was directly under the centre of the dome and the starburst of swords above. The edge of the mosaic was a wide circle of blue tiles. Every tile seemed to be of a different hue, perhaps reflecting the changeable colours of the ocean. Within this sphere was the intricate depiction of a large octopus. Its lapis eyes seemed almost to be gazing at Connor. A vision of Molucco Wrathe flashed into his mind. He pushed it away, turning from the octopus's hypnotic eyes to the eight powerful tentacles, which stretched out greedily to the edges of the circle.

Cheng Li turned the octagonal "key" over in her hands. "It's a puzzle indeed," she said. "It looks as if it might be a missing piece of the mosaic . . ."

"But there aren't any pieces missing!" Jacoby exclaimed.

"Yes," nodded Cheng Li. "I had noticed."

Connor crouched down on the floor to get a closer look. He ran his fingers over the mosaic tiles. The others were right. There were no missing pieces. It was a mystery. He began standing up again. Jacoby pushed past him and Connor momentarily lost his footing. Reaching out to the floor to steady himself, something strange happened. The floor moved.

Or, rather, the mosaic moved. Just a fraction, but enough for Connor to know he hadn't imagined it.

"Sorry, dude," said Jacoby.

Connor shook his head. "No worries," he replied. Now that he was steady on his feet once more, he reached out his hands and pressed down on one side of the mosaic. "Look!" he said, excitedly. "The mosaic turns over. Here, give me a hand, guys!" The mosaic was too large for Connor to turn alone, but with the others' help, it completed a full one-hundred-and-eighty-degree rotation, revealing a second face.

"This can't be right," Jacoby said. "Look, there's no design on this side. Just a mish-mash of different—".

"It *is* right!" Jasmine interrupted him. "Look, there's a gap! That must be for the key." She looked up to Cheng Li. "Captain, do you want to insert it?"

But Cheng Li smiled and extended the octagon to Jasmine. "You do the honours, Lieutenant Peacock," she said.

The others watched with bated breath as Jasmine inserted the octagon into the gap. It fitted into place with a satisfying snap. As it did so, the hundreds of tiles which made up the mosaic began flipping over.

"Way to go, Jasmine!" cried Jacoby.

They all watched as the tiles finally settled. Now they were looking at the same image of the octopus they had glimpsed from above. The key was located at the centre of the octopus's right eye.

"What now?" asked Connor.

Jacoby shrugged. "I have to admit, I'm a little underwhelmed." He turned to Cheng Li, who was staring intently at the mosaic, searching for a further clue.

"I don't think the key is correctly configured," Jasmine said, reaching across and extracting the octagon. She took it in her hands once more and began twisting its faces. "That's better! See how the squares of colour work better now? The shades of blue go in a perfect sequence from light to dark."

"Beautiful, Min," declared Jacoby. "But will it *work*?"

"Let's see, shall we?" Jasmine reinserted the key into the gap, giving the octopus back its eye.

Suddenly, the mosaic tiles began turning again. Once more, the four pirates watched.

"Do you think it's just going back to what it was before?" Jacoby asked.

"No," said Connor, shaking his head. "It's the same octopus as on the other side!"

"Not quite," said Cheng Li. "Look at the tentacles. Before, they were each extending out to the edges of the mosaic, like a star. Now they're in pairs, crossing over each other."

"You're right!" Jasmine said excitedly. "And can you hear that whirring? I think it's starting to move!"

They all watched and listened. Sure enough, the entire mosaic began slowly sinking beneath the floor of the Rotunda.

"What are we waiting for?" cried Jacoby, jumping onto the platform, and pulling Jasmine on alongside him. "Min, you're a genius!"

"Good work, Lieutenant Peacock," said Cheng Li with a smile, as she and Connor joined the others on the moving platform.

As the platform lowered, dust rose around them. It didn't appear that anyone else had made this journey for a good long while.

Within moments, the pirates' heads were level with the floor itself. The four of them found themselves surrounded by eight iron bars, which made them feel as if they were in a cage, but nonetheless ensured a smooth and steady descent.

At last, the mosaic platform came to a standstill. "It seems we have arrived," Cheng Li said, slipping between the bars and stepping out into the darkness to explore.

It took a few moments for their eyes to adjust to the dark as they each stepped off the platform. Jacoby was the last to jump off. As he did so, the makeshift elevator whirred into fresh motion and began to rise again.

"Hey," Jacoby said, "the podium's moving."

"Of course," said Jasmine. "It has to, so that if someone comes into the Rotunda, they won't notice anything different."

"Understood," said Jacoby. "But how do we get out of here? And, even before we come to that, how do we *see* anything down here?"

His question was quickly answered as they became bathed in a watery blue light. Looking up, Connor saw that the underside of the platform also featured the octopus design and that it was the octopus's eyes which were lit-up. As the podium rose up and fitted back flush with the floor above, the light illuminated the subterranean world. They found themselves in the middle of a corridor with a number of identical closed doors on either side.

"The cache must be inside one of these." Connor tried the door nearest to him. It was locked. He tried the next one along. Locked again. "They're all locked," he said. "How are we supposed to find this cache?"

"The doors are numbered . . ." Jasmine mused thoughtfully.

"And?" said Jacoby. "How does that help us?"

"I'll bet I know," said Jasmine striding ahead. She stood before her chosen door and turned the handle. It opened readily. "Just as I thought," she said, turning to the others with a broad smile. "The octagon key was a clue. It's in number eight."

199

CHAPTER TWENTY-FIVE

The Secret Cache

"What's it like in there?" Connor asked, catching up with Jasmine as she hovered on the threshold of Room 8.

"I can't see anything much," she said. "It's dark and decidedly musty inside."

"Spooky!" exclaimed Jacoby.

"Don't worry," Jasmine said, with a grin. "I'll hold your hand if you're scared."

"In that case, I'm really, *really* scared!" Jacoby said, reaching out his hand.

"Wait up!" cried Cheng Li, striding over to join them at the door. She folded her arms, her face severe. "I must remind the three of you that we are here on very serious business." Her dark eyes bore into those of her crew. "We are here to solve a *murder*. The murder of our headmaster, a leader of the Pirate Federation and . . . and a good friend. This is *not* a jolly little adventure. You're not schoolkids any more – you're professional pirates on *my* crew. I took a big gamble placing you three in such senior roles. Don't make me regret it."

"Sorry, boss," said Jacoby. "I guess we just got a bit caught up in the adrenaline-rush of cracking the code and all that."

"He's right," Jasmine said. "We do understand the gravity of the mission. Varsha was one of my best friends." There were tears in Jasmine's eyes as she continued. "I can't even bear to think about what she and Zak and Commodore Kuo went through . . ."

Cheng Li turned to Connor. He could tell she was waiting for him to say his piece. He took a breath then began. "There was no great love lost between me and Commodore Kuo. I'd be a hypocrite if I pretended there was. But no one deserves to die like that."

Cheng Li surveyed her crew-members once more. "All right," she said, "I'm glad we had this conversation. Now, let's proceed in a more appropriate manner."

The others stepped aside to give her room and she pushed back the door to the secret archive. As Jasmine had observed, it was dark inside, but the blue light from the corridor stretched in far enough to illuminate a table on which sat four hurricane-lamps, candles and a box of matches.

"Come on!" Cheng Li exclaimed. "Let's get some light in here." She lit the lamps, with Connor's assistance. They passed one each to Jasmine and Jacoby and stepped back, as the lamplight revealed the room to them. It was long and narrow, with shelves on either side, lined with rows of identikit boxes. At the end of the avenue of shelves was a pair of desks and a few chairs. Behind the desk were bookshelves, crammed tightly with volumes. Tacked onto the wall above them were several maps, punctured by coloured pins.

Cheng Li peered at one of the maps. "Fascinating," she murmured.

Connor appeared at her side. "These maps," he said. "They chart sightings of the Vampirate ship, don't they?"

Cheng Li nodded. "Who'd ever have imagined it?"

Connor smiled to himself. Certainly not Cheng Li, he

thought. He remembered telling her about *his* sighting of *The Nocturne* when they had first met. Her answer, in no uncertain terms, had been that it was impossible for such a ship of vampire pirates to exist. In spite of his confusion, he had known she was wrong. Now it seemed as if others within the pirate world had known the truth all along.

"Look at this," Jasmine said, joining them and placing one of the boring-looking archive boxes on the desk and lifting the lid. "It's full of notes, some handwritten, others typed, by those who've witnessed the Vampirates and their ship."

Cheng Li dipped her hand into the box and lifted out a sheet of paper. Her eyes ranged across the page. "To think this archive was here all along," she said, "right beneath the academy floor." She shook her head in disbelief, then set down the paper and picked up another.

"The word 'archive' sounds so dry and boring," Jacoby said, opening up what looked like an oversized gym locker. "But there's nothing boring about this!"

"What have you found?" Cheng Li called over.

"Just a few of my favourite things!" Jacoby yelled back. "Come and take a look!" The others turned as Jacoby wielded a pair of evil-looking swords at them.

"Swords!" said Connor. "What are they doing down here?"

"Jacoby!" The tone of Cheng Li's voice gave Jacoby a clear note of warning.

"Sorry . . ." said Jacoby. He dropped the swords and reached inside the locker again. "Man, this is like the cupboard of death!" He produced a couple of bottles, labelled *DANGER: TOXIC*, and waved them at the others.

"*Please* be careful!" said Cheng Li.

Connor at last managed to get a look inside the locker himself. "It's like some crazy science lab in there," he said. "Test tubes and vials and all kinds of strange equipment!"

"Of course," Cheng Li said, coolly. "They were experimenting."

"Experimenting?" the others asked in unison.

Cheng Li nodded. "Isn't it obvious?"

Jasmine's voice was low. "They were working out how to kill a Vampirate."

Cheng Li nodded. "Quite so, Jasmine. Thank goodness one of you has your brain switched on today. But they didn't finish their work. And now the baton has been passed to us."

"It has?" Jacoby exclaimed.

Cheng Li nodded. "It's our mission," she said. "*The Tiger* will be no ordinary rank and file ship of the Pirate Federation. We've been given a unique project. Our ship will blaze a trail as the first ship of the Federation designated for Vampirate assassins."

"Vampirate assassins?" Jacoby repeated, his eyes wide. "We're going to assassinate Vampirates!"

Cheng Li nodded patiently. "Yes. Starting with the one who killed Commodore Kuo."

"Isn't that going to be kind of dangerous?" said Jasmine. "How do we go into battle with *Vampirates*?"

"Just as we would go into battle with any other kind of enemy," answered Cheng Li, cool as ice. "We prepare. We leave nothing to chance. We read every last sheet of notes in this room. We absorb every last crumb of information gathered by the Federation over the years. We get up to speed on every one of their experiments and then we start continuing them ourselves. We need to know how to kill a Vampirate. But before we get to that, we need to think about how we attack them."

Jacoby's eyes were on stalks. "And this is an official Federation mission? How cool is that! Oh, I'm sorry, boss."

"You don't have to apologise," said Cheng Li. "It's all right to bring enthusiasm to a mission." She added, with some satisfaction, "My ship was singled out for the job."

"What's the timescale on this?" Jasmine inquired.

"Good question, Lieutenant Peacock," said Cheng Li. "This mission has priority alpha status. In other words, the Federation wants it accomplished yesterday. *But*," she stressed the word, "we must be fully prepared. And we will be." Her eyes were bright as she continued. "Let's not lose any time. Jasmine, you take charge of the archive boxes. Read through everything that's there and pull it together into a report for me."

"Aye-aye, Captain!" Jasmine saluted Cheng Li, then settled herself at the desk with the first box of papers, opening the desk drawers and finding a notebook and a pen.

Seeing the endless rows of boxes, Jacoby looked positively pained. "Don't worry, Jacoby," Cheng Li said. "I have something different in mind for you. I want you to go through all the weapons and scientific materials in that locker. It looks like there are notebooks in there too. You'll bring us up to speed on the experiments carried out to date. And then we'll continue them."

"Yes, boss!" Jacoby said.

Cheng Li grimaced. "Do stop calling me 'boss'," she said. "Either 'Captain' or 'Cheng Li' will suffice."

"Yes, bo . . . I mean Captain," said Jacoby, darting off eagerly towards the "cupboard of death".

Cheng Li turned to Connor. He met her gaze, trying to appear resolute, waiting to hear what role she had in mind for him on this unique and important mission. But when she spoke, her voice was different somehow, softer. "You're conflicted, aren't you?" she asked.

He nodded, flushed with relief. "Yes, I am. I know that it was a terrible, terrible thing that happened to Commodore Kuo. And don't get me wrong, I'm no lover of the Vampirates." He sighed, reaching out an arm to one of the archive shelves to steady himself. "But Grace has this connection to them and some of them *have* been good to her."

"You need to talk to her again," Cheng Li said. "She must break this connection."

Connor shook his head. "It's getting stronger and stronger all the time," he said.

Cheng Li frowned. "It's the boy Vampirate, isn't it? She told me about him. Lorcan Furey – that's his name, correct? Grace is falling in love with him, isn't she?"

If only that was the extent of the problem, thought Connor. Sure, it would be difficult to untangle but nowhere near as complicated as the true state of affairs. He couldn't tell Cheng Li about the latest development – the *real* reason why he'd left his sister to come back here. That Grace had started to believe that *she* – that *both of them* – had Vampirate blood in them. Cheng Li would think that both brother and sister were crazy. And, surely, she would be right.

"Well?" Cheng Li was still waiting for an answer.

"You're right," Connor said. "It's Lorcan. She has very deep feelings for him. And the captain too . . . though obviously her feelings for him are different."

"I understand," Cheng Li said. "And this won't be easy. We've been ordered to attack the Vampirates. There's no turning back for me. I must act as the Federation commands. And to honour my friend, John Kuo, I want to. But, if you want out, never mind the articles you've signed, you can walk away right now. I won't think badly of you."

Connor shook his head. "I don't want out," he said.

"Are you sure?" Cheng Li paused. "This is a one-time offer."

Connor nodded. "I mean it. I don't want out. I just wish we could make Commodore Black understand that not all Vampirates are the same."

"Maybe we can," said Cheng Li. "Maybe something we find right here in this archive will help us to persuade him of that."

"But if it was here," argued Connor, "wouldn't he already know?"

Cheng Li ran her fingers across one of the shelves. When she drew it away, her fingertip was caked in dust. "Look at that, Connor," she said. "It's dirt. Does Commodore Black strike you as the kind of man who gets his hands dirty?"

Connor smiled and shook his head.

"I care about Grace too," Cheng Li said. "And not only because she's your sister. I would never do anything to put her in danger. You have to trust me on this one. I know we've had our . . . *moments of difficulty* in the past. But we have to move on from that."

The words seemed so simple. She hadn't always been entirely straight with him in the past. Now, in spite of her present openness, was she still keeping secrets from him? It was a possibility. But then, he was certainly keeping secrets from her. His instinct told him that Cheng Li's team was the one he was supposed to be on. Together, they'd find a way to get Grace away from Lorcan and the others before anything bad happened. On that, he would trust her.

He reached out his hand. Cheng Li shook it.

"Right then," she said. "Let's get to work."

CHAPTER TWENTY-SIX

Perfect Day

"Are you sure you two will be OK?" Lorcan asked.

"Yes," said Grace, firmly. "We'll be fine, won't we, Mother?"

"Yes," Sally said, looping her arm through Grace's. "Just the two of us."

Mosh Zu nodded. "As it should be. It's a beautiful day. Enjoy it, my dear friends." Although he was smiling and his words were warm, they all knew the implications behind them.

Grace was keen to get going. "So we'll meet you at the churchyard just after nightfall?" she asked.

Lorcan exchanged a glance with Mosh Zu, who nodded.

"Yes," Mosh Zu said. "We'll meet you there."

Grace and Sally set off along the coastal path, up to the lighthouse. Birds swooped around them and pretty wildflowers grew on either side of the track.

"I think I might pick some of these flowers to take to Dad's grave," said Grace. She hoped that the mention of his name would start Sally reminiscing, but her mother stayed silent, preserving her energy for the walk.

All the way up, Grace wondered about who the new

lighthouse keeper might be. Would he – or she – know of Grace and her family? Would she be welcomed into the lighthouse? She wasn't sure if Sally would have the strength to climb up to the lamp-room but if, by any chance, she did, it would be wonderful to share with her the view from up top – and the memories of all those nights looking out to sea with her dad and Connor.

But as they neared the lighthouse, Grace stopped in her tracks. Ahead of her the main door was boarded up, with a chunky padlock strung across it.

"That's strange," she said, "and disappointing. I wanted to show you the view from the lamp-room. You get the best views of the bay from there."

"I'd have liked to have seen that," Sally said. "Dexter used to tell me about it. And I'd have liked to have seen it through your eyes, and Connor's."

Grace held the padlock in her hands, wondering if she had it in her to break it. If only Connor were here now, his brute strength might have done the trick. But she didn't have his physical strength. There was no way she could break the substantial metal chain.

Then a fresh thought occurred to her. She might not have Connor's *physical* power, but she had different powers of her own, powers that had begun to emerge during her time on *The Nocturne* and at Sanctuary. So far, these had been in the areas of thought connection and astral travelling but perhaps there was a chance that she could use them in other ways too.

"What are you doing, my darling?" Sally asked, seeing Grace's concentration.

But Grace could not answer. Her focus was directed onto the padlock, which weighed like an anchor in her palm. Was there a chance, just a chance, that she could persuade it to open? *Persuade* it, that was the word. She wouldn't force it, just coax

208

it, of its own volition, to open. As if it wasn't an inanimate metal chain but a large insect or a scorpion. As she framed this thought, she stopped seeing the rusty padlock at all. Instead, looking into her hands, she saw a red-black scorpion.

Open, she willed it. *Please, open for me.*

She watched as the creature's pincers began to move. It was opening! It was close . . .

"Grace!" Her mother's voice again.

She had to stay focused on the scorpion. To tease open its pincers. Just a little more . . .

But as much as she willed it, the pincers refused to open any further. At last, Grace sighed and admitted defeat as the scorpion disappeared and she looked down once more at a rusty padlock.

Sally put an arm around her. "Were you trying to break the chain?"

"Yes." Grace nodded. "But I couldn't do it." Tears were welling in her eyes. She had so wanted to take Sally into the lighthouse and up to the lamp-room.

"It's all right," Sally said. "We don't need to be in the lighthouse to feel close to your father."

Her voice was like balm to Grace's shattered nerves. "No, we don't," she said, releasing the padlock at last. "You're right."

"Well," Sally said, "Cook certainly did us proud, didn't she?"

They were sitting back on the beach, surveying their picnic spread of sandwiches, fruit and other tempting goodies.

"Yes," agreed Grace, popping open the lids to two bottles of pink lemonade and passing one to her mother.

"Cheers!" said Sally, chinking her bottle against Grace's.

"Cheers!" echoed Grace.

"No, no, my darling," Sally said. "That's not right. When you say cheers, you must look into the eyes of the person you're cheersing! Try again!"

"Cheersing?" laughed Grace. "I don't think that's an actual word, Mother."

"Don't be stubborn," Sally said. "Just because you haven't heard it before, doesn't mean it isn't a word." She lifted her bottle once more and gazed directly at Grace. Grace stared back and mirrored the gesture. Their vivid green eyes locked.

"Cheers!" exclaimed mother and daughter in unison, as their bottles chinked again. Then each took a swig of the delicious lemonade, which was already warm on account of the early-afternoon sun.

The plentiful picnic defeated them and they packed up the remnants back into the hamper, then stretched out on the beach.

"We should have brought along a blanket," Grace said.

"No." Sally shook her head. "I *like* lying on the sand."

Grace wrinkled her nose. "But sand gets everywere!" she said.

"Yes, my darling," said Sally with a grin. "That's the whole point of sand."

Grace laughed. She was having such a lovely time. Was this what it was like to share time between mother and daughter? She had nothing to compare it to. It felt like being out with a girlfriend, though really Grace's only true girlfriend was Darcy and they had yet to go off on a picnic together.

"What are you thinking about?" Sally asked her.

Grace shielded her eyes from the sun. "Just how special this is. How wonderful it is to have this time with you."

"For me too," Sally said. She hesitated, as if she was preventing herself from speaking. Then she shook her head and opened her mouth again. "I'm trying to keep things light and bright," she said, "because I don't want either of us to get upset and spoil this special day."

"Me too," Grace said.

"But still," Sally said, "I want to tell you how sorry I am,

Grace. You deserve so much more than this. So many more picnics on the beach and cliff-top walks. You deserve so much more of a mother than me."

"No," Grace said, looking directly into her mother's eyes. "No, you're everything I ever hoped my mother would be."

"Really?" Sally asked, a tear in her eye.

"Yes," Grace said, reaching out and hugging her. "Really."

They left the hamper on a rock and walked off along the beach, arm in arm. Not a soul was about and they had the long stretch of sand all to themselves. They were barefoot – both pairs of sandals now resting beside the hamper.

"Our one afternoon," Sally said, sadly, as they walked along the water's edge, "and we must spend it talking about the past . . ."

Grace nodded. She knew there wasn't much time left for them to say all they had to say. "What happened after Dad joined *The Nocturne*?" she prompted, gently.

"Well," Sally said, softly, "at first, things continued as before. I continued to serve Sidorio, just as Shanti did Lorcan. Sometimes, I confess, I wished that Sidorio might be a bit more like Lorcan. Shanti would tell me things that Lorcan had said to her and it was clear to me that they had a proper friendship, unlike Sidorio and me."

Grace couldn't help but frown at this. Sally shook her head. "It wasn't a romance, Grace. Not at all. But Lorcan and Shanti *were* friends. They talked. She was more to him than simply his blood supply . . ."

Grace remembered the terminology Oskar had used: MBS – Mobile Blood Supply.

"Sidorio," Sally continued, "remained aloof, formal." She shrugged. "But as time went on, it mattered less and less to me. I was spending more and more time with Dexter – my dear, darling Dexter."

Grace smiled. "What did you and Dad talk about when you were out together?"

"All sorts! He was such an interesting man. So different from all the other men I'd known. They were all show, with nothing inside, hollow somehow. Your dad was different. There were so many depths to Dexter. We never ran out of things to chat about."

Sally paused, reaching down and trailing some grains of sand through her fingers. "But increasingly," she said, "we talked about one subject more than any other. Our future." She sighed. "Dexter was so optimistic, so starry-eyed. He wanted to take me away, off the ship, to start a new life together. But I kept telling him that I had made a commitment to the ship, the captain and to Sidorio. He had known that when he bluffed his way aboard. And I'd told him time and time again, ever since. He knew what he was getting into – the choices I'd made."

"What did he say to that?" Grace asked.

Sally smiled. "He said that no decision was irreversible. He said that we should go and talk to the captain and see if he was willing to break the bond."

Grace was wide-eyed. "And is that what you did?"

"I kept arguing against it," Sally said, "but Dexter was very persuasive and, in the end, I thought: Well, he's right. There's no harm in asking, is there? And so yes I went – on my own, mind you – to see the captain . . ."

Sally's words failed. Grace looked over at her mother. Weariness was etched all over her face. The walk must have exhausted her. She should let her take a break. Grace sighed and reached over to brush a rogue strand of auburn hair away from her mother's green eyes. "Why don't you take a rest, Mother?" she said, leading her back towards the hamper and their shoes.

Sally closed her eyes gratefully, her fingers wrapping themselves around Grace's own. She squeezed Grace's hand weakly, then let her body relax. Before too long, Sally's breathing had lengthened and grown soft.

Grace watched her mother sleep for a while, amazed to be so close to her, yet to know so little about her. Finally, she pushed herself up to a sitting position. She looked out to sea, remembering her younger self walking here with Connor, collecting shells and skimming pebbles across the water; turning and waving up at their dad in the lighthouse. Suddenly, she felt an overpowering desire to see her brother.

Careful not to disturb her mother, Grace looked back up at the lighthouse. "Connor," she whispered. "Connor, where are you? I can't do this on my own."

CHAPTER TWENTY-SEVEN

The Visitor

It had been a long day and Connor had been desperate to get to his cabin and flop on his bunk. But, although he was dog-tired, as he lay on the bunk, he found that his mind was still spinning with thoughts. Thoughts which prevented him drifting easily off to sleep. He tried to shut them out, punched his pillow into a different shape and settled down again. But still sleep wouldn't come. He reached for a book and began to read. But in spite of his best efforts, his head was still spinning with anxiety. He set the book down in exasperation.

"*Connor?*"

The voice was instantly familiar. And close. Connor looked up to find Grace standing beside his bunk, looking almost as surprised as he felt.

"Grace!" he exclaimed. "How did you get here? How did you know where to find me? And to sneak into the cabin, without me noticing!" He pulled himself up against the pillows. "I guess I must have drifted off," he said.

"No," Grace said. "It may seem like I'm here with you, but I'm not."

Connor grinned. "Oh, I get it. I'm dreaming this. It makes

sense. I've been thinking a lot about you today, wanting to see you. So I've dreamed you up."

Grace shook her head. "No, Connor. You're not dreaming. I think I'm astral travelling." She smiled. "It's good to know you've been thinking about me, though. I've been thinking about you, too. Guess where I am?"

Connor frowned. What kind of a question was that? "You're here, in my cabin!"

"No," she said. "This is an astral projection of me. Look, I'll show you." She walked over and sat down on the bed beside him. He was puzzled. She appeared to be weightless.

"Here," she said, "don't freak out. Now, take my hand." Saying this, she extended her hand towards his. He reached out for it and wrapped his fist around her smaller one. He couldn't feel anything there; his fist had simply curled in on itself. Yet when he glanced down, he could see that Grace's hand still appeared to be beneath his. Now it was his turn to shake his head. "I really don't get this," he said.

"Like I said before, this is an astral projection of me," Grace said. "It's really me. I'm here with you and we can talk and stuff. But my physical body isn't there. It's separated from my mind. It's something Mosh Zu taught me. It must have become instinctive."

Connor was tempted to pinch himself and check he wasn't dreaming. But somehow what Grace said made sense and he realised that it was further evidence of her immersion into the other world – the world he needed to persuade her to separate from. However she was here, whatever had brought her to him, this visit was a gift. He realised that the main cause of his sleeplessness had been her; his anxieties about her and his need to talk to her. Well, now he had the chance.

"It's good that you're here," he said. "I need to talk to you."

She nodded. "I guessed that, Connor. We've always been

close, haven't we? I think, on some level, we're able to pick up on each other's moods; tell what the other one is thinking.

"Maybe," Connor said cautiously.

"We just need to refine that process, strengthen the connection," continued Grace. "So that we can communicate even when we are physically apart." She smiled. "Now, answer my question!"

"What question?"

"The one I asked you before. Where am I?"

He frowned once more. "You mean besides here?"

"Yes," she said. "Where is my physical body?"

"Tell me," he said. "It's late. It's been a difficult day. I'm not in the mood for guessing games."

Grace wrinkled her brow, but then smiled again. "I'm in Crescent Moon Bay, on the beach."

"*In Crescent Moon Bay!*" Connor's eyes were wide. "Are you serious? You've gone home?"

"Just for a visit," Grace said. "Mother wanted to see where we'd grown up. Oh Connor, we've had such a lovely time. It's been the most perfect day. She's been telling me all about how she met Dad. I was wrong, before, when I told you I thought he must be a vampire. They met on the Vampirate ship, *The Nocturne*. But he *wasn't* a Vampirate – he joined the ship to work in the kitchens, just to be near Mother! He was trying to persuade her to leave the ship!"

She was about to continue but he held up his hand. "Wait, Gracie," he said. "Slow down. You're going too fast."

"Sorry," she said, "but I have so much to tell you and this astral travel is problematic. I don't know how long I'll have to talk to you."

"Grace," he said, "look, if time is limited, then you really need to let me say some stuff to you." He reached out his hand to hers, then remembered it was pointless. "It's very important."

"OK," she said, acquiescing far more readily than he had expected. "Talk to me, Connor."

"Do you remember Commodore Kuo?" he asked.

"Yes, of course," she said. "The headmaster of Pirate Academy."

"That's right," he said. "Well, he's been murdered."

"*Murdered?*"

Connor nodded. "He and two students from the academy were murdered by Vampirates during a race to mark Cheng Li's investiture as Captain . . ."

Grace's face went dark. "You say he was murdered by Vampirates? How do you know?"

"His body was found. He was killed out at sea, we think. But his body was brought back to the academy, by whoever killed him. Grace, it was entirely drained of blood."

Grace bit her lip.

"It *has* to be Vampirates, Grace. You must see that."

She didn't protest. "It sounds like Sidorio," she said. "He's obviously growing his forces – who knows where he'll stop."

"*I'm* going to stop him," Connor said.

"No!" said Grace. "You tried that once before, remember? You set fire to his ship. But the fire didn't kill him, it only made him stronger. It was as if he fed upon it."

"It's different now," Connor said. "I'm part of a mission."

"A mission?"

"Yes. The Pirate Federation has given Cheng Li's crew a special mission. We're to be Vampirate assassins."

"Assassins?" Grace looked shell-shocked. "You're going after the Vampirates?"

"Yes," Connor nodded. "That's what I needed to talk to you about." Once more he reached his hand towards her, unable to restrain himself. "You need to get away from them. I don't want you to get caught up in all this."

Grace laughed, but it was a hollow laugh. "You don't want me to be caught up in this? You tell me you've been given a mission to assassinate people I care about, and then you tell me not to get caught up in it? That's impossible, Connor. How can you be so dense? I'm not going to stand by and let you attack the captain and Lorcan and Darcy. They're my friends!"

"Wait!" he said. "Calm down! That's what I wanted to talk to you about. I know the close connection you have with Lorcan and the others. I see that. And we're not going after them. Not to begin with. Of course, you're right, Kuo must have been murdered by Sidorio. It has his name written all over it. We'll go after him and this expanding crew of his, and we'll wipe them out."

"Wipe them out!" Grace exclaimed.

"Grace," he implored. "I've given this a lot of thought. I've talked to Cheng Li about it too. I've told her that not all Vampirates are the same."

"Cheng Li!" Grace exclaimed. "Can you really trust *her* after everything she's done?"

Connor frowned once more. "She's my captain now, Grace. Besides, there was a time when you trusted her too, remember?"

"Yes," Grace said, "and look where that led me! She won't stop at attacking Sidorio and his crew. She'll come after the other Vampirates – I know she will."

Connor nodded. "I hope that isn't the case, but I'm concerned it might be. Grace, I'll do everything I can to convince her, and the Federation, that the captain and his crew on *The Nocturne* are good . . . people, that they're not dangerous. But we have to be realistic about this. I don't know if they'll recognise the distinction. And I'm scared to death that you'll get caught in the crossfire. Please, please get off the ship. Stay in Crescent Moon Bay. I can come and pick you up from there. I'll talk to Cheng Li in the morning . . ."

"No." Grace shook her head.

"Look," he said, urgently, "I'll go and talk to her right now. I could set off tonight. We could be there by sunrise."

"No," Grace repeated. "I won't leave them. Not now."

"What are you talking about, Grace?" Connor was angry now. "Look, I'm trying to take care of you. All my life I've tried to look after you. I've indulged your strange fascination for them. But I should have nipped it in the bud . . ."

"Stop it, Connor. Don't talk to me like this! I don't need you to 'look after' me. I can take good care of myself, thank you. And for your information, you *didn't* let me do anything. It wasn't up to you to let me."

It was clear from Grace's face that she was as angry as Connor had been. Angrier than he'd ever seen her before.

"Grace, I only want you to be safe."

"Really?" she said. "Don't you want me to be happy? Because that's what I am, here with Lorcan and Sally. At least I was. I felt happier today than I have done in ages. The only thing that was missing was you. But now you've spoiled everything."

"Grace," he said, "we're caught up in something bigger than both of us here. When we went out to sea, when we got shipwrecked in that storm, we couldn't have known it. But something's coming. It's big and it's merciless, like a tsunami. There's no stopping it. We're all going to be caught up in it."

Grace sighed and shook her head. "I see that, Connor," she said. "But the fact is, it's already too late. If you think there's any easy way out for either of us, you're wrong."

"No!" Connor cried out. Grace's image was fading. Now, he could fully appreciate that this was only a vision. He began to

219

panic, wishing he had somehow handled this differently. But how? "Grace! You're fading! Don't go!"

"I have to!" Her voice was broken up now, as if there was static on the line. "I told you I didn't know how long . . ."

Then there was only silence. Grace's image had disappeared just as suddenly as it had arrived.

Chapter Twenty-Eight
Souls Reunited

Grace was back on the beach. Beside her, she saw that Sally was waking up. Her mind was in turmoil. Should she warn Lorcan and Mosh Zu about what Connor had told her? But she had so little time left with Sally – it didn't feel as if she could afford to waste a moment. Connor had said that there was no immediate danger, so perhaps it was safe to wait.

"There are so many things I want to say to you, Grace," Sally said, interrupting her daughter's thoughts. She sat up and put an arm around Grace's shoulders. "I never thought I'd get the chance and now it feels like I have to pack a lifetime of conversations into one day." She sighed and shook her head. "If I could leave you with one message, Grace, do you know what it would be?" She gazed intently at Grace. "Don't ever give up on yourself. Whatever happens. Whatever challenges you face. Don't ever stop believing in yourself."

Grace was stunned. It was as if her mother knew exactly what was going through her mind. She nodded. "I won't," she said. "Don't worry."

"It paid off for me, you know, when I went to see the captain."

Grace took a deep breath. Maybe now she would find out what had really happened between her mother and Dexter. Suddenly everything else seemed unimportant.

"The captain reminded me that the bond between a donor and a Vampirate is not one to enter into lightly. I told him I knew that. I told him that I had had to ask, but I understood that the die was cast. But he shook his head. He told me that he would make an exception in my case. He would let me leave the ship, with Dexter, just as soon as a new donor could be found for Sidorio."

Grace smiled in relief. "So Dad was right."

"Yes," Sally nodded. "Dexter was right. The captain truly is a remarkable man." She smiled, then turned her face towards the horizon. "Look," she said, "our day has come to an end. The sun is setting."

Grace turned her own eyes to the shore where the sun was sinking into the inky waters and the sky burning into sunset. "I wish we could just stay here," she said, "hold on to this moment for ever." And stop the conflict she knew was coming.

"Me too," Sally agreed. "But we have an appointment to keep. We said we'd meet the others in the graveyard."

Grace nodded. She remembered. The looming deadline had cast shadows over most of the afternoon. Yet still she wished that somehow the sand might magically reach up and bury her feet – and her mother's too – shackling them both to the beach and preventing them from ever having to leave.

"Come on, my darling," Sally said, already on her feet. Her sandals were in her hand and Grace thought that she had a new energy about her – strong yet peaceful. Perhaps this was what happened to all the souls as they finally shed the last of their ties. They achieved a moment of perfect peace and grace. As Grace reluctantly drew herself up onto her feet, she stole another glance at her mother. In the golden light of the fast-setting sun, Sally looked more alive and beautiful than ever.

This time, it did not take them long to walk up the cliff-path, past the lighthouse and to the small graveyard where Dexter Tempest had been laid to rest. Grace opened the lychgate and led her mother through the scattered graves until they came to the simple headstone bearing her father's name. There it was – a solid block of pink granite simply inscribed with his name and the dates of his birth and death. Grace reflected on some of the thoughts which had bubbled feverishly in her head recently. That Dexter might not actually be dead. That he could be a Vampirate! She shook her head, cross with herself. Now she knew these had been fanciful thoughts. Here was where his story had come to an end. She looked at the oblong granite gravestone, drawing a sense of calm from its solidity. It reminded her of her father.

Grace knelt and set the posy of flowers she had gathered earlier on the base of the stone. "These are for you, Dad," she said, "I hope you like them."

She stepped back, watching the sea-breeze run through the heads of the flowers, ruffling the petals and setting free their scent – all the better for her dad to smell them. Grace smiled.

"Would you like to be alone with him for a while?" she asked her mother.

Sally nodded. "Yes, my darling. If you don't mind, I think that's exactly what I'd like."

Grace nodded and turned to walk away. As she did so, she saw that the graveyard gate had opened once more. The others had arrived.

"Wait a moment!" Sally said. As Grace turned, her mother swept her into her arms. "Thank you," she said. "Thank you for bringing me here, for bringing me back to him." She held Grace very close, her breath a cool breeze in Grace's ear. "Thank you for everything, my darling daughter. I'm so glad I got this chance to know you."

Grace felt her mother's arms reluctantly release her, like the ocean forced by the tide to retreat from the sand. Grace did not linger. She knew what she had to do; to uphold her part of the bargain. She walked away, her eyes seeking out her companions, who lingered on the other side of the graves.

"Grace," said Lorcan, quickly stepping forward as she neared and putting his arm around her, "are you all right?"

She nodded. "She's ready," she said, looking at Mosh Zu, "isn't she?"

Mosh Zu nodded. "I think so."

"What happens now?" Grace asked.

"Let's wait here for a moment," said Mosh Zu.

Lorcan held Grace close as the three of them watched Sally from a distance. She was kneeling in front of Dexter's grave, her silhouette clearly framed against the block of pink granite. The moon was rising fast and, as it did so, the gravestone seemed to glow more brightly. It became almost luminous. Grace turned her eyes for a moment, about to ask Lorcan about it, but something compelled her not to take her eyes away from the grave, not even for a moment.

There was a second figure at the gravestone. A man. Who was he? Where had he come from? Grace's heart began to race as the man extended his hand to Sally and she looked up at him. Grace could tell she was smiling. And she suddenly knew why. She knew who the figure was.

"Dad!" she exclaimed. At the word, Lorcan drew her into his arms more closely. Grace twisted her head. "That's my dad," she said.

Lorcan nodded. "Perhaps his soul has come to help your mother to pass on."

Grace smiled, though her face was damp with tears. Now, she need not worry that her mother would be alone on her journey.

At the graveside, Sally was back on her feet. Dexter had drawn her into an embrace and was kissing her forehead. Sally held the posy up to him and he took it in his hands and brought it to his nose for a moment, smiling and nodding. Then he whispered something into Sally's ear. She smiled once more and took his free hand. They began walking away.

"Where are they going?" Grace asked. But her question was left unanswered. The night was darkening and it soon swallowed up the two figures walking arm in arm through the churchyard; souls at long last reunited.

After they had gone, Grace stood there, surrounded by the others, for a time, saying nothing. It was as if they were all still waiting, watching. But for what?

Suddenly, she saw a shaft of light extending out over the beach. The light had a different quality to it than the soft light of the moon. She glanced up to the deserted lighthouse, her former home. It had been dark before but now the lamp had been lit once more.

Up in the lamp-room, she saw two figures. She could clearly make them out as Sally and Dexter. They came and stood at the window, looking down over the bay. Dexter seemed to be pointing things out to Sally. Once more, Grace felt comforted at the thought that her mother and father were together again. Now they would never be separated.

At last, they turned and she knew they were looking directly out at her. She watched her father draw her mother more tightly into his arms. Then both her parents raised their hands and began to wave at her.

At first she thought they were asking her to join them, but then she realised they were waving goodbye. She lifted her own hand, though it felt suddenly as heavy as lead, and waved back.

As she did so, inside her head, Grace heard her mother's voice once more. "*Remember what I told you, my darling girl.*"

She nodded. Then she heard her father's voice, clear as day. "*I'm so proud of you, Gracie. Look after your brother. And trust the tide!*"

She nodded once more. She would honour each of these promises.

She was still nodding as the lamp began to turn. Its beam spun out across the beach then continued its arc around the bay. After a time, the light reached the churchyard itself. The light was so strong that Grace not only had to close her eyes but also to raise her hands to cover them. She waited for a moment, giving the beam time to move on, then uncovered her eyes. Looking back up at the lamp-room, she saw that it was dark again. The room was empty, the lighthouse once more deserted. Her parents had moved on.

Trembling, Grace broke free from Lorcan's hold and began running back towards her father's grave.

"Wait!" Lorcan called after her, but she was fast. The grave was drawing her like a magnet, glowing pink in the moonlight. Standing before it, she could not believe her eyes. There was a fresh inscription beneath her father's dates. It hadn't been there before; of this she was quite certain. But now, unmistakeably, there were the words:

AND SALLY, BELOVED MOTHER AND PARTNER. HOME AT LAST.

Grace's heart was beating fast. So fast she wasn't sure if she could contain it. She felt giddy and hot and nauseous and thought she would have to sit down. The pink gravestone was a blur in front of her eyes. Her body felt as formless as jelly. She reached out to steady herself but it was no good. She slumped to the cool earth in front of the grave. The last thing she was conscious of was the grass racing towards her, then everything went pitch black.

It did not take the others long to reach her. Mosh Zu was the first to speak. "So it ends," he said. "So it begins." He turned to Lorcan. "We must take her back to the ship now."

"I'll carry her," said Lorcan, bending down to lift Grace into his arms.

"Do you need help?" Mosh Zu asked.

Lorcan shook his head. "No," he said, cradling Grace's limp body. "No, she is light as a feather." He smiled at Mosh Zu. "Almost as light as the first time I carried her." Then, he turned his eyes back to Grace, gazing down at her, thinking how peaceful she looked. This was a good sign, he thought – a good omen as she embarked on the next stage of her journey.

CHAPTER TWENTY-NINE

How to Kill a Vampirate

Cheng Li had set each of her three young crew-members a different research task – to be completed within five days. At the close of the fifth day, Captain Li made her way back to the secret cache to quiz them on what they had learned. As she made her descent on the mosaic platform, she wondered how they had fared. Her expectations were of a thorough and well-thought through analysis from Jasmine and a wild but potentially brilliant range of ideas from Jacoby.

The unknown quantity was Connor. The fact that his sister had such strong ties to the Vampirates was still a concern to Cheng Li. She had to consider the possibility that, at some stage, his loyalties would be torn. He had assured her that he had no love lost for the Vampirates, in spite of Grace's relationship with them. But he knew something of them and their world. He had seen them as distinct "people". This was bound to challenge him as the mission continued. In battle, you needed to know as much about your enemy as possible, but then you had to stop viewing them as anything but a barrier to your goals. A barrier to be eradicated. Did Connor have it in him to do this?

Jasmine, Jacoby and Connor were waiting for her inside Room 8. With the minimum of preamble, Cheng Li took her seat behind the battered desk in the corner of the archive. "So, who's going to begin?" she inquired.

"Ladies first," said Jacoby, with a grin.

"Sure," said Jasmine, standing up and lifting a pile of bound papers. "I've made a full copy of my report for each of you," she said, distributing it to each of her comrades.

Cheng Li smiled. When you gave Jasmine Peacock a project, she always delivered – efficiently, thoroughly and on time. It had been the case throughout her career at Pirate Academy, and Cheng Li was delighted to see that nothing had changed now that Jasmine was a fully-fledged pirate.

"Very impressive," she said, smiling at Jasmine. She set the report down on her desk for in-depth reading later. "I asked you to read through the numerous reports of sightings of the Vampirate ship here in the archive. Tell me, Jasmine, what were your top-line findings?"

"The fact is," said Jasmine, "I have very serious doubts about the value of much of what I've read here." Intrigued, Cheng Li raised an eyebrow. Jasmine continued with calm and confidence. "Many of these reports are – well, it would be generous to call them *unscientific*. A large number of them are more akin to rumour, verging on ghost stories." She sighed. "I've included some of the more colourful accounts in the report for your passing interest, but I think you'll agree that they should be taken with a heavy dose of salt." She paused. "However, there's a core of more consistent sightings, which talk of a traditional galleon – but with several distinguishing marks. In particular, sails made of an unknown material. Few got near enough to definitively identify the material, but several witnesses talk of the sails having a leathery texture, intermittently sparking with light, and having a winglike motion."

As Jasmine spoke, Connor thought of his own encounters with *The Nocturne*. So far, nothing Jasmine had said outstripped his own knowledge of the ship. After all, he had actually been on board it twice. He knew that – and Cheng Li knew that – but he had no intention of undermining Jasmine's research.

"Another distinguishing feature of the Vampirate ship," Jasmine continued, "is a female figurehead who evidently comes to life after dark. There have been a few sightings of her diving into the ocean after the sun sets and then climbing back up onto the deck."

While Jasmine spoke, Cheng Li glanced over at Connor. It was enough to remind him that she knew he had seen this at first-hand. He thought of Darcy Flotsam, the pretty but nonethess supernatural figurehead who had become firm friends with his sister. He frowned, thinking of his strange visitation from Grace several nights earlier. Not for the first time, this mission was feeling rather too close to home. Cheng Li had assured him that there was time to get Grace to safety, that it wasn't *her* ship of Vampirates which would soon be under attack. But he couldn't help feeling that once the conflict got underway, things would move fast and in a fashion it would be hard to control.

"This ship has proved hard to track in any consistent way," Jasmine continued. "Pretty much all the saner accounts talk of it arriving in a thick veil of sea-mist and departing in a similar fog. We're not able, therefore, to gain a working knowledge of how fast it can travel. It seems very possible that it moves at a different rate of knots, and in a fundamentally different way, to a conventional vessel." She tapped the map behind her. "It could quite literally disappear into the mist at point A, here," she moved her hand far across the map, "and reappear soon afterwards at point B, here."

Cheng Li cut in with a question. "You seem to be talking about just one ship of Vampirates, Jasmine. Is that right?"

Jasmine nodded. "Based on what I've read, it certainly seems like historically we are talking about one solo ship of Vampirates. I think Connor can tell you more about how that situation may have changed recently. But certainly – in terms of the accounts I've read – the sightings, though sketchy, do have a common thread. Which leads me to think either it *is* one ship we are dealing with – with its winglike sails and figurehead who comes to life – or, as an outside possibility, a fleet of ships which look exactly the same and operate in the same way."

"A fleet?" Cheng Li said, intrigued at the thought. "Do you have anything to back up that line of thinking?"

Jasmine shook her head. "Not yet, no. It was my own thinking which led me there, based on several accounts of sightings in multiple locations in quick succession. No regular vessel could cover the oceans in this way." She shrugged. "But I guess that's the point, isn't it? We're *not* dealing with a conventional vessel."

"No, indeed," Cheng Li said. She nodded. "Thank you, Jasmine. I shall look forward to reading your full report later."

Jasmine nodded, smiled modestly at the captain, and sat down again.

"Shall I go next?" Jacoby seemed hardly able to contain himself.

Cheng Li smiled. "Jacoby, you have been researching the experiments to date into how to wound and, ultimately, kill a Vampirate."

"Yes, I have," Jacoby said, taking the floor. He had no neatly-bound reports to offer the group, but he had assembled a variety of props on the opposite desk.

"Well," he said, his eyes bright with excitement, "the cupboard of death was just packed with fun stuff." He began reaching for a few of the items at his side. "So, you've got your crucifixes, ranging from the plain to the ornate. This one's a particularly nice bit of silver, don't you think? Talking of which, check out these silver bullets! *Kapow!* Good for werewolves – and possibly Vampirates too." He dropped the bullets onto the desk and reached for their neighbouring objects. "Then you've got your Holy Sacraments – like the rosary or this bottle of holy water. And then there's our old friend garlic." Suddenly, he reached behind the desk and produced a roughly-tied bouquet of flowers. "Min, these are for you!" He threw them to Jasmine, who caught them and smiled, inhaling their scent.

"Wild roses," she said. "My favourite!"

"Not if you're a Vampirate," chuckled Jacoby. "According to one legend I came across, you can chain a vamp to his grave with wild roses. But none of the items I've shown you so far are likely to actually kill a vamp. They fall into the category of *apotropaics*." He spoke the word slowly, then – like a young and somewhat mad professor – wrote it down and underlined it several times on the nearby flip-chart. "The aim of goodies like these is to protect you against Vampirates, but according to everything I've been reading you need to get a little creative when it comes to all-out attack."

Cheng Li glanced at Connor. His face was hard to read. Was he thinking about the Vampirates he had met first-hand? Or had he somehow managed to create a mental distance from them? She resolved to keep a close eye on him as she addressed her deputy captain once more. "Good work, Jacoby," she said. "But now let's focus on how to kill a Vampirate."

"Absolutely," Jacoby said, "but remember, Captain, our aim actually isn't to *kill* a Vampirate."

"It isn't?" Once more Cheng Li raised an eyebrow.

Jacoby shook his head. "Vampirates are, *de facto*, already

dead – or *undead* if you prefer. Our aim is not to kill them but to *destroy* them."

"A fair distinction," Cheng Li admitted, with a nod. "All right then, tell us how to *destroy* them."

Jacoby turned over the flip-chart to reveal a page of wildly scrawled notes. "Our forebears have listed literally hundreds of possible ways. For instance, place a coin in the vamp's mouth and decapitate him with an axe. Or boil his head in vinegar. Or pour boiling oil on him and drive a nail through his navel."

"Now that's what I call a belly-piercing," said Jasmine with a shiver.

Jacoby grinned back at her. "In Romania, they favour removing the heart, cutting it in two, stuffing garlic in the vamp's mouth and then a nail in the head. But in Serbia, they opt for driving a nail through the neck and then cutting off the vamp's toes . . ."

Again, Cheng Li stole a glance at Connor. This time he caught her looking and he stared straight back. Perhaps he was made of stronger stuff than she had credited.

Jacoby continued brightly, evidently oblivious to such concerns. "Like I say, there were literally hundreds of ideas in the cupboard of death. But I've compiled my list of the big three." He turned the page on the flip-chart to reveal a series of fresh headings:

1. *Burning*
2. *Sunlight*
3. *Stake through the heart*

"OK." Jacoby tapped the chart. "*Numero uno*. Burning!"

As Jacoby babbled on, Connor thought of the night that he had used fire to attack the renegade Vampirates. It was the Vampirate captain himself who had told Connor which weapon

233

to use. And it had proved a success . . . to a degree. Several of the Vampirates *had* been destroyed in the fire. But not all of them, thought Connor, closing his eyes momentarily. These were very painful memories. He had had to turn on Jez – or rather the thing which Jez had become – and throw fire at him. It had been one of the hardest things he had ever had to do. And he had almost been relieved when he had learned that Jez had not perished in the fire.

"Connor?" Cheng Li said.

He opened his eyes with a start.

"I know it's late and you've been working hard, but please do your comrades the courtesy of not dozing off during their presentations."

"Yes, Captain, " Connor said. He could have told her, then and there, that fire was not a certain way to destroy a Vampirate – that both Jez Stukeley and Sidorio had survived his arson attack. But for now, he decided to let it go.

He kept his eyes open, but as Jacoby continued to discuss the whys and wherefores of exposing Vampirates to sunlight and staking them through the heart, Connor's own mind was focused elsewhere. He was thinking again about the Vampirate captain and how he had given Connor the information he needed to attack Sidorio and the rebels. This interested Connor in two ways. Firstly, because the captain had been willing to turn on the other Vampirates. In the coming conflict, would that still be the case? Or, this time, would the different Vampirate forces come together against a common enemy? The second thing which interested Connor about the captain's advice was that it had been wrong. Or, if not exactly *wrong*, inadequate. Fire had not proved fatal to certain of the Vampirates. Had they evolved beyond the norm – beyond even the knowledge and powers of the Vampirate captain himself? Or had he intentionally misled him? Connor didn't think so.

His thoughts returned to the healing ceremony he had taken part in – to restore the weakened captain's vitality after he had sacrificed himself to save so many others. How was he now? Grace hadn't spoken of him. Did that mean he was still missing, as he had been when Connor had left Sanctuary, or was he now back at the helm of the ship, back in charge of the "good" Vampirates?

Connor's thoughts were interrupted as Jacoby finally wound up his presentation. Cheng Li was clearly impressed. "Jacoby, you've done an excellent job. I think our next step is crystal clear. We need to find ourselves some Vampirates to experiment on before we finalise our attack strategy."

"You mean kidnap a Vampirate?" Jasmine asked.

"One won't be sufficient," said Cheng Li, shaking her head. "I think we'll want at least three in the first instance."

"Three!" exclaimed Jasmine. "How long will we keep them? And where?"

"It's all under control," Cheng Li said. "I've having some cages built on the deck of *The Tiger*. We'll keep them there. As to how long . . . well, as long as it takes to get a result."

"You mean until we succeed in killing one of them," said Connor.

"Uh-uh," Jacoby corrected him. "Not *killing*, dude. Until we succeed in *destroying* them." He turned to Cheng Li. "But where are we going to go to *find* these Vampirates?"

Cheng Li smiled. "Connor's been working on that part of the mission, haven't you?"

Connor nodded, clearing his throat. "As Jasmine's research indicated, the main Vampirate ship, *The Nocturne*, is hard to track." He paused. "But it is no longer the sole Vampirate vessel. Sidorio and the rebel Vampirates have taken possession of a prison ship. And whilst *The Nocturne* does seem to move in a very mysterious fashion, the rebel ship, *The Blood Captain*, is moving in an erratic but nonetheless trackable way along the coast."

"How do you know this?" Jacoby asked.

"They're not like the Vampirates of *The Nocturne*," Connor said. "*The Nocturne* has its own crew of donors on board." He realised as he spoke that he had just kicked the others' industrious research into touch. But he didn't care. He had two missions to accomplish here – to give Cheng Li what she needed to pursue Sidorio, and to protect Grace for as long as he could. "Like I say, there are donors on board *The Nocturne*, who supply blood to the Vampirates. This means that the ship never needs to attack elsewhere. But *The Blood Captain* is far less organised. Its crew is growing fast and they are wild and out of control. This makes them dangerous but, at the same time, vulnerable."

"Vulnerable?" Jasmine said, with a shudder. "They don't *sound* very vulnerable."

Connor stared at Jasmine. "They need blood," he said. "They don't have a supply on board ship so they have to go onto land to hunt their prey. They've left a trail of devastation along the coast. It wasn't hard to follow." Now, he produced his own map on which he'd charted the ship's course, appropriately enough, in red. "I think it's pretty clear the direction it's heading in."

"Excellent work, Connor," Cheng Li said.

"I haven't finished," Connor said. He had kept his trump card till last – literally. Now he reached into his back pocket and produced a clutch of playing cards. He leaned forward and fanned them out on Cheng Li's desk.

"Notice anything strange about these?" he asked his comrades.

"They're splattered with blood," Jacoby said. "Gross!"

"They're *wrong*," Jasmine said. "They're all from the same

suit – Hearts. But Hearts are red. And these are black. I've never seen a pack of cards like these."

Cheng Li stared at Connor. "Where did you get them?" she asked.

"They were found on the victims from the recent attacks. There were hundreds more."

Cheng Li picked up one of the cards. "It's identical to the one John Kuo was holding when we discovered him," she said. "Remember?"

Connor nodded grimly. That was one sight he would in all likelihood never be able to erase from his memory.

"It shows we're on the trail of his killers," Cheng Li said, looking at Connor with unbridled admiration. "Well," she continued, "I must say you have not let me down. Each of your three reports has in its own way been highly insightful and revealing." She sat back in her chair. "I'm going to stay here and do a bit more thinking tonight. You three may return to the ship now. You should still be in time for the second dinner sitting."

They needed no persuasion. It had been a long day and they'd been cooped up in the airless, subterranean lock-up for many hours.

The others were out in the corridor, when Jasmine suddenly came to a stop. "Sorry, guys, I forgot to tell Cheng Li something. Go on ahead – I'll catch you up." She turned back and, knocking, stepped back into the archive room.

Cheng Li was already deeply engrossed in her work. She glanced up at Jasmine, clearly less than delighted at the intrusion.

"Did you forget something?" Cheng Li asked.

"Yes," said Jasmine. "It's in your desk drawer. A notebook. I found it earlier, in the last of the archive boxes. I didn't think you'd want me to tell the others about it before you'd had a chance to look at it yourself."

Cheng Li was intrigued. She set down her pen and opened the desk drawer. Sure enough, inside was an old notebook. She lifted it out and set it on the desk. Glancing up again, she saw that Jasmine had already left the room. How strange!

As she opened the notebook, her heart skipped a beat. The calligraphy was unmistakeable. It was a terrible shock. Instinctively, she closed the book, then took a deep breath before once more opening the page. There was no doubt about it. The precise script. The distinctive turquoise ink. She knew what she held in her hand even before she read the title page.

The Journal of Chang Ko Li, January 2495

It was her father's journal. He'd begun writing it in January 2495, just a few months before he had died. Cheng Li frowned. Why had she never seen this notebook? How come it was here, in the secret archive? What revelations lay within this journal? And would they shed light on her father's death? Commodore Kuo had told her that Chang Ko Li had been killed in a tavern brawl. That was the accepted version of events. But was it the truth?

Cheng Li began furiously turning the pages of turquoise writing. Words and phrases leaped out at her . . .

First sighting . . .

A figurehead who comes alive after sunset . . .

Not a veil but a mask!

A second crew whom they call the donors . . .

Cheng Li's head was spinning. Her father's last months had been spent pursuing the Vampirates!

Suddenly, she became aware of another presence in the room. This time, there had been no knock, or else she had been too engrossed to be aware of it.

"Jasmine," she said, "thank you. This really is an incredible find!"

But when she looked up it wasn't Jasmine who stood before her. It was a young man, with translucent pale skin and hair as black as a raven's wing.

"And who might you be?" she asked, though already she had her suspicions.

"My name is Lorcan," he said. "Lorcan Furey." His sky-blue eyes bore into hers as he continued. "I've come to bring you a message from the Vampirates."

CHAPTER THIRTY

The Conundrum

Beguiling. It wasn't a word which came into Cheng Li's mind often, but it was the perfect word to describe the young man standing before her.

"So," she said, "the legendary Lorcan Furey."

He raised an eyebrow. "Legendary?"

"I've heard a lot about you," she said, with a smile. "And, from what I can see, you more than live up to your advance publicity."

In reality, of course, he *wasn't* young. That was the trick of it! He had roamed the earth and oceans for several centuries. His pallor hinted at the fact but, at the same time, enhanced his rare beauty – like the translucent marble of an antique statue, or the papery violet-tinged skin of a garlic bulb. Ironic, thought Cheng Li, given what they said about garlic.

His long dark lashes cast shadows over his sharp cheekbones, as he looked down modestly. "This isn't a social call, Captain Li," he said. "I have a message for you. From Mosh Zu, guru of the Vampirates."

"Mosh Zu?" she said. "I've never heard of him."

"There is much you don't know about us," answered Lorcan.

"But I'm eager to learn," said Cheng Li. "Why don't you sit down?" She indicated the chair on the other side of the desk. "That is, if you care to sit?"

"Assuming you don't have a handy velvet-lined coffin for me to lie in, this chair will do just fine," Lorcan said, settling himself down, opposite her.

"Vampirate humour!" Cheng Li smiled. "I wasn't expecting that. From what Grace told me, I had you pegged as the 'dark and brooding' type."

He smiled at that. "I'm sure I have my moments."

"I'm sure you do, Lorcan Furey," she said, feeling butterflies stirring in her stomach. "I'm sure you do."

I'm flirting with a Vampirate, she thought. What was the expression? *Flirting with danger.* Well, it didn't come much more dangerous than being shut in a confined space with a confirmed bloodsucker, even if he *did* have the kind of looks usually reserved for marble statues. What if he was hungry? Or was it *thirsty*? Never mind – it all boiled down to the same thing. Him leaning across the battered desk and sinking his teeth into her . . .

"We had better get down to business," Lorcan said, his rich brogue drawing her back from her internal monologue.

"Indeed," Cheng Li answered, hoping he had no clue as to the effect his presence was having on her. "You said you had a message for me. From this Mosh Zu." Her almond eyes focused intently on Lorcan's face.

"It's very simple, really," he said. "Don't start something that you cannot finish."

His words sent Cheng Li's heart racing. An electric current of adrenaline pulsed through her. Her first thought was that it might be fear, given that she *had* just been given a warning from the Vampirates. But she knew fear and this *wasn't* fear. What then? Attraction? Well, undeniably she was attracted to the youth seated across the desk from her, with his blue eyes, long lashes and sharp cheekbones. Yes, in another place and time, things could have become very interesting between them. But this feeling, this sensation, was bigger than either fear or attraction. Suddenly, she realised what it was, striking a pin decisively through the butterfly wings of her thoughts.

It was the fact that Mosh Zu, clearly one of the most senior Vampirates, had sent an envoy to her. *To her!* Not to Rene Grammont, much-respected old-guard of the Federation. Nor to Commodore Ahab Black, the mysterious and ambitious newcomer. No, Mosh Zu had sent Lorcan to *her*, Cheng Li. She couldn't have wished for a more potent sign that her power was on the increase.

Lorcan cleared his throat. "Do you understand the message?" he asked.

She nodded. "You know about my mission." She gazed at him, waiting for him to speak again. He stared back, seemingly quite happy at the silence between them. She was tempted to say something more, but she had to be careful. Already, there was something about Lorcan Furey that had her off-balance. Usually, this was the effect she exerted on others. How very strange, and not altogether pleasant, to have it turned back upon herself. There was a very real danger that he might draw her into saying more than she would wish, or that the Federation would condone.

He stood up. Evidently he was preparing to leave.

"Is that it?" she asked.

"I've delivered the message," said Lorcan. "My job here is done."

"Wait," Cheng Li said. Her words succeeded in halting his rapid exit. But now she was unsure how to proceed. "How did you get in here?" she asked. "In fact, how did you know where to find me?"

"Does it matter?" he asked. "I got here. I found you. I delivered Mosh Zu's message."

Cheng Li's mind was racing. She wanted to keep him in the room, though quite why she wasn't sure and she didn't have time to question further now.

"Shouldn't I send a message back to your master?" she said.

Lorcan turned again but shook his head. "That isn't necessary."

"I see," Cheng Li said, somewhat bitterly. "So this wasn't so much a message, rather a warning."

Lorcan shrugged. "I'm grateful for your time. And your attention. I trust you'll give due consideration to what I've told you."

"Yes," Cheng Li said. "Yes, I will."

He nodded and turned once more, making the last few strides towards the door. As he did so, she saw a piece of paper fall from the folds of his cloak. It fluttered free in the lamplight, then landed on the floor, white and fragile as a feather.

"Wait!" she cried, then could have kicked herself.

He was already at the door. He turned around, his blue eyes seeking hers through the lamplight, then locking onto them. "Yes?"

Cheng Li tried desperately not to look at, or even think about, the piece of paper on the floor. With the utmost effort, she assumed a casual tone. "I just wondered how Grace was getting on?"

"She's very well," Lorcan said, his voice softer than before. "I'll tell her you asked after her, if you like."

"Please do that," said Cheng Li.

"Was there something else you wanted to tell me?" he asked. His hand was already on the door. In a moment, he'd walk through it and out into the night. This was her last chance.

She thought of the paper on the floor. It was probably nothing of any importance. But even so. "No," she said, shaking her head. "No, there's nothing else."

He didn't move. Could he sense there was something she was keeping from him? Had he dropped the paper intentionally? Was he testing her?

"So how do you make your exit?" she asked. "In a puff of smoke? Or do you just vaporise?"

He grinned at her. "Much as I hate to be a crushing disappointment to you, I reckon I'll just take the door." With that, he turned, pushed open the door and stepped out into the corridor.

She listened to his footsteps fade. She didn't dwell on whether he was taking the strange elevator back up to the Rotunda or finding another way altogether to leave the academy. As he had said himself, what did it matter?

Cheng Li sat down at the desk, feeling the aftershock of her encounter with Lorcan Furey and the strange blend of fear and excitement his visit, his warning – but above all his presence – had instilled in her. For a time, she replayed their conversation in her head, thinking how much better she could have played it, how much smarter. But Lorcan Furey was a cool customer – a very cool customer indeed. She remembered Grace telling her about his evasiveness when she'd first joined *The Nocturne*; his ability to speak without saying anything; to talk in riddles. He's a conundrum, thought Cheng Li. A walking, talking conundrum.

She couldn't help but think of Grace and of the relationship between her and Lorcan. The way Grace had told it to her that night at the academy, it had sounded like an intense crush. Grace wasn't the first young woman, nor would she be the last, to fall for the rebel outsider within her midst. But Lorcan was more than a rebel outsider, she reminded herself. He was a demon, even if he *was* blessed with the looks of a demi-god.

As Cheng Li framed the thought, she glanced forward and caught sight again of the rectangle of paper Lorcan had dropped before departing. She lifted the hurricane-lamp and walked over to it, dropping to her knees. As she lowered the lamp to the floorboards, she saw that it was not, as she had first thought, a sheet of paper Lorcan had dropped but an envelope. It was lying face down. She lifted it and turned it over, seeing that a single name was scrawled on the front.

Grace

The envelope was plump, filled with several pages of notepaper, no doubt covered in writing. What did it say, she wondered, not wanting to rush the moment of opening, but to defer the pleasure. Was it a declaration of love from the Vampirate to his mortal sweetheart? Or, perhaps more likely, was he about to break off their relationship and within this envelope was the full explanation why? Cheng Li weighed the precious envelope in her hands, smiling at this intriguing gift which had literally fallen into her possession.

It was time to get out of this airless lock-up, to return to her comfortable cabin aboard *The Tiger* and reflect on the treasures this day had brought her. She was tired but elated. She had much to reflect upon.

She glanced down at her father's notebook. She couldn't resist lifting it and glancing momentarily at the pages of writing, all penned in Chang Ko Li's distinctive hand and equally distinctive turquoise ink. But she wouldn't read it here. Save it for later.

She tucked Lorcan's letter inside the journal, then placed it in her bag, zipped it and slung it over her shoulder. Lifting the hurricane-lamp once more, she headed back to the door, then stepped out into the corridor. She shut the archive door and continued on into the darkness, anxious to get back to her cabin as quickly as possible so as to unpack the satchel. She had no shortage of reading material tonight, that was for certain! Suddenly, she felt quite revived.

CHAPTER THIRTY-ONE

Fightback

Another night. Another dead-end coastal town about to be decimated.

Stukeley and Johnny monitored their approach from the bridge of *The Blood Captain*. They could hear the hungry mob below getting psyched up for action. Another night of feasting, revelry and utter chaos.

In the captain's cabin, Sidorio stood before the ceiling-high mirror, adjusting his new cape. It was an elaborate affair, comprising an array of animal pelts with chains of bones, topped off with metal spikes on each shoulder. Needless to say, it was bespoke. Lola had recommended a tailor and, though initially he had been sceptical, he had been easily persuaded that a) he looked irresistible in every sense of the word and b) as King of the Vampirates, he urgently required clothes befitting his fast-growing reputation. He had acquired the new boots, with matching spikes, from another of Lola's contacts. He grinned. In a short time, Lola had become indispensable to him.

He leaned closer into the mirror – checking to see if anything was stuck between his teeth. Then he ran a hand over his close-cropped hair. "Perfect," he declared, grinning at himself. Then he turned – noting with satisfaction the swish of his new cape – and headed out of the cabin to rendezvous with his lieutenants on the bridge.

As he made his way along the corridor, the crowd of rank-and-file Vampirates parted like the Red Sea. Their shrill voices fell to a respectful hush as he prowled past them and began climbing the stairs to the bridge. He threw open the door to announce his presence. The reverberating clang of metal achieved the desired effect. Johnny and Stukeley turned simultaneously.

"Evening, lads," said Sidorio.

"Good evening, Captain," said Johnny.

Stukeley nodded hello, his eyes bugging at Sidorio's elaborate outfit. "That's quite an outfit!" he exclaimed. "Is the cape, by any chance, a new acquisition?"

Sidorio nodded, proudly. "Lola helped me with the design." He struck a pose, allowing them to see the outfit in its full glory. "Do you think it's too . . ." He hesitated, searching for the word.

"Ostentatious?" offered Stukeley.

"Understated?" Sidorio roared.

Stukeley shook his head very slowly. "No, Captain. I think you can rest assured that it is in no way too understated."

"Excellent," Sidorio said, rubbing his hands together. "Are you both hungry? I'm very hungry."

Johnny nodded. "I am hungry like the wolf!" he said, giving a rather accurate impression of a wolf-call.

"Very good, Stetson," Sidorio said with a grin.

"Actually," Stukeley said, "it's good to see you, Captain. As we've got a few moments before we disembark, could we have a chat with you about some business?"

"All right," Sidorio said, his bored expression signalling a marked lack of enthusiasm.

The captain, never one to enjoy strategy discussions at the best of times, seemed more restless than usual tonight. But Stukeley could not afford to defer this discussion. "Have you heard the news that the pirates are building a force to directly attack us?"

"Really?" Sidorio's raised eyebrow indicated moderate interest.

"Yes," Stukeley said, nodding. "It's on account of the murder of Commodore Kuo, the headmaster of the Pirate Academy, and two of the students there . . ."

Sidorio smiled. "Lola's work."

Stukeley nodded. "Yes, indeed. The work of Lady Lockwood and the crew of *The Vagabond*."

Sidorio grinned. "Naughty Lola!"

Stukeley frowned. "The thing is, Captain, all our intelligence indicates that Lady Lockwood has slipped through the net and the pirates are coming after you instead. They remember your massacre of Porfirio Wrathe and his crew and think you were responsible."

Sidorio smiled. "I think I did kill *him*."

"Yes, you did," Stukeley said. "I was with you." He paused. "My point, Captain, is that the situation is changing fast. We need to prepare ourselves."

"For what?" Sidorio asked. "An attack from some prancing pirates?" His fingers traced the spikes on his shoulder-pads. "Bring it on! We'll make mincemeat of them!" He paused. "Or maybe, we'll start up our own winery, like—"

"It's great to see you being so bullish about this," Stukeley forged on. "Do you remember when we talked before about setting up a new command structure?" Sidorio stared blankly at his deputy. "Along the lines of a Roman legion?" Sidorio showed a flicker of recognition at this.

"We need more captains," Stukeley said, deciding to keep it simple. "One for each ship."

"*I'm* the captain," Sidorio said, his voice booming around the bridge and out into the corridor.

"Yes," Johnny said, coming to the aid of his fellow deputy. "You're in overall command. No one is questioning that. But, given the combination of this threat and how fast our own numbers are expanding, we need more ships and a captain and deputy for every last one of them. We need to start assessing who within the ranks has leadership potential."

Sidorio yawned, his gold incisors glinting in his open mouth. His breath, Stukeley noticed, was uncharacteristically sweet. Minty fresh. Wrinkling his nose, Stukeley returned his focus to their discussion. "I know this stuff might seem overly bureaucratic to you, Captain, but we must attend to these matters. This situation has been building for some time."

Sidorio shrugged, though whether from lack of an answer or pure boredom, it was unclear. Noticing another mirror on the opposite wall, he turned away from his lieutenants and strutted off towards it.

Stukeley and Johnny exchanged a glance.

"I'd give it up if I were you," Johnny muttered under his breath. "His mind is somewhere else altogether tonight."

"You can say that again!" Stukeley hissed, with a grimace.

"Would you two just relax?" Sidorio said, over his shoulder. "We are becoming an unstoppable force. Let the pirates come after us if they want. If they think they can prevent our rise, then they're wrong. Dead wrong." Sidorio turned back to the mirror. He puffed out his chest, alternately raising one pectoral, then the other, as if taking part in a private bodybuilding contest. "Are we nearly there yet?" he asked. "We don't want to be late meeting the others."

"*What* others?" his deputies asked in unison, their voices laced with concern.

Sidorio turned, smiling amiably. "Didn't I mention that Lady

Lockwood and her crew would be joining us tonight? We thought it would be a laugh to hunt together."

Stukeley frowned, turning away and looking out across to the beach. "Oh yes," he said, in a voice utterly devoid of enthusiasm. "Her ship has just pulled in."

"Excellent," Sidorio said, sniffing under his armpits. "Right-o, boys, time to drop anchor and make tracks."

"Before you go," Stukeley said, "can we at least finish our discussion?"

"I thought we already did," Sidorio said.

Stukeley drew on every last ounce of patience within his command. "Captain, this issue won't just go away. If the pirates are planning to attack us, and it seems they are, we have to be ready."

"All right then," Sidorio said, pleasantly. "What are you suggesting?"

Sometimes, Stukeley wondered if the captain, in spite of his many considerable powers, was blessed with the memory of a goldfish.

"About the legions . . . a captain for every ship."

"Yes, yes," Sidorio said. "I'll talk to Lola about that. Must go now. Don't want to keep the magnificent creature waiting." Already, he was at the door.

"Captain," Stukeley said, "forgive me, but Lady Lockwood isn't part of our command. Should you be discussing such matters with her?"

Sidorio glared at Stukeley. "Need I remind you who's in charge around here? I'll talk to *whoever* I want about *whatever* I want."

"Yes, sir!" Stukeley said, realising that he had overstepped the mark. Sometimes the better part of valour was knowing when to shut up.

But Sidorio had not yet finished. "As it happens," he said, "Lady Lockwood and I are discussing a merger."

"A merger?" exclaimed Johnny.

Sidorio nodded. "That's right, Stetson. I've asked her to join us. I like her style. I think she'll shake things up around here. What's the phrase?" He grinned and punched the air. "*A woman's touch!*" he exclaimed. With that, he turned and sallied forth into the corridor, unwilling to delay his date a moment longer.

Johnny turned to Stukeley. "*A woman's touch?*" he repeated. "What is he on about, *hermano?*"

Stukeley frowned. "The captain doesn't know whether it's dinner time or doomsday, mate. That's the state Lady Lockwood has got him in. We've tried to talk some sense into him, but it just goes in one ear and out the other. It's not like he had much of an attention span to begin with, but since Lady Muck came on the scene . . ."

"So what do we do?" Johnny asked.

"We take things in hand," Stukeley said. "We let the captain bill and coo with his lady-friend until he grows bored and finds a new toy. And, in the meantime, we take control of this enterprise. Before it crumbles in front of our eyes."

Johnny's dark eyes glistened. "I hear you, *hermano*. But do you really think we can do it?"

"We've got to try," Stukeley said. "I don't see that we have any other choice. Do you?" He strode out of the door, beckoning Johnny to follow.

Sidorio was standing with Lady Lockwood and her crew, dressed identically in black capes, when Stukeley and Johnny arrived on the beach.

"Ah, here they are at last!" Sidorio cried affably. "Boys, come over here. You remember Lady Lockwood."

"As if we could forget," Stukeley muttered, bowing elaborately.

"*Buenos noces, Capitan Lockwood.*" Johnny took Lola's hand and kissed it.

Lady Lockwood smiled sweetly at the boys, then turned to Sidorio once more. "Your deputies are *so* charming," she said. She stretched out her hands to her side. "And no doubt you boys remember Jessamy and Camille?"

The two women stepped forward to greet Sidorio's team. Stukeley and Johnny looked embarrassed, remembering all too well how the duo had played them for stooges over the course of several nights.

"Now don't worry, boys," Lady Lola said, "they promise to play nice tonight, don't you, ladies?"

"Yes, Captain," the pair chorused sweetly.

Stukeley turned to Sidorio. "Isn't it time we got this show on the road, Captain?"

"Sure," Sidorio nodded. He reached out his hand to Lady Lockwood. "Come with me," he said. "We shall hunt as a pair."

"You know," said Lady Lockwood, "I have people to hunt for me, darling. I generally prefer to drink my blood out of a priceless Venetian glass."

Sidorio was momentarily deflated. Seeing this, Lady Lockwood took his hand. "But I'm always open to a new experience. Come along, you brute." She turned to address her crew. "Have fun, everyone!"

Sidorio led Lady Lockwood over to the centre of the crowd and together, they gave the command. "Go feast!"

Stukeley and Johnny watched the hordes tear away. They stood there, surrounded by the rest of Lady Lockwood's sizeable crew which, Johnny couldn't help but notice, was composed entirely of beautiful women.

"Well?" Jessamy said, raising an eyebrow. "We were rather hoping that you'd lead the way, gentlemen."

Johnny grinned. "Ladies, follow me!" He started running across the beach, leading the elegant swarm of Lady Lockwood's crew in their matching black capes.

After their feasting was done, Johnny and Stukeley accompanied Lady Lockwood's crew to the beach. After Stukeley's initial scepticism, he had had a great time. Now that Jessamy and Camille were no longer trying to trick them and induce short-term memory loss, they were actually rather fine company. There were, he reflected, worse things than a night of feasting in the company of a pack of gorgeous female Vampirates.

After a short time, they were joined on the beach by their two captains – Sidorio and Lady Lockwood. Sidorio ran along, carrying Lady Lockwood in his arms, her skirts trailing behind. She whooped with excitement. "Put me down! Put me down this instant!" At last, he released her, gently, onto the sand. She caught her breath then turned to the others, a little flushed of face. "Well, *we* certainly had a good time tonight. How about all of you?"

There were nods and enthusiastic words from the ranks.

Lady Lockwood looped her arm through Sidorio's. "It seems as if our crews are highly compatible, doesn't it?"

He nodded, beaming at her.

"Should I go and sound the siren?" Johnny asked the captain.

"Not just yet," Sidorio said with a shake of the head. "It's still good and dark. We've had *our* fun, but we should let the others have theirs a while longer."

Suddenly, the night air was lanced by a blood-curdling cry.

"What was that?" Jessamy cried.

But they all knew the answer. They all knew the sounds of mortal cries. This was different. This was one of their own.

"It's starting," Stukeley said, calmly. "The town is staging a fightback."

"What do we do, Captain?" said Johnny, turning to Sidorio for leadership.

Silently, Sidorio stood up and strode across the beach, looking back at the town. His two lieutenants followed.

"Should we stay and fight?" Stukeley asked. "Or do you want to ship out?"

The first scream was now followed by another. Up on the hill, there was fire. A flowing river of fire. Torches. Flaming torches.

"Let's get out of here," Sidorio said.

"I'll sound the siren," said Johnny.

"No!" Sidorio shook his head. "No need. We're not waiting for any stragglers."

"Stragglers?" said Stukeley. "Captain, a moment ago, you were saying we should let them have their fun . . ."

"Things change," Sidorio said. "Those who make it, make it. As for the rest . . ." He shrugged. "Easy come, easy go."

Stukeley and Johnny stood rooted to the spot, shocked at the captain's attitude.

"Am I not making myself clear enough for you?" Sidorio cried. "Get back to the ship and draw up the anchor!"

"Yes, Captain!" Stukeley answered, leaping into action.

"Right away, Captain!" cried Johnny.

"I suppose we'd better beat a hasty retreat ourselves," said Lady Lockwood, turning to her crew. "Come on, ladies!" At her command, her crew began sprinting across the sand.

Lady Lockwood blew Sidorio a kiss. "Nighty-night, then. Thanks for inviting us to partake in the fun. I had a ball, Sid, an absolute ball. And I'm sure we'll be seeing one another again very soon!"

As Lady Lockwood and her crew fled in one direction, Sidorio and the crew of *The Blood Captain* raced to the other side of the beach, where their ship awaited them.

*

Vampirates were still clambering up the side of the mighty hulk as it began to swing around. Others now appeared on the beach. The final, surviving, stragglers had at last returned. Stukeley looked down at them. They were a sorry sight. One's hair had been set on fire and she was desperately trying to extinguish the flames. Another had been staked and was gazing mournfully down at the pole protruding from his chest.

"Wait for us!" cried one of the group.

"Swim for it," Johnny cried.

"I can't!" cried the staked Vampirate.

Sidorio was impassive. The ship was, according to his instructions, already pulling out.

"You can't just leave us!" cried the singed Vampirate.

"I can do whatever I want," Sidorio said, in a bored tone.

"You're our captain!" cried another. "You're supposed to look after us. The captain of *The Nocturne* would never have treated us like this!"

Sidorio rolled his eyes. "That's kind of the point, isn't it?" He looked down at the stranded crew-members with disdain. "You're Vampirates, aren't you? Show some spine. I could take on that town single-handed and leave them for dust . . . if I could be bothered." He yawned. "But now, I'm going to go and have a little snooze. *Hasta la vista!*" He turned and walked away across the deck.

On the beach below, the stranded Vampirates continued to cry out bitterly as *The Blood Captain* disappeared into the night. Behind them, accelerating across the beach, was a mob of angry townspeople.

The lynch-mob brandished flaming torches, stakes, pokers and whatever else resembling a weapon they had managed to lay their hands on in the thick of night.

But now, another ship approached the shore. Its captain

stood at the front of the ship, surveying the scene below. "How terrible," she said, turning to her deputy. "Did you see that? That other ship left these poor Vampirates for dust."

"Yes," said the deputy, "that wasn't very sporting, was it?"

The captain shook her head. "I think we ought to go and offer our help, don't you?"

Jacoby grinned at Cheng Li. "Yes," he said. "I think we've got room for at least three of those poor Vampirates right here on our ship."

They turned and looked at the three cages which had been constructed on the main deck for just such a purpose.

Cheng Li shook her head. "Talk about out of the frying pan and into the fire," she said. Then she turned again and began signalling to the desperate creatures on the sand.

Chapter Thirty-Two

Running on Empty

"Grace, I'm sorry to barge in on you like this. I knocked but you didn't answer."

Grace opened her eyes, groggily. Her vision was blurred, and it took her a moment to place the figure entering the room.

"Oskar?"

"Yes," he said brightly, moving towards her. "How are you doing today?"

Her vision was hazy. "I'm OK . . . I guess." But, as she said the words, she felt suddenly nauseous. The room seemed to be spinning around her.

"Here," Oskar said, sitting down beside her. She felt his hand grip hers. His touch was cool, like all the Vampirates . . . but no, Oskar wasn't a vampire. He was a donor. Grace's mind was racing. His touch was cool because she was so hot. She must have a fever. "Oh, Oskar," she said, "I'm not feeling too well."

"It's OK, Grace," he said. "I know. I know." He sat down on the bed beside her and kept hold of her hand. They sat like that for a while, saying nothing further.

After a few minutes had passed, Grace felt her breathing

begin to slow down and her temperature to cool. Her vision was becoming clearer. She eased herself up in bed.

"Well," said Oskar, "you certainly look better than yesterday."

"Yesterday?" Grace said, vaguely. "Did you come to see me yesterday?"

Oskar nodded and smiled, patiently. "And the day before and the day before that. Don't you remember?"

She shook her head, gripped by a coil of panic. "No, Oskar, I don't. I don't even know how long I've been here." She sighed. "I guess I've been a lot sicker than I realised."

Oskar smiled and squeezed her hand. "You've been here for five days, Grace. Five days and five nights. Ever since we left Crescent Moon Bay." He paused. "Do you remember what happened there?"

"Yes," she said. "Of course! My mother passed on. She was reunited with my dad – at least, their souls were reunited. They went away together."

"That's right," Oskar said. "And do you remember what happened next?"

She thought back to being there in the bay. To standing in the churchyard, safe in Lorcan's arms, watching her mother and father's reunion at Dexter's grave. And then seeing them walk away and then . . . The vision was dimming but she held on to it tenaciously. There had been a beam of light from the lighthouse and she had seen them up in the lamp-room, looking down at her and waving goodbye. And then the beam had begun moving across the beach and the bay until she had had to close her eyes. Darkness. Utter darkness. But no, before that there had been something else. The gravestone, her father's gravestone, had glowed red . . . no *pink*. It was as if it was calling her, summoning her. She had raced towards it. And she had seen the extra line of carving – Sally's inscription. And that was when the darkness had come. She had read the new words

259

and then everything had begun to blur and she had lost consciousness.

"I think I must have fainted in the churchyard," Grace said.

Oskar nodded. "That's exactly what happened," he said. "You see, you *do* remember! The others brought you back to the ship, back to your old cabin." He gestured around the room and now her eyes began to take it in too. It had been a while since she had been here, after her protracted stay at Sanctuary, but yes, this was her cabin – the one she'd been assigned after her initial arrival on *The Nocturne*, back when she hadn't even known the ship's name.

She was propped up in the canopied bed, its wooden posts bearing intricate carvings. To her right was the small washroom with its china basin, a washcloth folded over its side. Her eyes continued to move around the room – to the chair, on which her clothes were neatly folded. Close by the chair was the desk. As usual, its surface was crowded with pens, pencils, ink and notebooks – including the notebooks in which she had written down the crossing stories of the Vampirates she had met and talked to here and at Sanctuary. Beyond the desk was the lacquered chest of drawers, painted with strange characters, and bearing a silver hairbrush and mirror set. She remembered that mirror. The glass was missing from it.

Grace seized Oskar's hand. "How long did you say I'd been here?" she asked once more, starting to wonder if everything had been a dream – Lorcan's blindness, their trip to Sanctuary, the captain's healing ceremony, her mother's return and everything after.

"Five days," Oskar said. "Ever since your mother passed on and you fainted in the churchyard. Mosh Zu brought you here. Lorcan carried you."

So it *hadn't* been a dream. It *had* all happened. Why did it all seem so hazy to her?

"I'm sorry," she said, "did you say you've visited me here before?"

He nodded. "Every afternoon," he said. "Lorcan and Mosh Zu told me it was OK. They thought you would like the company."

"I'm very grateful," Grace said. "I really am. It's just so strange that I can't remember. It's like everything since the churchyard has been lost. And everything that happened before is all jumbled. I'm having trouble telling what's real and what's my imagination."

Oskar addressed her in his most soothing tones. "Don't beat yourself up about it, Grace. You've been through a lot in the past few weeks. It's only natural that your body would react at some point. You've been under so much stress. There had to be some outlet for that."

Grace heard his words, processing them as though he was talking about somebody else. It made sense, though she hadn't seen it that way from the inside. "I suppose you're right," she agreed. "Maybe I've been running on empty for a while. And it's taken its toll on me. Maybe this is like a cold bug or the flu or something."

"Exactly," Oskar said. "I'm sure it's nothing to worry about, anyhow. The most important thing is for you to rest up. You'll feel better soon, I'm sure."

"Thank you," she said.

He grinned at her. There was a second knock at the door.

"Come in," Grace called.

"Well, you sound better . . ." began Lorcan, entering the cabin. He broke off. "Oh," he said, "Oskar. I didn't know you'd be here."

"It's OK, isn't it?" Oskar asked. "You said it was all right for me to visit Grace, remember?"

Lorcan looked remote for a moment then nodded. "Yes. Yes,

of course I remember. I just wasn't expecting to see you right now, that's all." He paused. He seemed a little agitated.

"Would you like me to leave you two alone?" Oskar asked him.

Lorcan nodded. "If you wouldn't mind," he said.

Oskar shook his head. "No, of course not. Besides, I have to go and get ready for the Feast tonight."

"Is it Feast Night, tonight?" Grace asked.

They both nodded. This explained why Lorcan seemed so distracted. Like the other Vampirates, he was at his weakest just before the Feast. It was when his blood levels were at their lowest and his energy along with them.

"I'll go and get ready," Oskar said. He smiled at Grace. "But I'll check in on you again tomorrow, all right?"

"Yes, please," she said, smiling up at him. "Thank you, by the way, for what you said. You've made me feel a lot better already."

"Good," he said, with a smile. Then he nodded at Lorcan and made his way to the door.

"How *are* you feeling?" Lorcan asked Grace, sitting down where Oskar had sat before.

"A bit strange, to be honest," Grace said. "I can't remember anything since I fainted in the churchyard. Oskar said that you carried me back here."

Lorcan nodded. "That's right."

"Thank you," she said. "One way or another, you always seem to be rescuing me."

He shrugged and smiled at her tenderly. "Well, if you will keep getting shipwrecked and having fainting fits in churchyards, somebody's gotta look after you," he said.

"Well, I'm glad it's you," she said, reaching out her hand for his. His touch was cool, as always. But that was right. He *was* a Vampirate, after all.

"So," said Lorcan, "you and my new donor seem to be fast friends. What have the two of you been talking about?"

Grace paused.

"Or is it secret?" Lorcan asked.

"No." Grace shook her head. "No, we were just talking about what I've been going through. And how I'm feeling now. Oh, Lorcan, it's been so strange. I have this jumble of symptoms. One minute I'm really hot, then I'm ever so nauseous and then I guess I'm really tired because I seem to be sleeping so much."

"I know," he said. "But it's OK, Grace. It will pass."

Grace nodded. "That's what Oskar said too. He thinks it's just the stress I've been under, working its way out of my body. Some kind of flu, I guess . . ." She stopped speaking, noticing that Lorcan was looking at her very intently. "Lorcan," she said. "What's wrong?"

He continued to stare at her, then gripped her hand more tightly. "Grace," he said. "My dear, sweet, Grace. I have something to tell you." He broke off.

"Lorcan, what is it? You're scaring me. Please, tell me what it is."

He nodded. "It's time. It's way *past* time. I've been trying to protect you for so long, we all have, but you have to know."

Grace stared at him in wonder. What on earth was he talking about?

CHAPTER THIRTY-THREE

A Dangerous Trio

Cheng Li was staring at her father's portrait when she heard the knock at her cabin door. She turned and composed herself before calling out. "Enter!"

The door opened and Jacoby, Jasmine and Connor trooped inside.

Cheng Li raised an eyebrow. "Is it done?" she asked.

Jacoby nodded. "It's done. The experiments concluded earlier today. We're ready to share our findings with you."

"Excellent," said Cheng Li, "everyone grab a chair." She led them over to the round table by the window and they all sat down. Her three crew-members had brought notebooks with them, which they opened, ready to discuss their findings and to take the captain's next orders.

"So," said Cheng Li, "three nights ago, I brought you three lab rats. Talk me through your experiments and tell me what you've found."

Jacoby nodded. "Sure thing, Captain! Well, first we strung the cages with garlands of wild roses and garlic bulbs—"

"How decorative," Cheng Li cut in.

Jacoby grinned at the captain. "And you'll remember that

both plants have apotropaic properties – that is they help to protect against Vampirates. Or so we had been told. We wanted to test it out."

"And?" inquired Cheng Li.

Jacoby nodded. "I'd say it's an affirmative. Certainly, we didn't see any early attempts at escape. Of course, it's hard to confirm one way or the other, but I'd say that the garlands had some repellant effect, wouldn't you Min?"

Jasmine nodded. Cheng Li scribbled a note, then urged her deputy to continue.

"Next," said Jacoby, brightly, "we tested out the effects of sunlight. We wanted to see just what degree of harm this would do to them. We know anecdotally, of course, that a Vampirate whom Connor has met was temporarily blinded by the sun."

"How did these three fare?" Cheng Li inquired.

"They were definitely panicked by the idea," said Jacoby. "When we removed the covers from the cages that first night and told them we'd see them in the morning, all three were in a heightened state of agitation." He paused. "Of course, we didn't entirely take our leave, but observed them from a distance. As the sun rose, there were further signs of distress."

"They began to scream," Jasmine interjected. Her face showed her own distress. "It was horrible, really horrible."

"But," said Jacoby, "the sunlight appeared to be another apotropaic. It weakened them but it didn't seem to inflict significant harm. Overall, I'd say it had more of a sedative effect."

"Interesting," said Cheng Li, making another note. She glanced at Connor. "Perhaps different Vampirates react to the sun in different ways?"

Connor nodded. "It's possible," he said. "Besides, from what little Grace has told me, I don't think Lorcan Furey's blindness was caused by exposure to daylight alone. There appear to have been other underlying causes."

Cheng Li nodded, turning back to Jacoby. "There's no chance they were faking this sedative effect, in order to trick you?"

Her deputy shook his head. "No," he said. "Trust me, Captain, there was no fakery."

"After a time," Jasmine said, "we had to cover the cages in order to minimise their distress and prepare for further experimentation."

At this, Jacoby produced an object from his pocket and set it on Cheng Li's desk. "A wooden stake," he said. "We tested this on Vampirate One. You may remember him? Adult male. The largest of the trio. When I went into the cage, he was like a dead weight. I turned him around. He seemed to have been weakened by the sunlight but, even so, he put up a fight."

Cheng Li raised an eyebrow.

"He appeared to be in the full throes of blood-hunger," Jacoby continued. When I looked into his eyes, it was as if I was staring into a deep well, with a fire burning at the very bottom of the pit. Then things got really nasty."

"Nasty? How?"

"Vampirate One attacked me," Jacoby said, frowning at the memory. "He easily overpowered me and tore my shirt . . ."

"He was trying to expose Jacoby's thorax," said Jasmine. "This seems to be the Vampirate's preferred place for puncturing the skin to open up a blood channel."

Jacoby grimaced at the memory. "If it hadn't been for these two, Captain, I'd have been Vampirate brunch. Connor came into the cage and tried to pull Vampirate One off me, but the fiend proved too strong for him, too. He was scratching my chest as if he was deciding where to puncture it. I don't mind telling you – it was the single scariest moment of my life!"

Connor nodded. "The Vampirate was bearing down on Jacoby, his teeth extended. I made a fresh attempt to pull him off but he threw me across the cage."

"So how *did* you repel and subdue Vampirate One?" Cheng Li asked.

"Enter the Peacock," Jacoby said with a smile, turning to Jasmine, who took up the story.

"The night before, Jacoby had been telling me about the rumoured powers of aconite," said Jasmine. "It's a flowering plant, also known as monkshood or wolfsbane, which has been used for centuries as arrow poison by hunters in Ladakh and Japan, and even in human wars in China." Cheng Li scribbled away furiously as Jasmine continued. "In humans and animals, the poison works quickly, causing numbness to the mouth and a burning in the abdomen. This is generally followed by severe vomiting. Then the pulse and respiration steadily fail, leading to death by asphyxia. Aconite was listed as another apotropaic and, as I happened to be carrying a bag of petals I was taking to the lab, I decided to test it out right then and there."

"She was fearless!" Jacoby said, his eyes wide. "She ran into the cage and dropped the petals onto Vampirate One's head. The effect was instantaneous. He had me pinned to the floor but, as the aconite took hold, it was as if he was instantly paralysed. His hold loosened and he cried out in pain."

"Which led me to conclude," said Jasmine, "that aconite is not simply an apotropaic, like roses or garlic. It didn't just hold Vampirate One at bay. It seemed to act more deeply and inflict actual harm." As she finished speaking, she placed an innocent-looking sprig of white flowers on Cheng Li's desk, beside the wooden stake.

Cheng Li glanced from the flowers to the stake. "So," she said, "the flower works but the stake doesn't? Is that what I'm hearing from you?"

Jacoby shook his head. "The stake works all right," he said. "We just had to subdue the Vampirates before we brought it into play. We left them for another night and then exposed them to several bouts of light throughout the following day. This appeared, as before, to sedate them – the more light we exposed them to, the more pronounced the effects of the sedation. Then, we returned at sunset to test out the stake on Vampirate Two, the second male, but of a decidedly smaller build."

"Did he put up much of a fight?" Cheng Li inquired.

Jacoby shook his head. "I pretty much bowled straight into the cage and inserted the stake through his thorax. He opened his mouth but made no cry. It was kind of weird."

Jasmine nodded. "There was a high-pitched noise but it didn't come from his mouth. It was as if it was on a different frequency – rather like the sound glass makes when it shatters. And then, he literally disintegrated before our eyes."

Cheng Li was rapt with attention.

"That's right," Jacoby nodded. "One moment, he was there – the next he cracked like a mirror. His human form disappeared. There were shards all over the cage. And then the shards broke up further into this strange kind of metallic-looking dust." Jacoby glanced at his comrades. "That's when we made our first mistake," he said.

"Mistake? What mistake?" asked Cheng Li.

"Well, to be honest, Captain, I was kind of in shock at what I had done. We thought I'd been successful in destroying him . . ."

"You *thought* you had? It sounds pretty definitive."

Jacoby nodded. "That's what we all thought. So we decided to leave our experiments there for the night and we went off to dinner."

"It was only later," said Jasmine, "that, Kavan, the guard up on duty in the crow's nest, told us what he'd seen."

"Which was?" pressed the captain.

"He said that it was like a dust storm on the deck," answered Jasmine.

268

"A dust storm?"

"That's what he thought it was at first. He could see the metallic dust moving within the cage. Then it swirled out of the cage, as if the wind had blown it. And it continued to move. Only now, it took shape – the outline of a human form. Kavan said that as he looked down, the glittering dust became flesh again. Vampirate Two had reconstituted himself."

"Amazing," Cheng Li said. "But that was hardly your mistake. You couldn't have known."

"*That* wasn't the mistake, Captain," said Jacoby. "The mistake was what happened next. Like I say, we had all gone off to dinner. Kavan was up in the crow's nest. When he saw what was happening, he climbed down to try to catch Vampirate Two, but he wasn't fast enough. The captive escaped off the ship."

"Escaped?" Cheng Li exclaimed. "Where did he get to?" Her features grew dark. "And why is this the first time I'm hearing about this?"

Jacoby was red-faced. "The others did try to persuade me to tell you before, but I felt that you'd delegated responsibility for this task to me. I didn't want to let you down, Captain. I was confident we could recapture him."

"Oh, Jacoby!" Cheng Li said, exasperated. "But you didn't, did you?"

Jacoby shook his head. "I'm really sorry, boss."

Cheng Li nodded. "It's unfortunate, but understandable in the circumstances. So he got away. He's only one Vampirate. We still had the other two, right?"

Jacoby nodded, greatly relieved that the captain had taken this so well. Clearly, he should have listened to the others and told her sooner – it would have saved him a couple of long, sleepless nights.

Cheng Li was writing but, as she did so, she glanced up. "Although he escaped, you proved that the stake is a very powerful weapon, especially when used in conjunction with other techniques." She took the stake in her hand. "What wood is it made from?"

"Hawthorn," said Jasmine. "Our research suggests that hawthorn is especially toxic to Vampirates."

"Excellent work," said Cheng Li, "this is all starting to come together. So, how did you proceed?"

"We decided to further investigate the powers of aconite," answered Jacoby. "As Min described before, this substance appears to be highly toxic to Vampirates. The petals alone have a numbing, paralysing effect. They cause marked swelling around the eye and lip areas and there seems to be an even deeper effect internally. So we prepared a reduction of aconite and, that night, we administered it in the form of a drink to Vampirate Three – the sole female of the trio."

Cheng Li glanced up, waiting for Jacoby to continue.

"We destroyed her," he confirmed.

"With this aconite reduction alone?" Cheng Li said.

Jacoby nodded. "We call it the aconite-cap," he said with a smirk.

Cheng Li saw Connor wince at Jacoby's black joke. She had noticed how silent and withdrawn Connor had become as this interview had gone on. She knew that he had assisted Jacoby and Jasmine with their experiments but, as she had predicted, he had clearly found it hard to achieve the same level of objectivity the other two had brought to the task. Well, this was not a complete surprise. Clearly, she needed to have another word with him later. But, for now, she was anxious to hear the final part of their findings.

"At this point, we only had one remaining Vampirate," Jacoby said, "Vampirate One – the one who had attacked me before. We had covered his cage and had managed to weaken him with more of the aconite petals but we were unable to trick him into taking any of the poison orally." He paused. "So we had to resort to other means."

Again, Cheng Li raised an eyebrow.

"We staked him," Jacoby said. "Well, I say *staked*. It would be more accurate to say that we *stabbed* him."

Cheng Li was surprised. "You dispatched Vampirate One with a regular pirate sword?"

Jacoby shook his head. "Not with a sword, no. With a candlestick. Hang on a moment." He rummaged in his pack and produced the candlestick, setting it on the table, alongside the hawthorn stake and the sprig of aconite.

Cheng Li ran her finger over the candlestick, intrigued.

"He crumbled, much like Vampirate Two did," said Jacoby. "Only, this time, we watched and waited and he *didn't* reconstitute himself."

"You're absolutely sure about that?" said Cheng Li.

"Yes," said Jacoby, seeking the support of his two comrades. Both Jasmine and Connor nodded grimly.

"And what is this candlestick made of?" Cheng Li asked.

"Silver," said Jasmine. "We came across some accounts during our research of how silver has been utilised to destroy werewolves."

Jacoby nodded. "And we thought what's bad for werewolves might just be equally bad for Vampirates."

Cheng Li made another note, then began flipping back through her pages. "So you've tried every substance on your list, from garlic to silver?"

"Yes," agreed Jasmine. "And we have identified three substances from our list which have tested positive as highly toxic to Vampirates."

"So what can we conclude?" asked Cheng Li. It was clearly a rhetorical question. "We can conclude that though these substance wreak much damage in isolation, a combination of all three is likely to have the most destructive impact."

Cheng Li gestured towards the eclectic array of items set upon her desk. "Hawthorn, aconite and silver." She smiled. "A dangerous trio. Rather like the three of you!"

Jacoby grinned. Jasmine looked serious. Connor grimaced and then glanced away.

"So," Cheng Li continued, "our weaponry should incorporate all three of these substances."

"If possible, Captain," said Jasmine.

"What are you thinking?" Jacoby asked.

"Give me some time," Cheng Li said, standing and looking out of the window. "Thank you, all of you, for your very thorough work."

As day began to fade once more into evening, Connor was on the deck of *The Tiger*, practising some sword moves in an isolated spot. He was so engrossed that he did not hear the captain's stealth-like approach. She was able to stand and watch him execute his moves for several moments before he stopped and turned, at last aware of her presence. Their eyes met.

"Your swordplay gets better and better," Cheng Li observed.

"Thank you." He was clearly awkward in her presence and they both knew it.

"Put down your sword, Connor," Cheng Li said. "We need to have a little talk."

He slid the rapier back into its holster, set it on the floor and walked over to the deck-rail to join her.

"You didn't much enjoy the experiments we conducted on the Vampirates, did you?"

"You know the answer to that," he said. "It was hard. *Really* hard. Not so much for Jacoby and Jasmine but for me . . . yes. I don't know why."

Cheng Li smiled. "It's obvious," she said, "isn't it? It's because

272

you have had direct, personal, contact with some of the Vampirates. And you know how close your sister has grown to some of them."

"Yes," Connor said. "Yes, that's all true." He stared off into the horizon.

"I gave you an opportunity to remove yourself from this mission," Cheng Li said. "Remember? That first night in the secret cache."

Connor nodded, then turned back to face the captain. "I don't *want* to opt out of this mission," he said. "I want to be a valued member of this crew. More than anything, I want that." His eyes were wet with tears of frustration. "It's just hard for me to go down this route when Grace . . ." He changed tack. "I did talk to her, like we agreed I would. I tried to persuade her to leave them."

"You talked to her?" Cheng Li was puzzled. "When? How?"

He was stonily silent.

"Connor, this is important. Talk to me."

He sighed. "Grace has this ability to astral travel. I know how far-fetched it sounds but it's happened twice now. She comes to see me and we talk to each other. She isn't a physical presence – if I try to reach out to her, my hand slides right through her, but it *is* really her. I'm not imagining it. You have to believe me."

"I do believe you," Cheng Li said. "We've both come such a long way since we first met. There are many things I believe now which my younger self would have been distinctly dubious about." She smiled once more. "So, you talked to Grace and tried to persuade her to part company from the Vampirates?"

"Yes," Connor nodded. "But she is adamant that she won't." He couldn't tell Cheng Li the full extent of Grace's dark imaginings: that she – and he – were related to the Vampirates. He could never tell her that. Why did things have to be so complicated? All he wanted was to fit in somewhere, *here*. All he craved was to be a good and trusted pirate but now he was even failing at that.

"Connor," Cheng Li said. "You're doing your best. I see that. This isn't easy for you."

"I've let you down," he said. "You gave me a second chance and I've failed you."

Cheng Li shook her head. "Stop being so hard on yourself. You did exactly what I asked of you – you spoke to Grace. And then, although it was understandably difficult for you, you assisted Jacoby and Jasmine with their experiments."

"I tried," he said.

"It's going to be easier from hereon in," Cheng Li said. "Our experiments are over. Now, we start planning for our attack on Sidorio. On *Sidorio*, remember? We're *not* going after the Vampirates Grace is with. Neither she nor they are in any immediate danger."

"Not now, but . . ."

"You need to take one day at a time, Connor," said Cheng Li. "There will be plenty of time, *after* this mission is completed, for you to talk to Grace at length. And not simply by astral travel. I'll take you to wherever she is. I'll talk to her too, if it helps. But, for now, please be assured that she is safe."

He nodded. "Thank you," he said, attempting a smile. "I mean it. Thank you, for everything."

Cheng Li nodded. "You're welcome," she said, lightly. "And now, are you ready to hear about the next part of your mission?"

He nodded.

"I'm sending you back to Lantao," she said. The very word stirred pleasing memories in Connor's mind. "Yes," she continued, "I thought that might bring a smile to your face. You'll meet with Master Yin and commission him to make new weaponry for us. Fifty swords, made of silver – but also incorporating hawthorn and aconite. I think Master Yin will enjoy the challenge, don't you? And the trip will do you good too, I think."

Connor nodded.

"Prepare your things," Cheng Li said. "You'll leave first thing in the morning. And I anticipate you'll need to stay in Lantao for a week or so."

"Sounds good to me," Connor said, reaching for his sword and hooded sweater, both of which lay on the deck floor.

Cheng Li began walking away across the deck. Suddenly, she stopped and glanced over her shoulder. "Oh, I forgot to say before. Jasmine will go with you – to keep you company on the journey."

"Jasmine!" Connor exclaimed. He loved the thought of sailing to Lantao with Jasmine, of introducing her to Master Yin and his excitable daughter, Bo. But there were complicating factors . . . "Erm, how's Jacoby going to feel about me sailing off to Lantao for a week with his girlfriend?"

Cheng Li's eyes seemed to twinkle in the starlight. "Let me take care of the deputy captain," she said. "I have plenty to keep him busy here in the run-up to the attack." With that, she turned and strode off, bristling with purpose.

Connor lingered on deck for only a moment more, the sky darkening around him. Filled with a sudden, surprising surge of happiness, he jumped up and punched the air. Then he ran inside to start packing.

CHAPTER THIRTY-FOUR

The Chrysalis

"Grace," Lorcan said. "What you're going through at the moment, these strange physical symptoms. It isn't the flu. And I don't think it's stress, like Oskar says."

"What is it then?" Grace asked, urgently.

"You're in a stage of metamorphosis," Lorcan said. "And it's exerting a powerful force on your body."

"What *kind* of metamorphosis?" Grace asked, feeling suddenly alert.

"It's like when a caterpillar transforms into a butterfly," Lorcan said. "You know how that works? The caterpillar sheds her skin and the skin hardens to form a chrysalis which contains and protects the caterpillar while she changes into a butterfly." Lorcan nodded at Grace. "Well, right now you're inside that chrysalis. That's why everything feels so strange and confused to you. Grace, the most amazing changes are happening inside you."

Grace comprehended his words but she was still unsure exactly what he meant. "These changes," she said, "are they a good thing?"

Lorcan smiled and squeezed her hand. "I think you *will* feel good about them," he said. "But it's a major transformation, Grace. You need to pace yourself, to take one step at a time."

She took a breath. "All right," she said. "All right, I think I can do that. But you have to tell me more. I need to know what I'm becoming."

"Yes," he said. "Yes, I know." He glanced down, then back up at her eyes. "Grace, what I'm about to tell you is going to change everything for you. It's going to change the way you think about yourself and about me, about your mother and Dexter and Connor. Everything you thought you knew. Everything you thought you were. That's all about to change. I've been trying to protect you from this . . ."

Grace frowned. She had been feeling off-kilter before Lorcan had started speaking. Now, his words sounded ominous. "I don't understand. If the transformation is a good thing, what is there to protect me from?"

"The transformation itself *is* good," Lorcan said. "But like I say, it will change the way you think about things, about people who are close to you. That's why I wanted to be the one to tell you, but we had to wait until you were ready."

"I am ready," Grace said, sitting upright in bed.

"Yes," Lorcan said. "Yes, I know that now." He squeezed her hand. "I'll take this slowly, Grace. If there's anything you don't understand, just tell me, all right?"

She nodded, her heart racing with suspense.

"Grace," said Lorcan. "You're not a regular mortal."

"I knew it!" she exclaimed. "I'm a vampire, aren't I? And Connor is too!"

"Not exactly," Lorcan said. "Grace, you are both *dhampirs*."

"Dhampirs?" Grace repeated. "Are they a kind of vampire?"

"Yes," Lorcan nodded. "Put simply, you are half vampire. A dhampir is the child of a mortal mother and a Vampirate father."

Grace felt herself flush hot and cold but she was unsure

whether it was due to the metamorphosis Lorcan had referred to before or simply the shock of his revelation. A mortal mother and a Vampirate father . . .

"So I was right. Dexter *was* a Vampirate!"

Lorcan's eyes were intense. "I'll come to that later. First things first. You have to understand the implications of this. You and Connor are both dhampirs. Like Vampirates, you are blessed with immortality, but you are stronger. You do not have our weaknesses."

Grace tried to keep up. "I'm immortal?" she said. She understood the implications of the word but she could not equate them with herself. Lorcan had just told her that she was special, that she was going to live for ever, but she could not truly believe it. She felt unchanged from before – weak with fatigue and flu-like symptoms, perhaps – but otherwise the same old Grace as ever. But somehow she had always known she was different. She wracked her brains now for some evidence, searching for something to hold on to, something to make this feel real, concrete.

"Do I need to take blood?" she asked. "Is that why my body is changing right now? Will I need a donor?"

"I believe that's a matter of choice," Lorcan said. "I shall let Mosh Zu talk to you about that, in due course. He can explain it better than me. You're the first dhampir I've ever met."

Grace sighed.

"Don't rush at this," Lorcan said. "It's a lot to take in at once. You need to give yourself time."

"Is that why Sally came back?" Grace asked. "To prepare me?"

"Yes," Lorcan said. "Yes, I believe so."

"But I don't understand," said Grace. "If that's the case, then why did she leave before telling me herself? Why didn't she finish the story?"

"She wanted to," Lorcan said. "More than anything she wanted to, but she just couldn't in the end. That's why I said I'd do it for her."

"You?" Grace said, looking up at into his eyes, his azure-blue eyes. The eyes which had welcomed her to *The Nocturne* that very first night.

Suddenly, she found the fixed point in all this she had been searching for. "You!" she said once more, but this time it was no longer a question.

"What about me?" he asked.

Feverish as she was, she almost blurted out the words. *Now that I'm immortal too, you and I can be together. Always. There's nothing to stand in our way.* But in spite of her fever, an internal censor prevented her from speaking the words. Instead, she merely smiled. Suddenly everything made sense, pure and perfect sense.

But Lorcan did not return her smile. He was looking anxious.

"Lorcan," she asked, "what's wrong? What aren't you telling me?"

"Shhh," he said, managing a smile. "Did I say that anything was wrong? I told you before, Grace. This is a wonderful transformation you are going through. You just have to give yourself time." He turned his gaze from her, briefly. "I have to go now. The Feast will begin soon. Will you be all right on your own? I can stop by later, or have Oskar or one of the others . . ."

Grace shook her head. "I'm fine here." Then a fresh thought occurred to her. "Why don't I come with you? To the Feast! I came before."

Lorcan shook his head. "It's too soon," he said. "You need to rest."

"I'm tired of resting," Grace said. "From what I can gather, all I've been doing for days is resting. It would do me good to get out . . ."

"I'm sorry, Grace," said Lorcan. "But it's too soon. You have to trust me on this. You're experiencing a sudden burst of energy now but it's fragile. You'll need to rest again soon. Trust me."

She sighed but she knew it was futile. There was no one more stubborn than Lorcan Furey when he chose to be. All right then, let him go. Let him go to the Feast. But while he was away, she wouldn't sleep. She would sit up and think all of this through. She'd put the pieces of the jigsaw together and work out exactly what he was keeping from her.

"All right, then," she said. "I'll stay here and rest."

"It's for the best," he said, bringing the covers up over her once more. Ever the dutiful nursemaid.

He leaned close then and gazed down at her. She smiled up at him. He was so beautiful. Was this the moment she had been waiting for? Was he, at last, about to kiss her?

"I'll see you later," he said, then bowed his head and kissed her tenderly on her forehead.

In spite of her disappointment, his kiss was soothing. It left a pleasing chill on her fevered brow long after he had made his way to the door and out to join the others at the Feast.

After Lorcan had gone, Grace tried to hold on to everything he had said. But it had been so much to take in and she was incredibly tired, more tired even than in the aftermath of the near-fatal shipwreck. She fell into a deep sleep, full of strange dreams. Conversations she had had replayed in her mind. She awoke with a start, realising what she'd missed. Dexter Tempest wasn't a Vampirate. Her mother had been very clear about that. And if that was the case, then Dexter *wasn't* the twins' father.

Grace began rewinding the conversations she'd had with her mother. She couldn't be a hundred per cent sure but she didn't think Sally had once referred to Dexter as the twins' dad or father.

She had always called him by his name or simply "he". It was as if Sally had been giving Grace a message throughout their conversations, but Grace had only picked up on it too late.

So Grace and Connor *were* half-vampire: dhampirs. And their true father – their "biological" father – was a Vampirate. But who? Again Grace began reflecting upon her recent conversations and experiences. Sally had been Sidorio's donor but it was clear that their relationship was strictly business. She was, to coin Oskar's phrase, simply Sidorio's Mobile Blood Supply. But which of the other Vampirates could it be?

Grace felt her heart begin to race. Who had been the first Vampirate to welcome Sally with open arms? Lorcan. Who had been the one exchanging secret looks and smiles with Sally? Lorcan. Who, throughout their relationship, had blown hot and cold towards Grace – suggesting intimacy one moment, then just as suddenly backing away? Lorcan. And who had been even more evasive and furtive around Grace since Sally's arrival? Lorcan.

Was Lorcan the twins' father? He couldn't be. Could he? It would change everything . . . Just as he'd said.

CHAPTER THIRTY-FIVE

Return to Lantao

"Connor! Connor Tempest!"

As Connor jumped down onto the wooden pier he hardly had a chance to catch his breath before a small bundle of energy bounced into him and hugged him. Looking down, he saw the beaming face of Bo Yin, the swordsmith's daughter. "Connor! Connor Tempest! It *is* you!"

"Hello Bo," he said, shaking with laughter as Bo Yin released him from her clutches. "That's quite a welcome!"

"I'm very pleased to see you," said Bo. "I was on my way to the fish market. There I was, minding my own business, watching the taxi boats, and then I see Connor Tempest! What brings you back to Lantao so soon?"

"I have a new commission for your father," Connor said. "From Captain Li."

Bo Yin looked understandably puzzled. "A new commission? But all those other swords he made before, what happened to them? Was there something wrong?"

Connor shook his head. "Of course not," he said. "They were perfect, like all Master Yin's work. I've come to talk to him about something extra. Something special."

"Intriguing!" said Bo Yin, smiling from ear to ear. Suddenly her expression changed. "And who's this?"

They turned as Jasmine climbed out of the taxi boat, having concluded a lengthy discussion with its oarsman. Jasmine slipped down her sunglasses and strode along the pier. The oarsman seemed transfixed by her long tanned legs as she walked away. Joining Connor, she shook her head. "Makes you wish they had a course in negotiation at Pirate Academy!" she said, then caught sight of Bo. Smiling, she extended her hand. "Hello, I'm Jasmine Peacock."

"And I am Bo Yin. *Very* good friend of Connor Tempest."

"Really?" Jasmine said. "Well, any good friend of Connor's is a friend of mine."

Bo Yin nodded, a grin dancing on her face. "Come on!" she said. "Come up and talk to my father." She looped her arm through Connor's and led him briskly along the pier, the fish market already a distant memory. Grinning, Jasmine followed in their wake, soaking up the sights, sounds and smells of the bustling little harbour.

Bo Yin leaned in close to Connor and lowered her voice to a whisper. "Connor Tempest has a girlfriend," she said.

"No," Connor said, shaking his head. "Just a friend."

"Jasmine Peacock. *Beautiful* name. *Beautiful* girl!" declared Bo Yin.

"Perhaps, but—" began Connor.

"Lots to catch up on," said the irrepressible Bo, winking as she led him up the stairs to the stilt building which housed her father's workshop.

"Back so soon, Bo Yin?" came a familiar voice from beyond a beaded curtain.

"Yes, Pop. And I bring guests!"

"Guests? We're not expecting any guests! What's all this

283

nonsense?" In a moment, a hand appeared, then a face. And then Master Yin shuffled into the room, a diminutive figure. Seeing Connor, he smiled. "Ah, *that* explains the commotion. It looks like Bo Yin's wishes came true."

Connor blushed. "Good afternoon, sir," he said. "I'm sorry to arrive unannounced. This is my comrade, Jasmine Peacock."

"It's a great honour to meet you, Master Yin," said Jasmine, bowing before him.

"Welcome, welcome!" said Master Yin, shaking her hand. "It's a hot afternoon and you must be parched from your journey. Bo Yin, perhaps some lychee juice would be in order?"

"Coming right up, Pop!" said Bo Yin, hurrying into the kitchen.

"Well, my friends," said Master Yin. "Come and sit. Sit! Make yourselves comfortable and tell me, what brings you back to Lantao?"

"What do you think, sir?" Connor asked. It had been several minutes since he had handed Master Yin the note detailing Cheng Li's requirements and, so far, the swordsmith had made no response. Now, at last, he lifted his moonlike face.

"An intriguing proposition," he said. "For many years, I have crafted swords for pirate captains from all over the oceans. But this is the first time I have been asked to make swords for such a purpose."

"Are there really vampire pirates?" Bo Yin asked, her eyes wide with excitement and wonder.

"Yes." Connor nodded.

"Cool!" said Bo Yin. "Have you seen them? What do they look like?"

"Quiet, Bo Yin!" said her father. "I cannot think with your ceaseless chatter. Doesn't your pet need feeding?"

"Sinbad!" Bo Yin cried. "I forgot all about Sinbad. Thank

you, Pop." She jumped down from the table and ran out of the room.

Master Yin sighed and glanced down again at the note. Then, saying nothing, he set it back onto the table. Was this his way of saying no?

"I can help you," said the swordsmith, "but it will take time."

"We don't have much time," said Connor, unable to keep the anxiety out of his voice.

"This is a new departure," Master Yin said. "I cannot be rushed."

"How long do you need?" asked Jasmine, in a placatory tone.

"At least two weeks," said Master Yin.

"Two weeks!" Connor said. "We were hoping for half that."

Master Yin shrugged, extending his arms, his flattened palms raised upwards.

"Is there any chance," Jasmine said, hesitantly, "I mean, would it be at all possible to do this within ten days?"

Master Yin looked straight into Jasmine's eyes. "Ten days, you say? All right, then. Ten days." He turned to Connor. "And while I work on the swords, you will both be our guests here."

"That's kind of you," Connor said, "but we have our boat and provisions."

"No, no, no!" said Master Yin. "I am doing you a favour and now you will do me one. For ten days, you will be our guests. And for ten days, you will keep crazy daughter out of my hair!" He extended his hand to Connor's. "Deal?"

Connor grinned at the swordsmith. "Deal," he said, shaking the old man's hand.

"I think Miss Yin has a bit of a crush on you," said Jasmine, as they taxied back to collect more of their things from the boat.

"Really?" said Connor. "I think she's just grateful for some young company. Any company, in fact. Her father's *so* grouchy with her."

"Trust me, Connor. I'm a girl. I know a crush when I see one."

"Bo's only twelve," Connor said. "I'm fourteen."

"Girls mature faster than boys," Jasmine said with a smile. "And you can't deny that she's very pretty. You two are perfect for each other."

"Except," said Connor, shaking his head, "I've always had a thing for older women."

It was Jasmine's turn to laugh. "Really? That's news, Connor. So tell me who's your type? Captain Li? No, she's probably too *young* for you. How about Captain Quivers? Or Ma Kettle?"

"Not *that* old," said Connor softly, daring to look Jasmine straight in the eye. "Only a couple of years older than me."

"Really?" said Jasmine, her lips framed in a smile. To his surprise and delight, she didn't look away but instead held his gaze. He was taken back to the first time he'd seen her, limbering up for the morning run on the academy porch. Then, he had been dazzled by her silky black hair and her green eyes. Now he was more than dazzled. But Jasmine was Jacoby's girlfriend. And Jacoby was his friend. This couldn't happen. Could it?

"All settled, Connor Tempest?" asked Bo Yin, popping her head around the door to his room. She had caught him changing into a clean shirt and, as he turned to face her, bare-chested, she flushed with embarrassment.

"Sorry!" she said. "So sorry! I'll come back later."

"It's OK," he said. Maybe Jasmine was right. Maybe Bo *did* have just the tiniest of crushes on him. It was flattering. She was a nice girl. And, now that Jasmine had mentioned it, very pretty.

286

"I just wanted you to meet Sinbad," said Bo Yin.

"Sinbad?" Connor asked. Did Bo Yin have a brother he hadn't known about? Then he remembered. Bo Yin had mentioned Sinbad before. After her father had asked her if she had fed her pet. What kind of pet would Bo have, he wondered? A rabbit? A little songbird?

"Come on, Sinbad! Don't be shy!" said Bo Yin, crouching on her knees.

Connor came to kneel beside her, waiting expectantly.

Suddenly the most hideous creature he had ever seen in his life came scurrying into the room. A cross between a bat and a rat, it had mad luminous yellow eyes, rodent-like teeth and oversized ears. Stray wisps of hair stuck up from its forehead as if it had recently suffered a terrible shock. But strangest of all were the creature's paws. It appeared to have thumbs and fingers. They were all long and thin, curved and wizened like the fingers of a fairy-tale witch. But, on each hand, the middle finger was at least three times the length of the others. The creature gazed up at Connor, then glanced down and proceeded to sniff his shoes.

"Ha! Ha!" said Bo Yin. "Sinbad likes you! Sinbad likes your shoes!"

"What on earth *is* it?" Connor asked.

"He's an aye-aye," Bo said. "Isn't he cute?"

Connor shook his head. Cute wasn't the first word which sprang to mind.

As the sun set in Lantao harbour, Connor set the table for dinner, while Bo busied herself at the stove making laksa, assisted by Jasmine.

"Have a taste. Tell me what it needs," said Bo, passing a spoon to Jasmine. Bo watched intently as Jasmine blew on the broth, then took a sip.

"More shrimp paste?" inquired Bo. "Or lime juice? Perhaps some extra chilli?"

"Nothing," said Jasmine. "Absolutely nothing! Bo, this is the most delicious thing I've ever tasted!"

Bo beamed from ear to ear. "Maybe I can come back with you and be Cook aboard *The Tiger*."

"You'd get my vote," Jasmine said.

"Careful!" joked Connor. "She really doesn't need any encouragement."

"What's so funny?" Bo asked. "Cheng Li is a pirate. Jasmine Peacock is a pirate. Why not Bo Yin too?"

Connor flushed. He'd forgotten how seriously Bo Yin took her dreams of being a pirate. It seemed that the more Master Yin poured cold water on them, the stronger they grew.

"Of course you can be whatever you want to be, Bo," he said, with a smile. "But you wouldn't want to leave Sinbad all alone now, would you?"

Bo frowned and turned her back. Connor could tell he had upset her. He'd have to learn to treat her with more sensitivity. For now, he decided to go and check in on Master Yin. He found him inside the workshop, stirring a pan. Like daughter, like father.

"I'm sorry," said Connor. "I did knock but I don't think you heard me. Are you eating in here? Bo Yin is busy making the best-ever laksa."

Master Yin beckoned Connor over. "I'm not making soup, Mister Tempest," he said. He took a dishcloth and wrapped it around the saucepan, then carried the hot pan over to his workbench. A sword was waiting there. Master Yin picked up a paintbrush and dipped it in the pan, then began painting the tip of the sword with the varnish-like substance.

"What is that?" Connor asked.

"Take one silver sword. Paint with compound of aconite and

hawthorn. Silver, aconite and hawthorn. All poisonous to Vampirates." He lifted the sword and passed it by its hilt to Connor. "There!" he announced. "A recipe for success. The first of the fifty swords Captain Li requested."

"Wow!" Connor said, holding the sword in his hand.

"Yes, wow," said Master Yin. "Enough for one day, I think. My stomach is rumbling. What's that you say about laksa?"

CHAPTER THIRTY-SIX

A Conspiracy of Silence

Grace was waiting, alone, on the deck of *The Nocturne* as the sun set. It seemed to take an eternity. Were some sunsets actually slower than others or was it just that when you were waiting so urgently for the sun to set, the moon took forever to rise and darkness to come?

She was tempted to look over the edge of the ship, to see if there was any sign that Darcy was coming to life. But she didn't dare. She didn't want to give Darcy any clue that she was waiting for her and, whilst the figurehead was inanimate until the hours of darkness, her eyes, even while wooden and painted, were sharp.

So Grace was resigned to standing on the deck and waiting, listening out for the strange cracking sound as Darcy's limbs came back to life and then the splash as she dived down into the waters below for her nightly dip.

At last, she heard it. *Crack. Splash.* Grace's heart thudded. She'd been waiting all day for this meeting but now it was upon her, she felt exceptionally nervous.

She withdrew to the shelter of the mainsail so that she would control Darcy's first sighting of her. It felt a little cruel to play such tricks on a good friend like Darcy but she knew that she had to take her by surprise; it was vital in this situation.

She watched as Darcy climbed up onto the deck and retrieved the towel which had been left hanging for her earlier. As she began drying herself, Grace made her move, stepping free from the shadows.

"Good evening, Darcy," she said.

"Grace!" Darcy was wide-eyed. "You gave me a start. Where did you suddenly spring from?"

"I'm sorry, I didn't mean to give you a shock," Grace lied. "I just wanted to see you."

"It's certainly good to see you," Darcy said, smiling. "I've been worried about you, and I've been meaning to visit . . ."

Grace shook her head. "It's OK. Even if you had done, I think I'd probably have been asleep. I seem to spend most of the time sleeping at the moment."

Darcy nodded, drying her hair. "It's probably exactly what you need under the circumstances."

"Under the circumstances?" Grace asked, raising an eyebrow.

"After the shock of your mother and all that," Darcy said. She began folding the wet towel in her hands.

"Darcy," Grace said, looking her friend straight in the eye. "Darcy, I know."

Darcy looked suddenly awkward. She fumbled and the towel fell to the deck. "You know what? What are you talking about, Grace?"

Grace stooped to pick up the towel and pass it back. "I know that I'm a dhampir, Darcy – that Connor and I are half mortal and half vampire."

Darcy's eyes widened. "You know!" she repeated.

Grace nodded. "Lorcan told me."

Darcy's eyebrows shot up.

"You seem surprised," Grace said.

291

Darcy attempted a recovery. "No, not really. Well, how do you feel about this news?"

Grace smiled. "I'm fine with it. Happy, actually. I had my suspicions that I was . . . like you."

Darcy smiled back at her. "Yes," she said. "Me too. We've been good friends, since we first met, haven't we, Grace? And now, we're more like sisters!" She reached out and drew Grace into a hug, then hesitated. "Oh sorry, I'm still a bit damp! I ought to go inside and change my clothes."

"That's OK," Grace said. "I don't mind. You're right. We are like sisters. And sisters shouldn't have secrets from one another." She pulled back and stared once more into Darcy's huge brown eyes.

"Secrets?" Darcy asked, nervously.

"I need you to tell me something," Grace said. "And I need an honest answer."

"Of course," Darcy nodded. "But can it wait until I've sounded the nightfall bell and lit the deck lanterns? I don't want to neglect my duties."

"It won't take a moment," Grace said. "And, afterwards, I'll help you with the lanterns. Darcy, I know that Dexter Tempest wasn't a Vampirate – so he wasn't my true father."

Darcy froze. "Oh," she said.

Grace smiled to herself. Until now, it had only been a guess. Now, Darcy's expression gave her confirmation.

"Darcy," she continued. "I know that you know who my real father is. And I need you to tell me."

Darcy's eyes glanced nervously at Grace, then away in the direction of the bell. "I really ought to sound it," she said.

"Darcy," Grace said, gripping her arm. "You said it yourself. You're a good friend of mine, more like a sister. You *have* to tell me this."

Darcy frowned and shook her head. "It's not as simple as

that, Grace. I wish it were. But I'm under strict instructions not to talk to you about this." She sighed deeply. "That's why I haven't been to visit you in your cabin. I've been *desperate* to see you and know you're doing OK, but they told me I mustn't."

"They?"

Darcy nodded, without elaborating. "They know how loose-tongued I am, how hard I find it to keep things from the people I care about."

Grace sighed. She felt she was getting closer to the truth. If only she could crack Darcy.

"Darcy," she said, "if I tell you some names, you don't even have to say yes or no. You could just nod or maybe simply brush your hair away from your face. You could even go off and ring the nightfall bell. It wouldn't be like you were telling me anything. Simply doing your regular duties."

She looked intently at her friend. Darcy had the appearance of a cat cornered in a dark alley by a more dangerous predator. There was no time to lose.

"Mosh Zu," Grace said. Darcy stared back at her impassively.

Grace digested the information. Time to try another name.

"Sidorio," she said. Darcy frowned at the mention of his name but, again, was silent.

"The captain," Grace said. Darcy frowned once more. Again, she was silent.

Grace took a breath. The stakes had risen now.

"Lorcan," she said.

"Lorcan!" exclaimed Darcy.

It was a different reaction to the other names. Grace decided to push further. "Yes, Lorcan," she said. "It all fits. Every time we get close, he finds a reason to push me away. He's always looked out for me, to the point of going blind to save me. And I know that his blindness was in part psychological, because of things he was wrestling with – like having a daughter, perhaps, and

293

not being able to tell her the truth . . ." Darcy's mouth gaped open. Grace nodded and continued. "And when Sally emerged, during the captain's healing catharsis, there was something in the way she and Lorcan looked at each other. A deep bond between them. And a couple of times afterwards, I caught sight of them together and they seemed so close."

"They *were* c-c-c-close," Darcy stammered. "But that doesn't mean . . ."

"Yes?" Grace nodded once more. "Darcy, you're not betraying anyone by telling me the truth."

Darcy frowned again.

"You've already practically told me," Grace said.

"I have?"

"Don't you remember? I told you how I felt about Lorcan, that I had romantic feelings towards him. We were talking about you and Jez and me and Lorcan, remember?"

Darcy nodded.

"And you said that Lorcan *did* have feelings for me, but maybe not *those* kind of feelings . . ."

"Grace," Darcy said, "this is very complicated. Really, I'm not the one to talk to about this."

"It's true, though, isn't it? Lorcan *is* my father. It's OK to tell me. I'll deal with it." She smiled.

Darcy shook her head firmly. "I can't talk to you about this. I made a promise. And I have to honour that promise, even if it makes things difficult between us. Just try to understand that no one is trying to hurt you here. We all care for you very much. Everything we've done has been in order to protect you."

"Protect me? But how—"

"Grace, I really do have to sound that bell," Darcy said. "I'm so sorry that you're having to go through this. But please, wait for the truth to come to you. Don't go around like a bull in a china shop trying to force it out. It won't help."

And, with that, Darcy walked off purposefully to sound the bell.

Grace stood alone once more. No closer to the truth. If even Darcy had been sworn to secrecy then this must be very serious indeed.

Back in her cabin, Grace's mind went over and over her conversation with Darcy. Had her friend indicated that Lorcan was indeed the twins' father? She had certainly reacted more strongly to his name than to any of the others. And the more Grace reflected upon her own reasoning, as she had presented it to Darcy, the more concrete her case seemed. But, if Lorcan *was* her father, why were they all so intent on keeping this from her? Clearly he had some explaining to do. Her mother, after all, had loved another man – Dexter. But knowing Sally and knowing Lorcan, there must be a decent, reasonable explanation to this. Even if it was that her mother had simply loved two men – one mortal, one Vampirate. Grace could live with that. She could even live with the disappointment of knowing that Lorcan wasn't quite the person she had thought he was. He would still be a key figure in her life.

She just needed to know the truth. But how would she ever find it if the Vampirates had agreed upon a conspiracy of silence?

CHAPTER THIRTY-SEVEN

A Brutal Romance

Lady Lockwood awoke on her silk-covered chaise-longue, in a mild state of confusion. Above her, in place of her cabin's hand-painted ceiling, she saw stars. She turned and found Sidorio at her side, watching her intently.

"What's wrong, my love?" he asked.

"I'm on my chaise-longue," she said. "Which is usually in my cabin. But, unless I'm very much mistaken, I'm up on the deck of my ship."

He smiled softly at her. "You're not mistaken. I carried you up here, chair and all."

"*You* did?" She smiled quizzically at him. "Whatever for?"

He pointed above them. "There are so many stars out tonight," he said. "I wanted them to be the first thing you saw when you woke up."

"Oh Sidorio," Lady Lola said, sitting upright. "You're such an extraordinary creature – so capable of romance and gentleness one minute and of extreme evil the next."

"Thank you, my love," he said. He would never tire of her compliments. "So," he asked, "how did you enjoy our little outing tonight?"

296

Lady Lola smiled as she thought back to their earlier adventures. It was a good while since she had hunted blood prey for herself. Usually she relied on her very able crew and then drank, at her leisure, from one of her elegant Venetian glasses. Even with John Kuo, she had had his body drained before taking more than a taste of his blood. This, she knew, was not Sidorio's way. Though he humoured her by drinking from her antique goblets, he much preferred to take blood direct from the source.

So it seemed only fair that as he had deigned to try things her way, so she should step into his shoes and experience his world.

"It was rather exhilarating," she said, her face a little flushed. "Not something I'd necessarily want to do every night but, once in a while – especially with you." She paused. "It was wonderful to see you in action, Sid. You were utterly merciless, my darling. I'll never forget the way you punctured that thorax!"

He blushed, clearly embarrassed by her flattery.

She turned and found a decanter and two glasses on a table at her side. Once more, she gazed at Sidorio in wonder.

He shrugged. "I just thought you might be thirsty again when you woke."

She shook her head. "You really do think of everything. Can I pour *you* a glass?"

"Why not?" he said.

She thought how fragile the thirteenth-century glass looked in Sidorio's beefy fingers. He was far older even than the glass but he was so strong, so vital. Any moment now he would surely snap the glass in two. But no. He held it carefully there in his hands – the same hands which she had observed in their full brutality a few hours earlier. She noted with pleasure how he had learned to swirl the liquid in the glass – so as to release the finer subtleties of its 'nose' – and even to sip at it rather than to down the contents in one.

"You know," she said, "I think you and I are rubbing off on

each other." She sipped her own drink contentedly, then noticed he was watching her very closely. "What is it, my darling?" she asked.

"Nothing," he said. "Sometimes I just like looking at you."

"Oh Sid, come over here and sit beside me. It'll be a squeeze – you're such a brute of a thing – but I want to be close to you." She made room for him to sit on the chaise-longue. "That's it," she said, "you stretch your gargantuan legs out that way, and I'll just snuggle in close." She set her wine-glass down on the deck. "Comfy?"

"Yes," he said, planting a kiss on her head.

"You've not had very much affection in your life, my darling, have you?" Lady Lockwood said. "As great as you are, as pre-eminent in your world – in *our* world – I think you've been a little starved of close company and companionship. Am I right?"

Sidorio shrugged and drank from his glass. "I have Stukeley and Johnny to keep me entertained," he said with a grin. "And another few hundred crew reporting in to me."

"Well, yes. But they can't offer you the same kind of companionship that I can, now can they?"

Sidorio laughed and shook his head. "No, Lola. I'd much sooner look at you than their ugly mugs."

"Anyhow," she continued, "I meant farther back than that. Back when you first crossed. All that time spent alone, wandering the world, before you found your way to *The Nocturne*." She turned to look up at him. "And even then, you didn't really fit in. Their way of doing things could never be *your* way. It was only a matter of time before you and the captain came to blows."

He frowned. "Are you *trying* to make me feel bad?"

"Of course not. Quite the opposite. I'm just saying that you must have been lonely at times. And, frankly, so have I. Perhaps it's the price we have each paid for our greatness."

"Perhaps," he reflected, then asked, "Are you lonely now?"

"With you?" she said. "No! Never with you."

"Well, then," he said, with a grin. "We'll just have to spend more time together, won't we?"

Lola nodded and settled herself against Sidorio's chest, closing her eyes. She lay there, gently dozing under the starlight. Sidorio reached forward and drew the blanket over Lola's sleeping body. He didn't want her to feel any discomfort whatsoever. It seemed the most natural thing in the world to protect and care for her. But the thought unleashed a sudden spiral of panic within him. What was happening to him? Was he losing his edge? The thought made him suddenly jump up.

Lady Lockwood awoke with a start. "What's wrong?" she asked. Sidorio was pacing back and forth across the deck, finally coming to a standstill against the deck-rail.

"What is it?" She rose to her feet, wrapping the blanket around her shoulders and following him to the edge of the deck.

He paused, attempting to collect his thoughts. "It's *not* you," he began. "It's me. The person I am when I'm with you. I become someone else. I thought I was bad, evil. I'm comfortable with that. It fits me just right, like a well-worn glove. Then you come along and awaken all these thoughts and feelings in me. Feelings that I didn't think I had. That I was even capable of." He traced the chiselled outline of her cheek. "I don't like it, Lola – it makes me feel out of kilter."

She smiled. "I understand what you're saying, Sidorio, I really do. But don't you see? It's possible to love me, to care for me, and to still be evil. I am, after all. Think back to this evening, when we stalked that couple together. Wasn't *that* evil? And wasn't it fun?"

"Yes," he agreed. "It was fun."

"And wasn't it *more* fun because we did it together? It wasn't you on your own or with one of your crew. You were with *me* – the one you love and who loves you back. And we were both evil. Very very evil."

"Yes," he said. "Yes, we were."

"Trust me," she said, "if I seriously thought you were losing the capacity for evil, I'd throw you overboard in a heartbeat. It would bore me silly. But don't you see? The more evil – the more vicious – you are to everyone else, the more special your tenderness to me becomes. Does that make sense?"

He paused for a moment, considering her words, then nodded. "It has a certain, twisted logic."

"Exactly!" Lola said. "*We* have a certain twisted logic too. That's exactly what we have. We shouldn't work, but somehow we do. Ours is a brutal romance. You're evil. I'm evil. And together we are evil squared."

"You're right," he said, not entirely understanding but grasping the gist of her argument. He gazed at her with wonder. "Marry me!"

She laughed good and hard at that. "Oh Sid, you crack me up! You really do."

"I'm *serious*," he said. "Marry me! We can be together through all eternity – making each other's lives a joy and everyone else's a misery!"

Lola beamed, but shook her head. "A moment ago, I thought you were walking out on me. And now this? I don't know what to think!"

"Marry me!" he repeated, reaching out his arms to her waist and drawing her closer towards him. "We're a perfect fit. We were meant to be together."

She felt his strong arms about her waist, saw the strange light in his eyes. It was like a distant lighthouse guiding her home. He was right. They *were* a perfect fit. Unstoppable. He was everything she had wanted from the first moment she had seen

300

him – and, if truth be known, even before that. "Yes!" she said. "Yes! I will marry you."

"You're getting *married*!" Stukeley exclaimed.

"Isn't it wonderful?" Lady Lockwood said. "Look at my divine ring!" She flashed the hefty jewel before Stukeley's eyes.

"When?" inquired Johnny, bluntly.

"Soon," said Sidorio.

"*Very* soon," said Lady Lola. "What's the point in waiting around? We've both been around the block enough times to know when we're ready."

Stukeley couldn't even look at Johnny D. He painted on a phoney smile and gazed at the happy couple. "Well, I'm chuffed. Really I am. For both of you." He stepped forward and kissed Lady Lockwood on each cheek, then shook hands with Sidorio.

"Of course, it won't be a conventional wedding," Lady Lockwood said, "but we'd like you both to be involved, wouldn't we, darling?"

Sidorio nodded. "As my ring-bearers," he said.

Lady Lockwood nodded. "And Angelika and Marianne will be *my* ring-bearers." She passed her eyes across Stukeley and Johnny approvingly. "What a beautiful quartet the four of you will make."

"It would be my honour," Stukeley said, realising that he had no choice in the matter.

"Mine too," said Johnny.

"That's marvellous!" Lady Lockwood said, clapping her hands together. "What a happy little family we're all going to make!"

"Yes," nodded Stukeley, feeling strangely nauseous.

"Well, I'd better get back to *The Vagabond*," Lady Lola said. "There's so much to sort out." She turned to Sidorio. "Will you escort me to the door?"

He nodded.

"Goodnight boys!" Lady Lockwood gave them both a cheery wave.

"Congratulations," said Stukeley.

"Yes." Johnny nodded. "Congratulations!"

They watched as Sidorio held the door open for his fiancée, then took her hand and followed her out into the corridor.

As their footsteps receded, Stukeley became brisk with business. He marched over and closed the cabin door tight shut. "We have to think fast," he said.

"Yes," Johnny nodded. "Like the lady says, there's a lot to sort out in a short time. Should we wear matching suits, do you think?"

Stukeley grabbed Johnny by the shoulders. "Earth to Johnny! I'm not talking about the wedding arrangements. We've got far more important things to think about."

"We do?" Johnny asked.

"Of course!" nodded Stukeley. "This changes everything. Don't you see?' He met his friend's eyes. "Who's in charge of this operation now?"

"The captain," Johnny said. "Sidorio."

"That's right," said Stukeley. "And who's next in command?"

"You," said Johnny. "And me!"

Stukeley shook his head. "Uh-uh. Not any more! As soon as they're hitched, Lady Muck will have the run of things and we'll be left out in the cold."

"No," Johnny said. "The boss wouldn't do that to us. I got a feeling—"

Stukeley shook his head. "He won't have any choice in the matter. Don't you see the way she leads him around like a little poodle? Do this! Do that! Marry me! I bet she had this planned right from the beginning."

"No," Johnny said. "She distinctly said that *he* asked *her*. And the ring! You saw the ring he gave her."

Stukeley waved his hand. "Doesn't mean anything. She's a schemer, that one. She may come across like love's old dream, but deep down, she's as cold as ice. She's not in love with Sidorio. She wants his power base, that's all. No wonder they call her Black Heart. She's played him like a card-shark."

"No." Johnny shook his head.

"Yes!" Stukeley insisted.

Johnny shrugged. "Well, it doesn't matter now. The wedding is going to happen, and soon. You should try to be happy for them!"

Stukeley shook his head. "You can start picking out a nice suit for yourself if you like, mate. Why, you can even choose one for me, if it tickles your fancy." There was a dark look in his eyes. A look Johnny had never seen before. "But there isn't going to *be* a wedding. Not if I have anything to do with it."

"What are you planning now, *hermano*?" Johnny asked, shocked but fascinated.

"Watch and wait," said Stukeley, grinning darkly at his friend. "Like the man says – the path of true love never did run smooth."

CHAPTER THIRTY-EIGHT

Rendezvous at Ma Kettle's

It was a rainy night but that wasn't "Cutlass" Cate Morgan's only cause for concern as she joined the queue outside Ma Kettle's Tavern. She pulled her cloche hat lower over her distinctive Titian-red hair and glanced at her fob-watch. Looking along the line, she watched Ma's Chief of Security, Pieces 08, frisking the pirates ahead of her.

In spite of the very well-advertised change in policy, and the very rigorous security procedures, many pirates still hadn't got the message that it was now prohibited to bring any sword, knife or alternate hilt weapon into the tavern. She watched as Pieces expertly patted down a much-celebrated pirate captain and produced no less than eight pieces of weaponry. "You have yourself a wonderful evening, madam," said Pieces, patient and polite as ever. He placed the armoury in a crate for collection at the end of the evening.

"Come on!" Cate muttered under her breath, glancing once more at her watch. "Come on!"

It was only another five minutes before she made it to the front of the queue, but it seemed a lot longer.

"Why, is that Miss Morgan?" Pieces asked, poised to give her a very public greeting.

"Yes," said Cate, her voice low. "Good evening, Pieces. I'm here on a private matter so I'd be very grateful for your utmost discretion."

"Of course, Miss . . . Of course!" he said, winking at her.

Cate readily surrendered her épée and passed it over to Pieces, a banknote wrapped around the tip of the foil. "For your discretion," she said with a nod.

"That's mighty kind of you," he said. "Come on through!"

He lifted the velvet rope and Cate brushed past him into the bustling tavern. Once more, she glanced at her watch. Ten minutes late. Not ideal. Not ideal at all. She just had to hope she'd covered her tracks sufficiently with Molucco and that he wouldn't change his plans for the evening and make a sudden beeline for Ma's.

"Cate," said a familiar voice, as a hand lightly brushed her shoulder.

Cate jumped, then saw that it was only Sugar Pie, Ma's trusty second-in-command. She smiled nervously. "Hello there. How are you?"

"Just fine," said Sugar Pie. "Where's the rest of your crew? Any chance of Bart swinging by later?"

Somewhat flustered, Cate shook her head. "I don't think so. It's just me, as far as I know. I have a little business to conclude. *Private* business."

"Say no more," said Sugar Pie, tapping the side of her button nose. "Your secret's safe with me."

Cate smiled, then dipped her head and moved swiftly through the crowd, striding up the staircase to the line of curtained booths above. Only one of the booths appeared to be occupied. Her rendezvous awaited her. Cate took a deep breath, then parted the velvet curtain and slipped inside.

"I was beginning to think you weren't going to show," said Cheng Li, basking in the glow of candlelight. "Nice hat, by the way."

"Sorry," said Cate, removing the hat and shaking out her hair. "It took longer getting here than I'd hoped. The line outside was crazy."

"Well, you're here *now*. That's what matters." Cheng Li smiled. "Sit down, relax! I took the liberty of ordering you a tankard of Ma's Reserve Ale. It used to be your favourite."

"It still is!" Cate said, sitting down.

"You see," said Cheng Li, "that's one of the things I like about you, Cate. You're a constant in this fast-changing world of ours."

Cate's face was mask-like, save for one raised eyebrow. "Is that your way of saying I'm boring?"

"Boring? Why, of course not. Dependable. Good in a crisis. These qualities are not boring. Not from the perspective of a captain."

Cate visibly relaxed at Cheng Li's praise. Cheng Li nodded. "Drink your ale, Cate. You must be thirsty."

Cate lifted the tankard and took a sip. A frothy moustache formed on her upper lip. She was oblivious to it until she noticed the smile creeping across Cheng Li's face. Embarrassed, Cate wiped away the foam.

Cheng Li was drinking moonflower tea. She poured herself a fresh glass and stirred in a spoonful of manuka honey. "So tell me," she said, casually, "how's life aboard *The Diablo*?"

Cate shrugged. "Not so different from how you'd remember it."

"Oh dear," said Cheng Li, sipping her tea. "I had hoped that Molucco might have mended his ways just a little by now. But I suppose it's true – you can't teach an old sea-dog new tricks!"

"Molucco's Molucco," said Cate, choosing her words carefully. "He's another constant, if you like."

"Yes," agreed Cheng Li. "A constant pain in the—"

"I'm sure you didn't summon me here to bad-mouth Molucco," Cate said, a note of formality restored to her voice.

"No," agreed Cheng Li. "He's pretty low on my list of current concerns." She took another sip of tea. "No, Cate. I *invited* you here to talk about you." She paused. "To talk about your future."

"My future?" Cate echoed.

"Yes. Your future. Your goals. Your five-year plan. I assume you *do* have a five-year plan?"

Cate sipped her ale and shook her head. "Don't need one," she said. "I know exactly where I'll be in five years. I signed up to Captain Wrathe's articles for life."

"Oh Cate," sighed Cheng Li. "I can't help but think you're selling yourself a little short. As I said before, things are changing fast in our world."

"Yes," acknowledged Cate. "But as you also said before, I'm a constant. I don't believe in switching allegiances every five minutes, like . . ." She broke off, glancing down at the flickering candle.

"What were you going to say, dear? Like *me*? Or like Connor Tempest?"

Cate resumed eye-contact. "Connor had his reasons. I understand that. I like and respect Connor very much. Even so, I think he was wrong to leave."

Cheng Li raised an eyebrow. "We'll have to agree to disagree on that."

"How *is* Connor?" Cate asked.

"Thriving," Cheng Li said. "I must say that it gives me great pleasure to watch him evolve from a young drifter into a pirate of considerable talents. I suppose I can't help feeling a special bond with him. After all, it was I who fished him out of the sea that first night. But for me, he would have drowned – and a great pirate would have been lost."

Cate smiled. "You've done many things I'm somewhat dubious about," she said, "but I'll always be grateful to you for rescuing Connor. I'm sure all of his friends would say the same."

"Thanks," Cheng Li said. Her voice became intimate once more. "He misses you, Cate. And he misses Bart. Of course, he has good friends on the crew of *The Tiger*. And me, of course. But I'm occupied with the business of running the ship so much of the time, I can't give him as much attention as I'd wish."

Glancing at her watch, Cate drained the last drops of her ale. "Let's cut to the chase," she said. "What do you want from me?"

There was a discreet cough outside the booth. "Right on cue," announced Cheng Li. "Come in!"

Cate's face was a picture of alarm but, as the curtains parted, she sighed with relief. Sugar Pie leaned in and deposited another tankard of ale on the table. She put a finger to her lips, winked and backed out of the booth.

"I thought you might be thirsty," said Cheng Li, indicating the fresh tankard.

"I'd sooner hear what you have to say with a clear head, thanks," said Cate, pushing the tankard away from her.

"All right," said Cheng Li. "What I'm going to tell you now is quite confidential. Do you understand? You must not breathe a word of this. To anyone."

"Trust me," Cate said, "it won't play well for me if anyone gets to hear about this meeting."

"I mean *anyone*," Cheng Li said, "including Bart."

Blushing, Cate injected a note of steel into her voice. "Point taken. Please proceed."

"*The Tiger* is not just a regular pirate ship," said Cheng Li.

"And mine is not a typical command. I have had the very great honour of being given a top-level mission from the very highest command within the Pirate Federation."

Cate was wide-eyed. *Good*, thought Cheng Li. *Thought that would get your attention!*

"Our ship is to be the first ship of Vampirate assassins," she continued. "We have been charged with leading attacks on the Vampirates and purging the oceans of their menace for good. Our first target is Sidorio, the monster who slaughtered Commodore Kuo and the two academy students, Zak and Varsha."

At the mention of the slaughter, Cate dropped her head. "That was terrible," she said.

"Yes." Cheng Li nodded. "And make no mistake, worse will follow. Unless we act fast and decisively."

"Go on," Cate urged her.

"As I said before, my ship is no ordinary pirate command. We have a higher purpose. And we're already well on our way to completing our first mission."

"Congratulations," Cate said. "But I don't see where I fit into all this."

"Think about it," said Cheng Li, her limpid eyes glowing in the candlelight. "We're going to be fighting Vampirates. Not regular mortals but demons, monsters. My team has conducted extensive research into their vulnerabilities. We have identified three substances which are poisonous to them: silver, hawthorn and aconite." Cate leaned forward, clearly fascinated, as Cheng Li continued. "Even now, Connor is in Lantao, collecting a special batch of weapons from Master Yin."

"Master Yin," said Cate. "Impressive!"

"I only work with the best, Cate," said Cheng Li. "*That's* the point of this meeting. I've got the weapons. I've got the support of the Federation. Now what I need is an attack specialist. And, not to beat around the bush, we both know you're the best in the business."

"You want me to devise a strategy for attacking the Vampirates?" said Cate, clearly intrigued by the proposition.

"It would be your greatest work to date. Your crowning glory. It would put you right on the radar of the Federation, where you belong. But it's not simply about glory, Cate. It's about taking a stand, making a difference. Cleansing the oceans and making them safe for future generations. Can you really content yourself with chumming along with Molucco when a mission like this is calling you?"

It was obvious from her expression that Cate was torn. Cheng Li waited patiently. Had she said enough to convince her former comrade?

Cate shook her head and sighed. "I'm afraid there's no way Molucco would agree to it."

"He doesn't have to," said Cheng Li.

"I'm not going to break my articles," Cate said. "It's a point of principle. I won't break them. Not even for this."

"Fair enough," said Cheng Li. "As I said at the outset, I greatly admire your constancy. But let's think outside the box, dear. My support comes from the very highest level of the Federation. They can be very persuasive."

"What do you mean?" Cate asked.

"It's no secret that you've been scrimping and saving all the while you've served on *The Diablo* for your poor mother and sisters. We all know what a worry they are to you. I'd be able to offer you a very significant sum to join my team."

Cate shook her head. "This isn't about money."

"No," agreed Cheng Li. "It's about much more than that. But money wouldn't hurt. It could make your life – and your family's – a whole lot more comfortable."

Once more Cate paused to consider the offer. Then she

shook her head. "I appreciate everything you've said. I'm flattered. But my answer is no. I made a commitment and I stand by it." She stood up and stretched out her hand. "I didn't think I'd say this, but I've actually enjoyed seeing you again."

Cheng Li shook her hand. She was disappointed but determined not to let it show. "You too, dear. We really should keep in closer touch." She smiled. "Us girls must stick together."

At Cate's request, Cheng Li waited in the booth while she made her way discreetly back out of the tavern. She remained paranoid about the two of them being seen together.

"How did that go?" Sugar Pie asked, popping her head into the booth.

"Not exactly to plan," said Cheng Li.

"Oh dear," said Sugar Pie, collecting Cate's still full tankard. "Well, there's no need to rush off. Would you like another pot of tea? Or perhaps something stronger?"

Cheng Li considered, then shook her head. "No," she said. "No, I had better get back to my ship. It's all work and no play when you're the captain!"

Cheng Li collected her *katanas* and her father's cutlass from Pieces 08 and then set off along the walkway towards the line of waiting taxi-boats. Her favourite jacaranda tree was in flower and she paused for a moment to admire its lavender blossoms. They reminded her that to everything there is a season, a ripeness. As she cradled the blossom in her hand, she thought of Cate. The timing was wrong, that was all. When the time was right, her answer would be different. She lifted one of her *katanas* and sliced off a sprig of flowers, tucking it into her buttonhole. Then she hastened towards the end of the boardwalk, raised her hand and yelled, "Taxi!"

"Where to, lovely lady?" asked the lead ferryman.

"My ship, *The Tiger*. It's moored around the bay," she said, making herself comfortable.

"No *problema*!" said the sailor.

Cheng Li stepped into the water-taxi, unaware of the second sailor, crouching at the back of the boat.

"It's a beautiful night for a detour," said a voice behind her. The second sailor's accent was a world apart from his fellow's and yet somehow familiar.

"I don't want a detour," Cheng Li said. "And I shan't pay you extra for one. Straight around the bay, thank you very much!"

The first sailor turned and smiled at her, his eyes as dark as hers. "*Buenos noces*, little lady," said Johnny.

Irate at his over-familiarity, Cheng Li turned and found herself looking straight into the face of Jez Stukeley. It was then that she realised she'd stepped into the wrong taxi.

"Long time, no see," said Stukeley, with a grin. "We hear you've been taking a sudden interest in Vampirates, so we thought we'd take you out for spin."

Cheng Li looked from one face to the other, her heart racing. How on earth was she going to get out of this one?

CHAPTER THIRTY-NINE

The Invitation

"Stop this boat!" Cheng Li commanded, reaching for her twin *katanas*.

But Stukeley was swift. Before she could unleash the razor-sharp swords, he had caught her arms in a deadlock, forcing her to drop the swords. "I'll just keep those safe for the time being," he said. "Don't worry, you'll get them back later . . . providing you behave."

Cheng Li frowned. In life, Jez Stukeley had been one of the best and fastest fighters she'd ever seen. Clearly he had carried such talents over into the afterlife – or whatever dark place it was he resided in nowadays.

Johnny coughed. "Oh, I'm sorry," Stukeley said, his voice suddenly more amiable. "Where are my manners?! Allow me to introduce my good friend and compadre, Johnny Desperado."

"You can call me Johnny," said the good-looking sailor, winking at Cheng Li and doffing his Stetson.

"This here is Cheng Li," continued Stukeley. "Us two go a long way back, don't we?"

His question was left unanswered as Cheng Li glanced around her, quickly assessing her escape options. They looked decidedly limited. Johnny had expertly ridden the currents and they were already a long way from the comforting neon halo of Ma Kettle's. What could she do? Swim for it? It was a considerable distance to the shore. And wouldn't the Vampirates follow her into the water? Somewhere in her mind, she remembered hearing that Vampirates couldn't swim. But was that true? Hadn't Lorcan Furey dived into the ocean to save Grace Tempest? She couldn't afford to take any risks at this point.

"Where are you taking me?" she asked. Even if she felt devoid of options, it was vital that they couldn't sense her fear. Play for time, she told herself. Focus. The answer will come. She thought of John Kuo's lectures on *zanshin*. Then she thought of John Kuo's fate – his mummified corpse sitting in his office chair. This was not much comfort.

"We're just taking you for a little mystery cruise," said Johnny.

"I don't like mysteries," said Cheng Li. "Or, for that matter, cruises."

There was a laugh behind her. A familiar laugh. It disconcerted her that Jez Stukeley, a former comrade, was now a Vampirate and threatening her.

"Come, come," said Stukeley. "From what we hear, you love a good mystery, isn't that right, Johnny?"

Johnny nodded. "We hear you've been delving into the unexplained world of Vampirates."

Cheng Li frowned but said nothing. What was the point in denying it?

"Anyhow," said Johnny, "we figured, if you're so interested in Vampirates, why not do you a favour and come pay you a visit?"

"Exactly," said Stukeley, leaning close behind her, so close that she could feel his breath on her neck. "So here we are. Ready and eager to answer all your questions."

Saying that, he clambered out from behind her and came to

sit down on the seat opposite. Johnny remained standing, his hand on the tiller. "It's OK, mate," said Stukeley. "I reckon we can idle here for a bit, don't you? It's a beautiful night. And this is a highly picturesque spot, don't you agree, Mistress Li?"

Cheng Li grimaced, determined to retain some semblance of control. "Actually, it's *Captain* Li, now," she said.

"Oh, of course!" Stukeley continued. "I was forgetting myself. I am sorry."

"That's quite all right, Jez," she said. "Things have moved on quite fast since we last met."

Stukeley nodded. "Indeed they have. For both of us. And, as it goes, no one really calls me Jez any more. I go by the name Stukeley now."

Cheng Li raised an eyebrow. "As you wish."

She looked at him properly for the first time. He didn't look as *changed* as she might have expected. Paler certainly. A little thinner perhaps. It was evident in his face. Jez had always been a joker and his round face and dimples had somehow reinforced that impression, as though he was always thinking back to the last joke or about to launch into the next. Now, the cheekbones were sharper and he looked a little more serious. More handsome, too, she noted, somewhat to her surprise. But when she thought about it, they were all rather handsome – Lorcan Furey, Johnny Desperado and Jez . . . or rather Stukeley. In spite of the changes they'd been through, or perhaps because of them, they had a strangely alluring quality.

Stop it! she told herself. Stop this crazy thinking! Any more and you'll go down the same blind alley as Grace Tempest.

"What are you thinking about?" Stukeley asked her.

She looked into his eyes. They were the same twinkly eyes, she noticed, with some relief. "I was thinking about us," she said. "About you and me. Back when we were comrades aboard *The Diablo*."

315

Stukeley frowned.

"What's wrong?" she said. "Don't you like to think back to that time?"

He shook his head. "Not really. I've moved on. I'm a different person now."

"Perhaps," agreed Cheng Li, intrigued at how unsettled he appeared by this line of inquiry. "But don't you sometimes like to think about your life back then? About Captain Wrathe and your friends, Connor and Bart?"

Stukeley looked pained then closed his eyes. "No!" he said. "Be quiet!" He clamped his hands over his ears.

Johnny leaned forward. "He doesn't like to talk about those times, or those people," he said.

Cheng Li nodded. How interesting that he had reacted in this way. She filed away the information in case it came in useful later.

They continued drifting in silence for several minutes. They had reached an impasse, floating along on the currents, out in the middle of the deserted bay.

"I bet I can guess what you're thinking," Johnny said after a time.

Cheng Li glanced up. "Go on."

"Bet you wish you had some of your weaponry to hand."

Cheng Li frowned, staring at the *katanas* which Jez still held in his grasp.

Johnny shook his head. "That's not what I meant," he said. "I meant the weapons you've been developing to attack Vampirates."

So he knew about that too. In spite of her best efforts, Cheng Li was starting to feel anxious and gloom-ridden. Clearly, Sidorio knew of her plans and had sent his lieutenants on a night-time mission to dispose of her. Like they had disposed of Commodore Kuo. Damn it! Her career was just taking off.

Why now? But then, she supposed, if you raise the stakes, you raise the danger.

"So you know about my mission," she said, carefully.

Johnny nodded. "Of course. One of your prisoners escaped."

"Vampirate Two!" Cheng Li exclaimed, her heart sinking. She remembered her words of reassurance to Jacoby. "*So he got away. He's only one Vampirate.*" But of course he had gone to alert Sidorio and the other Vampirates.

Stukeley smiled at her. There was no trace of humanity – no trace of the Jez she had known. "Your goons had a nasty go at our little friend, Babyface, but he managed to put himself together again, find us and beg for our help."

"He wanted you to rescue the other two," Cheng Li said. Of course – when he'd escaped the other Vampirates had still been alive. "Why *didn't* you come and rescue them?" she asked.

"If it was up to me," said Stukeley, "that's *exactly* what we'd have done. But the captain had other ideas."

"Sidorio?" Cheng Li said.

"That's right. Our captain. Sidorio. King of the Vampirates."

"The one you've got in your targets," said Johnny.

Cheng Li thought of her meeting with Ahab Black. Her mission. The one which was supposed to bring her glory. Bring in Sidorio, the leader of the renegade Vampirates, the murderer of Porfirio Wrathe, John Kuo and the others.

"You're making a mistake," Stukeley said.

"Taking on the likes of you?" she said.

He shook his head. "That's not what I mean. Sidorio isn't the one you should be targeting. It wasn't Sidorio who killed Commodore Kuo."

"It wasn't?" Cheng Li was fascinated. Why were they telling her this? They didn't seem like the kind of people who'd feel the need to clear the air before they killed you. "Do you want something from me?" she asked curiously.

Stukeley shrugged. "We're here to share some information with you," he said. "That's all."

Cheng Li's heart was racing. No longer from fear, but from adrenaline.

"Who *did* kill Commodore Kuo?" she asked.

"Her name," said Stukeley, "is Lady Lola Lockwood. Also known as Black Heart."

"Black Heart!" Cheng Li exclaimed. Of course. She remembered the playing card Commodore Kuo had been holding when they had found him in his study. And the other, blood-tinged, playing cards Connor had placed on her desk.

"She has a ship called *The Vagabond*," said Stukeley. "And she's about to join Sidorio's forces."

"In other words," Cheng Li said, "*your* forces."

Stukeley nodded. "If you like."

Cheng Li's mind was racing now, as fast as her heart. "She's a threat to you." She was having such a rush, she thought her head might explode. "You don't want her to join forces with Sidorio because if she does, she'll threaten your position."

"You're good!" exclaimed Johnny. "One smart little cookie."

Stukeley raised his hand to silence his partner. "We're not talking about us. Or what we want. We're just putting you right. You were given a mission to kill Sidorio because you all think he killed Commodore Kuo. But that isn't the case. It was Lady Lockwood. We just thought it was important to set the record straight."

Cheng Li nodded. "I understand. You have an innate sense of fairness and justice." She paused to add, almost casually, "And if we were to target Lady Lockwood, you wouldn't stand in our way." She decided to chance her arm still further. "Indeed, perhaps you'd welcome it. Or even help us?"

Stukeley shook his head. "Absolutely not! Like I said before, we're only here to share some information with you. The thought of us helping you . . . no, no I can't even think about it." He grinned. "Oh, but we did want to give you something." He reached into his pockets. "Now, where did I put it?" He made a great show of patting every conceivable pocket.

Johnny laughed. "Don't you remember, *hermano*? You gave it to me for safekeeping." He reached into his own jacket pocket and produced an envelope, which he handed to Stukeley to pass on to Cheng Li.

She took the thick vellum envelope in her hands. On it, in immaculate script was written:

Cheng Li & guests

She raised an eyebrow.

"Why don't you open it?" Stukeley prompted her.

Intrigued, she turned the envelope over. It had been stamped with a wax seal and bore a coat of arms embedded with ribbons. "Very fancy," she noted.

"You don't mess around when it's the wedding of the year," smirked Stukeley.

"*Wedding?*" Cheng Li said. It was all coming together. As she drew out the card invitation, the final piece of the jigsaw locked into place. "So Sidorio is marrying Lady Lockwood?"

"Very good, Nancy Drew!" said Stukeley.

"*That's* why she threatens your position. They're going to be married and then they'll divide the spoils between them, and you two . . . well, your future will be uncertain, to say the least."

Stukeley shook his head once more. "Like I say, we're not here to talk about us."

"We just wanted to invite you to join the festivities," Johnny said. "Everyone loves a wedding." His eyes were bright.

"That's right," Stukeley said, his eyes fixed on Cheng Li's. "Everyone loves a wedding. Isn't that right, Captain Li?"

Now she understood. "You want me to come to the wedding and assassinate Lady Lockwood?"

"What a shocking idea!" said Stukeley, apparently deeply offended. But the expression in his eyes told a different story.

Cheng Li thought fast. "How do I know this isn't a trick?" she asked. "That you're not luring me there to kill me?"

Stukeley laughed good and hard at that. "Captain Li," he said, "if our intention was to kill you, you'd be dead in the water by now and we'd be long gone."

Cheng Li considered this. "But the invitation says 'plus guests'. You want me to bring my crew with me. You could kill us all."

"No one's talking about killing anyone," said Stukeley.

At least not aloud, thought Cheng Li.

"No," agreed Johnny. "Just come along, on your own or with your crew. Myself, I think it's more fun to bring a date to a wedding than to fly solo, but it's up to you. So come along, eat some cake, throw some confetti . . ."

"And then murder the bride!" said Cheng Li.

"Johnny," said Stukeley. "We ought to be getting Captain Li back to her ship. We've detained her quite long enough."

"Of course," Johnny said, attending to the steering once more. "You must get some rest, Mistress Li. Give you time to come up with the ideal wedding gift."

Cheng Li turned back to Stukeley. "Do you have any suggestions?" she asked. "After all, you know them both so much better than I do."

Stukeley shook his head. "I'm sure you'll come up with the perfect surprise."

So that was as much as he was going to help her. Well, given what he knew of her experiments, this must mean she was on the right track. Cheng Li thought of Connor and Jasmine, returning from Lantao with the silver swords dipped in hawthorn and

320

aconite. The perfect gift for a Vampirate bride. A poisonous sword through the heart.

"And afterwards?" she asked, turning back to Stukeley. "After the wedding, how can I be sure of a quick getaway? That you won't double-cross me and attack myself and my crew?"

"Don't worry," Stukeley said, "you do us the very great honour of attending the nuptials and we'll take care of the rest. Trust me!"

Cheng Li laughed lightly. "You're asking *me* to trust *you*?"

"You said it yourself. We're old comrades, aren't we?" He grinned at her. "Here, have your *katanas* back." With that, he slipped the deadly blades back into their holsters. "There now, Cheng Li. You have to trust me and I have to trust you. I believe this is what's known in better circles as mutual self-interest."

CHAPTER FORTY

Impossible Dreams

Once more, Connor wielded the sword of Chang Po in his grip. The last time he had held it, he had thought of Chang Po's history as a legendary pirate and the commander of the Red Flag Fleet and then of his own future. Now, all his thoughts were concentrated on the present moment as he looked down the length of the épée towards his opponent's weapon.

"*En garde!*" Jasmine cried, her rapier making contact with his épée. The battle had begun again.

Jasmine was an expert swordswoman. She had been schooled to the highest levels during ten years of combat workshops at Pirate Academy. This elite education combined with her natural athleticism made her a dangerous adversary. Connor felt like a rough streetfighter in comparison. No ten years of classes for him, just a few months at sea and the expert tutelage of Cutlass Cate, Bart and Jez. But Connor had a natural instinct for combat, as if he was born to the sword. As Jasmine parried him backwards, he remained cool and collected. He had a few surprise moves of his own!

Bo Yin watched the duel from the sidelines, greatly impressed by Jasmine's grace and precision. She had often tried out the swords herself – unbeknownst to her father. She had even smuggled some of his ancient books on swordsmanship into her room, reading late into the night – by the dimmest of light so as not to alert him. The problem was that she had no one decent to practise with. She had challenged some of the other local kids but, after showing some initial enthusiasm, they had rapidly grown tired of her games and moved on to others. Bo Yin sighed. If only Connor and Jasmine would stay longer, she could finally start to hone her skills.

"You win!" Connor cried, as Jasmine lunged at him, her épée perilously close to his heart.

"Three-two to me!" Jasmine cried, elated.

Bo Yin clapped her hands furiously.

Connor wandered over to her, putting down his sword. "I need a drink," he said, reaching for the bottle of water. "She's tiring me out!"

"I think you let her win, Connor Tempest," said Bo Yin. "You let her win because you like her."

Connor grinned but shook his head. "Trust me, Bo, Jasmine's a tough opponent." He smiled, extending the hilt of Chang Po's sword to her. "Why don't you see for yourself?"

"May I?" Bo Yin felt a shiver of adrenaline as she glanced down at the sword. She turned to Jasmine.

"Go on!" Jasmine said. "I'll be gentle with you, I promise!"

This time, it was Connor's turn to watch from the sidelines. True to her word, Jasmine was a little gentler with Bo than she had been during their earlier bout. But it was evident that the younger girl was also blessed with some real skill at swords. Perhaps, he mused, that was only to be expected from the daughter of a master swordsmith.

He sat back, watching the two girls sparring away. Jasmine was so lithe and elegant – like he imagined a leopard might be in a fight. Not for the first time, he found himself lost in a dream about himself and Jasmine. And, as usual, a picture of his friend, Jacoby – Jasmine's *boyfriend*, he reminded himself – swiftly rose in his mind. There were some things you didn't do, some thoughts you just didn't entertain. And yet, watching Jasmine now, sleek as a wild cat, he couldn't help but wonder what it would have been like if things were different.

His little fantasy was interrupted by a gentle tap on his shoulder. He turned around to find Master Yin at his side. The swordsmith had arrived in the room stealthily or perhaps Connor had been too involved in his impossible dream to notice.

"Come with me!" Master Yin said softly. He turned and shuffled out of the room again. Connor followed.

"Wow!" Connor said once more, surveying the long line of shining swords laid out in Master Yin's workshop.

"Yes, wow!" Master Yin smiled. "Fifty silver swords. Dipped in a compound of hawthorn and aconite. Fatal to Vampirates!" He grinned. "Though I say it myself, some of my very finest work."

At the end of the bench was a stack of what looked like tins of wood varnish. Connor lifted one up. "So each time we go into battle, we just paint on a coat of this compound?"

Master Yin nodded. "Yes. Just a sparing amount on the tip of your sword. Don't go crazy with it. Just a touch should prove most effective. I have prepared a detailed note for Captain Li." He reached amongst the tins and picked up an immaculately written page of instructions, which he gave to Connor.

"Well," Connor said, a little sadly. "I guess it's time we were packing up our stuff again."

"Yes," Master Yin agreed. "I'll have Bo Yin help me put the swords into cases, then we'll box them up for you." He turned and called over his shoulder. "Bo Yin!"

"Coming, Pop!" A moment later, Bo Yin raced into the

room. She was red-faced and a little out of puff. She still gripped Chang Po's sword in her hand.

Master Yin gazed at it, then lifted his eyes to his daughter's face. "Put away the épée, Bo Yin," he said. "I need your help packing up these swords. Connor and Jasmine are ready to return to *The Tiger*."

"So soon?" Bo Yin looked crestfallen.

"So, once more we find ourselves saying goodbye." Master Yin had come down to the quayside to bid farewell to his guests. "Miss Peacock, it was a pleasure to meet you."

"And you, Master Yin," Jasmine said. "Thank you so much for all your hospitality." She bowed formally, then found herself unable to resist hugging the old swordsmith. He might come across as an old curmudgeon, especially where his daughter was concerned, but during their ten days on Lantao, Jasmine had seen that this was just a façade. Deep down, Master Yin was like a teddy bear. Albeit one who had devoted his life to crafting deadly weapons.

"Goodbye again, sir," Connor said, shaking Master Yin by the hand.

"Travel safe," said Master Yin. "You and your comrades are sailing into uncharted waters with these Vampirates," he said. "Keep your wits about you and, rest assured, you could have no better leader than Captain Li."

Connor nodded. "I know," he said. He glanced about the harbour. "Where's Bo?" he asked. "We haven't said a proper goodbye to her."

Master Yin shook his head. "She was too upset," he said. "Bo Yin is very angry with me. Feels I am ruining her life by keeping her here with me." He sighed. "Perhaps she is right. But I made a promise, many years ago, to her dear mother and I intend to honour it. For a little while longer, anyhow."

"Well, tell her we said a special goodbye," said Connor. "And to Sinbad," he added.

"Yes," Jasmine nodded. "And please thank her again for that laksa recipe!"

Master Yin nodded. "Yes, yes, yes. Now get into the taxi-boat, please. You've already clocked up a good few minutes' waiting time."

"Poor Bo Yin," Jasmine said as they lifted the anchor and prepared their own boat for the sail back to join their comrades. "Do you think her father will ever allow her to pursue a career as a pirate?"

Connor shrugged. "Maybe. He seemed to be slightly softening this time. But she is still so young."

"She's only two years younger than you," Jasmine reminded him, with a grin.

"True," agreed Connor, hoisting the mainsail. "But if my dad was still around, I'm not sure he'd be too thrilled about me being a pirate." As the sail billowed out, he jumped across the deck to help Jasmine with the ropes.

"Funny," Jasmine said, "my parents' only dream for me was to follow them into piracy. You and I come from very different worlds, don't we?"

"Maybe," Connor said, finishing off the knots and finding himself so close to Jasmine, he could smell her honey-scented shampoo. "But does it really matter where you come from? Isn't the important thing where you're going?"

"Maybe," Jasmine said, standing up and drawing a stray strand of hair back behind her ear. Suddenly she grew self-conscious. "Connor, you're staring at me. What's wrong? Do I have a smudge of oil on my nose? Or worse, a zit?"

Connor smiled and shook his head. "No," he said. "No, you're perfect." The words were instinctive. "You really are absolutely perfect," he said.

The skin around Jasmine's dazzling green eyes crinkled. "No one's perfect, Connor," she said. "Don't be silly!"

"I'm not . . ." he began, reaching out to her, surprised at the boldness of his own actions.

She turned away, slipping her sunglasses down over her eyes and folding her arms, gazing out to sea. Puzzled, Connor stepped closer, daring to place his hands lightly on her waist. She jumped at his touch.

"What's wrong?" he asked. Then he heard a muffled sob. "Jasmine? Hey, are you *crying*?"

"No!" she said. "Yes! Oh I don't know! It's *so* stupid. I really didn't want to be a drama queen about this."

"About what?" he asked, his hands resting thrillingly around her waist.

"About these feelings I have. These things I shouldn't do. But that I really want to do."

Connor's head was spinning. "Jas, what are you talking about? What things?"

Jasmine turned around, as gracefully as a ballerina, still held within the circumference of his arms. She leaned in and kissed him on the lips, her arms draping themselves loosely over his shoulders. Connor was utterly taken aback. It was quite possibly the most magical moment of his life.

"Should we start thinking about dinner?" Connor asked.

They had been sailing for several hours and made excellent progress, spurred on by favourable winds. For Connor, the day had continued to have an unreal quality about it. Jasmine's first kiss had been the start of that. More kisses had followed. But they had talked too. This, in itself, wasn't new. They'd been friends for a while now and, of course, during their ten days on Lantao, they had chatted at length throughout each day. But ever since that moment, ever since that kiss, they had started talking in a different way, opening up about their pasts and about their hopes and dreams for the future. Their fears too: fears which ranged from what to tell Jacoby when they joined up with him again, to the surreal and unprecedented mission they would soon be embarking upon.

"Hey, Jas, did you hear me? Are you hungry?"

She turned and glanced over at him. "I guess so. What time is it?"

Connor was about to glance at his watch when he was distracted by a curious tapping noise. He paused, listening to see where it was coming from.

Jasmine stared at him, puzzled. "What are you doing?"

"Listen!" he said. "Do you hear that?"

"Hear what?" She focused her attention.

"There it goes again."

"Oh yes," Jasmine said. "What do you think it is?"

Connor walked slowly forward, trying to pinpoint exactly where the sound was coming from.

"Probably something got loose down below," said Jasmine.

But Connor could hear the tapping again. Closer and louder. He was crouched over a hatch now. He lifted it up and was not entirely surprised as a long finger poked out from below. Connor reached both his hands down, cradling the warm and furry body lurking below.

"Hello, hello," he said. "Ahoy there, Sinbad!" Bo Yin's pet aye-aye seemed delighted to see Connor again and to hear his own name.

"What's going on?" Jasmine walked across the deck to join him.

Connor turned, cradling the strange creature in his arms. "Looks like we have a stowaway!" he said.

"Looks like we have more than one," said Jasmine, as Bo Yin popped her head through the hatch.

"Sinbad Yin," she hissed, "you're a very naughty boy!"

"You're a fine one to talk," Connor said. "What on earth are you doing here, Bo?"

"I've run away!" Bo Yin announced, climbing up through the hatch and jumping up onto the deck, her hands on her hips.

"Of course you have!" Connor said, shaking his head but grinning.

"Please don't be angry, Connor Tempest!" said Bo, her eyes wide. "And please, don't take me back. I'll make a good pirate. You said so yourself."

Connor sighed, though he found it hard to stay exasperated with Bo. "I did mean it," he said. "But not now. Not yet."

"*Carpe diem*, Connor Tempest!" pronounced Bo Yin. "Seize the day!"

"What are we going to do with you?" Connor asked. He glanced over to Jasmine.

"Please don't take me back, Jasmine Peacock!" Bo Yin implored.

"We *can't* go back to Lantao," Jasmine said. "We've come too far already. We have to get back to Captain Li and take her the new weapons."

"Yay!" cried Bo Yin. "And then Bo Yin can join Cheng Li's crew!"

"We'll have to see what Captain Li has to say about that," said Connor.

"She's an old friend of the family," said Bo, smiling. "No worries!"

Connor couldn't help but grin at her irrepressible enthusiasm and determination.

Cheng Li stared down at Bo Yin, then spoke with surprising tenderness. "You shouldn't have acted so rashly. Your father will be upset and worried about you. I know how deeply you dream of becoming a pirate but you really shouldn't have done this without talking to him, and to me, first."

"When you know what you want out of life," said Bo Yin, "you just have to go after it. Think back, Captain Li. When you were younger, if someone had told you you couldn't be a pirate, would you have let anything stand in your way?"

"No," Cheng Li agreed. "But that was different." She indicated the portrait behind her desk. "My father was a pirate."

Bo Yin shook her head. "That's not what you're supposed to say."

"No?" Cheng Li raised an inquisitive eyebrow.

Bo Yin grinned, stepping closer. "You're supposed to say how much I remind you of yourself at my age."

Cheng Li laughed, but it was the warmest laughter Connor had ever heard from her. "Is that right? Well, Bo, I guess you're right. I do see a lot of my younger self in you. Though you are *a lot* cheekier than I ever was."

Bo Yin pressed on. "And this is the part where you tell me that you'll give me a try and, if I prove myself to be worthy, you will talk to my father and persuade him that this has happened for the best."

Cheng Li smiled. "You have this all worked out, Bo Yin, don't you?"

The girl nodded. "I have given these things much thought, Captain Li. I had a lot of time to think on Lantao."

Cheng Li considered the situation for a moment, then made her decision. "Bo Yin, under normal circumstances, I'd let your cheek and enthusiasm carry the day. But, you see, my ship is no ordinary ship . . ."

"No," agreed Bo Yin. "*The Tiger* is the best pirate ship, the very best . . ."

"No, dear, that's not what I meant. We have a special

mission. A very *dangerous* mission. It wouldn't be right to involve you in this. I'd never forgive myself if something happened to you."

Even now, Bo Yin was undaunted. "You're going to fight the Vampirates," she said. "I know *all* about it. That's why Connor Tempest and Jasmine Peacock came for new swords." She paused. "I can help!"

Cheng Li shook her head. "Bo, I'm so sorry to disappoint you, but you have no idea of the danger we're sailing into."

"Bo Yin is not afraid of danger. Bo Yin can help!"

Cheng Li was trying to remain patient. "Bo, how *exactly* do you think you can help?"

As ever, Bo was ready with the answer. "Bo Yin's father is mastermind of weapons, yes? And Bo Yin hasn't sat around without picking up a few tips from him. For instance . . ." She withdrew from her pocket a scrap of paper. "The formula for the poison to dip your silver swords in. When you run out, I can prepare more for you. As you know, Bo Yin is very proficient at recipes."

Cheng Li felt the wind had been taken out of her sails. Maybe this *could* just work. Of course, Bo would have to be kept well out of combat situations. That was imperative. But, so long as that was understood, where was the real danger? She could give Bo Yin a trial and, after the immediate business with Lady Lola Lockwood was concluded, she could talk to Master Yin and think again.

"All right," said Cheng Li. "You're in . . . for now! If you're half as good a pirate as you are a negotiator, you have a starry future ahead."

"Thank you, Captain Li," said Bo, giving her a salute. "I am honoured to join your crew."

Suddenly, there was a scuffle behind Bo Yin. A furry ball darted through the gap between her legs. Connor watched in disbelief as Sinbad mirrored his mistress's gesture, raising his strange hand to his head and saluting the captain.

"What *is* that?" asked Cheng Li.

"He's an aye-aye, Captain," said Connor.

"Very funny, Connor," said Cheng Li. "I see your mini-break to Lantao has done wonders for your sense of humour."

"Actually that's true, but he really *is* an aye-aye, isn't he, Bo?"

Bo Yin nodded, scooping Sinbad up into her arms. "He's my pet, Mistress Li. Say hello to Captain Li, Sinbad!"

Sinbad stretched out his wizened hand in Cheng Li's direction.

"I'm sorry," Cheng Li said, "*you* can stay, Bo Yin. But *The Tiger* is an animal-free zone. I'm running a pirate ship, not Noah's Ark."

Bo Yin frowned, then set Sinbad down on the floor. "Here's the thing . . ." she began. Connor sensed that another lengthy negotiation was about to begin.

CHAPTER FORTY-ONE

Changes

"I'm sorry," Connor said later as he and Cheng Li marched along the corridor. "You have to believe me. I had no idea she'd do this. And if we'd discovered her sooner, we'd have turned around . . ."

"It's OK," said Cheng Li, with surprising equanimity. "I don't think any of us could have stopped this happening eventually. It was only a question of time. Bo Yin is a very ambitious young lady."

"So you're going to let her stay?"

Cheng Li nodded. "For now. But we'll keep her away from any combat scenarios. I'll need your help in that."

"Absolutely," Connor agreed.

"Now then," said Cheng Li. "Where are these new weapons?"

"They're waiting for you in the armoury," Connor said.

"Excellent! Let's go and take a look!" Cheng Li marched along the corridor. As usual, Connor had to race to keep up

"Perfect!" declared Cheng Li, lifting one of the silver swords.

Perfect. The word took Connor back to the deck of the small ship. Jasmine standing in the sunlight. Her tanned shoulders turned towards him, her honey-scented hair. Just before that delicious moment when she had turned and . . .

"Connor!" Cheng Li's call brought his focus back into this room. "Didn't you hear me?"

"Sorry," he said, "I was distracted for a moment."

"We're about to embark on a dangerous and unprecedented mission," Cheng Li said. "You cannot afford to be distracted even for a split second."

"Yes, Captain!" Connor agreed. It was madness. Here he was, involved in the most dangerous pirate mission of all time, and all he could focus on was what it had felt like to be kissed by Jasmine Peacock, the prettiest girl at Pirate Academy. Where was she now? With Jacoby? Had she told him yet what had happened? His heart was racing.

Cheng Li strode purposefully forward. "There have been several important changes to our mission whilst you and Jasmine have been away."

"Changes?" Connor asked, Cheng Li's intriguing words pulling his focus back to the here and now.

The captain nodded. "We're going to a wedding!"

"A wedding? In the middle of a mission?" Connor couldn't help but be confused.

Cheng Li smiled. "The wedding *is* the mission," she said. "It seems that even Vampirates are inclined towards a little romance. Sidorio is tying the knot with a fellow Vampirate captain, Lady Lola Lockwood." She withdrew the wedding invitation from her jacket and flashed the card before his eyes.

Connor was dumbfounded. "How come *you* got an invitation?"

Cheng Li's eyes glistened. "Are you familiar with the expression, six degrees of separation?" she asked. As he shook his head blankly, she shrugged. "Well, let's just say that I'm unusually well-connected."

Connor didn't doubt that. "So we're going to this wedding?" He paused, light suddenly dawning. "And we're going to destroy Sidorio then and there?"

"Close, Connor, but not quite." Cheng Li pocketed the invitation again. "Our target has changed. I've discovered that Commodore Kuo wasn't killed by Sidorio after all. He was murdered, in such a brutal fashion, by Lady Lockwood. Do you remember what the playing card was that John was holding when we saw him for the last time?"

Connor's mind flashed back, a chill flooding his veins as he remembered the terrible sight of Commodore Kuo's body drained of blood, the strange playing card clutched between his petrified fingers. "It was a black Heart," he said.

Cheng Li nodded. "It's the madwoman's calling card. She even goes by the nickname Black Heart. That's why this mission is now codenamed Operation Black Heart." She turned to Connor. "Though, I still prefer to think of it as Operation Wedding Gift."

Connor's head was spinning as he absorbed all this new information.

"Come on," Cheng Li said, her voice softer all of a sudden. "I can see you're tired from your journey. Come and have dinner. It will be a good chance to catch up with your comrades."

Never one to refuse the offer of food, Connor followed Cheng Li out of the armoury and up to the mess hall – or cafeteria, as Captain Li preferred her state-of-the-art eating area to be called. There was no Captain's Table as such – Cheng Li preferred to eat with her crew, ensuring that she maintained day-to-day contact with the most junior recruits as well as her senior officers.

"Follow me," Cheng Li said, heading towards a table in the middle of the room. Connor saw that Jacoby and Jasmine were already seated there. They were laughing and Jacoby had his arm around Jasmine's shoulder. Judging from these signs, she hadn't told him yet. She glanced up at Connor and smiled, but there was something guarded about her. Connor felt confused and a little bit crushed.

"Welcome back!" cried Jacoby, jumping up and initiating their secret handshake. "I hear you got us some state-of-the-art weaponry!"

Connor nodded.

"And hey," Jacoby leaned closer. "Thanks for bringing Min home safe," he said. "I would have been out of my head with worry if she'd been off with anyone but you!"

Connor painted a forced grin on his face. But, as he turned, he saw something that turned the fake grin into a real one. Two familiar, but out of place, faces were sitting at the other end of the table. Bart and Cate.

"Guys!" Connor cried, racing over to hug them. "What are you two doing here?"

"We heard you were in need of some serious muscle," Bart said, as he embraced his old friend. "So good to see you again, buddy!"

"You too!" Connor was close to tears.

"We're on temporary loan," Cate told him. "Special dispensation for this mission. Ahab Black talked to Barbarro Wrathe, who talked to Molucco . . . well, anyhow, here we are, for now."

"I am *so* happy to see you guys," Connor said. "I'm only surprised they didn't send Moonshine over with you . . ."

As he said Moonshine's name, there was a cry from the food counter. "What's all this low-carb crapola? I *demand* a pizza!"

Connor turned around. At the same time, Moonshine looked up. Seeing Connor, he dug two fingers into his mouth. "I was feeling nauseous before," he cried. "Now, I'm *really* ready to hurl."

"It wouldn't be the first time," Connor called, remembering

all too vividly how Moonshine had vomited over him – twice! – during a particularly bad sea-crossing on board Barbarro Wrathe's ship, *The Typhon*.

As Moonshine threw aside his tray and stomped out of the cafeteria, Connor turned to Cate. "I was only joking before. What's the idea with Moonshine joining the team?"

Cate leaned forward. "It's politics, Connor," she said. "Pure politics. When Barbarro persuaded Molucco to loan us out, he insisted that Moonshine came too. He's under the impression it will be character-building for him!"

"Character-building?" Connor exclaimed. "Are you sure that Barbarro isn't secretly hoping a Vampirate will do us all a favour and finish him off?"

Bart laughed.

Cate smiled but shook her head. "As ever, the strategy re Moonshine remains very straightforward. Keep him as far away from the action as possible."

"All right," said Connor, "but please don't even think about pairing me up with him this time."

"Don't worry," Cate said. "I promise that won't happen."

Bart rested his hand on Connor's shoulder. "Let's not waste time talking about that little twerp. Grab some grub, mate, and bring us up to speed on your adventures! We've missed you like crazy, haven't we, Cate?"

Connor noticed that Bart's other arm was draped around Cate's shoulders. And she had made no attempt to remove it. Indeed, she was smiling very contentedly. Connor grinned. "Looks like you two have some stuff to fill me in on too!" he said.

"Get some food!" said Cate, trying hard to be formal but failing. To Connor's surprise and delight, she turned and kissed Bart just under his ear.

"Careful!" Connor joked. "Don't let Cheng Li see. This is a pirate ship, you know, not the Love Boat!"

On his way to the counter Connor passed Jacoby and Jasmine, who had already finished eating and were heading out.

"See you later, buddy!" Jacoby called. "Me and Min got some catching up to do, if you know what I mean." He winked at Connor, then punched his shoulder and continued on to joke with mates at another table.

Connor felt a headache coming on. Jasmine held back, then reached out and touched his wrist. It was the lightest of touches but thrilling nonetheless. "Connor, don't be angry at me," she said. "I couldn't just blurt it out the minute we got back. But nothing has changed. I *will* tell him. Everything we said to each other on the way back from Lantao holds true. I want this as much as you do."

Connor smiled and let out a deep sigh. "Thanks, Jas," he said. "That's a huge relief."

"OK," she said, slipping free her hand. "I've got to go now. But I'll come and find you later. I promise."

"OK," Connor said. Feeling hugely relieved, he stepped forward and grabbed a tray.

The next day, Cheng Li watched from the upper deck of *The Tiger* as Cate began putting the fifty members of the crew selected for Operation Wedding Gift through new attack formations. The captain's eyes ranged from Jacoby to Jasmine, from Connor to Bart to Bo Yin – who was surprisingly dexterous with her épée. If the early signs were anything to go by, she had taken on a prodigiously talented new crew-member in little Bo. Cheng Li smiled to herself. Everything was coming together very satisfactorily – in ways both planned and unexpected. She thought of something her father had once told her: *fate favours the brave.* She hoped Chang Ko Li's words would hold true.

CHAPTER FORTY-TWO

The Spell

Grace burst into the captain's cabin. It was still a shock stepping inside and finding that the captain himself was absent. Where was he? Was he ever going to return to *The Nocturne* – to the crew who loved and missed and *needed* him? But as anxious as Grace was to solve this mystery, there were other even more pressing questions that needed to be answered.

"Grace," said Mosh Zu, turning from the steering wheel. He smiled, evidently neither surprised nor disturbed by her sudden appearance.

She saw that Lorcan was here as well, standing in front of the hearth, staring into the fire. Now, he spun around and looked at her too, but he did not smile. He seemed anxious.

Grace looked from one to the other, wondering how best to broach her question. In the end, she dispensed with all pleasantries and simply blurted it out. "Which one of the Vampirates is my father? I have to know. Now!"

Her question was met initially with silence. Lorcan looked to Mosh Zu for leadership. Mosh Zu appeared to consider the matter, turning from the wheel and stepping closer into the cabin. "All right then," he said at last. "Yes, I believe it is time."

Grace felt her heart begin to race. At last, she was going to get some answers.

Mosh Zu sat down at the captain's table and gestured for the others to join him. As they sat down, he addressed Grace. "Grace, I want you to know that no one has been trying to keep things secret from you. It was clear to me that you were moving towards these important discoveries yourself. I saw no need to rush them. You were getting there in your own time."

"You mean through these visions I've been having?" she said.

Mosh Zu nodded. "The visions you've been channelling through your contact with Sally."

Grace nodded. "But that's just it," she said. "Ever since Mother . . . well, ever since we left her at the lighthouse, the visions have gone. I can't seem to find a way back into them."

Mosh Zu nodded. "That makes sense," he said. "As you know, Grace, your mother found it difficult to talk at any length when she came back. She desperately wanted to tell you her story – *your* story. I'm sure that was why she clung on so tenaciously for as long as she did. And though her speaking voice was weak, it seems to me that she found another way to tell the story."

Grace's eyes widened. "You mean my mother was *intentionally* conjuring those visions for me?"

Mosh Zu paused, then shook his head. "Not consciously," he said. "No, I would think not. But the subconscious is very powerful." He paused. "Remember how you were able to work with the ribbons in Sanctuary, tapping into the energies contained within them to unlock memories and stories others had imprinted there?"

Grace gasped. "You mean that I did the same thing, simply through holding my mother's hand?"

"Yes," Mosh Zu said, nodding. "Only, of course, your connection to Sally was even stronger.

"And now she's gone," Grace said, bereft. "And I won't be able to channel the rest of the story."

Mosh Zu smiled warmly. "What's that charming expression? *There's more than one way to skin a cat!*" His eyes were bright as he continued. "Tell me, through your conversations with Sally and your own visions, how far did you get?"

Grace's heart was racing now. "She told me about how my dad . . . I mean Dexter . . . how he joined *The Nocturne* as a kitchen porter and how they fell in love. She told me that she realised she'd been wrong to give up on her life beyond the ship and that she came to the captain and asked him to free her from the bonds of being Sidorio's donor."

Mosh Zu nodded.

Grace took a deep breath in, then out. "She said that the captain agreed to her request."

"It was not a decision he took lightly," Mosh Zu said, "but he could see her predicament and that her true destiny lay beyond this ship."

"And so," Grace continued, "he told her that she must wait until a new donor had been found for Sidorio. Once that happened, she would be free to start a new life with Dexter." She sighed. "And that's where she ended the story, that day we spent together in Crescent Moon Bay – that last, perfect day."

"So," Mosh Zu said, "that's where we will pick it up." He nodded towards Lorcan. "Perhaps you would care to begin?"

Grace's eyes turned to Lorcan, her first good friend aboard *The Nocturne*. He had come to mean so much to her and, whatever he was about to tell her, she knew there was no one she would rather hear it from.

"Word got to Sidorio that Sally had been to see the captain," Lorcan began. "That she had asked to be released from being his donor so that she could go away with Dexter." He shook his head, darkly. "Sidorio was incandescent with rage."

"Because he was losing his donor?" Grace asked. "But why? From everything my mother said, he only ever saw her as – what did Oskar call it? – a Mobile Blood Supply. Why would switching donors even matter to him?"

"You're right," Lorcan said. "At least, that's what we all thought. But evidently Sidorio had deeper feelings for your mother than he revealed. He couldn't stand the thought of her double betrayal – firstly through her relationship with Dexter and then through her decision to leave."

Grace couldn't believe what she was hearing. "Sidorio had feelings for my mother?"

Lorcan nodded. "The very strongest of feelings, Grace," he said. "Sidorio was in love with your mother. But it was an unrequited love. And so, it was all the harder for him to bear."

This was a lot to take in and adjust to, but Grace hung on Lorcan's every word as he continued. "Sidorio confronted Sally. She told him that he couldn't stop her from leaving the ship. Perhaps not, he said, but he'd find a way for her never to forget him."

Grace shivered at these words. She had a dark sense of foreboding about the way this tale was unfolding, but she had to stay with it, whatever the outcome.

Mosh Zu was the next to speak. "Love and hate are not opposites. They are merely different manifestations of the same intensity of feeling. What Sidorio did next may seem hateful to you, to all of us . . ." He broke off.

"What did he do?" Grace asked.

"You're sure you want to know this?" Mosh Zu answered.

"It isn't a question of wanting," Grace said. "I *have* to know."

Mosh Zu nodded. "Would you like me to show you?" he asked.

To *show* her? What did he mean? Mosh Zu stood up from the table and walked towards the fireplace. He beckoned to

Grace to join him. She did so, puzzled. Lorcan, who was sitting with his back to the fire, did not stand but turned around and rested his arms on the back of his chair.

"Look into the flames," Mosh Zu said, laying a hand on Grace's shoulder. Grace let her eyes fall on the flickering flames which licked around the edges of the hearth.

"Now," Mosh Zu said, "listen to the flames."

Listen to the flames? It was a curious instruction. But Grace did as he commanded, letting her attention focus on the hiss and crackle of the fire. Suddenly, the sound of the flames grew louder and all background noise was shut out. It was calming in a way, like listening to the waters of the fountain in the gardens of Sanctuary. The noise of the fire grew louder and louder in her head. Then she heard voices. The shock of it made her start, but Mosh Zu's voice reassured her. "It's OK. Stay with it, Grace. Listen closely." She obeyed his command. She could hear voices and music. Deeply rhythmic, somewhat familiar, music.

"Now." Mosh Zu spoke once more. "Now, look beyond the flames."

Grace did as he commanded. And suddenly it was as if a window had opened in the hearth – she could see the Vampirates and donors at Feast Night. They felt so close that she could almost reach out and touch them. But where was Sally? As she framed the question, the vision shifted and led her to where her mother was sitting, waiting at the long table. Grace caught her breath. This time, she was seeing things from a different viewpoint, no longer through Sally's eyes. It was fascinating to see her mother's face. She could see hope in it. Her mother knew she was leaving the ship, that her plans were coming together. That she was about to start a new life – and family – with Dexter. Her green eyes were bright with hope. She looked more beautiful than ever before.

Then, Sally dropped her head. Why? The vision shifted and Grace saw Sidorio enter the room. He instantly stood out, even amongst the crowd of other Vampirates. He strode over to the table and took his position opposite Sally. As he did so, Sally lifted her head and smiled at him. He nodded back, formally. If she had seen this vision before, Grace would have thought that what her mother had said – that Sidorio saw her only as a blood supply – was true. But now she heard Lorcan's recent words: "*Sidorio was in love with your mother. But it was an unrequited love.*" Yes, she could see it was true! Sidorio's face was mask-like, but it was not the face of someone devoid of feeling. Rather, it was the face of someone desperately trying to hide the turbulent emotions beneath.

Grace continued to watch as the Feast began. She could even hear the conversations going on around Sally and Sidorio. They, however, barely spoke.

"Are you ready to move on?" Mosh Zu broke in.

"Yes," Grace said, without turning away from the flames.

At that, the vision shifted again and she was watching Sidorio and Sally walking along the corridor, arm in arm, to her mother's cabin. Was she about to witness their sharing? But, as they entered the room, the door closed shut and Grace was left outside.

"Keep watching" Mosh Zu said softly. "You're not seeing this in real time. Time is passing."

Grace kept her eyes on the door. Suddenly, it opened and Sidorio stepped out into the corridor. Her heart began to race. Where was Sally? What had he done to her?

Sidorio's eyes ranged from left to right. At first, Grace thought he was simply anxious. Then she realised that he was looking for someone. But who? She heard him call out. "Over here! Come inside! Be quick about it!"

Now a figure approached. A woman, dressed in a long black cloak, carrying a bag.

Grace watched as Sidorio pushed open the door and pulled the woman inside. Now the door closed again but this time the vision took Grace right inside the cabin itself. Once more, she caught her breath. There was her mother, lying on the bunk. She looked peaceful.

The other woman sighed. "A real sleeping beauty!" she said, setting her bag down on the floor.

"Get on with it, witch," snapped Sidorio. "We don't have much time!"

"I'm no witch!" the woman cried angrily, throwing back her cape. "I'm a priestess!" Grace gasped. She felt as if she were hurtling along on a runaway train. Part of her wanted to jump off, but she knew that she had no option but to ride the vision out.

Witch? Priestess? Whichever, the woman now fell to her knees and began unpacking her bag. She lifted out a casket and set it with great care on the cabin floor. Sidorio hovered above her, his agitation and urgency obvious. Meanwhile Sally slept on, the expression on her face beatific. Grace imagined that she was dreaming of the new life awaiting her, so close she could almost taste it – like salt carried on the sea air.

It came as no surprise to see the medicine woman set out black candles on the floor and scatter tiny glittering discs around them. She had seen this part of the vision before. But now she heard Sidorio ask, "What are those?"

"Fish-scales," the woman answered. "An offering to my hungry gods."

The priestess reached out and took one of Sally's hands, enfolding it in her own leathery grasp. She began to chant. Her words were unrecognisable – strange, guttural sounds which lurched horribly between deep notes and high screeches. It was, thought Grace, an evil music. She feared for her mother and yet Sally lay there, seemingly untroubled and oblivious.

"Now we begin," the priestess said, turning to Sidorio and stretching out her free palm. "First, give me the mobius spiders."

Grace saw Sidorio reach into the casket and lift out two spiders, wriggling on a leaf. This too she had seen before. The priestess took the spiders in her hand, then dropped them over Sally's closed eyelids – first right, then left. As she did so, she chanted and, with her free fingers, tapped Sally's hand in a precise number of beats. "The spider's eye," announced the medicine woman. "For supreme vision, through fog and darkness."

After a moment's pause, she extended her empty palm again. "The vial!" she commanded. Grace watched as Sidorio reached into the casket once more and lifted out a small glass container. The woman seized the vial and, flicking off the stopper, upended it over Sally's pale lips – all the while chanting and continuing to percuss Sally's hand. "The vial of mountain air," she announced, "for unflagging stamina." Turning over her shoulder, she grinned, gap-toothed, at Sidorio. "Next, the coral!"

Sidorio took a branch of red coral out of the casket. The priestess placed it like a posy in Sally's free hand. There was more chanting, then the woman intoned, "Red coral, for good fortune till the end of days."

"Is it working?" Sidorio asked, bowing over Sally.

"Stop! Fool!" The woman pushed him away, angrily. "Do not interrupt my conversation with the gods! Give me the Kurinji plant!"

Sidorio delved back into the casket and carefully removed the tiny purple sprig.

The priestess snatched it from him and placed it on Sally's forehead. "The rare Kurinji plant, which flowers only once every twelve years, for a rarity of wisdom." Again, the priestess chanted and tapped at the hand. Still, Sally seemed to sleep, her body utterly still.

There was only one object left in the casket. The woman turned to Sidorio. "Last, the blackened heart of the sea eagle," the woman commanded.

Sidorio reached in and took out the charred offering. It looked disgusting but the priestess smiled as she received it, lifting it to her lips and kissing it. Chanting, she placed the blackened heart on Sally's thorax. "The heart of the sea eagle – for strength to never stand down from the fight," she announced.

"And now," she turned to Sidorio, "give me *your* hand." He readily extended his hand. The priestess clasped it tightly in her own, then brought it together with Sally's, which she continued to tap until the very last moment. Then, she pressed the two palms against one another and chanted once more. Her song seemed to grow louder and even more ugly as it reached its crescendo.

"Keep hold of her hand!" the priestess ordered. "Keep hold of her hand now and you will never be parted." Grace trembled, watching how tightly Sidorio clasped her mother's hand. Sally did not stir. At last the priestess laid her hand on Sidorio's shoulder. "It is done," she said. "I asked the gods and they have given their answer."

What did she mean? Grace thought she had an idea but she couldn't be sure.

The vision was fading fast, as if consumed by the hungry flames. Grace let it go, then turned to face Mosh Zu.

"What was the spell the priestess performed?" she asked.

"The answer is within you," Mosh Zu said.

Grace frowned. This was no time for riddles. And yet suddenly it came to her. Sidorio had said he'd find a way for Sally never to forget him. The priestess had said that Sally and Sidorio would never be parted. All at once, it was as clear as day.

Grace felt numb. "It was a pregnancy spell," she said, turning to Mosh Zu, hoping he would correct her. But he said nothing. Grace found herself shaking as she continued. "*Sidorio* is my father! He is, isn't he? He put a spell on my mother and that's how Connor and I were born." She could hardly believe she was speaking these words, yet somehow deep inside, she knew them to be true.

She waited for Mosh Zu and Lorcan to deny it, to tell her she was crazy, that it was another, quite different, spell. But still they said nothing.

At last, Mosh Zu reached out his hand to her. "Yes, Grace," he said. "You are quite right. Sidorio *is* your father."

CHAPTER FORTY-THREE

Fatherhood

Though she had guessed it, to have it confirmed by Mosh Zu left Grace reeling. It was the very worst possible outcome. Sidorio – *Sidorio!* – was her father.

Lorcan reached out and put his arm around her. "I'm so sorry, Grace," he said. "I know this isn't what you'd have chosen."

She was almost speechless. "Sidorio," she rasped, her voice weak, her body numb.

"Come and sit down," Mosh Zu said. "I know this is a great shock."

Lorcan held out the chair for Grace. She sat down, sighed but shook her head. "I think on some level I knew this," she said. "It was what I feared most, though confirming it takes away some of the fear."

Mosh Zu nodded. "Yes," he said. "I hoped that you would see it that way. It will take time to adjust: both to the idea that Sidorio is your father and that you are a dhampir, but I know you can work through both those things."

"Yes," said Grace, then a fresh thought occurred to her. "In fact, it *wasn't* what I feared most . . ."

Mosh Zu raised an eyebrow.

Grace reached out her hand to Lorcan. "It would have been much, much worse to discover that *Lorcan* was my father," she said.

Lorcan smiled at her and squeezed her hand. There were tears in Grace's eyes, but she wiped them dry.

"And besides, whatever Sidorio did, I'll never stop thinking of Dexter as my dad."

"Nor should you," said Mosh Zu. He smiled at Grace. "I want you to focus on the fact that you are very special." He paused. "You remember the different elements of the spell the medicine woman cast?"

She nodded, still a little dazed.

Mosh Zu continued. "She was talking about qualities that you and Connor possess. Supreme vision. Unflagging stamina. Good fortune. Rare wisdom. And, perhaps most importantly, the strength to never stand down from a fight. You have each been blessed with all these gifts. And I think we have already seen a number of them in action."

"Do you want some time to yourself now?" Lorcan asked.

Grace considered for a moment. "Perhaps," she said. "But first I really need you to finish the story. What happened *after* the spell was cast?"

Lorcan gripped her hand. "Are you sure you want to hear this now?"

Grace nodded, feeling determined. "It's best I know everything. Then I can start to move forward."

Lorcan gazed at her, his eyes wide with concern. He glanced at Mosh Zu, but the guru smiled and nodded. "All right then, we shall continue our tale." He rested his hands before him on the table. "When your mother awoke – alone, as usual, after the sharing – she had no memory of the medicine woman's visit, nor any realisation of what had happened. And so, life continued as normal. The time for Sally and Dexter to depart *The Nocturne* was approaching. The captain had identified a new donor for Sidorio and everything was set to proceed as planned." He paused. "But then your mother realised that something was happening to her, *within* her. Sally realised she was pregnant. The thought filled her with concern and she came once more to talk to the captain."

Grace frowned. "Didn't she think there might be a chance that Dexter could be the father?"

Mosh Zu shook his head. "No. Sally was most adamant about that. Indeed, it was a mystery to her just who the father could be. Then she remembered Sidorio's words to her – that he'd find a way for her never to forget him. Those words sent a chill through her." Mosh Zu stood and began walking around the cabin. "The captain came to see me and asked me to visit Sally on the ship. When I did so, I was able to confirm that she was indeed pregnant – and that she was bearing not one child but two. And I told her that, as these twins had a mortal mother and a Vampirate father, they would be dhampirs – powerful beings blessed with both vampire and mortal qualities." Mosh Zu smiled at Grace. "Even then, we knew that you would be very special. And we promised to look after Sally *and* her children, either on the ship or at Sanctuary." He shook his head. "But Sally didn't want that. All she wanted was to go away with Dexter, as planned. To return to the mortal world."

"And what about Dexter?" Grace asked. "How did he feel about it all?"

"A good question," Mosh Zu said. "I believe it was terribly hard for your mother to tell him what had happened, though she had had no control over the events. I truly think that she expected him to reject her. She had had a hard life before coming onto *The Nocturne* and her faith in people was fragile at best. But Dexter Tempest was not the kind of man to run from trouble or pain. He was, in the most instinctive of ways, a healer. He told your mother that their plan should remain the same. They should still leave the ship, but take the babies with them and bring them up together."

Grace's eyes filled with tears once more. "He agreed to bring us up as his own?"

Lorcan nodded. "I don't think he ever had a moment's doubt about that, Grace."

"Sally and Dexter came to see the captain and me once more," Mosh Zu said. "They told us what they wanted. We foresaw some problems, of course, but we could also see the sense of keeping Sidorio away from the children he had created. So we devised a plan to deceive him."

"To deceive Sidorio?" Grace asked, shocked. "How?"

Lorcan now took up the story. "Sally was to give birth at Sanctuary, where Mosh Zu would deliver her babies. But, as far as Sidorio knew, there was only one child, not two. And so, when the time came, we all journeyed to Sanctuary."

"*You* were there, at our birth?" Grace asked him.

"Yes," Lorcan nodded, his blue eyes full of emotion. He smiled at her. "Yes, Grace. I've been there since the very start."

So, thought Grace, there *is* a special connection between us. Going right back to the beginning.

"And Sidorio?" she asked. "Presumably, he was there too?"

"He arrived late," Lorcan said. "He had been out feasting on blood . . ."

"Out feasting!" Grace couldn't contain her rage. "While my mother gave birth?!"

"To be fair to him," Lorcan said, "he was unable to share Sally's blood while she was pregnant. And, besides, his late arrival at Sanctuary enabled us to enact our plan."

"When Sidorio arrived at Sanctuary," said Mosh Zu, "we told him that his baby had died shortly after delivery."

Grace gasped.

"He was devastated, as you can imagine," Mosh Zu continued. "He stood at the peak of the mountain and cursed the medicine woman for failing in her spell."

"And meanwhile," Lorcan said softly, "I had you and Connor in my arms, two healthy babes in swaddling clothes."

"You?" Grace said, once more marvelling at the way their lives had intertwined.

"Yes," Lorcan nodded. "I carried you both down the mountainside. I had a boat waiting there and I sailed off with you both to meet your dad. We met at an agreed location. And, Grace, he took you and Connor in his arms and I have never seen a happier man than Dexter Tempest at that moment." Lorcan placed his hand over Grace's. "I left him there and watched him sail off into the night. With you and Connor. My last words to him were to assure him that we would bring Sally to join him later. And you know what your dad said? He said that he would wait for as long as it took."

Grace bit her lip. "But she never came, did she? And he never stopped waiting."

Chapter Forty-four

No More Secrets

"I must tell Connor," Grace said. "As soon as possible."

Mosh Zu frowned. "I'm not convinced that Connor is ready."

"He has to know," Grace insisted. "He has to know who his real father is and what that makes us."

Mosh Zu considered her words, then nodded. "You are right. Of course you are. And perhaps *you* are the best one to tell him. But first we must ensure you are fit to do it." He paused. "I'm not just talking about dealing with the shock of what you've just learned, but also with your body's transformation."

Grace felt a chill run through her body. "Maybe Connor's going through the same transformation! Only it will be worse for him, because he won't understand it."

Mosh Zu shook his head. "Connor is not there yet. I always thought it would happen to you first."

"How can that be?" Grace asked. "We're twins, surely it should happen to us at the same time? How do you know it *isn't* happening to him?"

"You just have to trust me on that," Mosh Zu replied.

"When it begins for Connor, we will be there for him, just as we are for you. We will help him, and, of course, so will you."

"Well, all right . . ." Grace said. "Oh, this is such a shock . . . But in many ways it explains the feelings I've been having. Of not fitting into my life before. Of belonging to this ship, this world . . . of being connected to all of you. It will be more difficult for Connor. He hates this world. He's already run from it once." Her eyes were wide with fear for her brother.

Mosh Zu coughed lightly. "Grace, be assured that we will help Connor make the transition. But for now let us concentrate on you. Besides, our story is not yet at an end. If you're sure you want to hear it, then we should continue."

Grace had no hesitation. "I want to know everything," she said. "I've already waited too long."

"Very well," said Mosh Zu.

Once more, Lorcan spoke. "After the birth, Sally recuperated at Sanctuary," he said. "And back on *The Nocturne*, Sidorio seemed to have accepted that he had lost his child. Indeed, he seemed at last to have lost all interest in your mother. Perhaps in some way, he felt that the death of his child – as far as he knew – brought the affair to an end. He had a new donor and he began to get on with his life." Lorcan paused, a dark shadow falling over his face. "But then he found out that he had been tricked. To this day, we don't know who told him. Sidorio found out that he had not one child but two, and that neither of them were dead – but were, in fact, living far away from him."

"So he returned to Sanctuary to confront my mother?" Grace asked, her voice full of trepidation.

Lorcan took a deep breath. "Yes, Grace – and she was so brave. She didn't flinch. She admitted the truth. And she vowed never to reveal the whereabouts of her precious children – even when Sidorio threatened to kill her. Knowing that you and Connor were safe was all that mattered to her."

"But Sidorio knew about Dexter," Grace said. "Why didn't he simply seek him out and snatch us back?"

Mosh Zu nodded. "A good question," he said. "Sidorio employed some dark magic on Sally, but in return the captain and I froze his memories of Sally, right through to your birth. We took away all knowledge of his children."

"He doesn't know that he . . . *created* us?" Grace said.

"No," Mosh Zu said. Then his eyes darkened. "Though I sense a thawing has begun . . ."

"What did he do to Sally?" Grace asked. Mosh Zu was silent. Grace turned to Lorcan, who hung his head.

"What happened?" Grace repeated.

Mosh Zu looked at her with concern. "Sidorio attacked your mother. It was a very violent attack. He left her for dead and fled Sanctuary, returning to *The Nocturne*. Next, he attacked the captain, but was brought into submission. As great as his powers were then, the captain's were superior. And still are." He paused. "After the attack, Sally was very weak. I tried everything I could to heal her but we were losing her. The captain couldn't bear the thought that she would never see her children, nor they her. He came to Sanctuary." Mosh Zu hesitated. "Grace, it was then that he took the decision to save her in the only way he knew how. He drew her into his arms and allowed her spirit to become fused with his own. He vowed to carry her soul until it was safe to release her . . ."

Grace nodded. "Which was what happened during his healing catharsis?"

"Yes," said Mosh Zu. "Grace, I know the captain regrets not having set her free sooner. But he couldn't. He was too frightened for her." Mosh Zu paused. "I wish he was here now. I know that he would ask for your forgiveness."

A tear rolled down Grace's face. "But there's nothing to forgive! He *saved* my mother – you all did. You did everything in your power to give her one last chance." She sighed. "And you succeeded."

Mosh Zu looked up curiously. "We succeeded? How?"

"Because you brought the two of us together," Grace said. "The captain gave Connor and me that gift. We both got to meet our mother and she got to meet us. That would never ever have happened but for him – or you." She reached out her hand and squeezed Mosh Zu's wrist. "Thank you," she said. She let her hand rest there for a moment, then asked, "Please would you finish the story now?"

Mosh Zu nodded but it was Lorcan who spoke. "Dexter was waiting in Crescent Moon Bay, looking after you both. I gather you were quite a handful!" He grinned. "I journeyed one last time to Crescent Moon Bay to tell him what had happened. And also to offer to take you both back on board *The Nocturne*."

"You were going to bring us up on board the ship?" asked Grace, surprised.

Lorcan nodded. "Yes, but Dexter wouldn't even entertain the thought. He told me so in no uncertain terms. He said that he would be the one to bring you both up. That you were Sally's children and if he could not have another day with his dear Sally then at least he would always have a part of her – two parts of her – alongside him."

"And so you see," said Mosh Zu, "what I said before about love and hate . . . Though Sidorio acted out of hateful emotions, his actions led to something very different. For your true father was a man who didn't even know how to hate. The goodness of his heart transformed Sidorio's evil deed into a rare and wonderful blessing."

Grace was reeling from everything she had heard and yet, strangely, she also felt within her a deep sense of peace. At last, there were no more secrets. She knew who she was and who her parents were. And though they were both now gone, the depth of their love for each other and for each of their children, felt very real to her. In spite of the dark turns the story had taken. In spite of Sidorio being her father. *That* was going to take a long time to adjust to.

"I think I'll go back to my cabin now," Grace said.

"Would you like me to walk with you?" Lorcan suggested.

Grace nodded. "Yes, please, I'd like that very much."

"Good idea," Mosh Zu said, rising from his chair and turning to walk back to the steering wheel.

Lorcan and Grace took their leave.

Out in the corridor, Grace seized Lorcan's arm. "Let's go up on deck," she said, her eyes bright.

Lorcan readily agreed. So they pushed open the door to the deck and stumbled outside, where a strong breeze was blowing. It sent strands of Grace's auburn hair flying all over her face.

"You look like a spider's web!" Lorcan said. "Here, let me sort you out." He reached out his hand to brush the strands away. Almost immediately, a fresh gust of wind blew and her face was covered once more. They both grinned.

"Look," Lorcan said, "it's starting to rain! Maybe we should go back inside."

Grace shook her head. "It's only a summer shower. I'm not ready to go inside yet. I need to clear my head. Come on, it'll be drier under the mainsail."

"Good idea!" Lorcan said, reaching out for her hand. Together they raced across the wet deck until they reached the relative shelter of the vast, winglike mainsail.

"That's better!" Grace said.

Lorcan shook himself. "We're both soaked through," he said.

"Just like when we first met," Grace smiled. Then she shook her head. "Well, not when we first met, obviously, because I was a baby then . . ."

"It's all right," Lorcan said. "I knew what you meant. And you're right. 'Tis very much like the night we first properly met, you and I."

There was a new tone in his voice. He seemed somehow freer with her than before, as if by telling her the story and releasing his secrets, he could at last relax with her. Grace was delighted at this development. She glanced up at the rain, allowing the cooling drops to bathe her face and not minding one bit.

"Look," she said. "How strange! In spite of the rain, you can still see the stars. How bright they are tonight." She pointed but Lorcan didn't look. His eyes remained fixed intently on her.

"I can't think of a finer sight in the whole world than the one I'm looking at right now," he said.

In spite of being drenched, Grace flushed at his words.

Lorcan's eyes sparkled at her, brighter than ever before. It was as if the rare blue gems of his irises had been washed by the rain and buffed by the moonlight to a new intensity. "Grace, there's been something I've wanted to do for a very long time now, but things have kept getting in the way." He reached forward, bringing a hand to the side of her face. Then he gently but firmly drew her wet face towards his. He gazed at her, as if seeing her for the very first time. Then he brought his soft lips down to hers and kissed her.

She didn't want the kiss to end but, as it did, Grace drew comfort from the thought that it might be only the first of a million kisses between them. She had been given two precious gifts – the gift of immortality and, more importantly, the gift of someone to share it with. She felt as if all the hardship she had endured was ebbing away. At last, the tide was turning. Lorcan held her in his arms and she beamed up at him.

"It's strange," Lorcan said. "After everything you've heard tonight, I swear I've never seen you look so happy."

"I *am* happy," Grace said, surprised at herself. "Deep down in my soul, I feel peaceful and happy. I can hear my dad's voice. '*Trust the tide!*' That's what he told me. And I do, Lorcan. I trust that things are working out as they should. I know how much my mother must have suffered — and my dad too, waiting for her all that time. But now they're together again. It wasn't at all easy to hear everything you and Mosh Zu told me, but at least now I can put the past to rest and look forwards." She gazed into his eyes. "And we can be together."

"Yes," he said, kissing her once more. "Yes, my sweet Grace, that's exactly what I want too." Suddenly his face turned serious. "Grace, I forgot. There's one more thing."

"What?" she asked. Just when she thought all the secrets were out in the open, was there something more?

"Oh, no," he said, seeing her distress. "No, it's OK." He reached into the folds of his coat. "It's just that before Sally left, she gave me a letter for you. She knew she was running out of time and she wanted me to give it to you once you knew the truth."

"A letter from my mother?" Grace smiled with pleasure and relief.

"Yes," Lorcan nodded. "I've been carrying it around with me for days now, but you should have it." He continued to rifle through his pockets. "That's strange, I'm sure it was right here . . ." He unfastened the buttons of his greatcoat and turned it inside out to check its lining.

"*Which* pocket did you think it was in?" Grace asked.

"Why this one, of course," said Lorcan. "The one next to my heart." He tapped the lining with his long, pale fingers.

Grace frowned. "Well, there's your answer," she said, sadly, pointing to where the lining had frayed. "Look, it's worn away. I'm afraid the letter must have slipped out."

"Oh no!" Lorcan cried. "Oh Grace, how stupid of me. I am so sorry. What an idiot I am!"

Grace shook her head. She was bitterly disappointed but she didn't want him to know that, didn't want to spoil these perfect moments between them. "It's all right," she said. "Until a moment ago, I didn't even know there *was* a letter. And, after all, I know everything that happened now, don't I?"

"Yes," Lorcan agreed, nodding his head. "Yes, there are no more secrets to get in our way." He shook his head. "All the same, Grace, I am sorry. Where on earth can that letter be?"

"Shhh," she said, leaning in close once more. "I'm sure it will turn up sooner or later."

CHAPTER FORTY-FIVE

Position One

Cheng Li turned the envelope over in her hands. Her mind kept coming back to the letter inside. She had always suspected there was something extraordinary about the Tempest twins but this, *this* had exceeded even her expectations. It was even more of a gift because it had been brought to her by Lorcan Furey himself. She smiled. The Vampirates thought they were invincible, but they couldn't even deliver a warning salvo without making a grade A slip-up like this. No, if anyone could lay claim to invincibility, it was surely the pirates. And, amongst the pirates, she and her crew stood head and shoulders above their comrades within the Federation. They'd been given this special assignment to kill Kuo's murderer. They'd done their research. They had the weaponry, they had an unrivalled crew of the finest young warriors to sail the seven seas. And now, now she knew that amongst that crew, she had one very special warrior indeed.

She let the envelope rest in her hands. It was a powerful playing card, this. The question was – when should she elect to use it?

There was a knock on her door.

Cheng Li set down the envelope on her desk and covered it with the notebook Jasmine had found in the archive. "Enter!" she called, brightly.

Connor pushed open the door and, closing it behind him, approached her desk. "You asked to see me, Captain Li," he said.

She nodded. "Yes, I did. Please sit down, Connor."

He settled himself in the chair facing her desk. He couldn't help noticing that, though he knew he was a good few inches taller than Cheng Li, nevertheless she seemed to loom higher than him from behind the desk. He smiled to himself. She must have had the chairs adjusted!

"So," Cheng Li asked, "how's training been going this afternoon?"

"Really well," he said. "The new swords Master Yin made are awesome. They handle brilliantly."

Cheng Li nodded. "Of course. You get what you pay for from a master craftsman such as Master Yin." She drummed her fingers on the top of the leather-bound notebook. "And Cate – is she putting everyone through their paces?"

Connor nodded, smiling once more. "She's cracking the whip like only Cate can. It's great to have her here. And Bart too of course."

Cheng Li smiled. "Just like old times, eh? I'm pleased to have them on my crew too. Shall I let you in on a little secret, Connor?"

He shrugged. "If you like."

"I have plans to recruit Cate and Bartholomew to *The Tiger* on a more permanent basis."

"You'll have a job on your hands," he said. "They won't relinquish Molucco's articles without a fight."

Cheng Li smiled. "If only they were more like you, Connor," she said. "Well, we shall see what the future holds. I have a feeling that if we successfully conclude this mission, we'll be able to persuade them, and many others, to join our crew. There's no better strategist than Cate on any Federation ship. This is where she should be."

"What about Bart?" asked Connor.

Cheng Li made a tower of her fingers. "I think we both know that Bart has his limitations as a combatant. He's a wall of muscle but he lacks subtlety under attack. But, whatever the case, it's clear to me that Cate will go wherever he goes. Besides, he's your friend, isn't he?"

"Yes," Connor nodded. "He's my good friend." So, he thought, it might be kind of nice if you refrained from dissing him in my presence. Perhaps his thoughts were somehow transmitted to her because she now changed tack.

"Well, I didn't ask you here to talk about Bart or Cate. I wanted to talk to you about the mission."

"Sure," he said, nodding.

"I'm making some changes to the attack plan," Cheng Li said.

"Changes? What kind of changes?"

"Personnel ones," Cheng Li said. "It's absolutely vital that this mission is successful. The eyes of the whole pirate world are watching us. And the Vampirate world too. Our success – or failure – will echo across the oceans."

"We won't fail," Connor said.

"Of course not," Cheng Li agreed. "Especially as I'm moving you into position one."

Connor hesitated. "Position one?" he said. "That means that I'll be the one to assassinate the target."

"Correct," Cheng Li nodded. "*You* will eliminate Lady Lockwood."

Connor was shocked. For a moment, he said nothing.

"What's wrong?" she asked. "I thought you'd be ecstatic to

have this responsibility – a thrusting young fighter like you. This is the break you've been waiting for. You'll be the hero of the Federation if you pull this off – or rather, *when* you pull this off."

"I don't understand," Connor said. "Why me? Jacoby's your deputy. It was always going to be his position."

Cheng Li shook her head. "The plans were fluid. I've been mulling things over." She caught a glance of the corner of the envelope, peeping out from beneath the leather notebook. "And Cate and I have been talking. It's clear to us that you are the stronger fighter. Oh, make no mistake, Jacoby's good. But you, well you really are something of a prodigy, Connor."

"Thank you," he said. "But how's Jacoby going to feel about this?"

"That's not your concern. Leave Jacoby to me. I'll make him understand that there are bigger concerns here than personal pride. He's the deputy captain. He will understand that the success of the crew, the success of the mission, comes before everything."

She spoke with passion but Connor remained dubious. He was thinking guiltily of the kiss he and Jasmine had shared. First, he had stolen Jacoby's girlfriend, now he was usurping his role on the ship too. Some friend he was turning out to be!

Cheng Li gazed at Connor inquisitively. Above her, the portrait of her father, Chang Ko Li, seemed to stare down at him with the same penetrating eyes.

"Is there a problem, Connor? Something I should know about?"

Connor hesitated. He shook his head. "No," he said. "I'm just really uncomfortable about taking Jacoby's position from him."

Cheng Li ran her finger along the top of the envelope. Was

now the time to play her trump card? It would be a gamble. The letter could work in one of two ways. It could prove deeply motivational to Connor. Or else, it could send him completely over the edge. Though she knew Connor Tempest well, it was just too close to call. She decided to try another tack.

"You've killed before, Connor."

"I know," he said. "That isn't the problem."

"Are you sure?" she asked. "Because if you do have a problem with our mission, I need to know right now." She was pushing him hard, but she had to get the measure of him.

"I don't have a problem with killing," he stammered. "For a reason."

Cheng Li nodded. "All right, then. And you understand the reason here?"

Connor nodded.

"Humour me," said Cheng Li.

Connor frowned again. "The target, Lady Lockwood, is a cold-blooded killer. She murdered Commodore Kuo, and Varsha and Zak, in cold blood. She's on the verge of making an alliance with Sidorio. She must be stopped."

"Word perfect," Cheng Li said. "Connor, I know that at the outset of the mission, you were concerned on account of Grace's allegiance with some of the Vampirates. Is that what's holding you back?"

"No," he said. "No, I'm not keeping anything from you."

"I think perhaps I need to reassure you that our current mission does not, in any way, target the specific Vampirates whom Grace is close to. Therefore, your sister is in no immediate danger."

"I know that," he said.

Cheng Li glanced down at the notebook once more.

"What's that notebook?" Connor asked. "I'm sorry to be impertinent, but you keep looking at it as if it's really important."

Cheng Li shook her head, lifting it up in her fingers. "This old thing? Just some battered old diary Jasmine dug up in the archive. She thought I'd be interested to see it but," she shook her head, "it's nothing of consequence."

Suddenly she froze, realising that in holding up the notebook, she had uncovered the envelope. Glancing down she saw that the word *Grace* was clearly visible. Had Connor seen it? Cheng Li set the notebook down once more, covering the envelope. He didn't seem to have noticed, but she couldn't be one hundred per cent sure.

"Connor," she said. "I have a good deal of paperwork to crunch through before suppertime. I've told you my intentions. Go away and think things through. If you aren't happy with what I'm suggesting then it's imperative you tell me by nightfall."

Connor remained in the chair. He was thinking about Grace. About her attachment to Lorcan and the other Vampirates. About her deranged idea that they were Vampirates themselves, that their dad had been a Vampirate. He had to get her to see sense, to tear her out of their vile clutches. He had tried gentle persuasion but it had got him nowhere. Nowhere at all. But this mission, whilst not endangering Grace in any way, might finally show his sister the dangers she was facing. This in itself was good enough reason to take part.

"Connor," Cheng Li said. "This isn't some kind of zen meditation chamber. If you have thinking to do, take it out onto the deck, please."

He brought his eyes back to hers. "I don't have any more thinking to do," he said. "I'll do as you ask. I'll take position one. I'll be the one to assassinate Lady Lockwood."

Cheng Li smiled. "I'm very pleased to hear it. Well, off you go then. Go polish your sword and lay out your best clothes. We have a wedding to prepare for."

"Aye-aye, Captain," he said, standing up and giving her a salute.

"That reminds me," Cheng Li said. "I trust Bo Yin and that grotesque pet of hers are settling in all right?"

"Yes." Connor grinned. "Sinbad seems especially happy with his new abode. Perhaps you'd like to join us for his evening playtime later?"

"You're dismissed," Cheng Li said, sliding on her glasses and dipping her hands into her in-tray once more.

"I do so enjoy these chats," he said.

"Don't be cheeky," she said. "You may be in position one but I'm still captain around here, until further notice."

"Don't worry," he said. "I'm not in any danger of forgetting that." He nodded, then pushed open the door and exited into the corridor.

As the doors swung shut behind him, Cheng Li removed her hands from the in-tray and lifted the notebook and envelope once more. Standing up, she approached her father's portrait and raised her fingers to the small but distinctive scar above her father's right eyebrow. As she pressed lightly against the canvas, the painting began moving to one side, revealing a safe. Cheng Li deftly manoeuvred the cogs until the safe door clicked open. She placed her father's diary and Sally's letter inside, then closed the door and reset the combination – the latitude, longitude and geodesic height of the Pirate Academy. Smiling at her ingenuity, she touched the painting once more – this time at the centre of the ear-stud in her father's left ear – and it slid obediently back into position.

As it did so, she found herself staring once more at her father's face. It was as if he was smiling at her. "*Very good, Cheng Li,*" he seemed to say.

In life, Chang Ko Li had been decidedly short on words of encouragement for his prodigiously talented daughter.

Nonetheless, she felt sure he would have been swelling with pride now at how her career was shaping up. Turning her back on his image, she settled back down at her desk and opened up the attack plans for Operation Black Heart.

CHAPTER FORTY-SIX

Blood Wedding

In some respects, at least, it would be a conventional wedding. The bride had chosen the setting – the ruins of a small chapel, perched close to the edge of the cliff above Martyr's Cove.

"A chapel?" Sidorio had initially bristled at the thought.

"I know, " Lady Lola had said in her most soothing tones. "I know. But it's deconsecrated, darling, and trust me, we'll make it our own."

And she had not lied. The chapel building no longer had a roof or complete walls but the light of the moon revealed the skeleton of its former shape. Glimpses of the original stonework glowed silver in the moonlight, but relatively little of the stone was visible as around each column and architrave were coiled lavish amounts of ivy and black roses, interspersed with a variety of tribal fetishes, animal pelts and small skulls. Lady Lockwood's wedding designer had certainly risen to the occasion. Nature supplied the rest – the night sky, sprinkled with bright stars and a perfect full moon, made a dazzling canopy.

According to tradition, the groom arrived first. He was dressed in a striking outfit – to call it a morning suit was to utterly fail to do it justice. A bespoke creation by Lady

Lockwood's tailor, it had the approximate shape of a suit but the main part of the jacket was made of chainmail, the collar and tails of fur and, once again, there were thick leather shoulder-pads from which emerged metal spikes. "I think we've found your signature style," the tailor had said, presenting Sidorio with one final touch – a crown fashioned of bone and metal, which sat on his head rather like a laurel wreath. "Perfect!" the tailor had declared and Sidorio could only agree. Now, he looked not only like a groom but like a king – King of the Vampirates, as he indeed was.

Sidorio's dark eyes sparkled and his gold teeth glinted as he arrived at the ruined chapel. A string quartet were playing pleasingly discordant music – a rhapsody inspired apparently by the human scream – as Sidorio appeared at the top of the red carpet, accompanied by his ring-bearer. Johnny had been dressed by the same tailor but from his "off the peg" range. He cut a dashing figure in leather and chainmail. He wore his trademark Stetson, of course, but this had been glammed up with bone claws and feathers.

Sidorio was to have had two ring-bearers but the man originally scheduled to be his second ring-bearer, Stukeley, now stood at the other end of the carpet. From here, he would conduct the marriage service. He looked very much the part in a bespoke cassock. It was simple and black, with a line of small buttons, fashioned from bones, down the front. Around his neck, he wore a long gold chain, suspended from which was a pair of shrunken heads.

This was a strictly intimate and exclusive affair. Only a small, select and exquisitely-dressed crowd sat on either side of the aisle. Their chairs were covered in animal hide, with legs made from antlers. A table had been set up at the back of the chapel with an array of antique Venetian glassware and a line of bottles, supplied of course by the Black Heart winery. The hand-picked congregation would be treated to some of Lady Lockwood's finest vintages to toast the happy couple.

Later, there would be a party for the masses, beginning on board *The Blood Captain*, moored below in the bay. Then the party would continue off the ship, wherever the happy couple decreed. By this point, the "free bar" would have run dry but the happy couple were confident that the guests would be perfectly happy to fend for themselves.

The groom and his ring-bearer strode purposefully down the aisle, attracting smiles and admiring gasps from the assembled guests.

Sidorio nodded to Stukeley as he and Johnny arrived at the altar. "All set, 'Reverend'?" he asked.

"Yes, Captain," Stukeley nodded, exchanging a knowing glance with Johnny. "I was up all day learning the service."

"I trust you're word perfect," Sidorio said. "Everything must be just right for my Lola."

"Don't worry," Stukeley said. "This will be a night to remember." His dark eyes glinted. "We'll make absolutely sure of that."

"Very good," Sidorio said, turning to Johnny. "Stetson, you have the ring?"

Johnny nodded, patting the pocket of his long coat. "Right here, *Capitan*."

The music changed to the traditional wedding march, signalling the arrival of the bride. All eyes turned as she made her entrance, flanked by her two ring-bearers. The three women looked stunning in couture outfits. Angelika and Marianne were clothed simply but elegantly in tight-fitting sleeveless gowns. They each wore long gloves and their hair had been swept up and adorned with wild flowers and jewelled combs. Lady Lockwood's dress was more elaborate, tightly-corseted – in the style she favoured, with the whalebones exposed on the outside – and tight-fitting sleeves, coiled with snakeskin. The bottom part of the dress was a fairy-tale skirt composed of billowing layers of blood-red taffeta, which her two companions watched closely as she began walking along the aisle. Her face and upper body was covered by a black lace veil. On her head she wore a crown, fashioned to match that of the groom – but a touch smaller and more delicate, shimmering with rubies and black opals.

As Lady Lockwood, flanked by her ring-bearers, moved gracefully down the aisle, the congregation murmured in admiration. Her outfit had exceeded every expectation. Of particular interest was her rather unusual wedding bouquet.

For in Lady Lockwood's hands was a solid gold hand, with eighteen-carat rubies for fingernails, about which had been wrapped black roses and trailing ivy. Until recently it had belonged to one Trofie Wrathe. "Something borrowed, do you see?" Lady Lockwood announced with a grin, to her friends in the congregation.

At last, the bride and her entourage reached the altar.

As Sidorio reached out for her hand, Lady Lockwood passed her bouquet to Angelika. "Be sure to take good care of it, my dear!" she said, then turned back to Sidorio. "My, how handsome you look! You should always wear that crown, my love. It sets off your teeth perfectly."

He blushed at her praise. "You look more beautiful than ever," he noted.

The bride and groom knelt on the cushions placed before Stukeley. Marianne carefully arranged Lady Lockwood's voluminous train, then stepped aside to join Angelika.

Lady Lockwood's two ring-bearers were facing Johnny, who removed his dress Stetson and winked at them, amiably. Both women winked back. As their tattooed eyes closed, two perfect black hearts appeared on their faces. It was a shame, in a way, what was going to happen later, mused Johnny. There would have been some definite upsides to a merger of the two crews.

Sidorio glanced up at his other lieutenant. "Well then, 'Reverend'. Let's get this show on the road!"

Stukeley raised his hand towards the distant quartet and the music at once came to an end. Then he coughed lightly and stepped forward to address the congregation. "Dearly beloved! With great joy, we come together tonight to join this man, Quintus Antonius Sidorio, and this woman, Lady Lola Elizabeth Mercy Lockwood, in eternal matrimony."

The bride and groom's eyes locked upon each other.

"This marriage we bear witness to tonight," Stukeley continued, "is no ordinary marriage. For when I speak the words *eternal union*, I mean exactly that. These two are immortal and so can never die. And nor will their love." He surveyed the congregation, warming to his role. "And now, by the powers invested in me by . . . the groom, I will proceed with the wedding vows." He nodded towards Sidorio. "You're up, Captain."

Sidorio turned to face his bride, his voice ringing out across the ruined chapel and beyond. "I am immortal and so is my love. I am all conquering and so is my passion. I am as infinite as the oceans and as mighty as the night." His voice grew a little softer. "I promise you, my dear Lola, that I will be a loving and loyal husband to you. I will share with you my passion, my power and my love beyond tide and time."

Lady Lockwood's eyes sparkled brighter than the stars above as she began her reciprocal vow. "I am immortal and so is my love. I am all conquering and so is my passion. I am as infinite as the oceans and as mighty as the night. I promise you, my darling Sidorio, that I will be a loving and loyal wife to you. I will share with you my passion, my power and my love beyond tide and time."

Stukeley, feeling completely in his element, glanced to the attendants on either side. "And now, the rings," he announced.

Johnny and Marianne stepped closer, each dropping a ring into Stukeley's waiting palm. The rings were surprisingly simple – crafted in human bone with private messages, each decided upon by the bride and groom, inscribed on the inside.

Stukeley held out his palm, offering the rings to the bride and groom. "Each of you has rings for one another. Would you now exchange them?" He nodded and groom and bride lifted the rings from his palm and reached out to slide them onto each other's ring fingers. As they did so, Stukeley spoke once more. "These rings are an eternal reminder of this moment, and this night and of the promise you have made to each other, as you experience, now and forever, the oneness of your union as husband and wife."

Sidorio nodded, squeezing Lady Lockwood's slender hand in his own.

The rings exchanged, Stukeley geared up for his final crescendo. "Because they have so affirmed, in love and knowledge of each other, I do declare that Quintus Antonius Sidorio and Lady Lola Elizabeth Mercy Lockwood are now husband and wife!"

The bride and groom rose to their feet and embraced, Sidorio dipping Lady Lockwood low to the chapel floor. The congregation gasped in delight and broke out into spontaneous applause.

Sidorio grinned at his bride. "Hello, my Lady Sidorio," he said.

She beamed up at him. "Lady *Lockwood* Sidorio," she reminded him. "That's what we agreed, remember, my sweet?"

Johnny leaned across to Stukeley whispering, "Great job! You may have missed your vocation."

Stukeley grinned. "The doves!" he reminded his comrade.

"Oh yes!" Johnny reached excitedly for the gilded cage containing twelve White Rock doves. He passed this to Stukeley, who set it before Sidorio and Lady Lola and released the catch. Lady Lola reached inside, taking one of the creatures into her hands and caressing its delicate little body. The second dove padded out from the cage into Sidorio's hand. Together, the bride and groom joyously began releasing the snow-white doves up into the night sky. The birds circled prettily in the soft moonlight.

Stukeley nudged Johnny again. "The hawks!" he said.

Johnny presented the bride and groom with a second cage. This contained two Accipiter hawks. Sidorio opened the cage door and took out one of the hawks, passing it to Lady Lockwood. "What a handsome chap!" she cooed, to the congregation's delight, as the proud hawk rested for a moment on her wrist. Sidorio lifted out the second hawk. Then, bride and groom turned to each other and released the hawks, before melting into a deep kiss.

Above them, the hawks soared into the air and began attacking the twelve doves. They made short work of it. The sky began to rain with snow white feathers, spattered with blood. One of the doves' inert and bloody bodies fell and landed in Sidorio's hands. He laughed and presented it to his bride, who glowed with delight. It was the perfect symbol of their dark and eternal union. The congregation rose to their feet and clapped with wild enthusiasm.

The applause was accompanied by cannon-fire and the congregation gasped once more as a flood of tiny purple petals showered over them. The confetti fell like blossom from the night sky. It was the final *coup-de-theatre* in a perfectly executed ceremony which would be engrained on their collective memories for a long, long time to come.

As the confetti covered the bride and groom, Sidorio beamed at his bride. "Nice touch," he said, "*wife.*"

She looked at him questioningly. "What do you mean, *husband*?"

Sidorio scooped up some of the petals and sprinkled them over her face. "This!" he said with a grin.

"I didn't organise it," Lady Lola said. "I thought it was *your* surprise, my darling! Something you and your handsome lieutenants plotted!"

He shook his head. Lady Lola shrugged. "Well, it must be a little extra treat from our wedding designer. How thoughtful of Stefano and what a perfect end to a sublime ceremony."

"You have tears in your eyes, my sweet," Sidorio said. "How can you be sad at a moment like this?"

"I'm not at all sad, my darling," Lola said. "My eyes are stinging, for some reason."

Sidorio frowned. "That's strange. So are mine." He noticed with rising alarm that his new wife's eyelids were swelling up right in front of him.

"Actually," she said, "I'm really feeling quite strange. My lips are numb, my darling and, as great a kisser as you are, I don't think that's the reason."

"No," Sidorio said, experiencing the same numbness in his own lips and sensing it spreading rapidly through his body. Puzzled, he turned towards the congregation. They appeared to be suffering from the very same symptoms. It was as if they had frozen, like statues, their faces grimly contorting with pain. Suddenly fearful, Sidorio felt his own body become still, as if constricted by armour. Though his suit was tight-fitting, he knew it was more serious than that. He stared down the aisle, awash with confusion.

As he did so, a host of uninvited guests sprang forth from behind the ruined chancel and strode out into the knave. There were fifty of them – each bearing a sword. A specially-engineered silver sword, coated in a compound of hawthorn and aconite – the same substance which had floated down from the sky in the form of confetti.

"Let's make this quick!" ordered Cheng Li.

Connor leaped into the centre aisle, his eyes immediately assessing the scene. The elite crew of *The Tiger* began streaming into the chapel from both sides. Bart and Cate headed the troops on one side, Jacoby and Jasmine on the other. Connor glimpsed Moonshine's arrival, then turned and called to Jasmine. "How much time do we have?"

"There should be another cannon of confetti coming right about *now!*" Jasmine cried. Her words were drowned out as a fresh cannon sounded and the skies above began to rain down once more with purple petals. The congregation was literally petrified. Though the Vampirates could not for the moment move, they could see and hear exactly what was happening. They knew that something had gone very wrong at the wedding of the year.

At the altar, Johnny and Stukeley were experiencing the same physical pain as their colleagues. In spite of this, their eyes were bright as they stared straight down the aisle at Cheng Li and Connor. Things were proceeding exactly as they had planned.

"Come on, Connor!" Cheng Li urged. "You know what you have to do."

Hearing her words, Connor ran down the aisle, taking the same path that the wedding party had travelled along with such joy barely half an hour ago. He came to a stop, just in front of the newlyweds. Here was the groom, Sidorio, looking more formal than on their last encounter. More formal and more docile, though his eyes stared at Connor with a combination of ire and wonder.

Connor now turned his attention to Sidorio's bride. It was his first glimpse at Lady Lola. Connor knew all about her dark deeds but it was still disconcerting to see her like this – her eyes swollen, her lips engorged. He knew what he had to do. He was in position one.

"Do it!" Cheng Li cried.

He didn't take his eyes off Lady Lockwood for a second as he reached for Master Yin's specially-crafted silver sword. He was about to deliver a most unusual and unwelcome wedding gift.

CHAPTER FORTY-SEVEN

The Wedding Gift

"Come *on*, Connor," urged Cheng Li once more.

Connor lifted the sword and aimed it at Lady Lockwood's heart. Not the black heart on her face but her actual heart — which, from what he had heard, was a whole lot blacker. As he targeted the sword, he thought of Zak and Varsha and Commodore Kuo.

Sidorio managed to frame his numb lips into the word, "No", but he was powerless to prevent Connor from plunging the sword through Lady Lola's frozen body. It was a clean entry, piercing right through her. Lady Lola looked at him strangely, then her eyes shifted to her groom. The newlyweds' eyes met for one last time and then the bride's eyelids fell shut.

Connor couldn't meet Sidorio's glare. He had come to do a job and his job was done. He reached for his sword but, strangely, as he tried to withdraw it from Lady Lockwood's prone body, it resisted, as if lodged in stone.

"What's wrong?" Cheng Li asked, appearing at his side.

"It's the sword," he said. "It seems to be stuck."

"Try it again," Cheng Li said.

Connor reached out and gripped the hilt of the sword, employing all his strength to draw it back. It was no use.

"Let me try," said Cheng Li, stepping forward. She gripped her hands around the sword and pulled, but there was no movement whatsoever.

"Everyone," Cate called from down the aisle, "time to pull out. Quick! The effect of the aconite is starting to wear off."

Connor looked around him. It was true.

The congregation looked as if it was waking up after a communal coma. Heads were turning; limbs coming back into motion. The Vampirates still seemed stunned at what had happened to them but it wouldn't take long for their daze to turn to anger and their anger to transform into action.

"Everybody out!" Cate called, already back at the chancel of the ruined chapel.

"Leave the sword," Cheng Li cried, pushing Connor forward. "Let's get out of here!"

As they started running to catch up with Cate and the others, Cheng Li smiled at Connor. "Our mission succeeded, Connor. Great work!"

"Wait!" A thunderous roar arose as Sidorio leaped up and, regaining the movement of his legs and arms, flew after the escaping pirates.

"Run!" Cheng Li cried. Connor was at her side, at the cliff-edge, waiting to abseil down to their waiting ship. But, as they glanced back over their shoulders, they saw that Jacoby and Jasmine were still in the church. And Sidorio was blocking their exit.

"We have to go back!" Connor told Cheng Li. She hesitated, weighing up her options.

"You're right," Cheng Li conceded, running alongside him. "Cate, Bart, cover us!"

381

The pirate squad ran back into the melee of the church, where, at the altar, Sidorio had Jasmine in his clutches.

"Let her go!" Jacoby cried. "Take me instead!"

While Sidorio considered the matter, Jasmine shook her head and cried out to the other pirates. "Run! Save yourselves!"

"No way!" cried Jacoby, then turned back to Sidorio. "You heard me. Let her go!"

"Who are *you*?" Sidorio asked.

"Jacoby Blunt, deputy captain of *The Tiger*," cried Jacoby.

Sidorio's eyes spat flame at Jacoby. "You shouldn't even be here. You and your comrades weren't on the guest list."

Jacoby shrugged. "I know. And I wish I could say I'm glad I crashed your wedding but actually, it wasn't all that." He was playing for time – hoping that he or one of the others would work out how to extract Jasmine from Sidorio's clutches – but time was running out fast.

Behind him, Johnny and Stukeley were coming back to life. Cheng Li stalked over to confront them. "We have a problem here," she hissed. "We had a deal, remember? We've done our part. We gave the bride her wedding gift. You promised me and my crew safe passage from here."

Had the Vampirates tricked her after all? But no, to her surprise, Stukeley nodded. "I meant it."

"Well," said Cheng Li, "then *do* something!"

Her cry attracted attention from Marianne and Angelika, who were crouched over the slain body of their former captain. They were both in tears, staring down at Lady Lola's beautiful but lifeless face. Angelika still held the bridal bouquet. She looked sadly down at the golden hand.

"I'll be having *that*, thank you very much!" cried Moonshine Wrathe, reaching down and tearing it out of Angelika's confused clutches. Moonshine had had the advantage of surprise but now Angelika leaped up to face him, her teeth bared. As Moonshine blanched, recognising his assailant from her visit to *The Typhon*, Marianne reached out her hand and pulled Angelika back down. "Angelika!" she cried. "Look! Look at her eyelids!"

Moonshine stood there, his mother's golden hand now in his clutches. It was all he had sought from this mission and he was victorious. His mother would be overjoyed and his dad and uncle would never stop singing his praises. He couldn't believe how easy it had been! He glanced around, checking that none of the other pirates had witnessed the encounter. Then he ran off to safety, already rewriting his tussle with Angelika in far more epic and dangerous terms.

Still locked in conversation with Cheng Li, Stukeley suddenly became aware that Marianne was staring at him. Instinctively, he brutally shoved Cheng Li aside. "Get out of here!" he cried, adding under his breath: "Round up your squad. I'll do the rest."

Cheng Li nodded, instantly calling back her crew, with the exception of Jasmine, who was still locked, cowering, in Sidorio's arms.

Cheng Li waited for Johnny and Stukeley to make their move but, before they could do so, Connor stepped forward. Cheng Li cursed Connor for his heroic tendencies. "I'm the one you want," she heard him tell Sidorio. "I murdered your bride. If you have a score to settle, it's with me not her." What was he thinking of? Why did he have to go and complicate everything?

"*You!*" Sidorio bellowed, turning to Connor. There was a flicker of recognition in Sidorio's eyes and he released Jasmine and confronted Connor. "*You* killed her." The anger in his voice was balanced with deep sorrow. This came as a surprise to Cheng Li. It was as if the Vampirate had genuine feelings.

Cheng Li's eyes darted nervously from Connor to Sidorio to Johnny to Stukeley. Something had to happen . . . and fast! But she couldn't think of anything that would distract Sidorio now that he had Connor in his sights.

"Captain!" Stukeley cried. "Captain!"

His voice was loud, but Sidorio did not turn. He reached out for Connor.

"Captain!" Stukeley repeated.

"*You!*" Sidorio said, his hand grabbing Connor roughly by the shoulder.

"*Capitan.*" Johnny raced to Sidorio's side. "*Capitan.* Your wife, Lady Lockwood . . . I mean Lady Sidorio. She's not destroyed! She's waking up!"

At first, Cheng Li thought it was a brilliant ruse. She would have clapped her hands, if she hadn't been so intent on grabbing Connor and Jasmine and moving them on, whilst they had a brief advantage over Sidorio. But as she did so, she saw that Johnny's words were *not* a ruse. The murdered bride had indeed "woken up".

Both Sidorio's lieutenants and the bride's two ring-bearers were positioned on their knees around Lady Lola. Her eyes were open and, even now, she was pulling at the sword lodged in her chest.

"You came back!" Sidorio cried, running over to his returning bride in ecstasy.

"How can this be happening?" Cheng Li cried, turning to her crewmates for answers.

"The stabbing can't have been enough," Jacoby said, his eyes wide with panic. "Even with the combination of silver, hawthorn and aconite. It's like when we staked Vampirate Two – the one who reconstituted himself!"

"I thought you'd learned from that mistake," Cheng Li cried, shooting a sharp look at her deputy. "But it's happened again, hasn't it?"

"We thought we'd got it covered with the combination of the three toxic substances," Jacoby said, talking fast. "Look how effective the aconite was in stunning the crowd!"

"We didn't come here to stun the crowd," snapped Cheng Li. "Our mission was to kill the bride!"

"We need to stake her!" Jacoby shouted, thinking on his feet. "And we'll cut her head off too! That way, she can't bring herself back to life again."

"Jacoby!" Cheng Li cried out in exasperation. "Why didn't you work all this out before?"

"Don't worry, Captain," Jacoby said, sounding calm. "Connor and I will take care of it!" He glanced towards Connor. "Right, buddy?"

"Sure," Connor nodded. "Just one problem – I have no sword, except the one she's busy trying to extricate from her chest."

Jacoby turned to Jasmine. "Min, quick! Give Connor your sword!"

Jasmine threw her sword over to Connor, who caught the hilt in his hand.

"Head or heart?" cried Jacoby.

"Your call!" Connor answered. He just wanted to get this over with as quickly as possible. He thought he'd already completed his mission. Now he was having to kill, or rather *destroy*, his target a second time.

"I'll take the heart," Jacoby cried. "You take the head."

It sounded simple enough, but it was only as Connor ran alongside his comrade towards Lady Lockwood, that he faced up to the barbaric act he was about to commit. Slicing someone's head off! No, he told himself, not some*one*. Some*thing*. She might *look* human, but she wasn't. She was a monster. They all were. She had killed two innocent friends of his. She had killed Commodore Kuo. All in cold blood. And she wouldn't hesitate for even a fraction of a second before killing him.

Sidorio was bent over his bride, reaching out his arms to her, thrilled that she had miraculously revived.

"Captain!" Johnny and Stukeley cried simultaneously.

Sidorio turned towards them. As he did so, Jacoby seized his chance. He lunged at Lady Lockwood and plunged his sword into her heart. She let out a deep sigh and closed her eyes once more.

"Connor," Jacoby cried, "you're up!"

Connor's sword was stretched out. He knew what he had to do, but he was riddled with doubt.

"Connor!" Jacoby cried once more. "*Now!*"

Gritting his teeth, Connor leaped forward and sliced Lady Lockwood's head clean from her neck. The head rolled to one side. Jacoby grabbed it and started to run, as if in the middle of a particularly brutal rugby match. "It needs to be out of reach," he cried. "So she can't put herself back together . . ."

Sidorio turned from his lieutenants and, seeing what had happened, bellowed, "No!"

As he did so, Jacoby released Lady Lockwood's head onto the grass, which sloped down to the edge of the cliff. The head began to roll, gaining momentum as it went.

Sidorio watched, torn between the chance to rescue his wife's head and avenge the pirates' actions. It was no contest.

"And now," cried Cheng Li, "we get out of here!"

They ran back towards the cliff-edge, where their colleagues were already abseiling down the side. "Faster!" Cheng Li cried, watching Sidorio race after Lady Lola's head.

It was only Cheng Li and Connor left now, waiting for their lines to be free. They both watched as Sidorio flew to the cliff-edge, arriving just a nanosecond too late, as Lady Lockwood's beautiful head – veil, crown and all – was propelled from the edge of the cliff and hurtled down towards the ocean below. Crying out, Sidorio propelled himself over the cliff-edge and dived after his wife's head.

"Come on," Cheng Li said to Connor. They grabbed their

lines and began abseiling down the cliff-face as fast as they could. When they reached the shingle beach below, they raced towards the launch, where the others were waiting to return to *The Tiger* and make their escape.

Jacoby and Jasmine waved frantically at them from the launch.

Cheng Li waved back and gave them the thumbs-up signal.

"Behind you!" cried Jacoby.

Connor glanced over his shoulder. Sidorio had retrieved Lady Lola's head and, cradling it in his arms, was striding across the sand towards them.

"Quick!" Cheng Li cried, but Sidorio was already blocking their escape. Setting Lady Lola's head tenderly down on the sand, he turned to Connor, his eyes blazing fire. "You killed my wife," he cried. "Twice! And now I'm going to take my revenge. I'm going to kill *you*."

He reached out his hands and drew Connor towards him, his gold incisors extending from his mouth like daggers. Connor's strength, prodigious as it was, was no match for Sidorio's. The Vampirate tore at Connor's shirt, instantly exposing the flesh of his thorax.

"Wait!" Cheng Li cried.

Connor looked at her helplessly. Sidorio's grasp was paralysing. "Go!" he told her. "Save yourself and the rest of the crew!"

Cheng Li shook her head and shrieked into Sidorio's ear. "I said WAIT!"

"I heard you," Sidorio snarled, twisting his head towards her. "I was just ignoring you. Now, leave me to my kill."

Cheng Li stood still, her arms folded defiantly. "I don't think so," she said. "I don't think you want to do that. You're a little short on family right now. So you may not want to kill your own *son*."

Connor heard the words. He even comprehended them. But they made no sense to him. Then, he realised what she was up to. Cheng Li had employed some wild stratagems in her time, but this was really grasping at straws. Sidorio's *son*? As if. Even Grace at her most nutty hadn't suggested *this* as a possibility . . .

But as these thoughts rushed through his head, he felt Sidorio's grip on him release. He couldn't believe it, but Sidorio was actually letting him go. The Vampirate had turned to face Cheng Li. Now, Connor's heart was racing so fast it threatened to force its way out of his chest.

"That's better," Cheng Li addressed Sidorio. "You see. Even *you* are capable of being moderately civilised when the moment demands it." She reached out her arm and beckoned Connor towards her. Dazed, he nevertheless stumbled across to her, like a fish hooked on a line.

"Look!" Cheng Li addressed Sidorio. "Take a good look. This is your son. His name's Connor. His mother was Sally, your donor. Remember her? Of course you do. You loved her too once, didn't you? But you didn't know how to tell her and, while you were figuring it out, she fell in love with someone else – a mortal. A lighthouse keeper by the name of Dexter Tempest. She was planning to leave the ship and start a new life with him, a *real* life away from you."

Sidorio was transfixed at Cheng Li's words. They had a grim fascination for Connor too.

"So you found a way to ensure that Sally would never be free of you. You put a spell on her, which resulted in her becoming pregnant. Sound familiar?"

Sidorio nodded slowly, as if dark shards of memory were slowly rising from the depths of his mind. He waited for Cheng Li to continue.

"And she went to Sanctuary to have the baby, didn't she? And when you got there, they told you that the baby had died. And

388

you were heartbroken. But later you found out that they had been lying to you, playing a trick on you. And you took your brutal and final revenge on poor Sally."

"How do you know all this?" Sidorio asked.

A good and pertinent question, Connor agreed. But his head was pounding with other questions and it looked like Sidorio's was too. *Can this really be true?* Connor thought. *Am I the spawn of this monster? What does that make me? Where do I go from here?* Thought after unthinkable thought tore through his head like bullets.

"That hardly matters now," Cheng Li said. "What's important is that you know that your son is alive and well." She pulled Connor towards her before continuing. "And that he's coming with me."

Sidorio shook his head, looking intently at Connor. "He's *my* son." It was almost as though he had realised it for the first time. "He stays with me," he said defiantly.

Things had come full circle. Once more, Sidorio's arms reached out for Connor, though this time not to smother him but to embrace him.

"No!" Cheng Li said very calmly. "I told you before, Connor comes with me."

Sidorio shook his head. "You don't get to decide this, pirate," he said.

"Oh, but I do," said Cheng Li. "Have you forgotten, *Vampirate*, the other lie they told you? That there was only one baby, when in fact there were *two*? Twins. A boy and a girl."

"Twins," Sidorio said. It was almost a question. His eyes fixed on Connor's face and he suddenly had a brief vision of a girl on a mountain-side – a girl who looked very like this boy standing in front of him . . . "A girl." He felt a searing pain in his head, as though long-forgotten memories were forcing themselves to the surface, back at last into his consciousness. He remembered it all.

"Yes," Cheng Li continued. "A girl. And I'm sure you'd like to be reunited with her too, wouldn't you? Yes, of course you would." She paused briefly to draw breath. "So, this is how it's going to work. Connor is coming back with me now. We're going to find his sister. And, when the time is right, we'll arrange for you to see them both." She smiled at him. "You'd like that, wouldn't you?" she asked. "A chance to meet both your children properly?"

Sidorio nodded slowly.

"All right then," Cheng Li said. "Well, Connor and I are going to go now. But we'll be back in touch soon."

"How will you know where to find me?" Sidorio asked.

"I managed to crash your wedding, didn't I?" said Cheng Li. "I'm sure I can keep up with you."

Sidorio had one more question for her. "How can I trust you?"

Cheng Li smiled, feeling supremely powerful. "You can't," she said. "But you don't have a choice. If you don't let Connor come with me now, I'll see to it that you *never* meet your daughter."

It was checkmate. Sidorio relinquished his last hold on Connor and stepped back to allow them free passage.

"Here," said Cheng Li, reaching down. "Don't lose your head!" She lifted up Lady Lola's head and presented it to Sidorio. Numbly, he took it into his hands, staring down at his wife's beautiful features.

Lady Lola Elizabeth Mercy Lockwood Sidorio had, in every sense of the phrase, been cut off in her prime. He stared down at the black heart tattoo, willing her to open her eyes. Just one more time. If only he could see her beautiful eyes just one more time. He thought of their first meeting, on another beach not unlike this. He thought of the time he had trespassed onto *The Vagabond* and found her preparing for her blood bath. He thought of the times they had gone hunting together. And all the little things – like when she'd helped him pick out new clothes and shown him how to swirl blood in a glass and that perfect moment when she had agreed to become his wife. She *had* become his wife but, more than that, she had become his world. And now she was gone. Suddenly, Sidorio felt unbearably lonely. He let out a deep, keening roar.

Connor allowed Cheng Li to lead him out into the water. His head was spinning as they started swimming out to the launch. His body felt like a dead weight but his survival instinct had kicked in. It was the only thing enabling him to stay afloat.

"How much of that was true?" he asked Cheng Li.

"Every last word," she said. "Well, except that I'm not in any hurry to reunite him with Grace."

"You actually *believe* that monster is my father?" Connor said.

"Yes," Cheng Li said. "I'm afraid so, Connor – but chin up! Maybe you'll prove to be a shining example of nurture over nature."

"But he's a Vampirate," Connor said. "So what does that make me?"

"You're this half-vampire thingy," Cheng Li said, mid-stroke. "A *dhampir*, that's it. A dhampir!" She powered through another stroke. "Grace too, obviously."

"How come you know this?"

"It was all in a letter," Cheng Li said.

"A letter?"

"From your mother. I'll give it to you later. In private."

She had a letter? From his mother? How on earth . . . There were so many questions Connor had to ask but they were nearing the boat, where the others awaited them, and he had to think and talk fast.

"Does anyone else know about this?" Connor asked.

"No," Cheng Li said. "And that's just the way it's going to stay. Better all round."

"So what next?" Connor asked, sadly. "Do you want me to leave the crew?"

"Are you out of your mind, Tempest?" Cheng Li said. "According to the letter, you have extraordinary powers. You were a prodigy *before*. You just became my secret weapon. You're not going anywhere. You signed my articles for life and now it turns out you're immortal. You do the math!"

It was so much to take in. "I don't know what to say," Connor said. "I don't even know what to think."

"You don't need to say or think anything," Cheng Li said. "Just get back in the launch and come back to the ship with me. It'll take time but we'll figure this out. For now, you're a hero. Enjoy the ride!"

CHAPTER FORTY-EIGHT

The Dhampirs

My darling Grace,
You told me that you were compiling a collection of
Vampirates' crossing stories. Well, my dear daughter, this,
I suppose, is your very own crossing story. And your
brother's too . . .

Connor stared at his mother's handwriting. It was very tempting to simply destroy the letter without reading it. But he knew that he couldn't do that. Destroying it wouldn't change anything; it would just leave him in ignorance of the facts. Better to know the facts and then move on – whatever that meant now. Once more, he focused on his mother's handwriting.

This letter is for Connor too, my dear son. And this is why
I'm giving the full story here, though you and I have talked
through much of this already. I didn't get the chance to tell
Connor in person. I wish I had done, but he had another
journey to make. Please, Grace, give your brother this letter
when the time is right and help him to deal with its
aftermath . . .

393

Help me? I don't *need* any help, Connor thought. He felt a flash of anger towards Sally and Grace. Who were they to talk about him in this way? But he tried to still the anger and concentrate on the words in front of him. Soon, his mother's preamble gave way to the bones of her story and it became easier to read.

> *My story began when I joined The Nocturne as a donor. I thought this marked the end of my life but I was wrong. In many ways, it was only the beginning . . .*

Connor read on through the pages of his mother's letter, through the story of how she had joined the ship and served as Sidorio's donor. The idea of it made him sick to the pit of his stomach. Still, he kept on turning the pages, finding himself surprisingly touched by the tale of how his mother and father – his *true* father, Dexter – had met and fallen in love. Then Sally's story turned darker.

> *Now I need to tell you some things which I was not able to tell you in person, my dear children. These will be difficult for you to read, as they are for me to write, but please try to understand them. And, whatever you think, do not doubt for a moment the depth of my love for you, or your father's love for you both . . .*

And so he read on, uncovering the truth of how he, Connor Tempest, had been brought into the world. It had always been a mystery. His dad – the man he still thought of as his dad, and always would – hadn't talked of their mother. He had said it was too painful to think of her and not have her there beside him. Connor had always thought it must have been a brief marriage, ending in tragedy. In spite of his natural curiosity, he had cared for his father too much to push for answers. Now, here were those answers. And the truth was that it was indeed a brief union, never a marriage. It had ended in tragedy, but it had also begun there.

He and Grace had not been conceived out of love but through a voodoo spell. What did that make them? Something out of a fairy tale? Or a horror story?

And so you see that you are both dhampirs, which is to say that you have both mortal and vampire qualities. In time, your true nature will begin to show itself. I hope when it does you will be strong and that you will offer each other the support you each need and deserve. Dhampirs are very special beings, blessed with immortality and other gifts bestowed upon Vampirates but without the vampire's weaknesses. I suspect that you, Connor, will see this initially as a curse. If that is the case, then I can only apologise, from the bottom of my heart. I hope very much that, in time, you might come to see it as a blessing.

A blessing? How could she even use that word? He had come into the world through a violent spell and his biological father was a psychopath. *Well,* Connor thought ruefully, *at least now I know who I have to thank for my anger issues.*

He folded up the letter once more and returned it to the envelope. He felt numb.

He was sitting, alone, on the hillside looking down to the academy harbour. Down at the harbourside, festivities were underway. Music was playing and fireworks erupted into the night sky. There were celebrations as Commodore Black praised the bravery of Captain Li and her dynamic crew for their attack on Lady Lockwood, singling him, Connor Tempest, out as having a glorious future. If only he knew, Connor thought.

Perhaps he did. But no, he reflected. Cheng Li had said that she'd keep his secret. That he was her secret weapon. Would she honour her promise? As he watched her, down at the harbourside, he thought that this was a small worry in the greater scheme of things.

Captain Li was surrounded by Jacoby, Bo Yin and the rest of her young crew. Further along the jetty, Ahab Black stood deep in conversation with Barbarro Wrathe, Rene Grammont and Pavel Platonov. The other academy teachers, the captains who had survived the race, were ranged along the foreshore. Connor's eyes passed across the animated features of Lisabeth Quivers and Shivaji Singh. Further along, he saw Moonshine and Trofie Wrathe together, as always. Her golden hand had been returned and she was restored to her old self, Queen of the Pirates. Bart and Cate were also down at the harbourside, arm in arm. They were sharing a joke with Molucco Wrathe, and Scrimshaw, his pet snake, was curled about the captain's neck. And was that Ma Kettle, at Molucco's side, taking a rare night off from her duties at the tavern?

Molucco's loud and distinctive laughter echoed up the hillside. It seemed somehow to mock him.

Connor felt cut off from all of them. He had thought he belonged to their world, that he might find something approximating a home amongst this ragtag collection of pirates and adventurers. But he had been wrong. It had all been an illusion, now shattered with no chance of repair. He didn't belong anywhere. He was a mutant, a monster, an outcast.

"Hey, billy-no-mates, I've been looking for you."

He hadn't heard Jasmine approach, but now he turned as she sat down beside him in the long grass.

He gazed at her, wishing he could return her smile. But he couldn't. He felt as though an invisible wall had been erected between them. More than anything, he wanted to reach out to her but what was the point? There could be no kind of future for them now.

"You know what, Connor?" said Jasmine, wrinkling her nose. "I'm not really much into victory parades and that kind of stuff. And fireworks just give me a headache." She rested her head on her knees and smiled up at him. "It was gruelling what we went through back there," she continued. "And now it's over, well I just want to get back to normal, whatever normal is. To chill out with my friends, you know?"

He nodded, automatically. The word *normal* jarred with him. It didn't feel like a category he could place himself in any longer.

"You look tired," she said, "and battle-weary. I'm not surprised. You were at the heart of the attack."

"Yes," he said, looking at her and thinking how she looked more beautiful and inaccessible than ever. She belonged to a different world than him. They could never be together.

Then Jasmine Peacock did the simplest and most extraordinary thing. She leaned back in the long grass, patted her lap and drew Connor's head down to rest in it. And he did so, grateful for the warmth of her human touch. She lifted her hand and began stroking his hair.

"I don't know what's wrong, Connor," she said softly. "And I don't need to But you must understand that whatever it is – and whether you ever decide to tell me or not is up to you – you are not alone."

As she leaned forward and kissed him, a tear fell from his eyes and rolled down his cheek to mingle with the dew on the academy grass.

On the deck of *The Nocturne*, Grace lay in Lorcan's arms, looking up at the stars.

He smiled suddenly. "I forgot! I have a surprise for you." He gently released her and walked over to the mast. Grace watched him curiously. When he came back, he was carrying a parcel, wrapped up in brown paper and string. Crouching down again, he held it out to her. "It's not the best gift-wrap, I'll grant you, but I hope you'll like what's inside."

"What is it?" she said, her eyes glowing as she took the rectangular package into her hands. It was surprisingly light, given its size.

"Well, open it up and see, for goodness' sake!" Lorcan exclaimed.

Grace needed no further encouragement. She began untying the string and then unfolded the paper. As it fell away, she gasped. "Oh Lorcan, it's beautiful!"

In her hands, she held a painting of a scene on the very same deck. It was of two young people – a man and a woman. It was clear from their posture and expressions that they were very much in love.

"It's my parents, isn't it?" Grace said. "It's the picture Teresa painted of them."

Lorcan nodded. "Oskar told me about it," he said. "He's still firm friends with Teresa. He took me to her cabin. Grace, it's piled high with her pictures – she has to keep painting over old canvases to make room!"

Grace let out a breath. "Thank goodness she didn't paint over this one!" she said.

Lorcan rested his arms around Grace's waist. "She told me she would never *ever* have painted over this one. And she very much wanted you to have it."

"Oh Lorcan," said Grace. "I love it! Will you help me to hang it in my cabin? It will be like they're travelling with me always."

"Yes." He nodded, then kissed her.

She set the picture down carefully and then took Lorcan's hand as they sat back down on the deck together. Even then, she found herself gazing at the painting.

"What are you thinking about?" he asked, his finger gently tracing the curve of her cheek.

"Mosh Zu told me before that everything is unfolding as it should be. I couldn't believe him then." She turned to Lorcan. "But now I do."

"That's so good to hear, my sweet Grace. I was so frightened about how you'd react to all this. I thought that it would spoil everything, but I should never have underestimated you. I won't make that mistake again."

"Yes you will," she said.

He twisted his head and looked at her quizzically. She grinned. "Lorcan, we're both immortal. That means we're going to be spending a *lot* of time together. I think it would be a mistake to imagine it will all be plain sailing, don't you?"

He laughed. "Plain sailing? With our track record? You make a good point!" He leaned over and kissed her again. She was growing used to his kisses but, even though she knew an eternity of them lay ahead of her, she had no fear that she would ever tire of them. But after a moment, her smile turned to a frown.

"What's wrong?" he asked.

"I'm just thinking about Connor," she said. "I'm worried about how he's going to react to all this. It's easier for me because I want to be part of this world. I'm already connected to it in so many ways."

"That's true," Lorcan said. "But you and Connor are different people. He will react differently and shape his future accordingly. He'll find his own way. You have to trust that he'll do that."

"But I have you and Mosh Zu and Darcy and all the others to help me," said Grace. "And hopefully," she added, "the captain will return one day soon."

Lorcan nodded. "Yes, you do have all of us. But Connor has

his friends too, doesn't he? And *we'll* be there for him, waiting to help, as and when he has need of us."

His words were deeply reassuring. "Thank you," Grace said.

"You're welcome," Lorcan said. "But I'm only speaking the truth as I see it. Now, just for tonight at least, could we stop worrying about your brother and lie back and enjoy the stars?"

Grace nodded. She settled back onto the deckboards, snuggled closer to Lorcan and gazed up past the tall-mast and *The Nocturne's* vast winglike sails, their veins sparking with light as the ship sailed on.

Up above, the night sky was clear and the heavens were abundant with stars. Grace's eyes roved across the constellations: some familiar, others still mysterious to her. She remembered her dad telling her and Connor how sailors used the stars to navigate home by. Now, as she glanced up above, she imagined each of the lights as representing one of the special people in her life. Some gone now; others still with her. Sally. Dexter. Connor. Darcy. Oskar. Mosh Zu. The captain. Lorcan. Each in their own way had brought her to this special place. This place she now knew was home.

AN INTERVIEW WITH JUSTIN SOMPER

Is it true that the idea for VAMPIRATES came to you in something of a 'Eureka moment'?
It's completely true that the word Vampirates just dropped into my head one day. I feel enormously lucky about that. I knew from that moment that exciting times lay ahead but I had to knuckle down to some hard thinking and research as I knew very little about either vampires or pirates!

How easy has it been combining vampires and pirates into one story?
It was always going to be a challenge. The word Vampirates joins the two together brilliantly, but could I join the characters' worlds together as seamlessly? I did a lot of research into pirate history and vampire myth, searching for common ground. In the end, a connection surfaced all on its own. That connection is appetite – how far you live by rules and discipline and how far you give in to your baser hungers (whether for blood or violence, wealth or glory). In VAMPIRATES, there are characters who are very disciplined and others who are utterly out of control – in both the vampirate and pirate communities.

How much research do you do for the books?
Research is an integral part of my writing process. On most writing days, I'll be researching something or another – thank goodness for Google! This is especially true when I'm introducing a new character. Research helps me to find a note of authenticity even within the highly fantastical setting of the stories. Two examples – Sidorio's back story is largely true. Julius Caesar *was* kidnapped by pirates from Cilicia and he *did* trick them into freeing him, before turning on them and having them killed. And Cheng Li is inspired by a real-life pirate named Cheng I Sao.

How long does it take you to write a book?
It varies considerably. The first VAMPIRATES book, *Demons of the Ocean*, took about five years (!), if you include research time. *Tide of Terror* took about nine months. Then I was asked to write the (much shorter) mini-adventure *Dead Deep* for World Book Day, but that took me a whole four months, which shows that writing less words doesn't necessarily make you quicker! I'd say I now need

about seven months writing time, but then there's editing time on top of that. I know VAMPIRATES readers (and publishers) would like me to write faster, but I don't want to compromise the quality of my work.

Do you have a special place where you write?
I have an office at home with a "mood wall" featuring pictures relating to VAMPIRATES and its large cast of characters. This is the best place to write, especially when my dog Bailey curls up over my feet. I'm also quite productive on trains!

Is it true that you can swordfight?
On a decidedly basic level! I had my own introduction from the real-life Cutlass Cate. Like Connor, I got to try out a variety of swords and they really do seem to have their own personality. Because I write about swordfighting, there is an expectation that I know how to do it – I wish that were true! Earlier this year, I did have a fencing lesson with a former Romanian national champion, which was exciting and gave me the taste for more, if and when my writing schedule allows. Meantime, I'm shortly going to be visiting Japan and am looking forward to checking out the Sword Museum in Tokyo.

Do you have a favourite VAMPIRATES character?
I have a soft spot for so many of them – Lorcan, Darcy, Stukeley, Johnny, Cheng Li… The most fun scenes to write for *Black Heart* were those featuring Sidorio and Lady Lola. But I guess the characters I feel most attached to are Grace and Connor.

Your characters have some very memorable – and highly unusual! – names. How do you think them up?
It varies from case to case. With some, like Molucco Wrathe and Mosh Zu Kamal, it's all about the sound. With Cheng Li, I mentioned before that she was based on a real-life pirate named Cheng I Sao, so I didn't change her name much. Lorcan Furey sounded suitably Celtic and romantic and the 'Furey' is a tribute to a character in one of my favourite stories, James Joyce's *The Dead*. I'm always on the lookout for names. If I meet someone at a book-signing with a cool or unusual name, I'll often jot it down and file it away for later use.

***Black Heart* reveals a lot of the back story to VAMPIRATES. How hard was it to write?**
It was very hard to write – in places the hardest of the sequence to date. The problem with revealing a complex back story is that you need to convey a lot of important information but without slowing down the momentum of

the story. For me, the key was allowing Grace a very active way in which to explore her own history. Obviously some of the subject matter was highly emotional and this brought its own complications. But I was aware too that readers of the sequence wanted to know this stuff and had their own ideas about the twins' history. So I wanted to do justice to all that – I hope I have!

This book leaves Grace and Connor in a very different position from where they started out in *Demons of the Ocean*. What do you have in store for them next?

You don't really expect me to answer that, do you?! Actually, I'm just starting to map out the plan for Book 5 and I think it's going to be enormous fun. Now that the back story is out there and the twins are fundamentally changed, the story can move forward in some exciting new directions. It's going to be especially intriguing to explore how Grace and Connor each react to their discoveries about their family tree!

The book is dominated by Lady Lola Lockwood, the Highwaywoman of the Seven Seas. What inspired you to create her?

Very simple really. At the end of *Blood Captain*, I thought that the team of renegade vampirates was shaping up nicely with Sidorio at the helm, flanked by Stukeley and Johnny. But there was a gap – where was the female renegade vampirate to give them a run for their money? I decided that I had to rise to the challenge and, having created a cowboy – or vacquero – vampirate in Johnny, I thought that a Highwaywoman vampirate was the next logical step! I'm thrilled with Lady Lola. I like her combination of utter ruthlessness with that oh so proper brand of Englishness, which I've borrowed from British movies of the 1940s.

What is the best thing about being an author?

Firstly, the pure fun of the writing itself. I'm having a blast writing VAMPIRATES and entering daily into this crazy world of mad, larger-than-life characters. Secondly, receiving feedback from readers, whether it's face-to-face when I visit schools, libraries or literary festivals, or through the blog on my website (vampirates.co.uk).

And the worst?

I'm tempted to say deadlines, but really these are a necessary evil. I think the worst thing is probably those days when the writing just doesn't flow and you end up feeling frustrated. But really you just need to hold onto your sense of perspective. Tomorrow, as they say, is another day!

What has been the most surprising aspect of becoming a children's author?

I am genuinely blown away by how the books have succeeded internationally. The VAMPIRATES books are published in 25 countries, with more coming on-board all the time. It's amazing when I'm abroad and I dive into a bookshop – whether it's in Spain, Australia or the USA – and find my books on the shelf. Very exciting – and long may it continue!

Your books can be quite violent at times. Do you worry about their effect on readers?

I don't think that the books are overly or explicitly violent but when you are writing about pirates and vampires, there is bound to be an underlying menace. I am conscious of this issue and mindful of the wide age-range of my readership. I would never want to glamorise violence but at the same time it feels wrong to depict it too realistically in these kinds of books. It's an issue that's frequently on my mind as I write.

How many VAMPIRATES books will there be in total?

There will be at least six main novels in the VAMPIRATES sequence, plus a special collection of *Crossing Stories*, revealing untold secrets about the characters.

Is there going to be a VAMPIRATES movie or TV show?

I'm always asked this – especially by taxi-drivers and my brother-in-law Ray! There have been approaches and it's really just a question of finding the right partners to move things forward with. I'd love to see the world of VAMPIRATES come alive in another medium, but it's important to me that it's done in the best possible way and not rushed through for the sake of it. That said, I can't wait to step aboard *The Nocturne* or wander into Ma Kettle's tavern for real!

Do you have ideas for books other than VAMPIRATES?

Yes indeed I do, but I'm keeping them under wraps for now!